The House on Becket Lane

THE HOUSE ON BECKET LANE

A Novel

Of The Early Eighteen Hundreds

With Some Degree of Mystery

And A Touch Romance

ELIZABETH CHANTER

iUniverse, Inc.
Bloomington

The House on Becket Lane

Copyright © 2011 by Elizabeth Chanter.

All rights reserved. No part of this book may be used or reproduced by any means, graphic, electronic, or mechanical, including photocopying, recording, taping or by any information storage retrieval system without the written permission of the publisher except in the case of brief quotations embodied in critical articles and reviews.

This is a work of fiction. All of the characters, names, incidents, organizations, and dialogue in this novel are either the products of the author's imagination or are used fictitiously.

iUniverse books may be ordered through booksellers or by contacting:

iUniverse
1663 Liberty Drive
Bloomington, IN 47403
www.iuniverse.com
1-800-Authors (1-800-288-4677)

Because of the dynamic nature of the Internet, any web addresses or links contained in this book may have changed since publication and may no longer be valid. The views expressed in this work are solely those of the author and do not necessarily reflect the views of the publisher, and the publisher hereby disclaims any responsibility for them.

Any people depicted in stock imagery provided by Thinkstock are models, and such images are being used for illustrative purposes only.
Certain stock imagery © Thinkstock.

ISBN: 978-1-4620-3602-8 (sc)
ISBN: 978-1-4620-3604-2 (ebk)

Library of Congress Control Number: 2011912587

Printed in the United States of America

iUniverse rev. date: 8/12/2011

Acknowledgements

I would like to express my thanks and appreciation to the Members of the Cedar Creek Writers' Group, Shawnigan Lake, Vancouver Island, British Columbia, for their interest and helpful comments.
I would like to mention one member in particular, Elizabeth Symon, for her continual encouragement, chiefly because she was anxious to read the next episode of my notes so she could know what happened.

My thanks to Manuel Erickson for his considerable encouragement and helpful critiques.

My thanks to Judy Baxter, Library Manager Of the South Cowichan Library, and her staff in Mill Bay, Vancouver Island.

And lastly, my thanks to Walker Morrow, For his work as my copy editor.

Author's Comments

There is no such place as Becket Lane in Fulham; nor is there a village called Sutherfield in Sussex. Neither will be found on any map.

The Darley Arabian and Eclipse were real horses. All others are from the author's imagination.

CONTENTS

Number	Chapter	Page
1	Dashell	1
2	Dashell Visits His Aunt	3
3	Dashell Meets an Unknown Lady	7
4	Hannah and Johnny	10
5	Tragedies	13
6	Dashell Calls on the Unknown Lady—Twice	16
7	Dashell Has Afternoon Tea with the Lady Again	27
8	Dashell Spends Time At A Gymnasium	35
9	The Carriage Ride	38
10	And What Happened Afterwards	47
11	Dashell Is Summoned To Windsor	59
12	The Servants Wonder	65
13	Father and Son	72
14	Events Occur at Barrandale House	84
15	The Two Brothers	87
16	Dashell Dines With His Aunt	98
17	The Servants Are Concerned	103
18	Martin Gives Dashell A Warning	105
19	Dashell Attends To Business.	112
20	Dashell Dines With His Aunt Again	117
21	Happenings at Barrandale Park	122
22	Maxwell's Homecoming	129
23	Happenings At The House On Becket Lane	134
24	Dashell and Caroline	144
25	Dashell Returns To Windsor	157
26	Caroline Tells Her Story	162

27	Dashell Dines With His Aunt For The Third Time	173
28	Lord Barrandale Returns To London	179
29	More Happenings at the House on Becket Lane	189
30	Johnny Runs To Find Lord Lonsdale	200
31	At Becket Lane Again	205
32	At Grosvenor Square	212
33	More Happenings With Johnny	217
34	Thomas Wardlock	223
35	Father and Son	232
36	Wardlock Calls at Barrandale House	236
37	Johnny Again	243
38	The Death of Thomas Wardlock	251
39	Dashell and Caroline	256
40	Hannah and Johnny Tell All They Know	260
41	Dashell and the Others Continue To Talk	268
42	Lord Barrandale's Suspicions	272
43	At Becket Lane Again—and Elsewhere	276
44	The Cab Driver Tells All He Knows	290

Chapter One

Dashell

Lord Dashell Lonsdale was considered to be one of the most eligible bachelors in London. Twenty five years of age, the eldest of three sons, and heir of the wealthy Earl of Barrandale. He was a popular fellow and had enjoyed his time at Oxford University. His boyhood rowing on the Thames had stood him in good stead and he had been proud to row in the College Eights.

When he left Oxford he set up rooms in Curzon Street, a well-heeled area a few minutes walk from Barrandale House on Park Lane. Like many young men of wealthy family in those days he attended one of the several gymnasiums that were springing up in London, and continued with his boxing and fencing. He was an excellent horseman, a good shot, and could drive a coach and four. In short, he was everything that a young man of his position was expected to be.

He was almost six feet in height, and had pleasing features rather than being strictly handsome, with black hair and eyebrows. He had a scar on his right cheek near his eye, the result of a boyhood accident.

He resembled his father, Lord Randolph Barrandale, in appearance and manner. Sometimes when they walked together step for step with their hands behind their backs, discussing something or perhaps nothing much at all, it made people smile to see them.

Needless to say Dashell was looked upon as a great catch and Society matrons vied with each other with jealous intensity, parading their mostly willing—or sometimes unwilling—daughters in front of him.

He had no set picture of his ideal woman. He did not particularly mind if she was dark or fair, preferably not too tall, and not necessarily an heiress. He certainly did not want a simpering beauty with no thoughts of her own, nor did he want a shy violet. He had privately considered one or two possibilities, but in the end decided one had too much starch in her petticoat—too haughty—and the other had too much temper for his liking. He had one or two discreet dalliances but never met anyone who really attracted his attention or whom he felt was the right one. All this, he reflected ruefully to himself one day, certainly cleared the field of all runners and left nobody to win the race.

Chapter Two
Dashell Visits His Aunt

Dashell was getting bored with all this and decided to call on his Aunt Letty, Lady Smythe, his father's sister, whom he had not seen for a while. Her actual name was Letitia, which she had detested even as a child declaring it sounded like a sneeze, much to the amusement of young Randolph. The three brothers adored her and said she was their favourite aunt. "Favourite aunt, indeed," she would snort at them. "I am your only aunt."

She was the widow of Sir Charles Smythe, a well-known diplomat in his day, and lived in a small select house in Grosvenor Square. She was still a very attractive lady with the strong, yet feminine, Barrandale features, and her hair not yet fully grey.

Lady Smythe was reclining on her sofa one afternoon when her butler, Chadwick, announced Lord Lonsdale was here. She sat up joyfully and quickly patted her hair and arranged her shawl before saying, "Show him in, Chadwick. Show him in. Dashell, my dear, how are you?"

Dashell bent to kiss her cheeks. "Very well, thank you, Aunt Letty," he replied. "I trust you are too?"

"Yes, I am in my usual good health. Will you stay for tea?"

"Of course," smiled Dashell, "that's why I came."

"And how are your father and those brothers of yours? Sit down and tell me all your news." They chatted together until the butler came back with the tea tray. Lady Smythe poured out the tea with an easy grace and handed a cup to Dashell.

He watched her admiringly. "Aunt Letty, you are as beautiful as ever."

She picked up her cup and smiled. "Flatterer! Did you come here just to tell me that?" She leaned back against her cushions. "I hear about you from time to time," she continued. "Mrs. Cracknell is a great one for keeping me informed."

Dashell's eyes widened as he looked at his aunt over the rim of his teacup. "Dammit, Aunt Letty," he spluttered, "I can't go anywhere without matchmaking spies chasing after me. And don't pay too much attention to any gossip, especially anything from Mrs. Cracknell. People like her ought not to be allowed. And you should not be listening either," he added with mock severity.

"Don't be impertinent," she laughed. "A handsome, eligible young man like yourself is bound to attract plenty of attention. And think of your position. You should have many ladies after you."

"Don't I know it. Too many for my liking. I go to undesirable places just to shake 'em off."

"I am not interested in the places you may go to," said Aunt Letty, "but I don't blame you for trying to get away from them. I remember my younger days and all the young men I was introduced to; quite dreadful, some of them. It was such a relief when I met my dear Charles."

"I gather from that remark I have your sympathy."

"If they are dreadful, indeed you do," she chuckled, as she settled herself more comfortably on her cushions. "Help yourself to anything. It will save me passing the plate all the time." Dashell obligingly did so. He enjoyed the little shortbreads his aunt's cook made. He was extremely fond of his aunt, and she of him. She had a great deal of sense about her and she had not been the wife of a diplomat for nothing.

"You have no likelihood of becoming bethrothed then? Or met anyone who really took your fancy, if that is the way to describe it." Lady Smythe could be persistent.

"No, I have not. And it is not from the want of London Society trying either." He laughed rather grimly. "The number of girls who get trotted out past me, really, I feel quite sorry for them sometimes. And when I see their mothers!" He groaned and closed his eyes. "Anyway, I fortify myself by remembering that Father didn't marry until he was in his late thirties."

"Very wise, Dashell," said Lady Smythe approvingly, "but I am sure your father is hoping that one day you will announce your engagement."

"That, dear aunt of mine, makes it all the more difficult. I will not marry just anybody to oblige, not even Father, bless the man," sighed Dashell. "Surely there is someone, somewhere, whom I could meet and fall in love with. Properly, I mean, and not because it is expected of me. Someone who would love me and not just my wealth. But where do I go to find her?"

"It will happen," his aunt assured him. "Let events fall into place." After a moment or two of silence her talk took on a different tone. "Dashell, I want to talk to you seriously about something that troubles me a great deal."

"Oh? What can that be?" he asked, as he helped himself to the last shortbread.

"I have been hearing disturbing rumours concerning your brother Walden and his excesses, and from a more reliable source than Mrs.Cracknell. Has your father heard anything yet?"

Dashell shifted in his chair, all banter and amusement put aside. "Aunt Letty, this is serious if you have been hearing things. Quite frankly I have too, and my circle is very different from yours. Only a whisper so far but once people get bolder it comes out into the open, and I fear things are getting to that stage. Possibly it has reached Father's ears although he has said nothing to me." Then with a sudden flash of anger, "Walden is a damn fool. Does he not know what he is doing? Has he no thought for his family? Pardon my language, Aunt Letty, but he is."

"I agree with you," replied that worldly-wise woman. She put down her cup and brushed a few crumbs off her lap. "I am so glad you came for I was at the point of sending a note asking you to call."

"Thank you for warning me, Aunt Letty. I was actually considering going to Windsor soon. I would rather Father heard this from me than rumours get to him first." He stood up. "I will take my leave of you, dear aunt of mine," he said with a quirky little smile. "Don't get up, I can see myself out."

"Come again soon, or when you can," she said. "You young ones gad about so much."

Chapter Three
Dashell Meets an Unknown Lady

Dashell went out into the quiet square feeling anything but light-hearted. He was very angry and worried about his fool brother Walden. The fact was these were no idle rumours, and there was a great deal of truth in them.

He turned into Oxford Street with all its noise and clatter of hooves and wheels and it seemed to be more busy than usual. He walked along slowly, deep in thought, paying little heed to jostles by passers-by. He hardly noticed two women ahead trying to cross the road away from him.

Then all at once there was confusion. There were shouts and a child screamed, a horse reared, drivers shouted as they pulled up sharply, and a lady carrying a child tripped and fell at Dashell's feet. The child and its parents were crossing the road at the same time as the two women were crossing from Dashell's side of the street, thus passing approximately in the middle of the road, but the child saw something shiny and stopped to pick it up, unknown to the parents. The younger of the two women saw what was happening and the sight of a cab bearing down on them, and snatched up the child and ran back to the side of the road she had just left as it was the nearer one, her companion having continued to the other side. In her haste and anxiety the young woman stumbled and fell at the feet of a gentleman, and bumped her head on the pavement at the same time.

The driver of the cab jumped down and seized the horse's bridle. "Streuth, lady, I thought you were a goner then! Why, you were nearly under his feet!" The parents seized the child, scolded it, soothed its fears, and thanked its rescuer all at the same time. Drivers and passers-by called out to know if all was well, and on learning it was moved along again and the crowd began to disperse.

"My dear lady, please allow me to assist you," said Dashell gallantly, and holding her by the elbows lifted her to her feet with ease. "Are you hurt? That was a very brave thing to do."

The lady brushed the dust off her dress and looked at her grazed hands. "Thank you very much, sir, you are very kind. Yes, I am a little shaken, but that child is all right." She tried to look up at her helper but had to put a hand to her head, feeling a little faint.

Dashell held her by the elbow to steady her and found he was looking at the most beautiful face he had ever seen. Soft wavy brown hair, incredible sea green eyes, slightly prominent cheek bones in a heart-shaped face, and a lovely mouth. He was almost tongue-tied. "Lady, surely you are not alone?"

"No, I am not. My maid was crossing the road with me. She must be somewhere." The Unknown looked about and cried, "Oh, there she is. Hannah, I am over here!"

"Oh, Miss Caroline, Miss Caroline!" Hannah had managed to cross the road again and rushed up, breathless. "You did give me a fright! I thought you had crossed the road with me and then I looked round for you and saw you had fallen. For one dreadful moment I thought a carriage had gone over you. Dear child, please tell me you are still in one piece!"

"Yes, Hannah dear, I am," the lady said. "I managed to pick up that child and run back with him. But I am a little shaken and bruised, and this kind gentleman assisted me in getting up." She was feeling embarrassed at the attention from lingering passers-by and was very conscious of her helper's gaze.

Indeed, during this exchange Dashell had not taken his eyes from that lovely face. "Lady, do you have far to go? Please allow me to call a cab for you."

"Thank you, sir. We would be most obliged."

Dashell whistled and one soon came up. He helped the lady in and stepped aside for her maid, desperately wanting to know the lady's name but not knowing how to ask. "Where to?" asked the driver, and Hannah replied, "Becket Lane, house number twenty-nine." Then she stepped into the cab beside her mistress and Dashell closed the door after her.

"Thank you again, sir," said the Unknown, leaning forward a little. Dashell bowed in return, not really knowing what to say. He watched the cab turn round, which meant he could get a view of the Unknown again through a side window. Their eyes met as she turned her head.

He stood on the pavement and watched the cab until it was out of sight, completely oblivious to all the noise and traffic, then slowly resumed walking. All he could see was that lady with a beautiful face whom he had met so dramatically, whom he only knew as "Miss Caroline", and she had a maid called Hannah who seemed very concerned for her mistress. The lady had such grace and dignity, yet an air of sadness too, and he wondered if she had suffered some recent bereavement. And wonder of wonders he knew where she lived!

Dashell decided he would call upon her tomorrow and inquire after her. He would go in the afternoon which would be the proper time and perhaps take her a discreet bunch of flowers. He must introduce himself too. How rude of him not to have done so before, yet it had not been either the time or the place. He might be invited in or the lady might have put him out of her mind already. He would see. Then he realized he had no idea where Becket Lane was. He would have to take a cab when he called.

Walden, for the moment, had been forgotten.

Chapter Four
Hannah and Johnny

Hannah had been engaged by a lady named Mrs. Wardlock as nursemaid to look after her two little baby girls, Maude and Caroline, at their house on Becket Lane. She was a country girl from Sussex and her employment with Mrs. Wardlock was her very first position and she had stayed ever since. She was devoted to her mistress and was much loved by Mrs. Wardlock's two daughters. Perhaps a little on the plump side, with a round yet pleasant face, she was well described as "cuddly" by the children.

Johnny, her half-brother, was a servant boy at the same house. He was a typical Cockney boy, with a shock of hair, a ready grin, sharp-eyed, who saw everything and missed nothing.

When he was ten years old Johnny's parents died in a house fire and he barely escaped with his life. He went to live with his Uncle Joe Barlow, a cab driver for his friend, Mr. Paxton, who owned several horses and cabs, and his establishment was known as Paxton's Yard. Mr. Paxton allowed Johnny to live at the Yard, and the boy made himself useful by helping out around the place. His uncle used to tell him stories of being "on the road" as he called it, and often said it was astonishing what he overheard people say. "Just remember that, young Johnny-me-lad," he often said. "The good Lord gave us two eyes and two ears but only one mouth, and you have to learn to keep even that one shut."

When Johnny was about thirteen Uncle Joe died in an accident when his cab overturned. Johnny missed him very much, and without proper supervision he began to attend less at Paxton's Yard and got into bad company. He met up with a petty thief who called himself Fingers, who gave Johnny a lock-pick and showed him how to use it. One time a gang of boys got Johnny to help them rob a house, but things went wrong. He managed to escape being caught and ran all the way back to Paxton's Yard, but that incident gave him a bad fright.

Somehow Mr. Paxton got wind of Johnny's misdeeds—Johnny never quite knew how—and he had a talk with Mrs. Wardlock. The end result of that talk was that Johnny went to live at the house on Becket Lane. "Hannah might only be a half-sister," said Mr. Paxton, "but she is the only relative you have, now that your parents and uncle have gone. Mrs. Wardlock has very kindly said you could come and live at their house and make yourself useful."

Soon after Johnny arrived he spent one afternoon oiling squeaky hinges and sorting out a bundle of keys by seeing which ones fitted which locks, and labeling them accordingly. There was one locked door which intrigued him especially as none of the keys seemed to fit its lock.

"Why is that door at the top of the house kept locked," he asked Hannah.

"That door has been locked for years," she replied. "The rooms are never used and there is nothing there anyway."

"Oh," said Johnny, wondering why it was kept locked if there was nothing there. "I can't find a key to fit the lock."

"Well, it must be lost then. I don't know where it is."

"What about the other door kept locked, the one to the linen cupboard?"

"That door is kept locked because it swings open if not. Now run along, I'm busy."

Johnny saw very little of Mr. Wardlock, and if he did he put on a meek expression while the other one glared at him. Johnny took an instinctive dislike to him and thought there was "something very fishy about that gent."

Some while later Johnny gave Hannah quite a shock when he asked, "Do you fink Mr. Wardlock is Miss Maude's and Miss Caroline's real farver?"

She stared at him. "Whatever made you say that? Whatever made you think it?"

"Well, Miss Caroline looks very much like her muvver so it's natchural to fink Miss Maude would look like her farver, only she doesn't, and I would hate to fink either of them did anyway. Hadn't you noticed?"

Hannah came over to Johnny and sat down. "Yes, I had noticed," she said quietly. "Quite some time ago now. When the girls were still babies I naturally thought Mr. Wardlock was their father. I never thought twice about it. The mistress never said anything to me nor was it my place to ask. Yet for the first year or two she seemed very unhappy about something until she gradually relaxed and devoted herself to her children."

Her voice trailed off. "Now, Johnny," she continued briskly, "I have been telling you things that perhaps I shouldn't. If the mistress has a secret it is hers alone, poor lamb. Just remember what Uncle Joe used to say about keeping your mouth shut, and don't go annoying Mr. Wardlock, either. He is a strange man and the mistress had quite a time persuading him to let you come here."

Hannah turned her head at the sound of voices at the front door. "Hush now, here they are back from their walk. I must put the kettle on."

Chapter Five
Tragedies

When her daughters were old enough Mrs. Wardlock decided it was time for them to attend Miss Osgood's Academy for Young Ladies, somewhere in Kent. The application forms had been accepted and a list had been sent of all the items each pupil was expected to bring. Such excitement while so much sewing and making of garments was being done. They would be away for a whole year and Mrs. Wardlock assured her daughters she would be perfectly all right during their absence. They on their part promised they would write to their mother every week.

Tragedy struck, however, as their mother's health suddenly deteriorated and she died while the sisters were actually on their way home after completing their school year. Hannah had to greet them at the door with the devastating news. It was days before the girls could fully grasp the situation.

Hannah had been greatly attached to her mistress, but she didn't have to go and weep buckets of tears the way she did. Cor, she was getting to be the ruddy limit, she was, in Johnny's opinion.

Mr. Wardlock announced he had to go away because he missed his dear wife. He did go away but nobody missed him. Hannah was indignant. How could he miss his wife when he never took much notice of her anyway?

One young lady whom Maude and Caroline had met at the Academy called with her brother to offer condolences. Then the brother called on his own.

When Mr. Wardlock returned and learned a young gentleman had called on Maude he was furious. The next time the young man called he was told he was quite insensitive to come while Maude was in mourning for her dear mother, and was ordered out of the house. Maude wrote to the young gentleman apologizing for her Papa's behaviour, but she never received a reply.

Maude tried to speak to her Papa but he refused to listen. "You are quite heartless," she cried. A few days later she was found at the bottom of the stairs with a broken neck.

Johnny was sent to fetch the doctor, and together they carried the lifeless form of Maude upstairs and laid her on her bed. Mr. Wardlock followed them and remained in the room with Dr. Meldicott. Caroline and Hannah were devastated.

Afterwards, Johnny sat at the top of the stairs feeling rather shaky. So many deaths in his young life. He noticed a piece of black thread and picked at it for want of something to do and to his amazement found it was attached to a pin in the wall. He stared at it, mystified, not understanding at first, then twisted round and saw another piece of thread attached to a bannister. He got up and pulled the threads together and sure enough the two ends met, and slowly comprehension sank in. *Oh no,* he thought, *so Miss Maude can't 'ave thrown herself downstairs. Blimey, that means—e can't 'ave—'e can't 'ave done it. What would Miss Caroline and Hannah fink. I can't tell 'em wot 'e did.*

Just then Johnny heard the bedroom door opening. In a flash he leaned over the bannisters, slid down to the bottom of the stairs, and went to stand by the front door, trying to look as though he had been there all the time, just as Mr. Wardlock and Dr. Meldicott appeared at the top of the stairs. They came down slowly still talking when Mr. Wardlock caught sight of Johnny. "What are you doing there, boy?" he demanded. "You should be about your business."

"Beg pardon, I'm sure, Mr. Wardlock," replied Johnny meekly, "but I thought Dr. Meldicott might want me to run an errand for him." He had done this in the past and his answer roused no suspicions.

Dr. Meldicott sighed. "I don't understand how Maude could have done this. She always seemed such a sensible girl to me. I am sure, sir, you are quite distressed."

"Indeed I am," replied Mr. Wardlock. "She was such a dear girl. Pray say no more."

Johnny followed the doctor out of the house. "Do you know what 'appened," he asked innocently.

"Well, Johnny," answered Dr. Meldicott, "as far as Mr. Wardlock can tell, Maude must have wanted to speak to him once more, but overcome by her emotion she threw herself down the stairs. He heard a scream and ran out of his room."

Johnny snorted in disgust as he returned indoors. He crept up the back stairs and listened carefully, then slipped over to the front stairs. There was no longer any sign of the broken pieces of black thread.

He slowly went back to the kitchen and sat down to think. He knew he was not mistaken. The threads had been there and now they were not, and the only person to remove them would be the person who put them there. It was impossible for him to say anything. The master of the house to be accused by a servant boy? Why would Mr. Wardlock wish the death of one of his daughters? Johnny would be dismissed at once, and he could not abandon Miss Caroline and Hannah.

His tense, pale looks were put down to shock and grief.

Chapter Six
Dashell Calls on the Unknown Lady Twice

Dashell was still determined to call on the lady who occupied his thoughts so much.

After luncheon he stopped at a flower lady's stall and bought a pretty little bouquet. "For your lady love, dearie?" joked the flower lady. "Fresh every morning they are."

Dashell smiled back at her and hoped none of his cronies would see him. Their impudent questions would only belittle the Unknown. He hailed a passing cab and gave the address, thankful the driver knew his way and did not have to ask directions. He sat back and watched the passing scenario with interest, not knowing exactly where he was going.

The cab eventually went along Fulham Road towards Fulham Palace, the residence of the Bishops of London. Dashell could just imagine the incredulous looks on the faces of his friends if they thought he was calling on the daughter of a bishop.

The cab finally came to a place with a village green and then turned right into Becket Lane just past an inn, and went along a short way before stopping outside a house. Dashell stepped down and looked about. He asked the cab driver if he knew the name of the place they had just passed.

"It's called Parsons Green, sir," the man replied.

Parsons Green. *How appropriate,* Dashell thought. He ordered the cab to wait and turned his attention to the house. How odd to call it Number 29 when there were no other houses nearby, but the wrought iron numbers were firmly fixed onto one of the stone pillars of the gate. Somehow the house did not look inviting, and he felt dismayed. Did that sweet lady really live here?

Well, he had come all this way. He pushed open the gate and walked up to the front door. By the time he got there his heart was thumping. Was he being a complete fool after all? The lady could have a number of swains already, or a particular gentleman friend who would be consumed with jealousy. She could be betrothed, or there could be an even more jealous husband. But her maid had addressed her as "Miss Caroline". He knocked on the door and waited. As he had hoped, Hannah answered it. She looked rather anxious as though they did not get many visitors, but relaxed when she recognized him.

"Good afternoon, sir," she said, with her country burr.

"Good afternoon, Hannah. I overheard you being called Hannah yesterday," he said, with a disarming smile. "Is your mistress at home? I thought I would enquire after her to see how she is faring. Forgive me, but I do not know the lady's name."

"Her name is Miss Caroline Wardlock, sir. She is upstairs and I do believe she is asleep."

"Then please do not disturb her," said Dashell. "May I leave these flowers for her? And here is my card."

Hannah beamed at him as she took the flowers. "Thank you, sir," and her eyes widened as she saw the gentleman's name and title printed in gold on the card.

"Thank you," said Dashell. "Please inform Miss Wardlock I shall call again tomorrow."

"Indeed I will, sir. I mean your lordship." Hannah appeared a little flustered. "Good afternoon."

Dashell returned to the waiting cab disappointed he had not seen Miss Wardlock. At least Hannah did not say her mistress would not be at home the next day.

Hannah hastened to place the flowers in a pretty vase and arranged them carefully. She went up the back stairs and tapped on her mistress's bedroom door. There was no answer so she quietly opened it and placed the vase on the dressing table and tip-toed over to the bed and gently shook her mistress awake. "Miss Caroline, please wake up! You will never guess what has happened!"

"Caroline stirred sleepily. "Yes, Hannah, what is it?"

"Look at those pretty flowers!" Hannah cried, pointing to them. "That gentleman from yesterday has just called to see how you were. I said you were asleep and he said not to disturb you."

Caroline was now wide awake. She sat up and snatched the bed clothes to her. "You mean he is still here?" she exclaimed, aghast.

"Oh, no. He said he would call again this time tomorrow. And here is his card."

Caroline read the name in astonishment. "Lord Dashell Lonsdale." She caught her breath, remembering the event of yesterday.

The shouts, the noise and the confusion all came back. What a daring thing she had done, but that child had to be saved and she had not stopped to think. Then she had stumbled and fallen at a gentleman's feet, and he had lifted her up with complete ease. She still felt acutely embarrassed at the thought of it. Then there was the look on the gentleman's face, startling her with the understanding that had seemed to flash between them. She had put her hand to her aching head and felt herself swaying and his hand on her elbow had held her steady. Then Hannah rushed up and the gentleman insisted on calling a cab. When the cab moved off and turned round they had looked at each other again.

But Caroline was puzzled. "Hannah," she said, looking at the card once more. "How did this Lord Lonsdale know where to come? How did he know where I lived?"

Hannah thought for a moment, and then her eyes widened as she exclaimed, "Ooh, he must have heard me give the address to the cab driver."

"Oh," said Caroline. She slipped out of bed to look at the flowers and savoured the delicate scent of them. "I shall keep these in my room. If Papa saw them he might start asking awkward questions."

"And like as not throw them away," muttered Hannah under her breath, then added, "I shall make a nice cake for tomorrow."

Caroline laughed. "You seem so sure Lord Lonsdale will come."

"Of course he will, I am sure of it. He must be quite taken with you Miss Caroline, or why else would he have called just now?"

"But it was just a brief passing episode," protested Caroline. "He was merely being kind and helpful."

"I just hope he does not come late, that's all," said Hannah. "Well, I had best be getting downstairs again."

Caroline knew full well what Hannah meant by that first remark. She sighed to herself as she got dressed and brushed out her hair, and looked again at the flowers, so delicate and fresh. She felt a little chill of apprehension at the coming visit tomorrow, for she must be polite and ask the gentleman in. She would have to be careful.

By now Hannah would have told Miss Wardlock of his visit and given her the flowers, thought Dashell. He smiled and wondered what Aunt Letty would think of it all. Was this the event she had predicted would happen? If so, it was much sooner than either of them had imagined.

The next afternoon Dashell drove to Becket Lane in his own gig, which he left at the inn, and walked to the house. He had puzzled over the name Wardlock and it meant nothing to him.

Once more he knocked on the door. If Miss Wardlock was feeling better he would be invited in, as propriety and manners would dictate that he should be. They also dictated that he should not stay long, at least not on the first visit.

Hannah opened the door. "Good afternoon, Lord Lonsdale. Do please come in." Dashell's hopes were raised at that invitation: it meant the lady was at home and was willing to receive him.

"Good afternoon, Hannah, I trust Miss Wardlock is better?"

"She is, your lordship," she replied. "If you would come into the parlour I will inform her you are here."

While he waited Dashell noticed a water colour painting of two girls aged about fifteen and fourteen. One of them was Miss

Wardlock showing great promise of beauty even then, and the other must have been her sister, just as beautiful.

Caroline entered the parlour and Dashell turned to meet her as she came forward with one hand graciously extended. She was wearing a simple dress with her hair worn round her head and he thought her quite lovely. "Lord Lonsdale, how kind of you to call," she said. "Please forgive me for not being able to receive you yesterday. And thank you so much for the flowers, they are beautiful."

Dashell had already observed they were not in the room which meant she must have kept them upstairs.

"Thank you, Miss Wardlock. You are very kind. I trust you are feeling better?"

"Yes, thank you, Lord Lonsdale. Would you care to stay for tea?"

This was exactly what Dashell had hoped she would ask. He was only too delighted but gravely replied, "Thank you. That is most kind of you."

Hannah had been waiting by the door and Caroline turned to her with a smile, so with a bob she returned to the kitchen where there was a kettle already steaming on the range. Of course she had known the gentleman would come again, hadn't she said as much to Miss Caroline yesterday? Tea would be ready in next to no time at all.

Caroline invited her guest to be seated as she sat down herself. There was an awkward silence for a moment, and then they both began speaking at the same time which made them laugh and relax a little.

"I could not help noticing the watercolour painting on the wall," began Dashell.

Caroline glanced over to the painting. "Yes; Mother painted that a few years ago. The other girl is my older sister, Maude." She did not elaborate on their absence from the tea table and Dashell did not like to ask. He did not fail to notice the flicker of pain that crossed her face and cursed himself for causing it. This absence must be the reason for her sadness.

Hannah came in with the tea tray which she placed on the table and then went to fetch the cakes. Caroline began to pour the tea with the same easy grace that reminded Dashell of his aunt. He almost laughed out loud. Only two days ago he was having tea with Aunt Letty and so much had happened since then it seemed like an age. Hannah came in with the cakes, and left the room with another bob to her mistress. Caroline handed her guest his tea and offered him some cake.

"Thank you, Miss Wardlock," he said.

Dashell could not clearly remember everything afterwards that was said. He only knew his heart was not being itself, especially when Miss Wardlock handed him a second cup of tea and he contrived that their fingers should touch. She gave him a look and he wanted to tell her what lovely eyes she had. He did remember that Miss Wardlock mentioned her papa had a business somewhere in London and that he was out a great deal, and that they kept a quiet house. He was greatly attracted to this lady and found her delightful, but he was sure there was a mystery here and wanted to find out more about it.

They had finished their tea and Dashell felt he should go as he had noticed Miss Wardlock glancing apprehensively once or twice at the clock on the mantelpiece above the fireplace, almost as though she wished him away. He rose to his feet. "I have enjoyed myself, Miss Wardlock, and now I will take my leave. Thank you again for the tea." Was it his imagination or did she appear relieved at his going? Why? He had not overstayed his time and his manners had been impeccable.

Caroline was still the gracious hostess and rang the bell for Hannah who came and handed Dashell his hat and gloves. As he took them he asked the question he had been longing to ask ever since he entered the house. "May I see you again, Miss Wardlock?"

Surprisingly she appeared a little hesitant. "Why, yes . . . I—Papa does not like—we do not have many visitors," she stated, before recovering herself and saying, "Yes, you may." What on earth made her say that?

Dashell bowed slightly. "Today week, then." He must not make it too soon even though he dearly wanted to. "Goodbye, Miss Wardlock."

Caroline went back into the parlour and looked out of the window at the handsome figure walking down the path. She turned round as Hannah collected the tea things and picked up the tray. "There, I was right," said Hannah. "I knew he would come. And now he wants to come again."

"Now, Hannah," rebuked Caroline, "I am sure Lord Lonsdale was just being polite." To tell the truth she had been surprised at herself for agreeing he could come again, but the words had just slipped out.

She turned away from the window as Hannah left the room. The question she kept asking herself was why Lord Lonsdale wanted to come in the first place; it was just a chance meeting as it was. Now he had asked her if he might see her again but she wondered if he really meant it. He had said he would call next week but by then he could well have forgotten her. Perhaps he was just a man-about-town wishing to amuse himself for a while until he found someone else.

Dashell was walking along as though on air. He felt so elated because Miss Wardlock had agreed to see him again, and almost jumped out of his skin when a voice behind him called out, "Hey, Guv! Wait a minute!"

He whirled round expecting some vagrant but confronted a boy who appeared to be no threat at all. "Who are you and what do you want?" he demanded, angry at having his thoughts interrupted. He wanted to think about Miss Wardlock's sweet face and not have this cheeky one grinning at him. Also, according to the strict social mores of the day they should not even be speaking to each other and the boy should certainly not have been the first to speak. They eyed each other warily, the young nobleman and the young Cockney boy.

"I'm Johnny," explained the boy, "I'm 'annah's bruvver. Akshelly, I'm 'er 'arf bruvver. 'Er ma died and 'er pa married again, and that's why I'm 'ere. I live at the 'ouse too," he said with a backward jerk of his thumb.

"Oh? Well, now that you are here what do you want?" Dashell was still annoyed at the start the boy had given him.

Johnny became serious. "Are you the gent wot 'elped Miss Caroline the other day?"

"Yes, I am," Dashell replied. Why did this boy want to know anyway?

"Oh," said the boy. "And are you going to be seeing 'er again?"

Dashell stared at him, speechless. The impudence! And nor was he in the habit of being addressed as "Guv". "Yes, I am. But what is that to you, you cheeky little devil?"

Johnny ignored that remark. "If I wuz you I would be careful about calling at that 'ouse. An' don't come on a Saturday or Sunday, or of an evening."

"Why ever not?"

"'Cos 'er farver's a miserable old cuss, that's why. Like as not 'e'd order you away, like 'e did when a gent came calling for Miss Maude a while ago. Cor, what an upset that was, an' all." Johnny scowled at the memory of it.

Dashell was astonished. What kind of father would do something like that? "What happened to her?" he asked, remembering the sister's absence at the tea table. "Where is she now?"

"She's dead," answered Johnny bluntly. "So's 'er muvver."

Dashell was now beginning to realize why Johnny was speaking to him, that he was offering himself as an ally. The things Johnny was saying certainly explained some of the mystery and unhappiness Dashell had sensed in the house, and he was more determined than ever to find out more about it. He looked hard at Johnny. A likeable rascal perhaps would perhaps be a fitting description but Dashell felt the boy could be trusted. "Why are you telling me all this?" he asked.

"'Cos Miss Caroline is a very nice lady an' I don't want to see 'er upset."

"What do you suggest I do, for I wish to see her again."

"Well," began Johnny, scratching the back of his neck thoughtfully with one finger, "if I wuz you I'd go an' 'ave afternoon tea at the shop opposite the inn. They always go there on Friday afternoons about three o'clock. And they like going for country walks along the lanes as well as beside the river," he added helpfully. "You could try that for a start." His manner indicated that if neither option worked then he would think of something else.

Friday afternoon! That would be the day after tomorrow. Dashell's heart quickened at the thought of seeing Miss Wardlock again sooner than expected. "Johnny, I am very much obliged to you but I am very puzzled. Why is Miss Wardlock so apprehensive of her father?"

Johnny gave a guarded reply. "Just be careful, Guv, for 'er sake."

Dashell was thunderstruck; never had he expected this. He had heard of fathers being strict, sometimes with good reason, if truth be told, but this particular one sounded quite dreadful. And why discourage gentlemen callers? Most fathers were only too thankful to pass their daughters over to someone else. He stood lost in thought but was roused when Johnny reminded him a penny or two would come in handy. Dashell gave a short laugh. "Johnny, you have given me a great deal to think about." He put his hand in his pocket and pulled out a coin and tossed it into Johnny's eager hand.

After his astonishing conversation with Johnny Dashell returned to the inn and studied the tearooms across the road. A shopping area was hardly the place to walk up and down hoping for a glimpse of a certain lady, and Becket Lane offered even less scope; especially when Miss Wardlock had the kind of father Johnny said she had. He would come in his carriage next time and remain in it until he saw Miss Wardlock, then enter the teashop and make out he just happened to be there. It did occur to him that

Johnny could be leading him on and heaven help the scamp if he was, but somehow he did not think so.

He drove back to the stable yard at Barrandale House where he left the gig and walked back to his rooms, his thoughts in turmoil. About this time two days ago he had visited his aunt, reasonably care free and certainly heart free, and now he was anything but. His regard for Miss Wardlock had greatly increased even from such a brief acquaintance; her grace and modesty charmed him, as did her manners and conversation. He liked her attitude towards Hannah, her maid and companion, who obviously cared for her mistress.

Dashell did not know what to make of Johnny, who appeared to be his own master. He had been slightly annoyed at being addressed as "Guv," for he was used to the Barrandale servants addressing him as "Lord Lonsdale" or "your lordship" or just "sir." As boys the three brothers had always been taught to treat servants fairly as they were in no position to answer back. You must earn their respect, their father had often told them. The only one unable to fully learn this lesson had been Walden. *Walden!* Dashell sat up with a start. Good heavens, he had forgotten all about his brother. Miss Wardlock was a far more pleasant subject to think about, but he had promised Aunt Letty he would go and speak to him so he would go round to Walden's rooms later that evening.

Dashell relaxed in his chair again, his thoughts going back to the house on Becket Lane, a dismal place indeed. It was obvious from the outside that the house had been neglected for some time, and from the inside the impression was "shabby genteel". Families, even titled ones, could fall on hard times. Miss Wardlock mentioned her father's occupation somewhere in London so perhaps he was trying to restore his family's finances.

But Johnny had indicated Mr. Wardlock was not a pleasant father to his daughter and Dashell had sensed Miss Wardlock was cautious of her father. Was Mr. Wardlock the root cause of her unhappiness? Circumstances were puzzling and certainly did not add up.

An hour or so later Dashell went round to Walden's rooms but there was still no sign of him. A rather sour-looking landlord informed Dashell that Walden had been out of town for some time. That could mean he was at some racecourse or other. Which one? Ascot, Epsom, Doncaster, Newmarket. Probably each one in turn. Walden could be away for some time.

Chapter Seven
Dashell Has Afternoon Tea with the Lady Again

Friday came at last and Dashell was driven in his carriage to Fulham Village. If he was early he would see Miss Wardlock arrive, and if late he would see her leave. Hannah would be with her mistress of course, but that was to be expected.

He waited nearly twenty minutes before he saw Miss Wardlock and Hannah come along and enter the tea-rooms. They had not come from the house as he had thought they would, but from the opposite direction. So Johnny had been right! He got out of his carriage thinking how surprised Miss Wardlock would be to see him, and crossing the road he entered the tearooms trying to look as though he just happened to be there.

It was Hannah who saw him first, and Caroline turned her head to see who she was looking at as her maid-servant gaped in astonishment. She gave a little "Oh!" of surprise, her mouth remaining open in a way which Dashell dearly wanted to kiss, her pretty bonnet framing her face.

"I was just walking by and saw you enter," Dashell lied gallantly. "May I join you?"

"Of course you may," replied Caroline.

"I hope I am not interrupting anything, Miss Wardlock."

"Not at all. I was just discussing something with Hannah, but it can wait. But I did not know you moved in such exalted circles," said Caroline.

"Only when I know I shall find an angel," smiled Dashell, causing Caroline's resolution to be sensible to come tumbling down.

"Oh," she said, a little taken aback, and felt her face turn pink, while Hannah coughed.

Just then a waitress came up for their order and saved Caroline for the moment. Really, this persistent gentleman had a surprising effect on her, and had done so right from the first time she met him, if she was truthful with herself.

The waitress returned with the tea tray and for the second time Dashell watched Caroline pour out the tea. As before, when she handed him his cup he contrived that their fingers should touch.

Caroline's resolution held firm this time. "May I offer you some cakes, sir?"

Up until now Hannah had remained quiet for she was somewhat in awe of Lord Lonsdale, although he and her mistress seemed to be enjoying each other's company. But when some comment of his caused Caroline to laugh, Hannah impulsively placed her hand on Caroline's and said, "It's lovely to hear you laugh again, Miss Caroline," and then flushed, feeling she had spoken out of turn.

"I am enjoying myself, Hannah dear," responded Caroline, placing her other hand on Hannah's in turn. "Lord Lonsdale is very amusing, although I am sure he does not wish to be bothered by my small problems."

It was on the tip of Dashell's tongue to say he would love to be bothered by Miss Wardlock. He saw the gesture and it warmed him all the more to this lovely girl." There fell a little awkward silence which he broke. "May I have another cup of tea, Miss Wardlock?"

She smiled at him for his tact. "I shall be pleased to oblige."

By the time they had finished their tea the rooms were almost empty. Dashell had been surprised at how many people acknowledged Miss Wardlock, with a wondering look at him, as she smiled back at them. He was relieved to note that none of the men he saw could seriously be considered a rival, except one who had not stayed long because of the scowl on Dashell's face.

Caroline was feeling more relaxed now in his company and found he was easy to talk to, and on his part he enjoyed her straightforwardness with none of this silly simpering and fluttering of eyelashes which he found so irritating.

Caroline laid down her napkin. "If you please, Lord Lonsdale, we must be getting back."

"Of course, Miss Wardlock," said Dashell, "and please allow me to pay for the tea."

"Thank you. That is most kind of you."

"I have enjoyed myself immensely, Miss Wardlock," said Dashell. "Now may I walk you to your house? Although I know it is not very far away." They began walking side by side. "Incidentally, how on earth have you managed to cross roads by yourself all this time?" joked Dashell, looking round at the quietness surrounding them.

"With great fear and trepidation, if I recall correctly, sir," replied Caroline, matching his humour. "We shall not be crossing any roads at all on the way back, so please do not tease me. You have no idea how embarrassed I was the other day. How will you return? Cabs can be difficult to obtain sometimes."

"My carriage is waiting for me."

"Oh? I thought you said earlier that you were just passing by. Now it is my turn to quiz you."

"Yes," replied Dashell serenely. "I left my carriage so I could walk by. You are quite correct, Miss Wardlock."

"Sir, you lead me to believe you are not to be trusted."

"Where you are concerned, Miss Wardlock, I am definitely to be trusted." He looked down at Caroline, compelling her to look up at him, and when she did so he remarked, "Has anyone ever told you what lovely eyes you have, Miss Wardlock?"

Caroline, again taken aback, rallied and said, "So many that I have lost count and you have just given the lie to your own statement!"

"Ha! Brilliant, Miss Wardlock," he said, and they both laughed. They began to walk in silence until Dashell noticed a frown on Caroline's face. "Does something trouble you? Please forgive me if I sounded impertinent just now."

"It's not that, Lord Lonsdale," replied Caroline, "but we only met by chance a few days ago and we have not been formally introduced. I am not concerned about myself, for nobody knows me, at least not in Society, but you are known in much higher circles."

"You need not be concerned on my account, Miss Wardlock," interrupted Dashell. "And as for Society, you could put many a member of it in the shade. You are charming and graceful and have that inner strength which so many lack."

Caroline coloured up. "Sir, you misunderstand me. I was not looking for compliments, but merely stating a fact."

They reached the gate to the house, and as Dashell held it open for her and he did not fail to notice Caroline's quick glance of apprehension towards the house and the tense look which descended upon her once more. He frowned to himself and wondered again what was wrong.

They stood on the path admiring the beautiful pink cabbage roses growing along each side, enjoying their scent. "Mother so loved these roses," began Caroline. "They were her joy."

"She must have been a very special lady," remarked Dashell.

"Yes, she was. She and I were very alike and she was a perfect darling—oh!" Caroline said this with such an earnest expression that Dashell laughed outright. "Sir, I was not seeking a compliment again!"

"Miss Wardlock, you really are delightful! Please allow me to call on you again. Perhaps we could go for a carriage ride if the weather is suitable." Dashell misunderstood the sudden anxious look on her face. "And Hannah too, to make it proper," he added. "May I suggest Monday week, if that is not too soon?" That was not soon enough for him but he did not wish to alarm Miss Wardlock, and he was careful to avoid the end of the week.

"Thank you, sir. I shall look forward to it." Caroline said the words before she really stopped to think. They just came out, as they always seemed to do when speaking to Lord Lonsdale. But it was too late now. She turned round startled at the sudden noise of a blackbird as it flew out of a tree, calling loudly for its mate.

"Goodbye till then, Miss Wardlock," said Dashell, and with a slight bow turned away to walk back to the inn.

Caroline and Hannah slowly went up the front steps and into the house. "I wonder what Lord Lonsdale was doing in this area," mused Caroline. "What kind of business could he have to bring him here? I wonder if he lives round here, but that is not likely. Perhaps he was visiting a relative or someone. How else could he have seen us, Hannah?"

"I tell you, Miss Caroline," answered Hannah, "you could have knocked me down with a feather when Lord Lonsdale walked in. I could hardly believe my eyes. He was very pleased to see you again, anyway."

"Now, Hannah, don't go on so, or I shall suspect you of a little matchmaking. Lord Lonsdale's business is his concern only." It never occurred to Caroline, never even crossed her mind, that she was the business that concerned him. "I shall go upstairs and put my things away."

To tell the truth she wanted to be by herself to think. All her earlier resolutions to be sensible had vanished in the light of this second meeting with the persistent Lord Lonsdale, who made his admiration obvious. She glanced at the little bouquet of flowers he had given her. They were lasting well and she had already decided to press some of them. A foolish decision perhaps but there was little in her life at the moment. She sat on her bed and stared at the tips of her boots peeking out under the hem of her dress, recollecting her tea-time conversation and the second talk at the garden gate, wondering what on earth had possessed her to say the things she did.

She closed her eyes at the memory of her sister and the young gentleman who came calling on her for they had taken a great liking to each other. But Papa had been so unkind and unreasonable. Why? She could not allow Lord Lonsdale to be treated in the same manner.

Downstairs in the kitchen Hannah was giving Johnny his tea, and he appeared to be in a chatty mood. "What did you and Miss Caroline do today?" he asked innocently.

"We stopped at the tearooms on the way back from Chelsea, you know that," began Hannah, surprised that he should ask. "But you will never guess who we saw there!"

"Oh? Oo?"

"Why, Lord Lonsdale himself, the gentleman who called the other day. I was never more amazed in all my life. He said he was passing by and saw us enter the tearooms and thought he would join us. And what's more, he insisted on paying for the tea. Now that's a real gentleman. It's about time Miss Caroline met someone for there isn't much to look at round here, even though I shouldn't be saying that." She eyed Johnny suspiciously. "What on earth are you grinning at?"

Johnny's grin became even wider. "I knoo 'e'd be there 'cos I told 'im that's where you both went on Friday afternoons."

Hannah gave a little shriek. "You told him that? How could you? When did you speak to him, anyway?"

"I followed 'im down the road when 'e left the other day and said if 'e wanted to see Miss Caroline try going to the tearooms," said the unabashed Johnny. "And I also warned him 'im abaht calling 'ere," he continued, with a meaningful look at his sister.

Hannah stared at Johnny open-mouthed. "So Lord Lonsdale didn't just pass by, he came on purpose to see Miss Caroline. Oh, Johnny, I'm not sure you should have done that. Whatever would Miss Caroline think? Whatever did Lord Lonsdale think?"

"'E thought it very good of me. Gave me sixpence 'e did, which was very 'andsome of 'im, considering I only asked for a penny."

"Johnny!" shrieked Hannah again, which was all she could think of saying.

That evening Hannah made Johnny tell Miss Caroline of his part in Lord Lonsdale's happening to join the two of them for tea. Caroline could hardly believe her ears. "You told him where to find me and he actually gave you sixpence for telling him. How dared he!" *And he told me he came looking for an angel*, she thought furiously to herself. All the time he was being so charming he was probably quietly amused at her expense. "Johnny, how could you! I believed it was a chance meeting but you and Lord Lonsdale planned it between you. You are a pair of absolute rogues and it is all quite embarrassing for me."

"I dunno why you are so cross about it, Miss Caroline," complained Johnny peevishly. "We've gotta do somefink to get you out of this 'ouse."

"You know perfectly well we are doing something. And why expect Lord Lonsdale to help? He might not want to," Caroline added, with a feeling things were getting out of control.

"Oh, I fink 'e would. He likes you a lot. I fink 'e would love to help 'cos 'e's taken quite a shine to you."

Caroline began to feel desperate. "Now Johnny, you are talking quite out of turn."

"And when 'e came back wiv you this afternoon," continued Johnny, thinking he might as well make a full confession.

"What do you know about that?" demanded Caroline.

"I wuz behind the laurel bushes listening."

"You were what!" Caroline put both hands up to her hot face. "Johnny, you are absolutely impossible! You will leave the room. Now!"

Johnny obligingly did so, well pleased with himself. Even if Lord Lonsdale was not in love with Miss Caroline—well, 'e oughta be, because she was such a nice lady. And if Miss Caroline had any sense she would be in love with Lord Lonsdale, too.

Caroline remained sitting for several minutes still with her hands to her face trying to make sense of the thoughts spinning through her mind. Even though they had only met a short time ago she knew by the look in Lord Lonsdale's eyes that Johnny was possibly right. She had never heard of the expression "to take a shine to someone," and it did not suggest any comforting degree of permanency. But what was she supposed to do? She dared not return the favour, even if she wanted to, not with his social position and her poor background—and her Papa.

She wished she had not accepted the invitation of a carriage ride, but like other occasions it was too late now. Although she had led a quiet life with her mother and sister she knew this was not quite the correct thing for her to be doing, especially when there had not been a formal introduction. Lord Lonsdale might be attracted to her but he could still just be amusing himself, and if so where did that place her? And if Papa found out there would be a scene, a repetition of what happened to Maude, and Lord Lonsdale could be abused in much the same fashion.

For the umpteenth time Caroline tried to understand why Papa was so morose and cold and why all three of them had to be so cautious of him. She knew he went into the City every day of the week but had no idea what he did. Not even their mother had known. This was not really surprising as many husbands never told their wives what they did. Let it suffice that there was a roof over their heads and the bills were paid.

Home! This gloomy house? Since her mother and sister had died she felt as if a light had gone out and something sinister had taken its place.

Chapter Eight
Dashell Spends Time At A Gymnasium

Dashell went riding in Hyde Park early each morning to help time pass, but he knew he could not stay in the saddle all day. If he took to walking in fashionable places like St.James' Palace Gardens or Regent Street or again in Hyde Park, he was bound to meet up with some wretched female, with or without her mother, whom he would rather avoid. Therefore it would be much safer to keep to some male establishment.

He went to one of the gymnasiums that were springing up in London and made his way to the fencing area. It was crowded, as a certain Monsieur Lecroix from Paris had been engaged to instruct novices in the art of using French dueling foils. Dashell watched for a while then moved over to the boxing hall.

The owner of the establishment, an ex-boxer, prided himself in knowing all the names of the gentlemen who came to his hall. "Would you care for a few rounds, Lord Lonsdale?" he asked, looking round to see which sparring partner was available. "Here, Mike, come and give his lordship a few rounds."

Dashell went into the changing rooms and after a few minutes warm up at a leather punch bag stuffed with wool he felt ready to take Mike on. But Mike soon had him twice against the ropes.

"Begging your pardon, sir," apologised Mike, "but you seem off form today. You keep dropping your guard. Let's have another go." Then, after feinting a couple of times, he broke through Dashell's guard once more and knocked him to the floor.

"All right, Mike," cried Dashell, "you win." He sat up, gingerly feeling his jaw. "You certainly gave me a crack this time."

"Begging your pardon, your lordship," Mike apologised again, "but you have not been concentrating. No offence, of course."

"I know what's wrong with him," drawled one of the bystanders. "He's in love." Lord Norris, one of Dashell's friends, was grinning at him. "Someone spotted him buying a pretty posy the other day."

Dashell got to his feet, a splendid muscular young man but now rather red in the face. "Damn you, Norris," he laughed, shaking his fist at him, "I'll get you for this!"

Questions were fired at him. Come on, Lonsdale, who is she, this Certain Particular of yours? What's her name? Is she pretty? Where are you keeping her?

Dashell laughed back at them. "Do you think I would tell you vulgar lot anything, and have you bandy her name about?"

"What's going on?" cried others, pushing their way in. They had heard the cheers and hilarity and did not want to miss anything.

"Lonsdale's in love. He has a Special Someone but the plague-y fellow won't say anything about her."

"Don't let him near me!" cried someone in mock fear. "That disease is catching. I know it is!"

"He's right!" cried another. "I'm always catching it, but I always manage to find a cure!" Roars of laughter followed that remark.

Mike finally tapped Dashell on the shoulder. "Come on, sir, I'll get you back to the changing rooms before you get cold." Dashell thankfully followed him, receiving slaps on the back as he passed the others.

"Thanks for rescuing me, Mike," said Dashell, "I appreciate that."

"Any time, sir," grinned Mike as he gave his lordship a vigorous toweling.

Dashell emerged feeling refreshed after a cold sponge down and headed for the entrance lobby only to find that word had reached the loungers there. "Here he comes! Is she an heiress?"

"No."

"Then it must be love if she ain't rich!"

He had done his share of ribbing so he took it all in good part. Then he remembered something. In his younger days he and some friends had once crowded into a cab and told the driver to follow the carriage in front. In that carriage was the love-sick brother of one of his friends, and they all considered it a great lark to see where the brother went. He smiled to himself over that memory and it put him on guard, because some of his acquaintances could still think of doing the same thing to him.

Chapter Nine
The Carriage Ride

At last the longed-for day came and Dashell was in his carriage on the way to Becket Lane. He kept a close watch through the carriage's little rear window ready to quell any impudence from his acquaintances. Never would he allow Miss Wardlock to be treated in so cavalier a fashion, and any attempt to do so would be stopped in no uncertain manner. He also knew there would be some raised eyebrows at the neighbourhood to which he was travelling

The carriage stopped outside the house and Dashell eagerly went to knock on the door. Hannah opened it with a welcoming smile and showed him into the parlour. "Please wait, Lord Lonsdale. I will tell Miss Caroline you are here."

It had been a long time for Caroline to wait too. She felt more excited than she cared to admit at seeing him again, but she had a few words to say to him first. Sixpence indeed! She came downstairs just as Hannah ushered Dashell into the parlour.

"You look lovely, Miss Caroline," Hannah beamed at her.

"Hush now," she whispered, "Lord Lonsdale might hear you." She pushed open the parlour door which Hannah had not quite closed, to see Lord Lonsdale standing and holding something behind his back.

"Good afternoon, Miss Wardlock. You indeed look lovely."

"Good afternoon, Lord Lonsdale," she replied sweetly. So he had overheard!

"May I present these flowers to you?" he asked, bringing them out from behind his back.

"They are beautiful," said Caroline, looking at the fragrant blooms, "but I am not sure I should accept them."

"Not accept them?" stammered Dashell in astonishment, turning slightly pale. Then he saw the glint in Caroline's eyes.

"After our tea together a few days ago I had a very enlightening talk with Johnny and he confessed he told you when to find me in the tearooms; and I believe a small coin changed hands."

"Oh," said Dashell, turning slightly pink, still holding the flowers. So apparently Johnny had not mentioned his warning to him about Mr. Wardlock.

"Indeed you may say "oh" sir. And furthermore," continued Caroline relentlessly, "a certain gentleman said that very afternoon that, where I was concerned, he was to be trusted. You know who that gentleman is of course, but I am not sure he is correct about himself. Have you anything to say, sir?" And I will accept my flowers now, if I may." She looked at him quizzically. "You are looking quite flushed. Are you not well?"

Dashell looked at his tormentor. "I am perfectly well, thank you, Miss Wardlock."

"I think I have punished you enough. In fact I am feeling rather contrite."

"If this is punishment, Miss Wardlock, may I have more. Oh, I do love it when you look like that! How many gentlemen have those lovely eyes slain, or have you lost count again?"

Caroline gasped. "Sir, you are impertinent!"

"Oh?" Dashell's eyebrows went up in mock amazement. "Perhaps someone else . . . ?"

"My flowers, please," said Caroline with a smile that completely melted Dashell's heart and he silently gave them to her. "Thank you," she said graciously, smelling their fragrance. "The poor things must be quite giddy after being twirled about so much."

"I would have given them to you sooner had I been allowed to do so."

Caroline ignored that remark. "If you will please excuse me for a few minutes," she said, and slipped out of the room.

She closed the door behind her and lent against it for a moment or two struggling to regain her composure. What in heaven's name had come over her, engaging in repartee with a gentleman whom she barely knew? Would Lord Lonsdale always have this effect on her? Her mother would have been horrified, although she might have laughed afterwards. Taking a deep breath she went to ask Hannah to put the flowers in a vase. "I will take them upstairs and fetch my cloak."

"I can do that, Miss Caroline, "protested Hannah.

"I will take them," insisted Caroline. She was not going back into the parlour to be alone with Lord Lonsdale again. Goodness knows what else she might say.

She came down the front stairs wearing a cloak and bonnet in a pretty shade of green that matched her dress. She opened the parlour door with great composure. "Here I am, Lord Lonsdale. Please forgive me for keeping you waiting."

"You look charming, Miss Wardlock."

"Thank you, sir," she replied graciously.

"I think Hannah would agree with me." Dashell looked as though butter would not melt in his mouth, but Caroline refused to take the bait. "You have forgotten something, Miss Wardlock."

"I have?" she said in surprise. "What is that?"

"You forgot to give me one of your looks."

This time she gave him one of wide open surprise. Had Hannah made her earlier remark hoping he would hear? She recollected that the door had not been quite closed when she pushed it open. She glanced over to Hannah, who was patiently waiting, and decided to speak her later. Hannah and Johnny were two of a kind, it seemed.

With great dignity she took Lord Lonsdale's arm and they left the house. Then another thought struck Caroline with such intensity, something that had not occurred to her before, causing her to catch her breath and making herself cough. Had Hannah meant Lord Lonsdale to overhear her giving their address to that cab driver the other day? And now the two of them, Hannah and Johnny, were conspiring together, to nudge her in a certain direction. *Oh!* she thought, *just wait till I get hold of them later.* And one more thing: that wretch holding her arm had given her pink roses, so what was he implying by that? She was so furious that Dashell felt her arm shake in his.

"Are you not well, Miss Wardlock?" he asked. "I felt your arm tremble."

"I am perfectly well, thank you, sir."

"Oh. Well, you look rather cross about something."

"I do?" said Caroline, forcing herself to sound surprised, and turning to look at him.

"I thought I had found an angel but methinks perhaps I am wrong," he sighed.

Caroline felt she wanted to laugh. "Then perhaps I must be wearing my dark wings," she said, giving his lordship such a dazzling smile that it made him catch his breath.

When they reached the carriage Dashell's horse turned his head at the sound of his master's voice, and pricked up his ears. He was a dark bay, with wide-set luminous eyes and a slight "dish" face, denoting some Eastern blood. Dashell was very proud of him.

"Oh, what a beautiful horse!" exclaimed Caroline. "May I stroke him?"

"Of course you may," replied Dashell, surprised she should even ask. "I think he would like that. Do you ride, Miss Wardlock?" He had a sudden delightful mental picture of the two of them riding in the Barrandale country estate or along country lanes.

"Only a little," she replied. "I have not had much opportunity." She stroked the horse's glossy arched neck and soft velvety nose. "What's his name?" she asked. Surely she would be safe in asking a question like that, and expected something Eastern or Arabic.

"His name is Sparkle. Just like your eyes."

Caroline gasped at the unexpected answer and felt her face turn pink. Well aware of Dashell's smile of amusement, she ignored his proffered hand of assistance and stepped into the carriage by herself and sat down, followed by Hannah. Then Dashell got in and closed the door after him and the carriage moved off. His coachman obviously already had his orders.

"You are silent, Miss Wardlock," observed Dashell.

"I am at a loss for words, sir."

"Never!" And they both laughed.

Dashell seated himself opposite Caroline with Hannah next to her, recalling what a worldly wise uncle had once told him: "Don't stare at them, me boy," his uncle had said. "It annoys them and makes them cross and fidgety. Instead, look at their reflections in the windows. They don't always realise what you are doing so they are much quieter."

So Dashell settled himself comfortably against the upholstery and thoroughly enjoyed carrying out his uncle's advice, may his soul rest in peace, admiring what his blessed uncle would have called Caroline's charming roundness of shoulders and bosom, the line of her lovely throat and the gentle rise and fall of her breast as she breathed.

"Where are you taking us, Lord Lonsdale?" Caroline ventured to ask.

"Just a pleasant drive through Kew Gardens and Richmond Park. I thought you would like that. We can go through the villages of Hammersmith and Chiswick."

"That sounds quite delightful. It reminds me of the times we would walk to Chiswick and back along the riverside when Maude and I were little. We would pick wild flowers and see how many different kinds of birds we could see. Mother knew the names of them all; and she would sketch and paint the flowers when we got home. She taught Maude and me to do the same when we were older. Strange how it looks so different from a carriage; it makes the distance seem greater somehow. But I do not wish to bore you."

"Not at all," replied Dashell pleasantly, thinking that many people he knew would not know a thrush or a swallow even if they saw one. "You make it sound so idyllic."

They passed through Chiswick and followed the road alongside Kew Gardens. The Thames looked particularly splendid as a breeze stirred the leaves and made little ripples on the water. Dashell ordered the carriage to stop while they looked at the scenery. There were some young men in rowing boats and their voices could be clearly heard over the water.

"I know this part, too," remarked Dashell suddenly. "When I was younger I rowed a lot around Windsor and Eton with my brothers, and then later at Oxford. Have you heard of the newly formed Boat Races between Oxford and Cambridge, Miss Wardlock? We used to practice along this stretch of the river sometimes." He asked this question to test her knowledge and was agreeably surprised at her answer.

"Yes, I have heard of it," she said. "I believe it started in 1829. Is that correct?"

"Indeed it is, though how the devil you know surprises me."

"Sometimes when Papa did not notice, we would read his newspapers."

"I might have known there would be some mischief behind it," said Dashell, and wondered at her plaintive little sigh.

Caroline remembered many times seeing muscular young men straining at the oars with a cox calling the strokes. Could she have seen Lord Lonsdale in one of the boats and never known he was there? That thought made her smile and she asked him, "Were you ever in a Boat Race yourself, sir?"

"Yes, I did row for Oxford one year," Dashell answered with pride, "but we lost by a small margin. Cambridge won."

"You lost? How could you!"

For answer Dashell just looked at her and ordered the carriage to move on. But the fact that it was within the realms of possibility that Miss Wardlock could have seen him, even on practice runs, delighted him. They looked at each other, knowing each other's thoughts and Dashell smiled at her, but she coloured faintly and looked away.

They were now in Kew Gardens and Caroline watched the passing scenery with interest. "How much it has changed," she said, "and yet in some ways it has not."

"What do you mean?" asked Dashell curiously.

"The views and paths are mostly the same but I am amazed at how much the trees have grown since we were last here, like the ones over there," pointing to a small grove of silver birches. "I remember sitting in the shade there when we were little. It was so beautiful." She sighed again but a happy sigh this time. "Do you remember, Hannah?" she asked, turning to her maid servant.

"Indeed I do, Miss Caroline. I remember how you and Miss Maude used to play hide-and-seek and worry your poor mother to death if you were away too long."

Caroline saw Dashell give Hannah a quizzical look. "They were a pair of little imps sometimes, sir, especially Miss Caroline," Hannah added innocently.

Dashell's eyes widened., "I would never have thought it possible," he said solemnly. "Can you relate any particular incident?"

"Yes, your lordship," Hannah replied. "There was a time when we had been feeding some ducks on a pond with some scraps of bread and had started to walk away. But Miss Caroline, who was about five at the time, ran back because she wanted to look at the ducks again, only we did not notice at first. Poor Mrs. Wardlock saw Miss Caroline in the distance and was terrified she might fall into the pond. She called and called but Miss Caroline would not come."

"And how was the little miscreant brought back?" asked Dashell, as though Miss Wardlock was not there, yet well aware that she was quietly fuming.

"Well, sir, a lady and gentleman were out walking and heard Mrs. Wardlock calling, so the gentleman ran after Miss Caroline and caught her and picked her up in his arms"—*lucky devil!* thought Dashell—"and brought her back, but Miss Caroline was so cross, she cried."

Dashell burst out laughing. "I would never have thought she could be so troublesome, Hannah."

By now they had reached Richmond Park. "Beautiful, beautiful," murmured Caroline. "It has been quite a while since we were here, too, sir. Do you know that lovely view across the river, the one with the view of Windsor Castle in the distance? May we stop the carriage? I would love to walk to it again."

"Certainly," replied Dashell. He ordered the carriage to stop and they both stepped out.

"Would you like me to come with you, Miss Caroline?" asked Hannah.

"No thank you, Hannah. I think I shall be safe without you."

Dashell laughed. Never had he met a girl with such a sense of humour. "Well now, Hannah, you had better stay in the carriage or you will make your mistress cross again." Then he ordered Stephen to take the carriage to the top of the rise and wait there.

Dashell and Caroline started to walk along slowly. She had removed her bonnet and closed her eyes for a moment to enjoy the gentle breeze on her face just as Dashell turned to say something. He looked away as she opened her eyes.

Dear girl, he thought to himself, *how much I love you. Is it only about two weeks since we first met?* He felt he had known her much longer. She occupied his thoughts so much, had almost become the very air he breathed.

They reached the top of the rise and looked out at the view Caroline so well remembered; the one her mother had loved and painted, with the shadowy outline of the Round Tower of Windsor Castle in the distance. They both stopped to look. "Mother painted that view," began Caroline. "She loved the greeness of it. The painting is still hanging in her old bedroom."

"My father's estate is near Windsor," said Dashell, "and we have a view of the castle too." He smiled at her. "Miss Wardlock, I want to see you again. And again and again," he added softly, as she looked at him with widened eyes and quickened breath. "You are the sweetest and most beautiful woman I have ever met."

"Lord Lonsdale," faltered Caroline, "I thank you for your compliments, but you forget we have only recently met." Then all of Johnny's cheeky words came to mind and to her mortification she could feel her face colouring, well aware of Dashell's obvious delight and wonder in watching her.

"You are beautiful," he said again.

"Sir, this is grossly unfair of you!" cried Caroline, wishing desperately that Hannah was with her, and looked round for the carriage which now seemed so far away. "And do not tell me I can trust you for I am fast beginning to believe I cannot. You tease me too much."

"Then what else can I say, except that I love you," Dashell said. "Forgive me," he added as Caroline caught her breath, "I had not meant to declare myself so soon. I fear I have alarmed you."

"Sir," began Caroline, "before you say anything else, I should tell you I have no background. You can see how poorly I live." She began walking rapidly towards the carriage, taking Dashell by surprise, but he caught up with her and gently took hold of her elbow, turning her round to face him.

"Miss Wardlock, I feel I have distressed you but do my attentions offend you? Please do not send me away, for I cannot promise not to see you again."

Caroline smiled faintly when she saw the earnest expression on Dashell's face. "No, sir, they do not, but I am more distressed for you. I should tell you that when a young man called for my sister, Papa was furious and ordered him out of the house. He gave Maude the reason that we were still in mourning for our mother and that the gentleman should have been more considerate. Perhaps you can now see my concern that he does not abuse you also. Papa also threatened to cut her off without a penny if she thought of eloping. Poor darling, she was so upset."

Once more Johnny's warnings came back to Dashell. What a fiendish brute this Mr. Wardlock appeared to be. Why deny his daughters any happiness?

They continued walking in silence. "Lord Lonsdale," began Caroline, "I must thank you for such a pleasant afternoon for it has brought back so many happy memories."

"Thank you, Miss Wardlock," Dashell replied. "I have enjoyed it greatly as well. Now let me hand you into the carriage."

Chapter Ten
And What Happened Afterwards

The carriage drew up outside the house and the three of them made their way to the front door.

"Oh, look," exclaimed Caroline as they passed the roses, "some of the buds have opened while we were out. How lovely."

Johnny, of course, had been listening for their return and when he heard the sound of wheels he hid round the corner of the house and watched them go inside, grinning to himself.

Then he heard the sound of an approaching vehicle and peered round wondering curiously who it might be, and froze in open-mouthed horror as the cab stopped and Mr. Wardlock stepped out. He could hardly believe his eyes. *"Blimey! Wot the 'ell's 'e doin' 'ere. Wot's goin' on? 'E's never bin this early before."* The cab drove away and Johnny, wanting to warn the others of Mr. Wardlock's return, reckoned they would be in the front parlour by now. He grabbed some pebbles off the ground and threw them up at a parlour window. It was the only thing he could do.

Mr. Wardlock had not been feeling well lately and had been to see a doctor and he had decided to return home earlier than usual. Arriving at Becket Lane and finding a carriage outside the house did nothing to improve his temper. He approached the carriage and asked the driver who owned it, and Stephen had no choice but to say it belonged to Lord Lonsdale.

"I see," Mr. Wardlock sneered, with a glittering stare. What was a gentleman doing calling behind his back? He would find out.

The rattle of pebbles on the parlour window startled the others. Caroline and Hannah knew at once that only Johnny would have thrown those pebbles and that it must be some kind of warning. They looked at each other in unbelief and horror.

"It can't be," cried Caroline as she ran to the front window, aghast to see her Papa coming up the steps. "Oh dear heavens!" she cried. "He's here, Lord Lonsdale, I—" but she had no time to say anything more before the front door opened and then saw her Papa standing in the parlour doorway with a menacing look on his face.

Dashell has also been startled by the pebbles on the window and had been astonished at the reaction of the two women. Again he remembered Johnny's earlier warnings, the feelings and impressions he had had on his previous visits to the house, and the little remarks Miss Wardlock had made. He had thought her sadness was caused mostly by the deaths of her mother and sister, but now he was beginning to understand as the sight of Mr. Wardlock filled him with fascination and horror. Never had he seen such a repellant and unpleasant man. Not quite as tall as Dashell himself, but well-built, with cold pale eyes and a hard mouth. A very sinister person.

Dashell stared at the man before him. How could this creature be the father of the two lovely sisters whose portraits hung on the wall? He glanced at the painting and back to Mr. Wardlock and could see no likeness at all.

He looked at Caroline and was shocked again. Where was that bright and lively girl he had been with all afternoon? She was standing pale and wide-eyed beside Hannah, bracing herself for the coming scene, the very situation she dreaded might happen, now wondering how she could have hoped to defend Lord Lonsdale against her Papa's fiendish temper.

Mr. Wardlock moved further into the room, fixing his cold eyes on Dashell. The four of them stool immobile as though waiting for a cue to act their parts in a play. There was such an intense silence that the ticking of the clock in the hall could be heard quite clearly.

Mr. Wardlock spoke first, addressing Dashell. "Is that your carriage outside, sir?" he demanded, "and who the devil are you anyway?"

"Yes, it is," said Dashell. "And I am Lord Lonsdale."

"Indeed?" Mr. Wardlock sneered. "And how did you become acquainted with my daughter?"

Caroline spoke up, her voice shaking slightly. "Papa, I was in London a few days ago and had a slight accident. I fell down and this gentleman assisted me to my feet and kindly procured a cab for me."

"I see. So if this was a few days ago, sir, why are you here now?"

Dashell replied very evenly. "I happened to be near Fulham Road a day or so later and saw Miss Wardlock, so I enquired after her well being."

"Indeed," sneered Mr. Wardlock again. "A most fortunate coincidence. And I suppose you were told where to call." Dashell could have struck him. Did he always sneer? "And now, sir, explain why you are here today."

Caroline spoke up again. "Lord Lonsdale offered to take me for a carriage ride. It was my fault, Papa." She stopped short at the sight of his face.

"I was addressing this so-called gentleman, not you, Miss." Mr. Wardlock turned back to Dashell. "Is this true, sir?"

Dashell could feel his temper rising. "Yes, I did ask Miss Wardlock and the fault is entirely mine. Do not attach any blame to your daughter." He looked again at Mr. Wardlock and Caroline, then at the double portrait, still unable to see any likeness in looks or manner. Caroline saw the look of disgust on his face and turned away in shame, misunderstanding the look's meaning. But Hannah saw everything and knew exactly what Lord Lonsdale was thinking.

Mr. Wardlock now addressed Caroline. "And you accepted? When the cat is away the mouse will play, it seems, entertaining a gentleman behind my back. How inopportune for you I should come home early for once."

"Miss Caroline was not alone, sir. I was with her in the carriage." This time Hannah spoke up, standing with a protective arm round her young mistress.

"Be silent, woman!" Mr. Wardlock turned again to Dashell. "Are you a rake, a libertine, sir, that you offer carriage rides to young women without their fathers' consent or knowledge?"

"Do you insult me, sir?" Dashell knew that whatever his faults he was not that type of man.

Wardlock hesitated, realizing Lord Lonsdale was not a mere boy to be ordered out of the house, like that other caller, but that this was a much stronger personage. He therefore turned back to Caroline and mouthing in anger, screamed out, "You harlot! You shameless hussy! You . . . you common little piece!"

"Papa!" Caroline cried out like the words hurled at her were physical blows, putting her hands to her face as though shielding herself.

Dashell's jaw literally dropped open in amazement and then in one quick movement he came face to face with Wardlock. "How dare you, sir! How dare you! Would you now insult your own daughter?" He looked hard into Wardlock's face, his own suffused with anger, hands clenched at his side. Like the boxer he was Dashell saw the flinch, the first flicker of fear on the other man's face as the latter stepped back. In boxing parlance he knew he had Wardlock cornered. He then turned round to look at the other two and saw Caroline, her face deathly pale, obviously shaken by those terrible words.

Dashell turned to face Wardlock again, his eyes boring into the man, and began speaking in a very slow and menacing way. "I shall leave, for I will not give you the satisfaction of ordering me out of the house. But I will come back. And when I do, if I find that you have laid so much as one finger on this lady or hurt so much as one hair on her head, you will answer to me. Is that clear?"

Wardlock could not answer. His face turned a sickly colour and he stepped back again.

Caroline and Hannah were clinging to each other, the former staring at Dashell as though she did not know him. Who was this man? Where was the amusing gentleman she had been with all afternoon, who said he loved her? He had gone, replaced by a complete stranger.

Where was that darling girl he had fallen in love with? Dashell wondered, his heart almost breaking at the sight of her. What in heaven's name had that fiend done to her? He held one cold little hand in his firm clasp and kissed it, hoping to reassure Caroline, but she shrank back from him. "Hannah, take care of her," he whispered gently.

"Yes, sir," Hannah whispered back. She turned away with one arm round her mistress, hardly able to hold back her own tears. Caroline allowed herself to be led away but looked back at Dashell as she began going upstairs, her face still pale and stricken, so different from the happy way she had come down those stairs only few hours before.

Dashell watched them go, then picked his hat and gloves off the hall table and left the house. He completely ignored Wardlock. He strode down the path, still seething with anger. "To my rooms, Stephen," he ordered, and jumped into the carriage, slamming the door so hard, it rocked, as Stephen drove off white-faced.

Wardlock did not move at first as that terrifying young man had really shaken him. Then he slowly made his way into his downstairs room and closed the door behind him.

At the sound of the carriage leaving, Johnny, who had been outside the open window listening, or rather could not help overhearing all this time, peered round the corner of the house and watched it go. *Blimey*, he said to himself several times over. He leaned back against the wall of the house and mopped his face with both sleeves of his shirt. Thank goodness he had time to warn the others, not that it had done much good. He had heard the terrible accusations hurled at Miss Caroline and her cry in response, and Lord Lonsdale's thundering answers. What an upset this time, far worse than the other one. *Three cheers for you, yer lordship, giving His Horrible Nibs wot for. Should have 'appened to him long ago.*

Hannah had helped Caroline into her room. "I must go, dear. With that man here I shall have to prepare a proper supper," she whispered, knowing that Mr. Wardlock would still expect his evening meal. "Will you be all right?"

Caroline nodded, barely able to talk. When she heard Hannah close the door behind her, she threw herself on her bed and wept as she had never wept before, until she wondered how she had so many tears to weep. The shame of those words humiliated her, as did the look of horror on Lord Lonsdale's face. Did he really believe them, that she had just accepted that carriage ride because she was—all that? She bitterly regretted having done so now. She was guilty of a bad social error, made worse by knowing that Papa could be right.

She wept at the memory of the scene between Papa and Maude when her sister's gentleman called, and understood now why Maude had been found at the bottom of the stairs with a broken neck. Her life had been so lonely since. *Mother, Mother, Mother*, she moaned to herself, *why did you have to die?* She missed them both so much.

Lord Lonsdale had said he loved her but he probably did not mean it. The change in him still terrified Caroline; she was hardly aware when he kissed her hand, he was almost like a stranger. She doubted she would ever see him again, as he must be so disgusted with her and her background. She wept again when she remembered the scolding she was going to give Hannah, whom she had clung to for very comfort and support. All these thoughts came at one and the same time, going round and round in Caroline's head like the sails of a windmill, until she was exhausted.

When Hannah returned wearily to the kitchen she found Johnny sitting tense and silent. She had hardly gone through the doorway when a bell rang and she had to answer it.

"Wot did That Misery want yer for?" Johnny demanded when she came back. "Can't 'e just shut up? Cor, wot a swine," he muttered under his breath.

Hannah sat down and put her elbow on the table, resting her head on her hand. "Oh, Johnny, what a day. Who would have thought this would happen. Why did he have to come back earlier than usual? I had to count to ten before I could knock and open the door and be civil to him, believe you me. He said that in future he wanted all his meals on a tray in his room because he does not wish to be associated with such a person as his daughter. Huh. I am only too thankful his daughter does not have to associate with him, the hateful man. What he did and said to Miss Caroline was unforgiveable. If you could have seen her, she was so happy earlier and now she is probably crying her eyes out." Hannah paused to mop her own eyes while Johnny's mouth tightened. "But Johnny, you should have seen and heard Lord Lonsdale. He put the fear of God into that man and said that if he hurt her in any way he would come after him."

"Good," said Johnny. "That's just wot 'e needs." He had already decided not to tell Hannah he had heard everything through the open window.

Hannah got up with another sigh. "I had better start getting the supper, and thank goodness we had planned a cold one. We don't want any more trouble if it is late. At least I won't have to wait on Mr. Wardlock at table so I should be thankful for small mercies." She set about getting the meal ready, placed it on a tray and knocked on Mr. Wardlock's door, and without waiting for an answer, went straight in.

Mr. Wardlock was still looking shaken and the sight of him sent a shudder through Hannah. Forcing herself to speak, she said, "If you please, sir, if you would place the tray outside the door when you have finished then I will not have to disturb you," then gave a little bob and shut the door behind her.

Hannah remembered that Miss Caroline's cloak and bonnet were still in the parlour and went to fetch them. She closed the window and stepped on one of the pebbles that Johnny had thrown. It must have missed the glass and fallen on the floor. Thank goodness he had the presence of mind to warn them! Hannah was about to go upstairs and stopped with one foot on the bottom step. No, she would not go this way, Mr. Wardlock might hear her. She would use the back stairs as much as possible, at least when that man was in the house. Anyway, although she was anxious to go upstairs she must speak to Johnny first and tell him her plans.

"Johnny," she began, sitting at the table again and still holding the cloak and bonnet, "you and I have got to look after Miss Caroline like never before. I don't trust that man one inch, even after what Lord Lonsdale said to him, and we don't want any more trouble."

Johnny's eyes widened in alarm. "Oh, no! You don't fink 'e's goin' to do anyfing, do yer? Yer don't fink Miss Caroline will do anyfing like wot Miss Maude did?" His voice trailed off. He was thoroughly alarmed now; he had still never mentioned his suspicions about Miss Maude's death to Hannah.

"No, she won't," said Hannah decisively, "because you and I are not going to let her. Lord Lonsdale would never forgive us if anything happened to her. Oh, Johnny, if you could have seen them together. Those two are made for each other and now everything has been spoiled."

"Do yer fink he will come back?"

"Of course he will. He said so, didn't he? Need you ask."

"So wot should we do?"

"To begin with, I am going to sleep in the room with Miss Caroline at nights. Now, Johnny, I want you to take your boots off."

"Take me boots off?" he repeated feebly, staring at her.

"Yes, that's what I said. When we go upstairs I want you to do something for me as you are much lighter on your feet than I am, and I don't want Mr. Wardlock to hear you. Now I must go and see to Miss Caroline. I have left her alone long enough as it is." She went upstairs followed by a mystified Johnny, and tapped gently on Caroline's bedroom door and went in.

Caroline was still lying on her bed but sat up when she saw Hannah, who came and sat beside her and put a pair of soft arms around her.

"I came as soon as I could after I had to get his supper," said Hannah gently, holding her closely. She put a hand on the bed to ease her position and felt a damp patch on the bedspread. "Why, Miss Caroline, you have been crying quite a lot."

Caroline replied with a wan smile. "Oh, Hannah, every time I think I have run out of tears more seem to come. Did you see that look of d-disgust on Lord L-Lonsdale's f-face?" she said, hiccupping a little.

"Yes, I did, dear, but it was not meant for you. How could it be when he loves you?"

"Not any more, Hannah. I shall never see him again. Not after all those dreadful words said to me. How could Papa be so cruel."

"Yes, you will, dear," Hannah said, giving her another reassuring kiss, "and when he does he will not want to see reddened eyes and a puffy face."

Caroline sighed and shook her head. There seemed nothing more to say. Her nose was so stuffed up she resorted to sniffing, and Hannah got up to find her a handkerchief or two.

Johnny was waiting patiently in the doorway and saw Miss Caroline's pale face with its look of desolation, and remembered how she had been earlier that afternoon in the company of Lord Lonsdale. He then shifted his gaze and appeared to be staring at a blank wall with a wooden expression. But in actual fact he was making a silent and most solemn pact with himself that one day—he did not know how, when or where, but one day—he would get revenge on what Mr. Ghastly Geezer did to Miss Caroline, just see if 'e didn't.

Caroline sat up straight and in doing so caught sight of Johnny in stockinged feet. She could not help but smile at him. "Johnny, whatever are you doing standing there?"

He grinned back. "'annah's orders, Miss Caroline."

"Ah, yes that's right," agreed Hannah, "I told him to take his boots off so he would not be heard moving about. Now, Miss Caroline, I am going to be very firm about this but I am going to sleep in this room with you. I can sleep on the couch tonight and then tomorrow Johnny and I can bring in another bed." She paused as Caroline stared at her. "I promised Lord Lonsdale I would look after you, and quite frankly I do not trust your Papa."

"But Hannah, whatever do you think he would do?" asked Caroline, wide-eyed.

"He could do anything, and what's more he is not going to get a chance." How could Hannah tell her dear young mistress the real reason for her concern, something she had never even told to Johnny. She would never forgive herself if anything happened to Miss Caroline. "So when we go to bed I shall lock the door. That's why I want Johnny to fetch a few things out of my room. He is much lighter on his feet than I am, and we don't want to arouse any suspicions. Also, we will use the back stairs as much as possible except when we have the house to ourselves. That way, Miss Caroline, you will avoid having to meet your Papa."

"Why, Hannah, you sound so decisive, and I do agree with you, but I will still need to have meals with Papa, although I don't think I could bear it after all the horrible things he said to me."

"You won't have to, dear," Hannah replied. "He told me he wants all his meals to be taken in to his room on a tray in future. He also said he does not wish to see you again."

"Really, Hannah? Oh, what a relief. I can hardly believe it."

"Well, I think that's settled. Now, Johnny, you have been patiently waiting. I want you to get some things for me and anything else I can get tomorrow. Remember to be quiet, especially opening and closing drawers and doors."

Johnny quickly returned with the things Hannah wanted and now felt it was his turn to speak. "Miss Caroline," he began, clearing his throat nervously, "I dunno quite 'ow to say this, you bein' upset an' all, but you've gotta be careful goin' down them front stairs. We don't want yer fallin' like . . . like . . ." he trailed off lamely, being short of words for once.

"Why Johnny, whatever do you mean?" Caroline asked.

"Well, er—yer 'ave bin crying a lot," Johnny again floundered to a stop, not daring to give his real reason. "Please, Miss Caroline, promise me you'll be careful." He was blissfully unaware of the fact that he, a mere servant boy, was begging the lady of the house to promise something, and Caroline was too preoccupied to notice it herself.

"Of course I will be careful, Johnny," said Caroline, rather surprised at his words. Poor Maude must have been more heartbroken than she realized. "Anyway, I shall not be using them much if we are taking the back stairs." The thought of meeting Papa was enough to make her keep away from the front stairs altogether.

It was now beginning to get dark and Hannah reminded them that they had not yet had their supper. Johnny perked up at that but Caroline was not so sure. "I don't think I could, Hannah. I don't feel hungry."

"You must, dear. Don't let your Papa think he has the upper hand. Besides, Lord Lonsdale will want to see you in good colour when he comes."

Caroline felt a faint hope rising. "Do you think he will come back?"

"Of course he will. I am sure of it. Now we had all best be going downstairs. I must pick up that tray too, before your Papa comes out and wonders what I have been doing."

Johnny, who was halfway down the stairs, called back softly, "I'll get it, 'annah. I'm still in me socks."

Down in the kitchen Caroline remarked, "This reminds me of the time when Maude and I had our teas in here when we were little. We always loved it, it was so cozy." Then she had a frightening thought. "Hannah, suppose Papa does ask to see me, after all. I shall have to go, although I could refuse to see him."

"If you do, I shall go with you," Hannah replied grimly. "And if he tells me to go away I shall refuse to do so. I must keep my promise to Lord Lonsdale. Now, Miss Caroline, supper is ready so try and eat at least something."

Lord Lonsdale did not return the next day, nor did he come the day after that. By the third day Hannah and Johnny were exchanging grim anxious looks with each other, and were tight lipped about it, too.

Chapter Eleven
Dashell Is Summoned To Windsor

Dashell sat back in his carriage. Never in his life had he been so angry. Meeting Mr. Wardlock in that manner was a shock, especially after such a pleasant afternoon, and the character of the man was quite different to the one he had imagined. Of course he had paid heed to Johnny's warnings and had wondered at Miss Wardlock's fears and apprehensions, and now he understood them. Good grief! What kind of a fiend was that man to hurl insults at his own daughter—if she was his daughter?

He still smarted at the insults to his person for he had always believed himself to be a gentleman, by disposition as well as birth. But the insults to Miss Wardlock had been his breaking point. He was almost glad he had threatened Wardlock the way he had, even in his own house, which was actually a great social faux pas on his part. He knew he had terrified Miss Wardlock. That look on her dear face! He had meant that carriage ride as a generous gesture and nothing else, just to get her out of that house for a few hours or so. Hannah had come as well and they had all enjoyed it, and now it had been turned into something sordid.

Dashell sat with his elbows on his knees and his face in his hands, unable to endure thinking of her as Miss Wardlock any more, but now as Caroline. What an awful name. Ward. Lock. It made the house sound like a prison. *Caroline, my darling,* he thought, *what did I do to you? I should never have declared my love for you so soon. I only alarmed you. If I had not kept you talking we could have returned sooner and avoided that terrible* scene. *It could have waited, but you were so beautiful. Caroline, you must forgive me.*

He sat up straight. If some minor mysteries had been cleared up, an even greater one had emerged. Looking from Wardlock to Caroline then to the painting on the wall and back again, Dashell had not seen any likeness in looks or manner. It was impossible that man could be the father of those two sisters. Stepfather, yes. Real father, no. Did Caroline believe him to be her father? Did she not realise he could be her stepfather instead? He would return to the house the next day to see her, even if he had to beg her to receive him. And if Wardlock was not her real name, what was? Who was she? Whose daughter had he fallen in love with? What an impossible position to be in.

He had every intention of returning the next day, as he could not leave Caroline to suffer alone. He had twice nearly ordered the carriage to turn back, but realized each time it would only make matters worse. Thank heaven for both Hannah and Johnny, he knew they would look after their mistress.

The carriage finally came to a halt outside his rooms and Dashell thankfully stepped down. He had a sudden thought: "Stephen, did that Mr. Wardlock speak to you at all at Becket Lane?"

Stephen looked at his young master's haggard face and wondered what had happened back at the house. It must have had something to do with the arrival of that man, for he had overheard certain words through the open windows, although if he was asked he would deny hearing anything. "As a matter of fact he did, sir. He enquired who owned the carriage and I had to say it belonged to you. I hope that was all right, sir." Stephen was rather apprehensive, as Lord Lonsdale was in quite a rare mood.

"Yes, of course, Stephen. You had no alternative but to answer. But tell me, what was your impression of Wardlock? You may speak freely." Master and servant were on good terms and understood one another.

"Well, sir," began Stephen, "I thought him a very ugly customer, quite a nasty piece of work. Fair gave me the shivers, the way he spoke." *My sentiments exactly*, thought Dashell. "And what's more, sir," Stephen continued cautiously, "when he approached the carriage Sparkle turned his head and flattened his ears at him."

"Did he indeed," said Dashell with a grim little laugh. "Well, it is said animals always know these things." He moved forward to stroke Sparkle's arched neck then remembered how a more gentle hand had done the very same thing earlier that afternoon, and his arm fell back to his side with a clenched fist. Stephen saw this and wished he had kept quiet, but how was he to know? If he incurred his lordship's wrath, then so be it.

Dashell had been standing with his back to the entrance to his rooms but turned round at the sound of the door opening and approaching footsteps. It was Walter, his manservant, coming out with a letter in his hand, who had to use all his training to remain impassive at the sight of his lordship's face. "This letter came for you, sir, shortly after you left," Walter said. "George brought it round from the house. I beg your pardon, sir, but I had no means to give it to you sooner."

"That's quite all right, Walter," said Dashell, taking the letter. He recognized his father's handwriting at once and noted that the letter had been marked "Urgent". It must have come by special messenger. He turned away and tore the letter open, while Walter cocked a quizzical eye at Stephen, who frowned at him and shook his head slightly.

The note was a brief summons from Lord Barrandale for Dashell to come to Barrandale Park immediately, with that last word underlined. Lord Barrandale did not often issue these summons but when he did he expected absolute obedience. What the devil could be wrong? His father could not be ill for his handwriting was quite strong. Dashell felt he already knew the answer and he swore under his breath. To him the more urgent commitment was to Caroline. This note could not have come at a more inopportune time, although his father could not have known. With a heavy heart he turned round to two impassive servants. "Walter, Stephen," he began.

"Yes, sir?" they replied together.

"I have to return to Barrandale Park. Tonight, in fact. Stephen, would you take Sparkle to the stables and see to him and then bring him back here, saddled, in an hour's time. And would you also enquire of Matthew if there has been any message from or concerning Mr. Walden."

"Very good, sir," replied Stephen, and drove away.

At least, thought Dashell, he could honestly say to his father that he had been enquiring after Walden for several days. He entered his rooms feeling torn in two between his love and concern for Caroline and his very real affection and regard for his father, and come what may he knew his father had to come first. He would have to send a letter to Caroline explaining his absence and just hope she would understand.

Walter had followed his lordship indoors, waiting for orders. "Lay out some fresh linen for me, will you," said Dashell. "I will change before I go."

"Very good, sir." Seeing Lord Lonsdale so tense and edgy made Walter cautious and he was glad to have something to do.

Dashell went slowly into the living room wondering how much more he could take. What had started out so well that day had now turned into a nightmare and it was not over yet. He did not hold out much hope of there being any message from Walden. He was fairly certain that was why the summons had come. He remembered his conversation with his aunt some days ago and felt uneasy. He poured himself a brandy and water and swallowed a mouthful, then put the glass down, went over to a small writing table and pulled out some paper. He must write to Caroline. He was about to write "Dear Miss Wardlock" and stopped; he would not address her by that awful name. It was not quite socially correct but he would address her as "Miss Caroline".

Dear Miss Caroline,

On returning to my rooms just now I received an urgent summons from my father requesting me to return to Windsor immediately and of necessity I must go. I do not know how long I shall be away. Please forgive me for doing this. Trust me when I say I shall be thinking of you.

Yours ever,
Lonsdale

Only a brief note but perhaps it was better not to make it too long. Picking up his glass he finished the contents.

Walter appeared in the doorway. "I have prepared the things you requested, sir."

"Thank you," said Dashell. "That letter on the writing table, Walter, take it to the Post Office tomorrow without fail."

"Very good, sir."

Dashell went to his bedroom where Walter had poured out some water into a basin and began splashing his face. In actual fact contact with Wardlock had made him feel soiled all over and he wondered what had induced Caroline's mother to marry him. How that brave girl survived amazed him, but did not the act of saving that child prove her bravery? He again felt a surge of relief to know Hannah and Johnny were with Caroline. There could not be two better people to look after her. He stripped to his waist to sponge himself, while his manservant stood ready with a towel, admiring the well-muscled back as his lordship dried himself off. Dashell glanced at the clock on the mantelpiece. Time enough yet.

"Will you require anything to eat, sir, before you leave?" Walter ventured to ask, as he handed his master a clean shirt. Dashell just shook his head. He was in no mood for any fussiness. Fortunately Walter sensed this and quietly helped Dashell finish dressing.

Stephen was at the front door with Sparkle when Dashell came out. "Any message at all, Stephen?"

"No, sir. Matthew has nothing to report."

Damn! Dashell swore under his breath. He had thought that would be the answer. It was time Walden put in an appearance anyway, unless he had turned up at Barrandale Park. Now that was a possibility. Ascot Racecourse was only a few miles away from the Park, if there were any races going on right now.

Without wasting any more time Dashell mounted and rode away.

Chapter Twelve
The Servants Wonder

Both servants stood watching until Lord Lonsdale was out of sight. "I hope he'll be all right," said Stephen suddenly, as though speaking to himself.

"Why ever not?" asked Walter, staring. "What do you mean?"

"Well, it's beginning to get dark and he has to cross Hounslow Heath and that can be dangerous."

"Anyway," persisted Walter, "what the hell has been going on? Has his lordship quarrelled with his lady-love?"

"Oh, shut up, Walter," said Stephen irritably.

"Hey, I'm only asking," Walter retorted. "He was as happy as a lark when he left earlier and then he comes back like a thundercloud. Of course something has happened. And I'll warrant Mr. Walden has something to do with Lord Lonsdale's return to the Park, for why else would he be asking about him?"

Walter certainly had a point and would have rattled on but Stephen stopped him.

"I must tidy up here first," said Walter, "and then I'll come round for supper."

As Stephen walked back to the house he brought to mind what Reuben, Lord Barrandale's coachman, had told him when Stephen first became coachman to Lord Lonsdale. Reuben had driven into him that a coachman was very often the only person who knew where the master really went and therefore had to be completely trustworthy.

Not that there had been anything untoward about this afternoon's drive, but while waiting outside the house Stephen had heard raised voices and had been able to make out some of the words spoken, quite dreadful some of them, and all because of that awful man unexpectedly appearing. Then his lordship had come out in a furious rage, which was quite unlike him.

The trouble was Walter wanted to know why Lord Lonsdale had returned the way he did; and Matthew would want to know more about his lordship's summons to return to Windsor because there was obviously something going on there.

Stephen reached the stables at Barrandale house feeling thankful there was plenty of work for him to do, most of which he could leave until tomorrow.

Walter must have been thinking the same way that he could tidy up tomorrow, for he appeared surprisingly quickly, not wanting to miss anything.

"Oh," said Stephen, surprised to see him so soon. "Well, now that you are here I can lock the stable gate. You go in while I clean myself up."

As no member of the family was in residence and there was therefore no table to wait on, the servants' meal could be leisurely. They always ate in silence and talked when they were finished and could relax.

"So, Stephen," began Matthew, "how did the day go? And why did Lord Lonsdale come back so angry?"

Stephen looked at Walter: he must have told Matthew already. He sighed to himself. He had better get it over with. "Yes, it was a pleasant drive out to Kew Gardens and then into Richmond Park."

"What? All by himself?" quipped George, a footman, cheekily, and promptly got silenced by a look from Matthew.

"No, there was a lady with him."

"What's she like, this lady?" asked Janet, the cook. "Is she pretty?"

"Pretty?" repeated Stephen, "She's more than that. She's beautiful."

"So you went for this drive," encouraged Matthew, who was quite a romantic at heart in spite of his impassive exterior.

"When we were in Richmond Park Lord Lonsdale and the lady went for a short walk, while I waited with the carriage with the maid."

"Oh, so they were alone together then. At last," said George.

"Yes, they were," retorted Stephen. "Lord Lonsdale is a gentleman, you know."

"Well, I don't know." George could be quite flippant sometimes.

"That's quite enough sauce from you, George," said Matthew sternly.

George encountered a steely look from Stephen. "Sorry," he muttered.

"Well, as I was saying," continued Stephen, "I waited with the carriage, and the maid took a short walk by herself. She seemed a decent person and spoke civilly to me. Then Lord Lonsdale and the lady returned and we drove back to the house."

"Had they quarrelled at all?" asked Matthew, who hated upsets of any kind.

"No, the whole drive was very pleasant."

"So what made Lord Lonsdale angry?" asked Walter, who was determined to find out.

Stephen hesitated. Now came the hard part. "The trouble started when the lady's father returned unexpectedly. He asked me who the carriage belonged to and I had to tell him, and he went into the house looking very displeased."

"So he could not have known his lordship would be visiting," suggested Walter.

"I suppose not. I have no idea. Anyway, I heard raised voices."

"Could you hear what was said?" asked Matthew. "Well, go on," he urged, as Stephen fell silent.

Stephen might well hesitate. The trouble was that he had heard the insults screamed out to Lord Lonsdale and the lady. He also knew that anything he said would be repeated for some time to come. He could not betray either Lord Lonsdale or the lady, who could quite possibly become the future Lady Lonsdale, so like the loyal fellow he was he would deny hearing anything. "No, I couldn't make out the words," he finally said, "and I have never seen Lord Lonsdale so angry."

"Ah," said Walter. He had been waiting for this. "What happened then?"

"When we got back to his rooms Lord Lonsdale asked me if the lady's father had spoken to me at all, and I said that he had asked who owned the carriage." Stephen left out the rest of the conversation he had with Lord Lonsdale as he had an uncomfortable feeling that he had already said too much. "Then Walter came out with that letter from Lord Barrandale."

"That's right!" cried Walter. "When I handed him the letter I almost gasped at the sight of his expression. He read it and then said he had to return to Barrandale Park at once."

"So in other words he has had two upsets today," remarked Matthew, feeling rather sorry for his lordship. "I wonder what really took place at that house?" he wondered. A rhetorical question as they would probably never know. He looked at his empty cup. "Any more tea, Janet?" he asked hopefully.

"I warrant that letter was about Mr. Walden," declared Walter, "for why else did Lord Lonsdale ask if there had been any message."

"Aye, maybe you're right," said Matthew. "Perhaps there's trouble brewing there as well."

"How was he with you, Walter?" asked Stephen.

"I was very careful, I don't mind admitting," he replied. "I kept on thinking of all the boxing he does. And he left me a letter addressed to the lady, by the name of Miss Wardlock, which I have to take to the Post Office in the morning. First thing, he said."

"Really?" said Matthew. "Mind you do that."

"I don't need reminding," replied Walter stiffly. Matthew could be officious sometimes.

Stephen felt relieved about that letter. For some reason he could not explain he hoped all was well between Lord Lonsdale and the lady, whom they now all knew as Miss Wardlock. Stephen knew it was none of his business, as he was only a servant, but somehow he could not help feeling concerned. Only time would tell.

"Do you think Lord Lonsdale is in love with this lady?" enquired Janet.

Stephen smiled as he recollected Lord Lonsdale's attentions to Miss Wardlock. "Yes, I think he could be."

"I wonder if she could become the next Lady Lonsdale," mused Matthew. "Who is she anyway? What is her background? Her family?"

They were all interested now, for this did concern them. If Miss Wardlock became Lady Lonsdale, she would be the new mistress and the future Lady Barrandale when in time Lord Lonsdale inherited the title.

"It's about time Lord Lonsdale settled down," mused Matthew again. "He must be twenty-five by now. I wonder how and where he met her? Any ideas, Stephen, or you, Walter?" They both shook their heads. "Wardlock sounds such an ordinary name," continued Matthew, who prided himself on his knowledge of family names, "and who would want to live at Fulham? It's not a fashionable neighbourhood."

George remarked, unfortunately, "Perhaps Lord Lonsdale does not mean well by her."

Matthew cried out in protest and the others gasped at George's audacity, and none of them was prepared for Stephen's response. He jumped to his feet, slamming the palms of his hands down hard on the table, startling everyone and making the tea cups rattle. "How dare you say that?" he cried, his flushed face showing how angry he was. "I have seen Miss Wardlock and you haven't and I say she is a lady,"

"Hey, you two!" shouted Matthew, alarmed at Stephen's response. "Stephen, sit down will you. And you, George, what the hell has got into you. Any more from you and I will have to take you severely in hand."

"And I'll tell you something else, George," put in Janet. "Being a lady with a capital L does not necessarily make a lady a lady, if you know what I mean, and if this Miss Wardlock is a lady as Stephen says, then that's good enough for the rest of us, so keep that smirk off your face or I'll wipe it off for you."

George turned pale at these strong rebukes, and went very quiet as Stephen still glared at him. "I'm sorry," he muttered, feeling rather ashamed of himself.

"It must have been something awful, that letter," Matthew continued. "I don't want to keep harping on about it but usually anything concerning Mr. Walden spells trouble. I've heard enough about him from the others at Windsor."

"You could be right, Matthew," said Janet. "I've got a feeling something awful is going to happen."

"Please, no!" cried Matthew in alarm. He knew Janet's 'feelings'. Trouble was, she was often right.

"I can't help it, Matthew, but I just have this creepy feeling."

All the others looked interested. What do you mean "creepy?" they wanted to know.

"Never mind now. You will know when it happens," was all the information she would impart, glancing apologetically at Matthew, who put his elbows on the table and his head in his hands, and groaned.

Time was getting on and Walter decided he should leave.

Stephen lit the stable lantern he had left outside the kitchen door. "I'll unlock the gate for you, Walter," he said.

"That was some talk tonight," murmured Walter. "Whatever got into George, I wonder?"

"I don't know," replied Stephen tersely. Neither of them really liked George. "Here, take the lantern, you can bring it back tomorrow."

"Thanks," said Walter. "Good night."

Stephen closed and locked the gate behind Walter and went up to his small room above the stables, first taking another lantern from the harness room. He did not have to make a last minute check of the stalls since they were all empty.

Chapter Thirteen

Father and Son

Dashell had ridden off knowing he only had a certain amount of time before it got quite dark to cross Hounslow Heath and reach the village of Hounslow. It was only a few miles from Chiswick, which was so near to Kew Gardens where he had been with Caroline that afternoon. *Caroline, my darling, why did I delay you by talking? That terrible scene could have been avoided.* He cursed himself again for causing her so much hurt.

Caroline never left his thoughts and Dashell would have been heart-broken if he had known how much she had wept, or how much she believed she would never see him again. He smiled to himself as he recalled their repartee when he had presented her with those roses and teased her when she asked the name of his horse. What a darling she was. So alive and so sweet. So unlike anyone else he had met.

Dashell had wanted to meet Mr. Wardlock in order to ask for her hand in marriage, and to enquire about her background, believing her to be of good family. But now everything had been turned upside down. His love for Caroline had not changed but Dashell was determined to get the truth out of that man somehow. He had to clear the mystery for Caroline's sake too. The next time he saw her he would ask her to relate her story, for there was so much he wanted to know. Dashell then reminded himself that he had not considered enough the full reason for his return to Barrandale Park. Whatever it was, he would find out soon enough.

He stopped briefly at an inn for a meal, then left to finish his journey. There was still about ten miles to ride.

It was past ten o'clock when Dashell walked Sparkle the last mile along the avenue up to the house. His father must have gone to bed early, for there was no light at his window. He dismounted stiffly at the stable gates and rang the bell. The sudden clang echoed round the yard and startled the stablemen, who came running out, one with a lantern.

"Lord Lonsdale," cried Reuben, when the gates were swung open. "We were not expecting you, or we would have kept watch for you."

"That's quite all right, Reuben," said Dashell. "James, take care of Sparkle will you. He has been in harness today as well as the ride here. I expect he would enjoy a good feed."

"Yes, of course, sir." James could not help wondering what brought his lordship home this late, unless it was that letter a groom had taken to the Post Office that morning.

A footman came out with a lamp and Dashell went along an inside passage to the main hall. He looked into his father's study just to make sure his father was not there, then into the library, but his father was not there either. Although the word "immediately" had been underlined in his father's letter perhaps Dashell was not expected quite so soon. He sighed as he rang the bell for Simmonds.

Simmonds appeared quickly, begging pardon for being in his house robe. "I have just been told of your arrival, your lordship. Lord Barrandale retired early. He wished to be informed when you came. Shall I do so, sir?"

"No, Simmonds. I shall go up to his room myself. But before I do I want to ask you a few questions. Can you tell me what this is all about?" Simmonds was a trusted servant and Dashell wanted to obtain his observations first.

"Not a great deal, sir. His lordship received a letter this morning which seemed to trouble him. He did not reveal its contents to me, nor did he say who it was from, nor did he take me into his confidence." Simmonds coughed slightly. "His lordship enquired if anything had been heard from Mr. Walden." *I knew it*, thought Dashell. *It sounds as though Walden's creditors are catching up with him at last.* "Lord Barrandale wrote a letter to be sent to you at once by special messenger," continued Simmonds. "That is all I can tell you, sir."

"Thank you, Simmonds," replied Dashell. He then asked, "How has my father been keeping since I last saw him?"

"His lordship has been in his usual excellent health, sir." Simmonds looked at Lord Lonsdale's tired face. "Do you require any refreshments, sir?"

"No thank you. I had a meal on the way here. I shall see myself to bed." In his present mood Dashell did not want servants around him. "I shall look in on my father before doing so."

"Very good. Goodnight, sir."

Dashell took his lamp and went upstairs. What a day! He was tired out mentally and physically, and that house on Becket Lane seemed so far away. He rather hoped his father would be asleep and knocked gently on the bedroom door, not really wanting to be heard, before opening it carefully and looking in. The room was in darkness and Dashell smiled to himself when he heard gentle snores. Well, that was that. At least he had tried. Quietly closing the door he went along to his own room.

In five minutes he was in bed and his last thoughts were of Caroline. *Dearest, darling girl, forgive me for leaving you, I had to come home.* He took comfort from the fact that Walter would take his letter to the Post Office in the morning.

He spent a restless night and woke up feeling not much better than when he had gone to sleep. A footman came in with hot water and towels and after Dashell got dressed he opened a window overlooking the gardens and breathed in the fresh country air. It was good to be home again but he wished it was under happier circumstances. Looking out on the gardens what must he needs do but picture Caroline there as mistress.

Dashell went along to his father's room knowing Simmonds would have informed him of his son's arrival. "Good morning, Father."

"Good morning, Dashell," said Barrandale as they greeted each other like the good friends they were. "Simmonds informed me you had arrived late last night."

"Your letter arrived at my rooms while I was out, and I came as soon as I could."

Barrandale regarded Dashell keenly and noted he looked white and strained.

"Sir, does your request for me to come home have anything to do with Walden?"

"Yes, it has," his father replied, "but I will inform you of everything after breakfast."

After breakfast they went along to Barrandale's study where his lordship unlocked one of the drawers of his desk, pulled out a letter, and handed it to Dashell. "I received the letter about this time yesterday and upon reading it I wrote to you immediately."

Dashell took the letter and saw it was from a well-known firm of moneylenders. He looked significantly at his father. The letter was short and to the point, merely stating that their representatives would be calling at Barrandale Park the next day, which would be today. He handed it back to his father. "So it has come to this," he said slowly. "Had any rumours reached you, sir?"

"No they had not. Had you heard anything?"

Yes, I had heard something," confessed Dashell, "and that was why I have been asking at Walden's rooms as to his whereabouts, but nobody knows anything. Nor has there been any message from Walden himself." Dashell realized that he should have spoken to his father sooner but he had had a much sweeter subject to occupy his mind. He referred again to the letter. "I see no particular time for today has been given."

Barrandale had noted that fact too, and it annoyed him. "I have informed Simmonds there will be certain people calling and to show them in at once."

It was not until after luncheon that Simmonds finally ushered two men into the study. Father and son rose to their feet with a feeling of apprehension, knowing more or less what to expect, yet fearing the unknown. Dashell's eyes widened when he saw them. They looked the same ilk as Wardlock. Was this the kind of business that man was in?

"I am Lord Barrandale," said his lordship by way of introduction, "and this is my son, Lord Lonsdale. Be good enough to state your business."

The two men bowed briefly in acknowledgement. "I am Mr.Lee," said the first man, without bothering to say the name of the other man. "No doubt you received our letter? I have here a writ served against your son, Mr.Walden Romford, for moneys owing to us."

"Show me the writ," said Barrandale. He gave a start and almost blanched when he read the amount, then silently handed it to Dashell, who turned equally pale. He could hardly believe his eyes.

Sixty thousand pounds! *Sixty thousand pounds!* Dashell repeated to himself. An enormous amount. A small fortune. Aghast, he looked at this father. What had Walden done? The absolute fool, getting himself into the hands of moneylenders. How could all that money be repaid?

Barrandale drew himself up proudly. "You can attest that this amount is correct?"

"Yes, we can," said Mr.Lee.

"How much time do we have to repay the moneys owed?"

"We can give you two weeks, after which, if there is no repayment in full, we will press charges. We do not wish to cause an open scandal of course," said Mr.Lee smoothly, trailing off his words, thereby indicating that was exactly what would happen if they did not get their money.

Two weeks! Was that all the time they had? Barrandale struggled to marshall his thoughts. He would have to raise that money somehow or else he stood to lose everything. "Very well. You will be paid in full. You have my word as a Barrandale."

The two men smiled knowingly at each other. They had heard such words in the past. "We have stated our business, Lord Barrandale. Good afternoon. And to you, Lord Lonsdale."

"I will show you to the door," said Dashell. He could have rung the bell for Simmonds but he wanted these two out of the house as soon as possible.

He hurried back to the study to find his father slumped into a chair. Dashell took one look at him and hastily poured out some brandy, and with one arm round his father's shoulders he held the glass to his lips and forced him to drink some. For the second time in two days Dashell had to endure seeing someone he loved being grievously hurt. His father suddenly looked years older and it almost broke Dashell's heart. *Damn you, Walden, for doing this.*

Barrandale struggled to sit upright in his chair. "We must think how to repay that sum of money. I have given my word."

"How can we repay such a sum?" queried Dashell. "This could lead to an open scandal. How can we avoid it? I am so desperately sorry this has come about."

"Thank you for your concern, but sit down while I try and think." Barrandale's voice sounded a little firmer. "We must begin by selling Rosewood Manor, and thank goodness it is not entailed."

"Sell Rosewood Manor!" cried Dashell in amazement. "But you love that place! It belonged to Mother. It was her birthplace and she loved it too," and then stopped before saying, "I had hoped to live there with my future wife." But the words could never be uttered now.

"Please, Dashell, do not make it any more difficult for me than it already is," said Barrandale. "I would rather agree to the sale myself than have Rosewood Manor taken out of my hands. I will not let Barrandale Park fall into the possession of those men. I shall also sell the townhouse in London, for it is far too large now and it would be better to find a smaller place. I think you would agree with me on that."

"Yes, I do," replied Dashell with a heavy heart. What else could he say? He had pictured Caroline at the townhouse too, but could see the logic of the sale. "Do you think the two sales will bring in enough money?"

"It is impossible to say, but I could face possible ruin. Park Lane is a very good area, yet of necessity I must have a town house." Dashell looked at his father, whose face was still stricken. He could see now how much his father needed him and that he had been right to come home. "We will discuss everything further this evening," said Barrandale, "but do not mention anything in front of the servants."

"I need hardly tell you, sir, that I am very concerned for you. And I must add that I admire your fortitude."

"Thank you, Dashell. As to my fortitude, I am bringing to mind our family motto: "Courage at all times", although its application at the moment taxes me a great deal," replied Barrandale with a wry smile.

After dinner, which they both hardly touched, they spent the rest of the evening quietly talking until they retired for the night.

The next morning after breakfast Barrandale returned to his study where he had already spent some time and Dashell went to join him and watched as his father wrote some letters and wondered again at his fortitude.

Barrandale finished his last letter and laid down his pen. "Dashell, please listen carefully. I must ask you to go to London for me. I want you to do certain things that I would not entrust to anyone else."

"Of course, sir," replied Dashell, but with a sinking heart. His return to Caroline seemed to be put further away.

Barrandale glanced at his son, half smiling. "I will give you these three letters. The first is to my bank to borrow the sum of sixty thousand pounds against the sale of Barrandale House and Rosewood Manor. I have also offered Barrandale Park as collateral. The second letter is to some estate agents requesting them to make arrangements for the sale of the two properties, and to give notice to the tenants at Rosewood Manor that the lease will not be renewed. I have also asked the agents to look about for a smaller townhouse within a certain area, which I have outlined."

Barrandale slowly pushed the two letters aside and picked up the third. He held it in his hands for a moment or two, while

Dashell watched his father, motionless. Then looking straight at Dashell said, "This third letter is to the Commanding Officer of the 53rd London Regiment. I have bought Walden a commission. What he makes of himself is up to him. I am also disinheriting Walden. If anything should happen to you he cannot be allowed to inherit after me."

Dashell felt his blood run cold. "So that is final." He kept silent for a moment, before saying, "I remember reading something about that regiment in *The Times* the other day. It is being sent to India fairly soon, I believe."

"That is correct," Barrandale replied. "Now I will go outside for a while. I feel some fresh air will do me good."

"I'll come with you, sir, as I do not like to leave you alone."

The morning which had begun so well with high white clouds was now changing, with a strong wind bringing up low grey ones with a threat of rain, and there was now a sultry feel in the air.

"Would you like me to return to London this afternoon, sir?" asked Dashell. "There is still time."

"No, tomorrow will do. Besides, I would like your company for one more day, if you can forgive an old man his foolishness. It can be lonely sometimes."

"I am very attached to you, sir, and would gladly help in any way I can."

"I am deeply touched, my son." Some large raindrops caused them to look up at the darkening sky. "Come," remarked Barrandale, "I think we had better return to the house. How overcast it is becoming. I do believe we could have a storm."

They returned through the rose gardens. Some petals suddenly scattering in the wind caught Barrandale's attention. "Alicia, your mother, loved these roses. She used to say the dark red ones were her favourites because their petals looked just like velvet. I still miss her, you know. I could not bear it if I could no longer walk here. I hope one day, Dashell, you will find such a love as I did," he concluded with a long sigh.

Dashell felt a stab of pain in his heart. He wanted to cry out that he already had, only she loved pink ones, but this was not the time to say anything. He took some comfort from the fact that Caroline must have received his letter and wondered what the darling girl would make of it. More large splashes of warm rain fell, so all he said was, "Come, sir, we must hurry indoors before we both get soaked." So Barrandale allowed himself to be hastened along and they barely reached the terrace doors before the rain fell in earnest.

After luncheon Barrandale returned to his study for a few more minutes while Dashell went ahead to the library. "I will join you shortly," said his father, "I will not be long." Actually it was longer than Barrandale thought he would be before he finished and put away his writing materials. He glanced up as he heard a faint distant rumble of thunder amidst more dark clouds. It was just as well Dashell had delayed his journey. He locked the desk drawer and went to join his son in the library.

"It is coming on more to rain," he observed, going over to a window to watch the strengthening wind ruffle the trees. "We really are in for a storm. How fortunate you did not set off for London after all. Don't you think so, Dashell?" There was no answer. "Dashell?" Barrandale moved over to his son's chair and saw to his surprise that he was sound asleep. He was about to put a hand on Dashell's shoulder to awaken to him when he hesitated, then slowly moved to his own chair and sat down.

For several minutes he quietly watched Dashell. He knew his son was as concerned as he was over this wretched affair and had probably spent a restless night too. He recollected that Dashell had already looked tense and troubled about something when he came to talk the morning after his arrival, before those two men called. There was another rumble of thunder, closer this time, but Dashell did not move.

Another thought that had often come to Barrandale's mind was how long it would be before Dashell announced his engagement. He knew Dashell was considered to be a great catch and could have his pick of anyone he chose, although as yet he had given no indication of settling down. Once news got around of the reduced

Barrandale fortune Dashell's chances would greatly change, and his stock in the marriage market would drop completely. Who would want to marry the heir to a newly impoverished earl, however respected his name? And yet marrying an heiress, if one rich and willing enough could be found, would solve all their financial problems, and nothing need be changed. But that would take time and there were only two weeks in which to repay Walden's debt.

If Barrandale compelled Dashell to sacrifice himself by forcing him into one of these loveless marriages it would cause a rift between father and son that might never be healed. It would alienate Dashell's other brother, Maxwell, who idolized Dashell. In other words he was in danger of losing all his sons, a prospect as grey and dismal as the falling rain outside. He would rather be penniless. Before long his own head began to nod.

They both awoke with gasps of surprise. The thunder, which had slowly been coming closer, now crashed violently overhead, accompanied by vivid flashes of lightning.

"My apologies, sir," said Dashell, as he sat up and rubbed his eyes. "I had no idea you had come into the room. I must have fallen asleep." He stifled a yawn and stretched himself.

"Indeed you had," observed Barrandale, also stifling a yawn. "In fact you looked so comfortable I did not like to disturb you."

"I must say, sir, it was as well I did not set out for London after all," remarked Dashell. "I would have been drenched," unknowingly echoing his father's words.

Later, when they retired for the night Dashell said, "I will set off early in the morning, sir, so I may not see you. I do not know when I shall be back, probably not for a day or two."

There was one last thing Dashell had to do before he went to bed: he must write again to Caroline to explain his further delay. Would she be so angry and offended at his cavalier behaviour that she would no longer wish to see him? That was a chance he must take. He went back to his father's study and drew out some writing paper.

Dear Caroline,

Once again I must write to you concerning my absence and beg you to forgive me.

As I explained in my first letter I had to return to Windsor at my father's urgent request, and now I have much business to attend to on his behalf.

Those words I spoke to you in Richmond Park, please believe me when I say I meant every single one of them. You have never left my thoughts. When I call again, as I surely shall, I beg you to receive me. Please do not refuse me.

Until then, yours ever,
Lonsdale.

He addressed and sealed the letter and put it with those his father had written, then rang the bell for Simmonds.

"My father has already gone upstairs," Dashell explained when Simmonds came. "Now, I believe Lord Barrandale has spoken to you already about the recent turn of events concerning our family?"

"Yes, he has, sir. And may I say how deeply regretful I am, for I have served his lordship many years. It is all quite distressing that this has happened."

"Yes, I know, Simmonds," agreed Dashell patiently. "It is for all of us."

"And I can scarcely believe the change in his lordship, if I may say so." The poor fellow was so overcome he was compelled to pull out his handkerchief and blow his nose. Then remembering his position, he enquired with composure, "Is there anything further you require before you retire, sir?"

"No, but I do need to speak to you. I shall be leaving for London early tomorrow morning and I do not know when I shall return as I have a great deal of business to attend to for his lordship. I want you therefore to keep an eye on my father for me as I am quite anxious for him, so do not hesitate to call a doctor if you feel it at all necessary. And if he protests, just say you are following my orders," he added with a faint smile. "Also, would you order breakfast for me at eight o'clock and tell the stables to have my horse ready. That is all, Simmonds, thank you. Good night."

"Thank you, sir. Good night, sir."

Chapter Fourteen
Events Occur at Barrandale House

At around the same time that Dashell went up to his bedroom at Barrandale Park, Matthew was checking up on everything at Barrandale House, as he always did each night. He was just about to cross the hall to put out the lamps when there was a thunderous knocking at the front door. He flung the door open and stared in stupefaction at the sight of Walden standing there with a woman of questionable propriety on his arm. Matthew could hardly believe his eyes.

"Well, don't just stand there like a stuffed owl, man. Aren't you going to let us in?" demanded Walden. He placed his hand on Matthew's chest and roughly pushed him aside, making the door swing back and Matthew with it as they moved past him. Neither Walden nor the woman could stand up properly and they certainly smelled of liquor.

Matthew tried to remonstrate. "Mr. Walden, sir, what is this? You cannot bring her here."

Walden turned round and the woman had to turn with him, causing hiccupping laughter from her. "Why not? Is his lordship here? No? Then of course I can come in. And don't you dare speak to me like that."

Matthew recalled all the unpleasant stories about Mr. Walden that he had heard over the years, but he was compelled to answer, "No, sir, Lord Barrandale is not here."

Walden and the woman were endeavouring to mount the stairs together, but at the sight of the outraged Matthew watching them they collapsed with mirth.

Matthew called up to Walden. "I have to inform you, sir, that Lord Lonsdale has been enquiring as to your whereabouts for some time."

Walden, who was now sitting on one of the treads, peered at Matthew through the bannisters. "The devil he has," he said, slurring his words, "Where is he, anyway?"

"He is at Windsor, sir."

"Well, may the devil take him and keep him there." At last the two reached the landing when Walden called down to the scandalized Matthew, "Go and get us some wine. And take that sour look off your face, and damn you for your insolence."

Matthew had no choice but to obey. He stalked to the kitchen, selected a bottle of wine, not too good a one, placed the bottle and two wine glasses on a silver tray and stalked out again without saying a word to Janet. One look at his face and she kept silent.

Walden and the woman stopped outside the late Lady Barrandale's suite and Walden managed to open the door at the first attempt. Matthew came up with the tray and knocked on the door, and entered without waiting for an answer, and was shocked to see Lady Barrandale's things being used by that woman. "Is there anything more, sir?" he enquired stiffly, staring straight ahead.

"Yes. Fetch me one of Lord Barrandale's dressing gowns."

"Very good, sir." Again Matthew was forced to obey. Never in all his years in the service of the Barrandale household had he beheld such a spectacle as this. The fact that Mr. Walden had the audacity to bring that woman into the house, let alone that particular suite, appalled him. He returned with the required garment and handed it to Walden, then turned to leave the room, but was thrust forward sharply by a hand in his back. "You forgot to say goodnight."

Matthew turned round in protest only to have the door slammed in his face, and then jerked open again. "Bring me some hot water at half-past ten in the morning," snapped Walden, before slamming the door again. Matthew heard drunken laughter again as he returned to the kitchen.

"What's up, Matthew?" Janet asked quietly. "That was Mr. Walden, wasn't it?"

Matthew could only nod his head and it was quite a few minutes before he could speak. Eventually he was able to tell her everything that had happened. "It was shameful, and in her ladyship's own rooms."

"Whatever would Lord Barrandale say?" wondered Janet, aghast.

"I don't know," Matthew moaned. "Say nothing about this to the others."

"Don't forget Lord Lonsdale was asking about Mr. Walden the other day," Janet reminded him, "so we will have to send word to him somehow."

"Aye, you're right," said Matthew. "I did inform Mr. Walden about that. Not that it did any good."

"I wonder how long they intend staying," queried Janet. "Just Mr. Walden, I mean," she added hastily. "Surely he is not going to keep that woman here. Nor can we ask him to leave." Matthew could only shake his head in disbelief.

They both spent a troubled night, and in the morning Matthew quietly informed the other servants that Mr. Walden had arrived late last night bringing an 'undesirable' with him. They listened in horrified silence, amazed that one of the sons of the House of Barrandale could stoop to this. "There is real trouble brewing," Matthew warned them, "and Lord Barrandale will have to be informed sooner or later. You are all to keep quiet about this. Is that understood?" He looked round sternly at them and waited for each one to say "Yes." Then he remembered to add that Walter would have to be told as well, with the same admonition to keep quiet.

Chapter Fifteen
The Two Brothers

That same morning Dashell set off for London with all those letters and documents in one deep pocket of his riding-coat.

The whole countryside had a refreshed look after the storm and its much needed rain. He rode past a row of thatched cottages and one garden had a clump of forget-me-nots hanging over a wall. It was that scene that gave him the thought of sending some flowers to Caroline. This time, he would send that precious letter he had for her by cab, together with a bunch of forget-me-nots and some pansies. Pansies in the language of flowers meant, "My thoughts are always of you".

Dashell rode on through South Kensington until he came to the Barracks at Hyde Park. Without dismounting, he handed over the letter that would seal Walden's fate to an orderly. "Would you have this letter taken to your Commanding Officer," he said, and went away with some mixed feelings of relief and gloom.

He next went to St.Paul's Cathedral where he knew he could find several flower sellers. To his joy he found one that had both kinds of flowers and made his purchases, and was fortunate enough to hail a passing cab. After speaking to the driver and giving him the precious letter for the address, he laid the bouquets of flowers tenderly on the back seat of the cab, and closed the door. "Here," he said, giving the man a coin, "keep the change."

"Thank you, sir," stammered the man, "thank you kindly." He stared at the shilling in his hand and drove off cheerfully on his errand.

Dashell watched the cab leave, then remounted and made his way to Barrandale House.

At half-past ten Matthew went upstairs with the hot water and towels. Walden was still feeling the effects of the night before and was in a bad mood. "Bring up some sandwiches and the key to the wine cellar." he ordered.

Determined not to be ruffled Mathew turned to face Walden. "Lord Barrandale has entrusted the key to my care, sir, therefore I cannot let you have it without his express permission. Will that be all, sir?"

"Am I to understand that you are disobeying me?" demanded Walden.

"Not at all, sir. I am obeying Lord Barrandale."

With that parting shot Matthew left the room pleased with his small victory, until Walden shouted at him over the landing banisters. "Bring me some more sandwiches and a decent bottle of wine when I ring for them. These are not nearly enough. And be damned to you!"

"What are we going to do?" asked Janet when Matthew returned to the kitchen. "How long do you think they will stay?"

"I don't know," he sighed. "It's a terrible situation, I can tell you, and it's hardly my place to ask them to leave. I just wish one of their lordships would turn up."

The words were hardly out of his mouth when there was a clatter of hooves in the stableyard. "That must be Lord Lonsdale now," cried Stephen, and seized his coat and ran outside.

There was a curt "Good morning" to Stephen as Dashell handed him the reins. Lord Lonsdale seemed to be in a blacker mood than ever.

Dashell strode along the inside passage to the front hall where Matthew was waiting to speak to him. "Good morning, Matthew."

"Good morning, Lord Lonsdale," replied Matthew as he helped Dashell out of his riding-coat. He glanced at the expression on his young master's face and his heart sank, but he had to speak up. "May I speak to you, sir, about a most distressing incident that occurred here last night?"

Dashell closed his eyes as though in protest. "Really, Matthew, can it not wait? I have so much to attend to today for his lordship."

"I beg your pardon, sir," replied Matthew, "but it concerns Mr. Walden."

Dashell stiffened as he turned away but slowly turned back towards Matthew. "What did you say? Mr. Walden is here?" He stared at Matthew, completely taken by surprise. After all the times he had been enquiring after him and leaving messages, Walden had turned up here on this day of all days.

"Yes, sir. Mr. Walden came late last night bringing with him a woman of—er questionable propriety."

"He did *what?*" Again Dashell could hardly believe his ears. To call not knowing who was in residence then Walden must be absolutely depraved. "Where are they now?"

"They are upstairs in the late Lady Barrandale's suite," answered Matthew, looking at his lordship's darkening face.

"I think you had better tell me everything that happened last night. Come into this room." Dashell went to a small salon near the front door followed by Matthew, but left the door open, and listened carefully as the old servant related everything, from the time of opening the front door to being shouted at this morning. He left nothing out. Just then George came out with a tray carrying the sandwiches, a bottle of wine and two glasses.

"This is the tray ordered by Mr. Walden, sir," explained Matthew.

"George, take it back," said Dashell.

Dashell removed his coat and tugged off his cravat and handed them to Matthew, then took the writ out of the pocket of his riding-coat and placed it inside his shirt and went upstairs with a cold measured tread that boded ill. Matthew watched him go and the look of fury on his lordship's face sent a chill down his spine.

Dashell entered the suite without knocking, closed the door behind him and stood with his back to it. Walden literally gasped on the sight of his brother standing there like some Nemesis. "What the devil are you doing here? Matthew said you were out of town."

"I was. I came in this morning. Who is she?" asked Dashell, referring to the woman. "Some moll of yours?" But before Walden could answer Dashell told her to get out.

The black looks of the two men frightened the woman who hastily dressed and left, going downstairs a lot faster than she had come up. She swept past Matthew with a deliberate disdainful sniff, and he thankfully closed the door behind her.

The two brothers were alone at last. "What do you mean by coming in like that?" hissed Walden furiously.

"Where the devil have you been all this time?" countered Dashell, ignoring his question. "I have been looking for you for several weeks."

"I have been at Doncaster and Newmarket and had some good winnings," answered Walden truculently, as though he had really achieved something. "Why were you looking for me anyway?"

"I will answer that question later," said Dashell. "Matthew told me just now about your arrival last night and all your despicable subsequent behaviour. You utterly disgust me." His eyes never left Walden who was beginning to be unnerved by his brother's cold anger.

"Oh, did he? I can come here if I want to," said Walden, with another attempt at being truculent.

"Not with the likes of that woman. And you let her use Mother's things?" Dashell stooped to pick up a discarded garment watched by a sulky faced Walden. "Have you become so depraved?"

Walden turned to pour out some more wine but the glass was seized out of his hand and the contents flung in his face. "What the—!" he spluttered, as he staggered back. He glared at Dashell as he wiped his face with both hands. "Would you insult me, sir!"

"Would you insult our dead mother, sir!" blazed Dashell in return. Walden's face reddened as he began to realise the enormity of his behaviour.

"Now I will tell you why I have been looking for you," went on Dashell relentlessly. "There have been rumours circulating for some time about your debts and excesses. Three days ago Father called me home at short notice and the next day we had a call from some moneylenders. Now explain to me how you got involved with them."

"Yes, I owed money all round," Walden admitted, "and my creditors had been pressing me for some time and I had to pay them off."

"So you went to the moneylenders. Lee and Macy, of all people. Did you not know what exorbitant interest they charge?"

"I had to honour my debts, didn't I?"

"Honour your debts?" Dashell almost shouted. "Have you never heard of "Honour thy father and thy mother"?"

"Oh, for goodness sake!" cried Walden, resenting that he was being forced to explain everything to his brother. "Don't get pompous with me."

"Me! Pompous!" Dashell was rendered speechless. He stared at Walden, wondering if this was all some terrible nightmare and that he would soon be waking up.

"Yes, you were! Or still are!" continued Walden angrily. "You used to walk round with Father with your eternal "Yes, sir; no, sir; yes, sir; no sir;" wagging his head from side to side as he spoke. "It fair turned my stomach to hear you."

What brotherly love that still remained between them was fast disappearing. Dashell thought of all the pain and hurt Walden's behaviour had brought on the family. The sight of their father; the effect on Maxwell's future; and the possible ruin and loss of the country house and estate; and Walden was also the reason why he had been forced to leave Caroline to suffer alone. Dashell looked at the brother he now hardly knew. "And you were always insolent."

Walden just shrugged his shoulders, and it was that gesture that finally made Dashell lose his temper. Without warning he struck Walden across the mouth with one hand and then again with the other in quick succession. The shock and impact sent Walden reeling back. He fingered his mouth and tasted blood.

There was no going back now. They sized each other up, being much the same height and weight and each one ready to give as good as he got. With a roar Walden made a run at Dashell and they began to exchange heavy blows which Dashell easily parried, until he eventually seized Walden by his shirt and slammed him back against the wall and held him there, their faces just inches apart. Walden tried to break free but Dashell was too powerful.

"Let me inform you, my dear brother, just what has been happening because of your unbelievably crass and selfish stupidity. We have been given two weeks to pay off your debts if we are to avoid an open scandal."

"What do you mean scandal?" panted Walden. "How much is the debt?"

"You mean you don't know?" Dashell was incredulous. "Sixty thousand pounds, let me tell you. Six-ty thou-sand pounds," repeating each syllable clearly.

Walden gave a cry of anguish. "It can't be that much!" He tried to break away from his brother's grip again, but was kept in place.

"Now let me tell you what we have to do," Dashell at last told him. "We have to sell Rosewood Manor, Mother's old home. We have to sell this house and look for a smaller one. We also have to sell family jewels, furniture and paintings and valuable books. We may even have to sell off some land. Many servants will have to go. Maxwell may not be able to go to Oxford, and how the devil we are to tell him that, I do not know. And any shortfall will have to be made up from Father's own capital. Now perhaps you realise the trouble and near ruin you have brought on us all."

Dashell finally let Walden go, who slid down to a sitting position on the floor, completely shaken and demoralized. But Dashell was merciless. "The most heinous thing you did was to nearly break Father's heart. In fact you nearly killed him. When I think of that dear man, who aged ten years or more before my very eyes, I could almost kill you, but I will leave that for the Army to do."

Walden lifted up an ashen face. "Army? What do you mean—Army?"

"Father has bought you a commission," said Dashell bluntly, "and you can be sure enough money was found for that. And I had great satisfaction in taking Father's letter to the Commanding Officer of the Barracks at Hyde Park on my way here this morning. And for once in your life you will have to learn the meaning of "yes, sir; no, sir." I should also tell you that according to the newspapers your regiment will be leaving for India fairly soon."

Walden remained sitting on the floor, unable to move, all the words he heard leaving him completely numb.

Dashell finally tossed the writ to Walden, who seized it with trembling hands and read it through. "Oh, dear God, what have I done?" He struggled to his feet not daring to look at his brother.

"I don't understand you, Walden," said Dashell, "you are not the brother I used to know. And how, in the name of wonder and everything else, have you managed to rack up such a debt? Have you nothing to say?"

"What is the use of saying anything. It is all over now. I cannot undo it," said Walden hoarsely. "Why go on about it? What does is signify?"

"Because I loved you as a brother and that is how I shall endeavour to remember you. That is, if I bother to think of you at all." Dashell bent down and picked up the crumpled writ and put it back inside his shirt. He looked at the clock on the mantelpiece. "It is nearly twenty to one. I shall give you until half past one to leave."

Walden raised his head at that. "Would it do any good if I spoke to Father?" he asked, knowing even as he said it, it was a forlorn hope.

"None at all," answered Dashell unsympathetically. "He is going to disinherit you." He paused before adding, "If there is anything you want from your old room at home I shall see that you get it."

Walden looked round at his brother as a cold fear gripped him. "I take it I am to leave for good?"

"There is no alternative." Dashell looked at Walden and actually felt pity for him. He opened his mouth to speak but no more words would come. Instead he left the room and silently closed the door behind him and went downstairs, more saddened and sorrowful than he cared to admit.

Dashell sank thankfully into an armchair, his elbows on his knees and his face in his hands, so exhausted in heart and mind that he could have wept. For the third time in as many days he had to endure seeing someone's distress. He still had to go to the bank and estate agents with his father's letters and eventually return to Windsor, and he still had to speak to Maxwell. He had to do all this before he could return to Caroline.

Something else came to mind: he would have to call on Aunt Letty before any gossiping busybodies did. It was a constant source of wonder and amazement how rumours and gossip got around, but they did. He had better write a note asking if he could dine with her tonight.

At twenty-five past one there was still no sign of Walden. At precisely half-past one Dashell went out into the hall just as Walden opened the door upstairs. He slowly crossed the landing and came downstairs. When he was halfway down Dashell opened the front door. Walden went outside and down the steps and turned round when he reached the bottom, but the door had already been shut. That was the last time the two brothers ever saw each other.

Dashell returned to the salon and rang for Matthew. "Matthew, see that George takes this letter to Lady Smythe, and to wait for an answer."

"Very good, sir." Matthew hesitated and could not help saying, "I beg your pardon, your lordship, but I am deeply troubled by today's events. That they happened at all is most distressing."

"Yes, I could not agree more," said Dashell, knowing what the old servant was really trying to say.

"I take it Mr. Walden has gone for good?"

"Yes, he has, Matthew, for good."

Matthew fell silent, then seeing his lordship's strained face ventured to remark, "May I suggest you take some refreshments, sir. This situation must be trying for you too."

"Perhaps you are right. Those sandwiches will do as there is no time for anything else. And bring me some tea."

Matthew went away surprised at the request for tea. Lord Lonsdale looked as though he needed something much stronger.

Dashell leaned back in his armchair, thankful that perhaps the worst was over because he would have had to confront Walden sooner or later. His anger and grief had been released and he now felt emotionally drained and exhausted, for he never imagined his relationship with Walden would end this way.

Matthew came in with the tea tray which he placed on a low table by the chair and poured out a cupful. "Thank you, Matthew," said Dashell. "Come back in half an hour, will you."

Dashell drank some tea and ate a sandwich without much enthusiasm, eventually placing the empty cup back on the tray. Then there occurred something which he would ever after regard as a miracle. Some means or process, not fully understood, which had been known through the ages, but he knew by the feeling in his heart that Caroline had received his letter and had understood the message of the flowers, and that her own heart had gone out to him. It sent a thrill through him and he actually put a hand over his heart. "Caroline," he murmured, ""Oh, my darling girl, God bless you. May you forgive me for having to leave you."

It was like a blessing, a benediction, a sunny break in a bank of gloomy clouds. It revived him. He took more refreshments and he felt better. He closed his eyes and let his thoughts dwell on that sweet face. The way Caroline had laughed at him during that carriage-ride. Her earnest words in the rose garden when he had laughed at her. How he longed to hold her in his arms and comfort her. He actually gave a start when Matthew knocked on the door.

"You asked me to come back in half an hour, sir," said Matthew, privately pleased to see that Lord Lonsdale looked better; a cup of tea could do wonders for a person. He also noted some of the sandwiches had been eaten. "George returned with the message from Lady Smythe that she will be pleased to see you tonight." Dashell was thankful about that, but he was not looking forward to it.

"Matthew, I have to go out and will require the carriage. I have to inform you that Lord Barrandale is putting this house up for sale and will be seeking a smaller property in London somewhere. Would you therefore have inventories compiled of all items in every single room. And would you instruct Stephen to do the same for the stables. I am going to the estate agents now to make the necessary arrangements, and no doubt their representatives will come to look over the place. I will have to leave you to handle that as I shall be returning to Windsor soon. That will be all, Matthew."

Within ten minutes Dashell was on his way to the estate agents' office and spent more time there than he thought he would as formalities required so many details. By the time he left it was too late to call at the bank so he returned to his own rooms.

"I will not be requiring the carriage tonight, Stephen, but have it ready on hand tomorrow morning. That is all."

Walter had been awaiting Lord Lonsdale's arrival with some apprehension ever since one of the maids had been sent to warn him of some "goings on," saying that Lord Lonsdale was in a blacker mood than ever.

"Good afternoon, Lord Lonsdale." Walter helped his lordship out of his coat, noting his taut, tired look. "I have to inform you, sir, that during your absence Mr.Martin Ellersby called round here twice asking for you."

"Oh?" said Dashell, surprised, as he smoothed down his shirtsleeves. "Did he say why?"

"No, sir, but he seemed anxious to speak to you."

Dashell was intrigued. If his friend Martin exerted himself that much to call round twice then it must be important. Something must be troubling him. He would go round early in the morning as there would be time before he called at the bank. *How much more will I have to deal with,* he wondered with a sigh. *Why does everything happen at once?* "What did you tell him?"

"Just that you were out of town, sir, and it was not known when you would return."

"Thank you, Walter," said Dashell, relieved his servant had been tactful. "Would you lay out some fresh clothes for me as I am dining with Lady Smythe tonight." He was not looking forward to having to tell his aunt what had been happening, but tell her he must. Lord Barrandale might be angry if he did and Lady Smythe might be equally angry if he did not, especially if the gossips got to her first. He would just have to take his chance.

Before leaving he locked the remaining letter for the bank in his writing table, then instructed Walter to compile an inventory of all items in all rooms within the next few days. Then he left for Grosvenor Square.

Chapter Sixteen
Dashell Dines With His Aunt

"Good evening, Chadwick," said Dashell, as Lady Smythe's butler opened the door. "No need to announce me, I will go straight up." He went quickly upstairs, knocked on the door of the salon and went in.

"Dashell, how kind of you to come," cried Lady Smythe in welcome. "Though I don't know why you wish to dine with an old lady like me."

"Because you are my favourite aunt," he smiled as he bent to kiss her on both cheeks.

"Humph. Blarney." she retorted. But the shrewd old lady missed nothing. She sensed that this was not purely a social visit. "What is it, Dashell? I can see something is troubling you, which must be why you asked to come round tonight."

"What I so like about you, Aunt Letty, is your straightforwardness," said Dashell as he began pacing about. "Oh, it is all so horrible and appalling."

Lady Smythe watched her nephew with growing anxiety for she had never seen him like this before. She sensibly remarked, "The best place to begin is usually the beginning, but before you do is this likely to take a long time?"

"Yes," answered Dashell, pausing mid-pace.

"Then may I suggest we dine first. I had a feeling this would be preferable."

"You are very perceptive, Aunt Letty."

"Yes, I have been told that on many an occasion," she replied with a faint smile.

They dined in silence and Lady Smythe noted with surprise that Dashell did not have his usual robust appetite. When they finished they waited while Chadwick cleared the table.

"We are alone now, Dashell, so begin." Lady Smythe settled herself comfortably on her favourite sofa and braced herself for she knew not what.

So Dashell began his narrative from the time of receiving his father's summons to the shutting of the door behind Walden, and then calling on the estate agents and the ensuing results.

Lady Smythe listened in growing horror to Dashell's description of the physical effects of the stress on his father, and his description of Walden taking a woman into Lady Barrandale's suite, and at the exchange of words he had with his brother. All this had taken its toll. "I can scarcely believe what you have told me," she exclaimed, putting her hand to her flushed face. "Oh, that stupid, stupid boy! Did he never stop to think what he was doing? His behaviour has been absolutely despicable. I am almost at a loss for words."

"Yes, I know," agreed Dashell. "I can hardly convey to you my feelings at having to send my own brother out of the house."

Lady Smythe, who had been walking about, stopped in front of him. "You had to," she declared emphatically. "You could not have done otherwise. Oh, my poor Randolph. My poor Barrandale. He does not deserve this."

"Walden's excesses have not exactly been unknown," commented Dashell, "and the moneylenders will be repaid within the time limit they allowed us, so there will be no threat there."

"But malicious gossips are going to have a field day. You know the ones I mean, those who enjoy other people's misfortunes."

"Father has already warned me that some may discontinue their friendships."

Lady Smythe snorted in contempt. "Let them, for that proves their friendships were not worth much in the first place. In fact we would be well rid of them. And you say Walden's regiment is going to India?"

"Yes, according to the newspapers."

Lady Smythe muttered something that sounded like, "The shameless hound. He deserved everything he got. He will get no sympathy from me." Then she asked, "How is your father taking it?"

"Stoically, as one might expect, knowing him, but underneath he is deeply wounded."

"Oh, my poor Barrandale," Lady Smythe moaned again. "I could almost weep for him. Do you think it would do any good if I went to see him?"

"No, I think not. He would prefer to be alone for the time being."

Lady Smythe nodded slowly in agreement. "Thank you for coming to see me, painful as it must have been for you. I am so glad you did for I understand your reasoning behind it. What will you do next?"

"Tomorrow morning I will go to the bank and then to the moneylenders to pay off the debt. Then I shall return to Windsor to see Father."

"That will be tomorrow afternoon?"

"Yes."

Lady Smythe looked at her nephew. "If I may say, Dashell, could you not leave returning until the next day? You look so tired, even exhausted." She put her hand on his shoulder. "I am terribly sorry that so much has been placed on you. Please reconsider my advice, Dashell. Do not wear yourself out. Do not let fatigue make you ill, because your father has need of you. Come and dine with me again tomorrow evening and tell me how you got on during the day."

Somewhat reluctantly Dashell agreed. "All right," he said. "So much has already happened and there is still so much to do and think about. I will come again tomorrow evening and leave early the next day. That's a promise."

They both fell silent after so much discussion, preoccupied with their own thoughts.

Dashell leaned back on the cushions, his own again reverting to Caroline and wondered for the umpteenth time what she was doing and how soon it would be before he could return to her. He had promised his aunt to wait one more day, and he could see the sense of that, which meant he would return to Windsor on Saturday. He could call on the house on Becket Lane on the way but he remembered Johnny's warning not to call on a Saturday or Sunday. He certainly did not wish to meet Wardlock again, not if that man was going to vent his anger on Caroline once more. He must avoid that all costs. Then he would wait for Maxwell to come home from Eton. It was amazing how everything worked out, and he felt so much easier in his mind now about Caroline. Yet he would have left her for a whole week or even more by then; and supposing he had been wrong about that precious incident after all? He must let her know he was planning to call and prayed she would not refuse to see him.

Lady Smythe began speaking again. "About Maxwell," she said. "I have some money of my own, perhaps I could offer to help him go to Oxford."

Dashell was horrified. "Absolutely not, Aunt Letty. Father would never permit it, nor would Maxwell accept it. Anyway, there may be hope yet. We must wait until the two sales have been completed and a new place purchased. We could end up in some out of the way place and be regarded as aristocratic paupers," he added bitterly.

"You will realise too, Dashell," Lady Smythe said in her matter of fact way, "that this will reduce your own inheritance. I suppose that had occurred to you."

"Yes, it had," he admitted, "but like Father, and you, I believe keeping the family together is more important." Then he held his breath, wondering if even this wise lady would make some infuriating remark about finding a rich heiress. "I think it is time I left anyway, Aunt Letty," he said. "Thank you letting me talk to you, for it has taken some of the load off my mind. And try not to worry too much."

"Worry!" exclaimed that worthy woman, "that is exactly what I shall do. How could I do otherwise? We must hope and pray for the future, though heaven knows it will be hard."

After Dashell had seen himself out, Lady Smythe sat for a long time as a feeling of depression descended upon her. She roused herself when Chadwick came to ask if she required anything before retiring for the night.

"No thank you, Chadwick," she said. "Lord Lonsdale will be dining with me again tomorrow evening. And I shall not be "at home" to callers for the next few days."

Chapter Seventeen
The Servants Are Concerned

When Dashell had left to walk over to his aunt's house, his manservant had hurriedly tidied up before taking the note Dashell had written to Martin Ellersby's rooms. Then he hastened to Barrandale House to catch up on any news. He was horrified when the others told him that the two gentlemen had quarrelled, with Mr. Walden being sent out of the house for good.

"Now listen, all of you," Matthew began. "We all know what a terrible day this has been and I, for one, never wish to see another like it. Lord Lonsdale has informed me that this house is to be sold and a smaller one bought. He has also ordered inventories made of all items in every room. And that includes the stables, Stephen."

"That's right," put in Walter. "I am to do one as well."

Matthew looked on them all again. "Lord Lonsdale has not informed me in so many words, but it is my belief that the House of Barrandale has fallen upon hard times."

There were gasps and cries of horror from the servants. "But what about us and our positions here? Does this mean we could be laid off? What will we do?"

"Lord Lonsdale has not said anything about that to me," continued Matthew, "but even with a smaller house I am sure we will still be needed. We can only wait and see."

"Well, I never," said Janet at last, after a long silence. "To think it has come to this."

Walter had been glancing at the kitchen clock for several minutes. "It is getting late," he said. "I had better be going now, Matthew. I must be there when he gets back."

This signalled the end of the evening and with heavy hearts the others began making their way slowly upstairs.

Stephen had gone to the stables to look in on Sparkle. "Well, old fellow? Comfy, are you?" These late night visits were jokingly described by the Barrandale stablemen as "Tucking 'em up for the night", making sure all was well with the horses before they went to bed.

Stephen had something else on his mind: the fact that nobody had mentioned Miss Wardlock. Not that there was any particular reason anyone should, but he had the odd feeling she had been left out, particularly after the others' earlier interest in her.

"You met Miss Wardlock, didn't you, Sparkle, and she liked you too. What will happen now, I wonder. It's none of our business of course, old lad, but I do hope things will work out between our master and that pretty lady." He stayed for a few more minutes, then with one final pat on Sparkle's rump he picked up his lantern, bolted the stable door behind him and went up to his room in the loft.

Walter had returned quickly and had busied himself about. "I left your note at Mr. Ellersby's rooms, sir," he informed Lord Lonsdale when he came in. "I was told he was out and would not be back until much later."

"Thank you, Walter." Dashell could not help smiling to himself. A night out for Martin would mean a following late morning, and he was not an early riser at the best of times. Well, he would find out sooner or later what it was all about.

Chapter Eighteen
Martin Gives Dashell A Warning

The next morning Dashell ordered the carriage for ten o'clock and was driven round to Martin Ellersby's rooms. Martin was still asleep but was rudely awakened by Dashell shaking him.

"What the blazes! Oh, it's you," he groaned, yawning and blinking sleepily. "How the devil did you get in?"

"Your landlord let me in," explained Dashell. "You told my manservant you wanted to see me and I sent him round with a note to say I would be calling today."

"I know he did, but I did not expect you to call at this ungodly hour," complained Martin, still yawning and stretching. He hoisted himself up to a sitting position and rubbed his eyes before looking at Dashell again.

Dashell surveyed him critically. "You look like the morning after the night before."

"If you are going to be rude I shall go back to sleep."

"Oh, no, you're not. Walter said you had called round twice, so why do you want to see me?" Dashell was getting impatient as he had so much to do.

"Ah, yes, that's right," said Martin, brightening up as he remembered. "Do sit down, old lad," he added, vaguely waving his hand at a chair. "I can't stand you towering over me so early in the morning."

"Early!" cried Dashell, "it has long gone ten o'clock," but he obliged by sitting down at the end of the bed. "Now talk, will you."

"All right, all right, don't rush me." Martin twisted round to rearrange his pillows, and leaned himself comfortably against them. He regarded Dashell thoughtfully, "I say, are you all right? You don't look your usual cheery self. In fact, you look like the morning after the night before."

"Get on with it Martin, please," said Dashell, "I can't stay all day waiting for you."

Martin became serious at last. "Well, to begin with, you have been very conspicuous by your absence. People have been asking me concerning your whereabouts because they know we are friends and I don't know what to say to them. Nobody has seen you for some days. And where the devil have you been anyway?"

"Father called me home last Monday and I have had to attend to family matters for him. He is not well."

"Oh," said Martin, thinking to himself that only accounted for less than one week. "Is that what I am to say to them? How is Lord Barrandale by the way?" he added anxiously.

"As well as can be expected," replied Dashell evasively.

"Oh," said Martin again, noting Dashell's tight-lipped expression. "I suppose that would explain your absence quite a lot."

"Why would my absence cause so much interest anyway?"

"Because you are popular," cried Martin airily, "because you are sought after, my lad, especially by the ladies. In fact quite a few matrons have been baying and casting about for your scent. And another thing, someone has been trotting out a new heiress. Not bad looking either, so I have been told."

"I am not interested," was Dashell's blunt response.

"Eh?" said Martin in open-mouthed surprise. "Let me give you some worldly advice, my lad. One way to call off the matrimonial hounds is to find yourself a sweetie-pie, like I did."

"You have? Well you do surprise me. And are congratulations in order?"

"Almost," replied Martin with a smile. "I have popped the question and it just needs full parental approval." Then beaming at Dashell he said, "Her name is Miss Angela Nicholls, and I would like you to be my best man. The wedding will not be for a few months anyway."

"Well, that should give Miss Nicholls enough time to change her mind," said Dashell, and laughed when Martin sat up indignantly. "I am honoured that you should ask me, and I will if I can. But have you considered asking Ellis to be your best man?"

"Ellis! Ask him!" Martin was almost speechless. "He's hopeless. He never opens his mouth except to eat."

"You do him an injustice, my lad. It is amazing how coherent and intelligent he is when he is away from you. Your infernal chatter always puts him in the shade."

"Well, of all the nerve." Martin glared at Dashell and put on a show of hurt pride and dignity.

Dashell was getting impatient again. "Is that all you really wanted to see me about?"

"Oh, no, there's more. Getting back to sweetie-pies, there's a rumour going around that you have a woman somewhere."

Dashell gasped before he could stop himself. "I beg your pardon?" he said, stiffening.

"Apparently there was a most interesting and delightful scene some days ago at a certain gymnasium. I heard all about it, and I wish I had been there," sighed Martin, gazing up at the ceiling. "I would have added my weight too, you know. And what do you expect when you were spotted buying pretty flowers," he added. "To some people that would mean only one thing."

"But that was just harmless ribbing," said Dashell, remembering that scene only too well. "I have done my share too. We all have."

"Ah, yes," replied Martin gravely, "but it is very different when it reached certain salons, when certain ladies have got hold of it."

Dashell gaped at him, and then his eyes narrowed. "What do you mean?" he asked.

"One of the men who had been at the gymnasium was laughing about it a day or two later with some friends at his house. "Y'know, a men only session." Martin paused and shifted his position.

"Go on," prompted Dashell.

"Well, this man has a thoroughly unpleasant sister who had been listening on the other side of the door to all the male chatter." He paused again as Dashell's lips curled up in disgust and contempt. "Yes, I agree. No decent girl would do such a thing. Anyway, she must have made some slight noise because his favourite hound, which he had in the room with him suddenly pricked its ears and looked towards the door. That made him suspicious, so he tip-toed over and flung it open and there she was, caught red-handed. It seems the sister has always had a nasty habit of listening at key holes. Well, whatever he said to her in front of all those men in the room made her furious, and apparently she later repeated everything she heard to her friend, Susanna Hepplewhite, who told her mother."

Dashell stared at him as the full import of what Martin said dawned on him. "What! Those w-w-witches!" he cried. "Pardon me, but by no stretch of the imagination can Lady Hepplewhite and her daughter be considered ladies. I know what type of salons they frequent." He stopped short and strode over to the window and stared outside.

This news absolutely stunned him. Something so unexpected. This despicable behaviour of one wretched girl! If those harridans ever found out the whereabouts of Caroline they would call on her on some pretext or other just to look her over; and in her lonely, vulnerable situation they would make what they would of it. His angel! To be insulted by those Hepplewhite women and others like them, not one of whom could hold her candle to Caroline's sun. Thank goodness she lived in quiet little Parsons Green, they would never think of looking for her there. But there could be the chance sighting and recognition of himself, a casual remark by someone who knew someone, and so on.

That original chance meeting with Caroline would be acceptable, but to call a few times without having been formally introduced and then the carriage ride however innocent it was, even with her maid with them, and also having afternoon tea with her in her home and without a female chaperon, and all this without a family member's knowledge, he could just imagine what would be made of that. And he had threatened a man in his own house. In fact, in the eyes of Society at that time with its very strict rules of propriety he had committed more than one faux pas, even if his manners towards Caroline had been impeccable. His behaviour, being a man, would be overlooked, but Caroline's, being a woman, never. What had he done? It was this thought that so filled him with shame and horror, that he could unwittingly be the cause of her disgrace, and that meant the possibility of a second scandal for the family; and how was he to explain that to his father, especially just after denouncing Walden for his behaviour.

Martin had been watching Dashell carefully and the latter's tense looks and clenched fists filled him with wonder, and he whistled softly to himself. Dashell slowly turned round and came and gripped the top rail of the brass bed end. "So there is someone," Martin remarked quietly, as one man to another.

"Yes, there is," replied Dashell, looking Martin straight in the eye, "and she is every inch a lady and I hope to marry her. Has there been any mention of a name?"

"No."

"For her sake, are you sure?" Dashell gripped the rail even harder as a look of understanding passed between the two friends.

"I am sure. There has been no mention of a name."

A wave of relief swept over Dashell as he whispered hoarsely, "Thank God."

"That is why there is so much speculation and gossip," said Martin. "They cannot find out who she is and they cannot find you. Whoever she is and wherever she is, be careful. Those women are going round with eyes like hawks."

Dashell sat down on the edge of the bed again. "Martin, I am forever in your debt. Thank you for your timely warning and for not prying. And now I must go."

"Not yet," said Martin quickly, "there is something else you may like to know."

Dashell again stared at him. "What else can there be?"

"Last night Tony Renfrew got hold of me and swore blind he had seen Walden coming out of some nefarious eating place trying to look inconspicuous. Walden did not see him but his face looked like he had been kicked by a horse."

"Oh?" said Dashell, looking bored and unconcerned, which did not deceive his friend. "Perhaps I should tell you that I am returning to Windsor tomorrow and will be away all week, maybe longer." Then looking straight at Martin said, "Barrandale House is up for sale and so is Rosewood Manor."

Martin's eyes rounded like saucers. "I say, that will make for even more speculation."

"Father has decided it is too large now and we shall be looking for a smaller place somewhere still within London. I cannot tell you any more just now."

Martin opened his mouth to ask something but instead said, "You had better make arrangements that nobody is admitted to the house without a letter of introduction from the estate agents. That should do away with any triflers. You know how nosey people can be. They might just go to look and see what they could get out of old Matthew."

"I never thought of that. Martin, you are brilliant."

"No, I'm not," stated Martin. "I just have a suspicious mind. Now, just to rehearse. Lord Barrandale is not well and you have to attend to family matters for him and you are returning to Windsor and will be away for several more days. Right? Not that it is anyone else's business anyway."

"Yes, that should do. Incidentally, I would appreciate it if you informed Ellis also."

"Right you are," said Martin. "Now if that is all, would you obligingly go away like a good fellow and perhaps I could get back to sleep."

Dashell laughed and went to the door and then grew serious again, "Martin, I beg you, say nothing to anyone about the lady, not even to Ellis. It's not that I do not trust either of you but the less said the better."

"You have my word."

After Dashell left Martin rearranged his pillows again and slid down to a more horizontal position. Underneath his nonsense and flippancy he was a sincere person and had great admiration for his friend. In fact he would go so far as to say that Dashell was the finest man he knew. *If you need friends, old lad, Ellis and I are right behind you.* He thought over what had been said. Called to Barrandale Park; Lord Barrandale not well; family matters to attend to; Barrandale House and Rosewood Manor to be sold; and Walden's face bearing the marks of what could only be Dashell's handiwork because no one else would have done that. And Dashell's seeming indifference had not fooled him. Walden's exploits were fairly common knowledge anyway. Hmm, there was a lot more to this than met the eye.

When the news that Barrandale House was for sale became widespread there was going to be even more speculation, and he would be in more demand than ever. The more he denied any knowledge the more people would suspect he did know something, and it occurred to him that perhaps he should find some reason to leave London for a while.

He would go and visit his father and tell him of his engagement. That was a clever idea. He must persuade his brother Ellis to come with him. He enjoyed imagining the situation of people not being able to find either of them. Serve them right.

Then he wondered who the lady was whom Dashell had found. Well, whoever she was he was obviously in love with her, which would explain why he was not interested in any heiress.

It was not long before Martin went back to sleep.

Chapter Nineteen
Dashell Attends To Business.

Dashell went outside with his heart aching even more, if it was possible. Thank goodness he had paid heed to his aunt's plea to stay one more day otherwise he might never have had this conversation with Martin. The only way to protect Caroline was to keep away, at least until he was completely free from immediate family affairs.

He had not thought he would be so long with Martin and as time was passing on he would go to the bank first.

The interview with the bank manager was not an easy one, for he was astounded at the request for a loan of sixty thousand pounds after reading Lord Barrandale's letter. He never expected this particular client to be in such a situation. After some necessary pertinent questions to protect the bank's interests the manager finally agreed to his request. With a great sense of relief Dashell left the bank with a draft for sixty thousand pounds.

His next call was to the estate agents' office to speak of his concerns about viewing entry for interested people. He was assured viewing would be by appointment or authorised letter only. Another reason to thank Martin.

Dashell returned to Barrandale House. He had informed Matthew earlier he did not know when he would be back for luncheon. Sandwiches would do again, he had said, and smiled when he gave the order. Was he hoping for another miracle?

A slightly harassed Matthew informed him that some gentlemen from the estate agents were already in the house looking around as a preliminary measure. They had also brought some information sheets about houses for sale in different parts of London.

"I am going out again Matthew, and have ordered the carriage for two o'clock. I will return directly to my rooms, and this evening I will be dining again with Lady Smythe. I will be here for breakfast tomorrow morning before going to Windsor, and I will be away for several days. Any viewing of this house will be by appointment or authorised letter only. That should do away with any triflers. That is all, Matthew."

"Very good, sir," replied Matthew, hoping he did not sound too thankful.

Dashell finished his luncheon. There was no further miracle; only the memory of yesterday's.

At two o'clock Dashell was on his way to the moneylenders' premises; the last call and perhaps the worst one. When he arrived a clerk approached him with an insinuating smile.

"I am Lord Lonsdale," Dashell said. "I have come to pay off a debt." At the sound of his name two men silently appeared from behind thick curtains, the same two men who had come to Barrandale Park. He stared at Mr.Lee, who now had a gap where his two front teeth had been knocked out, causing him to speak with some difficulty.

"My dear Lord Lonthdale," lisped Mr.Lee. "What a thurprith to thee you. I had not exthpected you tho thoon. You mutht excuth my manner of speaking. It is quite dreadful the kind of people one meethts. Do come into my offith." He held the curtains aside and Dashell had no choice but to go in, shuddering inwardly at the man's familiarity as he did so. He felt the same kind of revulsion he had experienced earlier in the week and wondered again if Wardlock was in the same line of business and half-expected him to appear.

"Do thit down, my dear thir."

"I prefer to stand," replied Dashell coldly. "I have come to pay off the debt incurred by my brother. Here is the writ you left with us, and here is a draft in the sum of sixty thousand pounds. You will find it all in order." He wondered briefly if Walden had been in this same room and how he had got into their clutches in the first place. He also felt disgust at the way the draft was fingered for soundness and even held up to the light for signs of a watermark. "Do you doubt our integrity?" demanded Dashell, becoming incensed.

"You would be thurprithed how many people try to detheive uth," replied Mr.Lee with a deprecating shrug. "We do have to be careful. However, I agree thith doth appear to be in order." Mr.Lee took the writ, crossed it twice and wrote the word 'paid' between the lines and signed and dated it. "May I congratulate you on your promptneth, Lord Lonthdale. It hath been a pleasure doing bithneth with you."

Dashell took the cancelled writ. "Good day to you."

"Thood you require our athithtanth in the future . . ." lisped Mr.Lee hopefully.

Dashell left him talking, thankful to get outside again. He also wanted to meet the man who had removed Mr.Lee's front teeth, if only to shake hands with him.

At last all immediate financial dealings were over. The debt had now been paid. There was no going back for the wheels had been set in motion and the family was now committed to repaying the bank loan. He was driven back to his rooms.

"I will not require the carriage tonight, Stephen," he said. "I shall be returning to Windsor tomorrow morning, so would you have my horse ready saddled. That is all, Stephen."

"Yes, sir. Thank you, sir."

Walter met Lord Lonsdale inside and helped him out of his coat. "Has anything happened in my absence, Walter?" he asked.

"No, sir, nothing at all."

After he left Martin that morning Dashell had forced all thoughts of Caroline out of his mind so he could concentrate on all he had to do. The effort had been intolerable but now everything came flooding back. Now he had to write to her once more to say he still did not know when he would be able to return to see her again. She would probably be so disgusted at his cavalier behaviour that she would never wish to see him again. He could not bear the thought of losing her, not when he had just found her.

Dashell pictured her face again, the way she turned her head, the curve of her throat and bosom, the way she moved, her direct way of looking at him, her laughter, and those lovely eyes. She was so refreshingly different. He knew there could never be anyone else for him. Surely after he had explained his absence she could find it in her heart to forgive him.

He tried to think of what to write but everything he thought of sounded so commonplace. It was how to begin that was so difficult. He remembered again that time yesterday when he had felt that warmth in his heart, that sweet conviction. Of course, that was it, that was where to begin! He went to sit at his writing table.

Dear Caroline,

Yesterday morning I sent you a letter and some flowers and from the feeling in my heart I knew you had received them. My only wish was that I had been able to give them to you myself and see you again, but that was not possible.

I am returning again to my father's estate. I am also anxious about his health.

My continued thoughts and love for you.

Yours ever,
Lonsdale

He wondered what Caroline would make of it all. He could hardly blame her if it sounded like a string of excuses. He stayed at the writing table a while longer unwilling to move, his thoughts once more drifting back to Caroline, wondering how long it would be before he could take her in his arms, if ever, and kiss her.

A knock on the door shattered his dream. "I have laid out some fresh clothes for you, sir," said Walter, "and I have some hot water ready for you,"

"Thank you, Walter." Dashell knew this was his servant's way of saying time was getting on. "Would you post this letter tomorrow morning?"

Chapter Twenty

Dashell Dines With His Aunt Again

"Come in," called Lady Smythe when Dashell knocked on her salon door. "Oh, Dashell, my dear, you look so tired."

"Indeed I am, Aunt Letty," he admitted as he bent to kiss her cheek.

"I have been wondering all day how you have been getting on. Do sit down. We can have an early meal and then talk."

After they finished their meal they sat on more comfortable chairs, each with a small glass of port. Lady Smythe was partial to a glass of port on occasions and she felt quite justified in thinking this was one of them.

"I hardly slept a wink last night," she began, "Everything kept going round and round in my head like a windmill, and it was impossible not to worry. But how did you get on?"

"Well," said Dashell, "I am glad and thankful that the debt has been paid off. I have the cancelled writ, signed and dated by that Mr.Lee himself. I went to the bank first, of course, and spoke to the manager and requested this loan of sixty thousand pounds. I must say he was quite astonished, but after some careful questioning he did grant the request."

"I hardly like to ask, Dashell, but how difficult will this repayment be?" queried his aunt. "Will the two sales cover it?"

"I doubt it."

"You mean that estate and household items will have to be sold off?"

"Yes," replied Dashell simply, "leaving Father to make up the difference."

Lady Smythe just shook her head. "Anything else?"

"Yes. I called at the estate agents and they sent representatives round to our house almost immediately. They also agreed to make appointments or write letters of entry, so that should do away with triflers."

"I still cannot believe this is really happening. So much, so suddenly. It's like our world has fallen apart. I just feel numb."

"Well, I did learn something when I happened to meet Martin Ellersby recently" said Dashell, casually. "He asked me to be his best man at his forthcoming wedding. Another thing he told me was that Walden was seen one evening with a bruised face trying to look inconspicuous."

"I knew it!" cried Lady Smythe, "I wonder if that could be the reason."

"Wonder what, Aunt Letty?" asked Dashell, mystified.

"One afternoon the other day," she explained, "I heard a carriage pull up and looked out of the window and saw that awful Lady Mathers getting out. She knocked on the door and I thought she was going to force her way past Chadwick. The audacity of the woman! The impertinence! To think she could come to my house to see what she could find out. I cannot stand the woman."

"I don't understand," said Dashell. "What do you mean? Find out what?"

"Her son and Walden know each other, or at least they used to, and that fact makes me think even less of Walden, if that is possible. She must have heard something and that was why she came here. Anyway, she did not get past Chadwick and shortly afterwards her carriage drove away. She's a friend of that equally detestable Hepplewhite woman."

She turned to reach for her wine glass, not noticing how the glass in Dashell's own hand nearly slipped. Surely they had not found Caroline already! Was that the reason why Lady Mathers had called, to see what she could find out about Caroline and not Walden? In either case she would have been sent packing in no uncertain terms, but it gave Dashell a terrible start.

He realized the awful possibility that the Barrandale family could be on the brink of two scandals, not one. He had thrashed Walden for causing the first one and now he was the possible cause of a second one through no real fault of his own, but that would not stop the vicious, spiteful gossip escalating, especially when people found out that Caroline was virtually alone with no female companion except a maidservant, who would not count; and never mind an unsympathetic step-father. This could almost completely finish his father. A muscle twitched in his jaw. He would like to find that girl who listened at keyholes and wring her neck.

His aunt's sharp cry of concern brought him back to reality. "Dashell! Whatever is the matter? You frighten me, looking like that. You look dreadful."

"I beg your pardon, Aunt Letty. I did not mean to alarm you, but I was thinking of everything that has happened since Father called me home. I feel as though I have been at full gallop the whole time and now am hardly able to draw rein." He fervently hoped this explanation would satisfy his perceptive aunt.

"Oh, Dashell, I am so sorry for you, believe you me."

"I know, bless you," he said gently.

She glanced at him. "Come and sit down, if you please. I want to discuss something with you. Now," she continued, "are you still planning to return to Windsor tomorrow?"

"Yes, I am. Why?"

"Because I am going too. I do not wish to stay here by myself worrying about your father because he has been on his own too much. My mind is made up, Dashell," she said firmly.

"Then I would not dream of arguing with you, Aunt Letty, not if you have already made up your mind."

"Well, that's that," said Lady Smythe decisively. "I shall order my carriage for eleven o'clock and I trust I may have your escort. Oh, Dashell, I am so afraid for the future," she added. "How on earth will we all survive? How will our family make good its losses?"

"I have no idea," replied Dashell truthfully. "We shall have to start taking stringent measures and economize somehow, but it could take years. Be brave. I shall kiss you on both cheeks for good measure, and Aunt Letty . . ."

"I know. Try not to worry," she sighed.

"Just think of the family motto."

"Oh, drat the family motto. Whichever dotty ancestor thought of that probably never had to contend with anything like this."

Dashell could not help laughing. "There you go already. That's the spirit."

"Humph," said his aunt, but she smiled at him.

"Good night" he said. "Now I must go. I shall see myself out."

Lady Smythe sat down again, thinking about her nephew. *I wonder who the lucky girl will be who will win your heart; that is, if anyone would consider you now. Oh, Walden, you have wrecked all our lives, including your own.*

Dashell had made up his mind about something and spoke to Walter about it when he returned to his rooms. "You will have heard from Matthew by now that Barrandale House is up for sale." Dashell knew the servants kept each other informed.

"Yes, sir," replied Walter carefully, "he did pass on that information to me."

"I have decided to terminate the tenancy of these rooms and will move into Barrandale House, at least for the time being," continued Dashell. "Would you see to everything with the agency, Walter? I will inform Matthew of this myself. I shall be leaving for Windsor tomorrow and could be away several days."

It was much the same at Barrandale House at breakfast. "I have to inform you, Matthew, that I am terminating the tenancy of my rooms on Curzon Street and will be moving in here, at least for the time being. Walter is making all the arrangements and if he requires assistance, please provide it. I know this is not the best time to be doing this but I am sure you understand the circumstances."

"Indeed I do, sir," replied Matthew. He understood this to be an economic measure.

Chapter Twenty-One

Happenings at Barrandale Park

It was around the same time when Dashell had left Martin Ellersby's lodgings that Lord Barrandale had been taken ill.

Lord Barrandale had sent a note to the family solicitor requesting him to call. Anything could happen to Dashell while he was in London and under no circumstances was the Barrandale estate to pass to the second son. The solicitor duly came and discovered his client wished to alter his will, and was privately horrified to learn his client was disinheriting one of his sons.

After the solicitor had left Lord Barrandale had gone upstairs to his room not feeling too well. The shock of receiving that fateful letter on Monday and all the ensuing circumstances; the enforced changes to pay off the debt; the anxiety of possibly losing the beloved house and estate; and sleepless nights; had all proved to be too much for him.

Lord Barrandale did not appear for tea at four o'clock. A footman ran upstairs to his lordship's suite and found him collapsed on the floor and immediately raised the alarm.

Simmonds, remembering Lord Lonsdale's instructions, sent for a doctor. His lordship was helped onto his bed by Simmonds and the footman, protesting feebly all the time. He tried to stand up and nearly collapsed again.

"I have sent for a doctor, your lordship," said Simmonds.

"Why? I do not need a doctor."

"I beg your pardon, sir, but before he left for London Lord Lonsdale said I was to send for a doctor if at any time I deemed it necessary."

Barrandale blinked at Simmonds in surprise. "Oh, he did, did he?" He passed a hand across his forehead. "I think I should lie down after all." He submitted patiently while Simmonds and the footman put him into bed. He lay back against the pillows and closed his eyes. Simmonds ordered the footman to stay in the corridor within call and went downstairs to await the doctor, not liking the situation at all.

The doctor duly came and was shocked at Lord Barrandale's appearance and examined him very carefully. "What have you been doing?" he wanted to know, and learned his lordship had been under great stress the past few days and had little sleep.

"Probably just a case of sheer exhaustion," the doctor said. "I shall order complete bed rest and leave some cordial to help you sleep, enough for three nights." The doctor paused, knowing this patient of old, but there was no protest.

He left the room and spoke to Simmonds. "I do not think he is in any danger and he has a strong constitution. I am relying on you to administer the cordial, one phial every night. In fact he could have the first one now. Let him sleep as much as he wants and only give him light meals when he requires them. I shall call again tomorrow afternoon during my rounds."

"I am relieved to learn there is no immediate cause for concern," replied Simmonds, and after seeing the doctor out he went back upstairs to give his lordship the cordial.

Lord Barrandale watched Simmonds pour it out. "Fuss about nothing," he muttered, but obediently swallowed it. "I will try and get a little sleep now," he said, and settled himself down. "Thank you for everything, Simmonds."

"Thank you, sir," replied Simmonds, with a slight bow.

There was concern in the servants' quarters, however. Usually Lord Barrandale was in the best of health, and now this? In fact, he had not been the same since that letter came on Monday. Then Lord Lonsdale had arrived late that evening after being summoned to come. Then those two shifty looking men had come the next day. A pall of gloom had settled on them, much like the one at Barrandale House in London.

The doctor called again the next afternoon and found his patient very much better, and the next day Lord Barrandale felt well enough to get up; but remained in his suite.

This was the situation that awaited Dashell and Lady Smythe when they arrived at Barrandale Park. Simmonds was genuinely pleased to see them. "Welcome home, Lord Lonsdale. Welcome, Lady Smythe."

"Thank you, Simmonds. I am pleased to be back. And how is my father?"

Simmonds coughed slightly and related everything to them. "He has not been in any danger, sir, just very tired. He has not been downstairs for two days." Dashell and his aunt exchanged anxious glances.

"I will go immediately to see him," declared Dashell. "Would you serve tea for us in his suite, Simmonds?"

"Come in, Dashell," called Barrandale in response to Dashell's knock. They looked at one another, each one silently appalled at the other's appearance. "I saw from the window you had arrived. Welcome home." There was another knock on the door and Lady Smythe swept in.

"Randolph!" she cried, with tears in her eyes. "Simmonds has just told us what happened to you. I am so very sorry."

"Welcome, Letty, my dear," as they kissed each other. "I am much better now. But did Simmonds send for you?"

"No, I came of my own accord. Dashell has told me everything and I could not bear to think of you being alone."

"I will have Simmonds serve tea here," said Barrandale.

"I have already asked him to do so," said Dashell.

"Oh, you have, have you?" Barrandale's eyebrows went up in mock severity. "Dashell, I am fast getting the impression my authority is being usurped. And what is this about you issuing orders to Simmonds before you left for London? If you were still a little boy and not the size you are now, I would seriously consider putting you across my knee."

"I am relieved to know your good spirits are returning, sir," chuckled Dashell, as Lady Smythe laughed.

"Now, I am sure you two will wish to refresh yourselves after your journey here, and I will expect you back here at four o'clock for tea."

Dashell and his aunt left the room together. "He always did put on a brave front, didn't he?" she whispered, "and did you see how much weight he has lost? How much will you tell him about Walden calling at the house?"

"I shall have to mention it of course, and will try to make light of it, but Father always has this uncanny knack of knowing if I am holding anything back."

After their tea Lady Smythe left them, saying, "I know you two have a great deal to talk about so I shall find myself a book in the library."

So Dashell related to his father everything he had done while in London beginning with the surprise encounter with Walden and the consequences. "I sent him out of the house, sir," he stated briefly, "and told him about your letter to the Commanding Officer at the Barracks in Hyde Park."

Barrandale merely nodded, regarding his son shrewdly. "Please continue."

Dashell then described calling at the bank, the estate agents, and the moneylenders, and handed his father the cancelled writ.

"So that part of it is over and finished with," said Barrandale, "and that gives me some measure of relief." He put the writ to one side to be locked away later.

"And here," continued Dashell, "are some information sheets about houses in and around London. I also ordered Matthew to draw up inventories of all the rooms; and as an economic measure I am terminating my tenancy on Curzon Street and will reside at the house for the time being."

"I see," said Barrandale, "and do you still intend to reside at the new house, where ever that may be?"

"Only if I need to keep an eye on you, sir." countered Dashell with a smile.

"Hmm," replied Barrandale, also smiling. "However, there is still a great deal for us to discuss."

Barrandale joined the other two downstairs for their evening meal and they talked in front of the servants about anything except the family situation. But once they finished and retired to the library their anxious conversation resumed for the rest of the evening.

Eventually this tired Barrandale and he bade goodnight to his sister and requested Dashell to accompany him upstairs. He sat thankfully on his bed. "Would you pour out the last draught of that cordial, Dashell?"

Dashell did so and handed the glass to his father but Barrandale shook his head. "No, I want you to drink it."

Dashell stared at him. "You want me to drink it?"

"Dashell," replied Barrandale steadily, "when you arrived this afternoon you looked exhausted, even haunted, almost as though you had the hounds of hell on your heels. You have obviously been worried about everything and have been stretching yourself to the limit and I cannot afford to have you ill. And if I may also make the observation, you had something on your mind when you came home in answer to my summons before we even knew what was going on. Now drink it. And that is an order," he added with a faint smile.

Dashell's thoughts flew immediately to Martin and his warning, and then to Caroline, and all the worry caused by Walden, marvelling again at the astuteness of his father, and he knew he also desperately needed some rest for his body and mind, so he obeyed without a word.

"Thank you, Dashell," said Barrandale quietly. Now I would advise you to go straight to bed, and please ring for Simmonds for me."

When Simmonds came to attend his lordship he noticed the last of the cordial had gone. "Do not be concerned, Simmonds," said Barrandale, "I have given it to my son. Would you see that he is not disturbed in the morning. I shall not expect him down for breakfast, or even for luncheon."

It was not until about half-past three the next afternoon that a rather sheepish Dashell appeared in the library. He had in fact awakened during the morning, gone back to sleep, awakened again and lay in a comfortable doze.

"I trust you had a good sleep?" enquired Barrandale.

"Yes, thank you, sir, I did. I can hardly believe I slept so well and for so long, and I feel so much better for it. I must thank you again for your consideration." Dashell went outside onto the terrace and took several deep breaths to chase away the last of his sleep.

After dinner that evening Barrandale requested Dashell to accompany him to his study. He seated himself at his desk, his forearms resting on it and his hands lightly clasped together. "I am pleased you are rested, Dashell," he said. "Yesterday you were not, so I did not press the point. You will now tell me exactly what transpired between Walden and yourself last Wednesday morning."

Dashell turned pale and stared at his father in dismay. He suddenly felt as he used to feel as a boy when called into the study to explain some misbehavior or other. He knew his father had this uncanny knack and he also knew that steely look in his eyes only too well. "If I withheld anything, sir, it was only to spare you more pain," he said at last. There was no use denying it.

"Thank you for your consideration but I will be the judge of that. Was it so terrible between the two of you, then?"

"Yes, sir," admitted Dashell, tight-lipped and still pale.

"Then tell me," ordered Barrandale. "The pain of not knowing can be worse than the pain of knowing. You may sit down if you wish."

There was no way out. Dashell sat down and related the whole incident, from Matthew speaking to him and then to the shutting of the front door behind Walden. Barrandale listened quietly, never taking his eyes off him, but Dashell knew he was hurt.

When Dashell finished his father merely said, "I would like to be alone now. Please make my apologies to your aunt."

Dashell paused at the door. "I tried to spare you, sir."

"Good night, Dashell."

Lady Smythe glanced up when her nephew entered the library. "Father is going straight upstairs and asked me to make his apologies to you," said Dashell.

"Is everything all right, Dashell?" his aunt enquired, knowing the two of them had a long talk together.

"I knew Father would know. He insisted I told him everything."

A little later Barrandale made his way slowly to his bedroom and rang the bell for Simmonds. While getting ready for bed he issued a certain order to his manservant.

"I shall attend to it in the morning, sir."

Chapter Twenty-Two
Maxwell's Homecoming

Father and son met again at the breakfast table the next morning and neither of them mentioned the evening before, but Barrandale did speak of something else.

"Mitchell, our estate manager, will be leaving soon."

"He will?" queried Dashell. "Nothing untoward there, I hope."

"No. Mitchell spoke to me some while ago that he had heard of an extensive estate in the North of England that would be requiring a new manager as the old one was retiring. He applied and went for an interview and was accepted. He said he would put everything in order before handing over our estate to a new man. Incidentally, none of the servants leaving of their own accord or being let go, will be replaced."

Dashell looked up in surprise. "Mitchell will not be replaced? But who will manage the estate?" He caught the look in his father's eye. "You mean you wish me to manage the estate?"

"It will not be financially possible to hire a new man," Barrandale pointed out, "and there is no one else I would rather ask, or even could ask."

"Yes, I will accept," stated Dashell, after a brief pause. "So that means I must discuss everything with Mitchell before he goes."

"There is one other matter I must mention," continued Barrandale. "Maxwell has left Eton, but he is staying with friends for a few days before coming home. He did write and ask if it would be all right and of course I said it would be. He should be here tomorrow."

Later that evening Dashell asked his father if he might speak to Maxwell first when he arrived. "Do so, if you think it will make it easier for him," replied Barrandale. "Poor lad, he is bound to take it very hard."

The next day Dashell and his aunt waited in the hall and eventually there was the sound of a trap pulling up. Dashell was not looking forward to this: to see one more stricken face. He went outside to welcome his brother.

Maxwell bounded up the steps with all the impetuosity of youth, a young man yet still a boy.

"Hello, Father!" he cried. "Oh, it's you, Dashell. Has anyone ever told you how much like Father you are getting?"

"Yes, people have," laughed Dashell in spite of himself, "and welcome home, by the way."

"Aunt Letty," cried Maxwell. "I did not expect to see you here," giving her a hug.

"It's going to be so cruel," she whispered to Dashell, and his heart sank.

"Oh, it's wonderful to be home again," continued Maxwell. "I can hardly believe I have finished with Eton. We were all talking about what we were going to do. Is Father here or is he in London?"

"He's here," said Dashell.

"Oh, then I must see him," and he turned to go.

"Maxwell, wait, I must speak to you." Dashell made it sound like a command.

Maxwell turned round on his heel. "What do you mean? Father is not ill, is he?"

"Come outside with me and I will try to explain." Dashell led the way towards the river followed by a very puzzled Maxwell, and they sat down on a wooden bench. Maxwell had no idea that Dashell was thinking this was the last time he would have to explain anything to anybody, except Caroline of course. The last time he would have to see someone's world fall apart.

Slowly and carefully Dashell told Maxwell of the trouble befallen the family brought about by Walden's debts, and which had caused such a financial drain upon the estate. Maxwell was stunned, he was completely unprepared for this, and Dashell watched as the colour drained from his brother's face.

"Are you saying Walden, our very own brother, did this?" Maxwell asked incredulously.

"Yes, Walden, our very own brother, did," repeated Dashell wearily.

"And he has been disinherited and is going out to India in the Army?" He stared at Dashell, shocked at such swift retribution. "And you say it may not be possible for me to go to Oxford?"

"Yes, Maxwell," said Dashell. "Father does not think there will be enough money for you."

Maxwell, still struggling to comprehend, burst out, "But Walden knew I had plans to go to Oxford and study architecture. What am I supposed to do now? What am I to tell all my friends? They will probably laugh at me now," he concluded bitterly.

"Maxwell, I do understand what it is like, because this has altered our lives as well. It has been a great shock to Father. The possible loss of the estate and all it holds dear, and how many servants will have to be let go, and how much else will have to be sold to help pay off the debt."

"How could Walden be such a complete damn fool?" Maxwell stood up and stared out across the river where all three brothers had gone rowing in earlier days. Boy-like, he kicked at a stone, then picked it up and hurled it as far as he could into the river. He whirled round. "I hope he gets killed!" He came and sat down again. "I'm sorry, I should not have said that," he muttered. "But why couldn't Father tell me this himself?"

"I asked Father if I might speak to you first, and he agreed."

"Oh," said Maxwell, not fully satisfied.

"Maxwell, do not direct your anger at Father. He has had enough."

"Oh," said Maxwell again. "I will go and see him."

"You will find him in his study. And be careful, Maxwell. For all his surface fortitude he is deeply hurt; and you will see a great change in him."

Maxwell nodded, then silently turned and walked up to the house, knocked on the door of the study, and slowly opened it. "Father? Father!" he cried, and ran towards him.

Dashell watched Maxwell go until he was out of sight, then turned round with a long weary sigh. What a wretched home-coming it had been for him. Only time would tell what the outcome would be.

Now at last all immediate family business was over for him. He had done all that he had been asked to do. Now he would have to turn his attentions to managing the estate. He went back indoors and found his aunt in a comfortable chair in the library overlooking the terrace.

She glanced up when he entered "How did Maxwell take it?"

"Not very well, which is understandable. He went to see Father and I warned him what to expect."

Later that evening Maxwell drew Dashell to one side. "Poor Father. I can't really be angry, can I?" he whispered.

The next day was quiet, each person occupied with individual thoughts, and in the evening they played cards together.

Just before they retired for the night Dashell casually remarked to his father, "If you do not require me tomorrow, sir, I plan to return to London. I have some unfinished business I wish to attend to. I can speak to Mitchell the day after."

"Of course," replied Barrandale "You must forgive me for taking up so much of your time." He had noticed the long silent sighs coming from Dashell, who was obviously thinking about something else even as he concentrated on his cards, and he had glanced curiously at his son from time to time.

Dashell had been well aware of his father's glances, but the time was not right to say what was on his mind. He had to speak to Caroline first.

Ever since that summons from his father days ago, he had wanted to see her, and now could hardly believe that time was nearly here. How could he ask Caroline to forgive him for what must have seemed like cavalier desertion on his part, even when he explained, if she agreed to listen to him. That dear face, when she turned to look at him as she went upstairs on that terrible afternoon. How he had wanted to kiss away all hurt! None of his letters had been acknowledged or answered, not that he had expected them to be, nor had they been returned to him unopened, either. He turned cold when he remembered his conversation with Martin and his warnings.

Chapter Twenty-Three
Happenings At The House On Becket Lane

That afternoon when Lord Lonsdale had left the house so angry, Caroline still felt shocked over the very scene she had so wanted to avoid for his sake, far worse than the one involving Maude. Those hateful words hurled at her in front of Dashell were so humiliating. Had she done such a terrible thing to warrant those accusations from her Papa? Lord Lonsdale had been quite the gentleman and had done nothing to disgust her, but the change in him terrified her.

For the hundredth time Caroline tried to understand why Papa behaved like he did, and there was now something about him that was beginning to fill her with dread, something nameless she could not put a finger on. She therefore made no real demur when Hannah insisted on sleeping in the same room with her. Yet she was aghast when Johnny showed them how to wedge a chair underneath the doorknob to prevent the door being opened from the other side.

"Whatever do you think Papa is going to do?" she cried.

Somehow neither Hannah nor Johnny could give a satisfactory answer, which left their young mistress looking at them in astonishment.

Johnny still remembered that black thread. What if Mr. Nasty tried to kill Miss Caroline in the same way? Not if he could help it. He planned to wait until early morning, creep up the back stairs and then to the top of the front ones to see if any thread had been tied across. He went to bed feeling much easier in his mind, and resolved to do this every morning.

The next morning Caroline opened one of the drawers of her dressing table where she kept the dried petals from the flowers Dashell had given her, all sweetly smelling. She had stitched a little sachet for them, a pretty thing made from scraps of lace and ribbon. She opened it and let the petals fall into a dish and wondered if she would ever see Dashell again. Perhaps not, after that dreadful quarrel, although Hannah did her best to convince Caroline she would.

There were other thoughts too. When she and Dashell had walked back from the tea-rooms and stood looking at the roses, she had turned round when that pair of blackbirds flew out of the tree. It was not the birds that had caused her to turn round, but a sudden conviction that her mother and sister were standing close by, but in no way to frighten her. Why had that happened when she was with Dashell? Was it to warn her or encourage her?

There was one more thing. The next time Dashell came, if he did, she must in all honesty tell him that she and Maude had long suspected the person they referred to as "Papa" was not their real father. Both she and Maude once tried to approach their mother about this, who admitted he was not their real father. But who was? they had cried. Their mother became quite upset and promised them that one day they would know.

After their mother's death the two sisters had gone through her writing-table and had not found any family papers. It was not until after Maude's death that an unbidden thought crept into Caroline's mind, that the two sisters had been born out of wedlock, hence their mother's silence. Oh, the shame of it if it was true! Slowly she picked up the dish and replaced the petals gently back into the sachet. She would always keep them, come what may, and in the years ahead would look back on a love that almost was.

How could she think that a gentleman in Lord Lonsdale's position would be interested in her, even if she did know her real father's name. He said he loved her and he probably did, but for how long? Aristocratic gentlemen were notorious for their philandering. Of course it was just a passing fancy, in spite of the words he professed. She put her hands to her face to stem the tears welling up. *Oh, Dashell, it might have been better if we had never met.*

At first Caroline believed Dashell would return, but after two days without a word her fortitude began to falter. Had his love cooled already and he had changed his mind? Perhaps she had placed too much faith in him after all.

Hannah and Johnny had been exchanging grim anxious glances. "I could have sworn he would have come back by now," she whispered to Johnny, "wherever can he be?"

"I dunno," was his disgusted answer.

On the morning of the third day Caroline came downstairs and, with an air of determination, announced to Hannah, "I am going out for a walk to get some fresh air."

"Would you like me to come with you, dear?"

"No thank you, Hannah. I would prefer to be alone." Caroline would not admit that she had made up her mind to forget Dashell. "I shall go into the village for those groceries we want and some sewing thread I need."

It was a beautiful day and Caroline decided to take the long way round to the village. She walked along hardly seeing a soul until she reached the village, and then it seemed that every other person she met was a friend or an acquaintance. "Caroline, my dear, how are you?" or, "I trust you are keeping well, Miss Wardlock?" Progress was slow for she liked meeting people and chatting, and it helped her forget her troubles. By the time she made her purchases the church clock was striking twelve. *Goodness,* she thought, *Hannah will be wondering where I am.*

She walked quickly back to the house. "I'm here, Hannah," she called. "I did not mean to be so long."

Hannah had been listening for her and came hurrying out. "Miss Caroline," she cried, "I thought you were never going to get here. Come into the kitchen quickly!" She took the packages from her young mistress and almost pushed her along. "Look!" cried Hannah eagerly pointing to the table.

Caroline looked and then gasped. "Oh!" There lay the flowers and letter sent by Dashell. "Oh!" she cried again. Joyfully she picked up the forget-me-nots first, and then the pansies, and held them to her face. She knew at once the messages they were meant to convey. So Dashell had not forgotten! But why had it taken him nearly three days?

"How did they get here? Did Lord Lonsdale himself bring them?"

"No, he didn't." Hannah's words came tumbling out. "Not long after you left there was a knock on the door and I thought you had forgotten something. I opened it and there was a cab-driver with the flowers and the letter in his hands. "Does a Miss Caroline Wardlock reside here?" he asked, and I said "yes". Then he said a gentleman in town had hailed him and directed him to deliver these flowers and letter to this address. And here we were quite sure he had forgotten you!"

Caroline felt mortified. Just when she had made her resolution to forget Dashell, he had sent this message. She eagerly tore his letter open and read it through quickly, and with a cry turned to Hannah, "Dashell mentions another letter! 'My first letter' he says. So this is his second one. I don't understand it. What happened to the first one? It must have gone astray, perhaps lost somehow, though I own that must be unusual. Or perhaps someone forgot to post it. I feel ashamed of myself now for doubting him so much."

"I always said he would remember you, didn't I?" Hannah reminded her, "though I do think he took his time about it."

By now Hannah had put the flowers in water and placed them on a tray. "There," she said, "I will take them upstairs for you, and by the time you come down lunch will be ready. It won't hurt us to be late for once."

"Thank you, Hannah. It was my fault for taking so long in the village. I had no idea this had happened." Caroline went upstairs to her bedroom followed by Hannah with the tray. Hannah placed the vases on the dressing-table and then went downstairs again. Caroline slipped off her cloak and bonnet and picked up each vase to smell the delicate scent of the flowers again; and they had been purchased only a short while ago! She read Dashell's letter again. *"Those words I spoke to you in Richmond Park..."* So he thought of them as well! Once more her resolution to be sensible had been set aside. She returned downstairs with a much heightened colour, to Hannah's silent satisfaction.

"We must tell Johnny, Miss Caroline, if you please, for he has been concerned for you. And we have all been so worried because someone forgot to post a letter."

"That was kind of Johnny. Of course we shall tell him."

Johnny came in later and listened in wonder as Caroline explained Lord Lonsdale's supposed silence because of a missing letter.

"Tell yer wot, Miss Caroline," said Johnny. "After supper I'll go an' see the postman. I know where 'e lives an' I'll just see wot 'e sez."

"Thank you, Johnny," said Caroline, "although I am not sure there is anything else he could say."

After supper Johnny set off for the postman's cottage and found the man sitting on a bench in his little garden, "watching his taties grow."

"I hafta arsk yer somefink," said Johnny. "This morning Miss Wardlock 'ad a letter delivered by a cab-driver. She said the letter mentioned annuver one which she should have 'ad by now."

"There was a letter for the lady yesterday," said the surprised postman. "Didn't she get it?"

"No, she didn't. "Oo did yer give it to, then?" Johnny demanded, as a dreadful suspicion crept into his mind.

"Well," explained the postman, "I was walking to the front door with the letter in my hand when suddenly Mr. Wardlock was there in front of me. He took it from me, looked at it and put it in his pocket. He must have seen it was addressed to Miss Caroline Wardlock. 'Here,' I said, 'what about my penny?' He handed me a penny as though he could not bear to part with it. I almost had to pull it away from him. Oooh, I don't mind telling you he gave me quite a turn. There he was, looking at me like Death Warmed Up. I couldn't move, and by the time I could he had gone off in the cab that was waiting for him."

Just the sort of thing that mean old devil would do, Johnny thought to himself. Here they had been wondering why nothing had been heard from Lord Lonsdale when all the time that crafty old buzzard had the letter. "I've got an idea," Johnny said. "You know that old hollow tree stump at the end of the carriage lane by the road? Well, if any other letters come could yer leave 'em inside the tree? and Hannah or me will come an' get them. We can leave a few pennies there so you won't 'ave to come and arsk."

The postman was rather taken aback. "I don't know about that, Johnny. I am under oath to deliver letters."

"You will be delivering letters. It's just that we don't want Mr. Wardlock finding out. It won't be for long anyway." By Johnny's reckoning once Lord Lonsdale returned there would be no further need for this arrangement.

"I'm sticking my neck out about this, but I'll do it," agreed the postman.

"Cor, you're a real brick, you are," said a relieved Johnny. "I must be getting back. Say hello to yer missus for me." He dashed away leaving the postman scratching his head. Running all the way back to Becket Lane Johnny was filled with mounting dread. How much longer could the three of them stay in that house? The sooner they left the better.

The two women were anxiously awaiting Johnny's return and Caroline started up when he came in. "Have you any news?" she asked eagerly. "What did the postman say?" She caught her breath when she saw the troubled look on Johnny's face.

"I dunno quite 'ow to tell yer this, Miss Caroline," said Johnny, still panting from running, "but there was a letter for you yesterday," and repeated what the postman told him.

Caroline's reaction was of horror and disgust at her Papa's duplicity. So this was his way of revenge, to make her think

Dashell had deserted her! It was no use wondering what was in the first letter, it was the second one that allayed her doubts about Dashell and told her his love was constant. That is, it would be until she told him the truth about herself.

Once or twice lately she had the thought of asking her stepfather who her real father was. There must be a marriage certificate between him and her mother with her previous name on it. But now when she caught sight of Papa his very looks filled her with dread, and even if he did know her real father's name he very likely would not tell her. To think her future happiness depended on speaking to him. The very thought made her shudder.

A rising anger took hold of her. "How dare he do this?" she said, careful to keep her voice down. "How dare he?"

"Miss Caroline," Hannah began tentatively, "you could speak to him about the first letter. He may still have it."

"No, Hannah, that would not be a wise thing to do. Papa would know at once that Lord Lonsdale had written again mentioning the first letter. I will not say anything, and that will make him think the matter is over and that I never knew anything about it."

"That horrible man," muttered Hannah, seeing the sense of it. "The sooner we leave this house the better, even if I am speaking out of place."

"Yes, I know," agreed Caroline, wondering how long it would be before Dashell did return. "In the meantime we will continue with our plans. If Lord Lonsdale has not called or written within two weeks, then we leave. And Johnny," she added, turning to him, "I must thank you for your help. That was a wonderful idea of yours about putting any further letters in the tree."

"I'm only too 'appy to 'elp, Miss Caroline," he grinned. *Anything to beat that old geezer.*

The clock in the hall chimed ten o'clock. It had become their habit to retire to bed before Mr. Wardlock did, to avoid meeting him. So Caroline and Hannah went upstairs and Johnny went to his little room more determined than ever to keep his early morning vigil.

Caroline and Hannah spent the following days sorting out what they were going to take with them when they left. Johnny said he would take anything not needed to pawnshops in the East End of London. After that stolen letter Caroline had no inhibitions about what they were doing. Besides, they needed all the money they could get.

Likewise, all the clothing belonging to her mother and sister was sorted through. Her mother's clothing was far too small for Caroline and was given to charity. Maude's clothing fitted her well enough except for a few alterations.

"Hannah," Caroline declared, "I can hardly believe I am doing this. I wonder I can bear to wear Maude's things."

"Now, now, Miss Caroline," said Hannah a little sharply, "we have discussed this already. We must trust we are doing the right thing because the alternative is to stay here and none of us want that. So what else are we to do?"

"As usual you are right, Hannah," she sighed.

When she went to the Village, as the locals called it, people would say to her, "Miss Wardlock, I fear you do not look in your usual bloom." Others were more forthright. "Caroline, my dear, it is time you got married, a nice lady like you. I am sure some gentleman would be pleased to meet you." Caroline hated that kind of remark and usually made some tart reply that she was not willing to marry just anybody, and make some excuse to get away.

She walked slowly towards the church they had always attended and slipped inside. It was the organist's practice time and parishioners would often go in just to listen. She sat down to enjoy the music and let her thoughts roam, for there would not be many more opportunities for this. She remembered joyous Christmas and Easter services and happy Harvest Thanksgivings, joining the choir as extra voices to go carol singing round the local villages. She and Maude had loved it when it snowed, the flakes showing up so prettily in the light of the lanterns they carried. Then there were all the Charity Teas organized by the ladies, as well as those when visiting clergy came.

Now Caroline would be leaving all this, and those two precious people who almost never left her thoughts. As she looked round the church she caught sight again of the words on the reredos screen behind the altar: "I am the Resurrection and the Life", and thought of that time in the front garden when she felt her mother and sister were close to her, and now it had a new meaning. She was not to think of them as lying in some dark, dank corner of the church graveyard but that they were alive in the spiritual sense. She closed her eyes and let her own spirit soar with the music, and by the time she left the church she was positively smiling.

Johnny's arrangement with the postman did bear fruit. After four days there was a letter but only from a friend Caroline had made at the Ladies' Academy; a kind girl who would have been horrified to know her letter had been delivered under such subterfuge. Caroline wanted to see Dashell again, and yet as the days passed she became more apprehensive, her mind full of what she had to tell him. Yet great was her joy when she received Dashell's third letter, only that he was still unable to say when he could return to see her.

Unknown by either Caroline or Hannah, Johnny had some thoughts of his own. He remembered that after the mistress died no personal papers of any kind had been found, which puzzled the two sisters as they had long suspected Thomas Wardlock was not their real father. He was such a strange man with an uncertain temper that they had hesitated to approach him themselves.

Johnny knew unless Miss Caroline knew her real name it would be impossible for Lord Lonsdale to marry her. So what could they do? Nothing, as far as he could see. If the three of them were planning to leave the house then it did not give much time for him to carry out what he had in mind. Fortunately tomorrow was Friday when Miss Caroline and Hannah would go to the Tea Rooms as usual. He would try to leave the inn early, where he had part time work, nor would he mention anything to Hannah just yet.

Luck was with him, for Johnny was able to leave the inn early, and he ran back to the house to carry out his plan. Without a qualm, or batting an eye, or a twinge of conscience, he set to work to thoroughly search Mr. Wardlock's bedroom and downstairs sitting room.

Johnny recalled the petty thief named "Fingers" whom he had met in London, and what that man told him. "Remember how things were before you move them." He searched in all possible and impossible places and found nothing. He went downstairs, and with the lockpick Fingers had shown him how to use, which he had always carefully kept hidden in his room, Johnny opened Mr. Wardlock's desk but found nothing of interest. Either the papers he hoped to find were hidden somewhere else, or they never existed in the first place.

Despondently, Johnny went outside to busy himself in the garden, reckoning Miss Caroline and Hannah would be back from the Tea Rooms soon. He wondered if he should tell Hannah what he had been doing, and if he did, he would certainly speak to her on her own. It would be no use raising Miss Caroline's hopes only to disappoint her.

Chapter twenty-Four
Dashell and Caroline

Mitchell, the estate manager, was informed Lord Lonsdale would speak with him the next day, for Dashell felt he had waited for this day long enough.

At last he was on his way to Becket Lane. Sparkle, sensing his rider's excitement, needed no urging. The rhythm of his swift canter drummed out the beloved name. Car-o-line, Car-o-line, Car-o-line. But suppose she refused to see Dashell? His letters torn up, or remained unopened, ready to be handed back if he ever did call. The flowers he sent, thrown away. Hannah forbidden to open the door to him, or if she did, having it slammed in his face.

Dashell left Sparkle at the Bishop's Head Inn and, still apprehensive, walked back to the house. His hands shook a little as he opened the gate. His heart pounded as he walked up to the house and knocked on the door. It was opened by Hannah and her face beamed a welcome.

"Why, Lord Lonsdale, sir, please come in."

"Hannah, dare I hope that Miss Caroline will see me, or is she angry with me? I must be allowed to explain my absence to her."

"Why, bless you, sir, come inside and I'll tell Miss Caroline you are here. She is in the back garden somewhere." She bustled away leaving Dashell thankful he had actually been invited in and not sent away.

Caroline was walking about in the garden recalling all the times she and her mother and sister had spent in it. Not much longer and she would be leaving all this, taking one cherished memory with her: a certain dear face with a scar on one cheek. Even if she did see Dashell again it would only be to say goodbye. She sighed deeply as she turned away and saw Hannah coming towards her with some degree of haste.

Hannah pulled up, breathless, and just said two words: "He's here."

"He's here?" repeated Caroline. "Oh, you mean . . . ?" *Then I must see him just once more,* she told herself.

"Now don't keep him waiting," Hannah said, "he's anxious enough as it is. He's expecting you to be angry with him," but by then Caroline had run past her.

Dashell stood up when he heard Caroline coming. Her quick light footsteps slowed to a more decorous pace as she neared the door, then stopped outside, her heart beating fast and not just from running. She came slowly into the room and they looked at each other. Dashell held out both his hands in mute appeal as Caroline slowly came forward, astonished at his looks. And he, not knowing what she had in mind, took her hands in his and held them close to his chest, she with one cheek against them and he with his chin in her hair.

Neither of them spoke at first. Dashell was so glad to see Caroline again, now the agonized waiting was over at last. During his ride he had tried to think of what he was going to say, to rehearse some kind of speech, but now no words would come or even seem appropriate. He wanted to say that she had earth on her boots and a leaf in her hair and that he had fallen in love with her all over again.

"Can you forgive me, dearest?" he whispered at last.

Caroline groaned to herself. *Don't call me names like that, Dashell,* she thought, *nor will you after I tell you what I must.* Out loud she said, ""What must I forgive you?"

"For leaving you the way I did," he replied. "I had to. My father summoned me home that same afternoon and I had to go. I have had so much to do since I last saw you."

"Is that what happened to you, Dashell? You look so tired. Oh, I'm sorry, I should not have said that."

"I know, Caroline, my darling," he replied, and wondered why she tried to pull her hands away. "I wrote a brief letter to you explaining I had to return to Windsor that very evening. Then I wrote again the next day and sent some flowers."

"Yes, I know. I was out when they came and Hannah told me a cab-driver had brought them, and I must thank you for them."

"And you understood their meaning?" he asked anxiously.

"Perfectly. Dashell, may I have my hands back, please?"

"Not yet. I like holding them. I could stand here for ever. And then I wrote to you again saying I would still be away."

"Yes, you did." Caroline, remembering her resolution, gently pulled her hands away and he reluctantly let them go. "I should tell you, Dashell, that I never got your first letter."

"What?" he cried. Did Walter fail to post the letter? But he was far too reliable.

"Come and sit down, Dashell," Caroline said, "and I will try and explain." They sat down on a sofa half facing each other. "It was not until I got your second letter that I learned about the first one."

"That means you heard nothing from me for days!" exclaimed Dashell. "Caroline, my darling, you must have thought I had indeed deserted you. But I do not understand how you did not get the first letter."

"I can explain," began Caroline, not caring now in what light this made her Papa appear after his duplicity. She outlined briefly how Johnny had gone to ask the postman if he remembered delivering the first letter, and how Papa had taken it and not given it to her later. "I do not know what he did with it," she concluded.

Dashell listened with rising anger. What a score he had to settle with this man! "What I said in the letter was very brief, just that I had been called away and did not know when I was able to return."

He frowned, realizing for the first time that Caroline looked pale and that her attitude was cool, and thought she was indeed still hurt and offended. He tried to hold her hands again but she refused to let him, and rather childishly put them behind her back. "Caroline, what is it? Are you still angry with me?"

"No, of course not."

However, he knew something was wrong. "Please let me explain," he said, getting to his feet, as Caroline watched him in silence. "I have already told you, I believe, that I had a summons from my father to return to Windsor immediately, and when my father says "immediately" he means just that," and Caroline smiled back tentatively. "I am the eldest of three brothers and Walden, the second one, had been very extravagant and got hopelessly entangled in debt, so much so that moneylenders gave us only two weeks to repay." He glanced at Caroline as she gave a little gasp of horror. "I had to return to London to make all the necessary financial arrangements and on my return to Windsor I learned of my father's exhaustion. Then I had to wait to speak to my youngest brother. I have told you this, Caroline, in trust that you will respect my confidence, and for you to know what occupied so much of my time."

"Dashell, I am so sorry," she said. "Of course I understand now. I had no idea what could be keeping you, I could only have faith you would return. No wonder you looked so tired and strained just now, with all that you had to do."

"I was apprehensive too. I thought you might send me away."

Caroline felt tears brimming up because that was exactly what she had to do. *Dashell, if you only knew how my heart is breaking,* she thought, *but I do have to tell you to go.*

Dashell waited, hurt at her silence. "When we were in Richmond Park you told me my attentions did not offend you, and now you behave as though they do, for I believe I have detected a degree of coolness. What has made you change? Is there anyone else?" he asked. "Say there isn't, Caroline. I could not bear to lose you."

"No, there is not."

"Then why?" he cried.

Caroline remained seated on the sofa and held her hands firmly together on her lap, but that did not quite stop their trembling.

Swallowing hard she began hoarsely, "Dashell, you did honour me by declaring your love for me even after so short a time, but before I can answer your questions I must ask you some. First, I wish you to make your intentions clear to me."

"My intentions? My intentions?" he repeated blankly, staring at her. "What in heaven's name has got into you? Did you think you were just a passing fancy? That my love was only worth that much? Caroline, every time I awoke, every time I fell asleep, my thoughts were of you, in spite of what other things I had to think about."

He came and sat beside her again but made no attempt to touch her, and she looked at him with widened eyes. "Forgive me, Caroline, but this meeting of ours is not going as I hoped and prayed it would. Something has upset you, but to put your mind at rest my hopes are to marry you."

Caroline closed her eyes for a brief moment. Now she had her answer to everything. All her doubts had been set aside. Dashell was a man of honour, which made what she had to say even more difficult. With a deep breath she said, "Dashell, again you do me an honour, but there is something I must tell you." She could feel her lips trembling.

"Go on, I am listening," he said, regarding her in surprise.

"You will remember the first time you came into this room you remarked upon the painting of my sister and I."

"Yes, I did," he agreed, looking at the painting and back again to Caroline, wondering what all this was leading up to.

"Then you met Papa a short while later." Caroline forced herself to be calm, to forget those shameful words, as though it was just an ordinary meeting."

"Yes, I did," he replied grimly. "He has not hurt you, has he?"

Caroline gave her head a little shake. "I have hardly seen anything of him since then; but to continue. Hannah told me afterwards that you had compared his looks with mine and then the portrait, and surmised that perhaps Thomas Wardlock was not my father, but my stepfather." She paused a moment, looking at her hands on her lap.

"Yes, as a matter of fact I did," said Dashell, "but what of it? Many people have stepfathers, and stepmothers too, for that matter."

Taking another breath, Caroline said, "I know he is my stepfather and as the name Wardlock was ours also people naturally thought Maude and I were his actual daughters." She stumbled to a halt knowing her next words would destroy any happiness she might have had with Dashell. Then looking straight at him with those lovely clear eyes, she said, "Dashell, I do not know the name of my real father. Neither Maude nor I knew. Mother would never talk about it."

It was out at last. That knowledge that had haunted the two sisters so much; and the fact their mother would not talk about it. Refused to talk about it. She had become visibly upset once when they tried to press her, she had left the room and returned with reddened eyes and begged them not to mention it again. Why, oh why? Did it mean there was some dark shameful secret? She saw Dashell's eyes stare and harden, then open wide in amazement then recoil in horror, as differing thoughts raced through his mind at the full implication of her words took hold.

"Caroline!" he cried. "What are you saying! I just assumed you knew. In fact I was going to ask you. I just don't know what to say. You have taken me completely by surprise."

Caroline stood up and went to look out of the window. She shivered with cold and began rubbing her bare arms with her hands. She heard Dashell get up and open the parlour door and braced herself to hear the front door close behind him as he walked out of her life for ever.

Instead she heard him ring the little bell on the hall table to summon Hannah and was able to hear him say to her, "Your mistress is feeling cold, Hannah. Have you something warm she can put round her?" Hannah murmured some reply, went upstairs and came down with a shawl and two handkerchiefs.

"Come, Caroline, come and sit down," said Dashell as he gently placed the shawl round her shoulders. "Now dry your eyes."

Caroline did so, trying to sniff elegantly. "Dashell, you must understand I had to tell you and that there can be no marriage between us. For that same reason I am not able to marry at all if I do not know my real name."

Dashell, still at a loss for words, got up and moved to the window trying to marshall his thoughts as Caroline watched him in desolate silence. He knew exactly what would happen if he, a Barrandale, dared to introduce Caroline into Society; a woman who could not name her own father. The scandal would be horrendous. Everyone would turn away in disgust. They would both be shunned, doors slammed in their faces, they could be forbidden entry into places. This time friends would turn away. "I've always liked you," they may murmur, "but there are limits to one's friendship." Gossips like that awful Lady Hepplewhite would have a field day and Caroline's reputation would be shredded. And how could he go to his father and say, "Sir, I have found the woman I wish to marry, but she does not know her background or who her father is." His father would be appalled and rightly so.

Again, the scandal! The proud Barrandale head could never be raised again. It would be like taking over where Walden had left off and Dashell could never be so cruel as to do that.

"What did you mean, your mother would never talk about it?" he suddenly asked, and saw Caroline turn white as she lifted her chin.

"I have no idea why." Caroline did not dare say she and Maude had wondered if they had been born out of wedlock, hence their mother's refusal to talk.

"Have you ever tried to make your own enquiries? Tried to find out by other ways?" Even as he asked, Dashell knew the difficulties women would have doing this.

"Yes, we did," Caroline replied. "Maude and I were going to try, but hardly knew how to set about it. And then Maude died," she added with a sigh. "All we really know was that Mother was an only child and that she came from somewhere in Sussex. Her maiden name was Frobisher. I remember when some newcomers were introduced here, Mother remarked that Frobisher was her maiden name, and it always remained in my memory even though I was only about eight years old at the time. Hannah told us Mother had tried to say something to her before she died, but to no avail, she simply did not have the strength to speak. If only she had been able to it might have saved a lot of heartache."

Dashell came to sit by Caroline again but made no attempt to touch her. "The obvious place to start would be to approach your stepfather because he must know. It would even help to know where your mother and he married, which church. There must be some record of it." He frowned. "He has not hurt or threatened you, has he?" he asked again.

"No," said Caroline, shaking her head. "I hardly see him." She felt it wiser not to say that Hannah slept in the same bedroom with her; that she had promised Johnny not to use the front stairs when Papa was in the house; nor that Johnny had shown them how to wedge a chair under the door handle.

She stared into space, re-living that awful scene. Those hateful words. How angry Dashell had been and how he had terrified her. "Dashell, I should never have gone on that carriage ride with you. I never thought Papa would take that meaning."

"We both enjoyed it and that is how we will both remember it," he said gently.

"Those shameful words. I was so humiliated. Looking back I can see Papa knew what he was saying. Taking advantage, almost as though he wished us hurt, as though he wished you to see me that way."

"Caroline, my precious one," Dashell chided, "do you think I would give heed to words spoken by a vindictive, spiteful old man? Have faith, dearest, I know we are meant for each other. Let me remind you that I fell in love with you the first time I set eyes on you and again when you entered this room just now. I could never love anyone else as I love you. But what about us?"

he continued. "What are we going to do? Have you thought of that?"

"Of course I have!" cried Caroline. "Do you think I would not? But I had to speak up before our love went too far." There, it had slipped out, almost before she realized it.

"Our love," said Dashell quickly. He turned her face to him so he could look into her eyes. "Did you say our love?"

"You know I did. And you are not being fair." She turned her face away. "It is useless for us to continue. We must not see each other again. In fact, it might have been better if we had never met in the first place."

"Don't say that," said Dashell so harshly that Caroline was startled. He wondered gloomily whom he would have married and could only picture a loveless marriage with someone; while Caroline could only see an empty future for herself. They each knew what the other was thinking: that their love was doomed even before it began. He stood up as Caroline got to her feet and put his arms round her and held her close to him.

"Dashell, I should not be letting you do this. You are making it very difficult for me."

"Let us have this moment, Caroline. It may be all we will ever have."

Caroline glanced at Dashell and saw the look in his eyes as he took her face in his hands. "Dashell, no!" she cried, pulling herself away hastily. "We must not be foolish. It is better this way."

"All right, my wise one," he said regretfully, letting her go. "But let me at least understand this. If we learn of your true parentage would you marry me?"

"Yes, I would," replied Caroline, "provided your family found me acceptable."

"I will begin by approaching Wardlock to try and get the truth out of him. If he will not tell me, I will find out some other way, even if I have to search the records of every parish church in Sussex. There must be proof in one of them."

"But that could take days, or weeks, or even months," Caroline said hesitantly, "but perhaps it would be possible to find out after all," as a light of hope dawned in her face.

"For our happiness, I would do it," said Dashell. "I would never be at peace again if I did not. Do you think I could leave to you wonder for ever?"

Caroline smiled gently at those remarks. "But would you be able to? To find the time, I mean. Did you not say your father needed you?"

Dashell saw the point of that and his heart sank. "There is something else too. When we find out who your family is they may not approve of me, an impoverished heir who has very little to offer."

"I have even less, Dashell. I have nothing. I cannot possibly bring you a dowry."

"When shall I approach your stepfather?" asked Dashell, becoming practical again. "I understand evenings are not good."

"No, not evenings. Saturday daytime would be better even though I wish it could be sooner. I shall say nothing to Papa about you being here today or that you will be calling, in case that makes him angry." She did not add that, according to Hannah, he seemed to be ill-tempered most of the time anyway.

"May I call again before then?" asked Dashell. "There is still so much I want to know about you. Wednesday, perhaps? I have to speak to our estate manager tomorrow before he leaves, and that is the only day."

"Of course you may. Come for luncheon if you wish, what simple country fare we have. That reminds me, I never offered you any tea. Would you care for some?"

"Not now, thank you," he replied. "We have both had a troubled time. I must be back for the evening meal tonight, and my father is a stickler for punctuality," he added with a smile.

Caroline closed the front door behind Dashell but did not run to a window to see him go. So when Dashell looked back as he shut the gate he could see no movement.

Caroline went to sit quietly by herself to think and perhaps even dare hope for their future. Eventually she rang the bell for Hannah.

Hannah came in with the tea tray and was astonished to see her mistress alone. "He's gone?" she could not help exclaiming.

"Yes, he could not stay, but Lord Lonsdale is coming again on Wednesday," explained Caroline. "I have invited him to come for luncheon. Thank you for the tea, and now I would like to be by myself for a while."

Johnny had been working at the inn that day, and made his way back to the house for his tea.

"He came back," Hannah said, without feeling it necessary to explain whom she meant.

"I know," remarked Johnny. "He left his horse at the inn."

"He didn't stay all that long either. Didn't even stay for tea."

"Yer mean e's gone an' left er?" asked Johnny incredulously.

"Oh, no. He's coming back on Wednesday for luncheon, so we can take that as a good sign."

"Oh," said Johnny, sounding relieved. He eyed Hannah thoughtfully, reckoning it was time to confess what he had been doing and lowering his voice asked, "Where is Miss Caroline now?"

"In the parlour by herself. Why?"

Keeping his voice down Johnny explained what he had been doing last Friday afternoon, while Hannah listened in surprise, until he finished with a dogged, ". . . An' I don't care if yer do fink it wrong of me."

"Knowing what we do about that man, like you, I don't care," said Hannah, "But how on earth did you think of searching like that?"

"We-ll," said Johnny with a knowing grin, "let's just say I knew a certain gent in London and I've fergotten 'is name."

Hannah gave him a dry look and said, "Humph."

"We've gotta find those papers somehow," persisted Johnny. "Where could 'e 'ave put 'em?" He paused, scratching his head. "P'raps there aren't any. Maybe they don't exist."

Hannah pressed her lips together before answering, "Oh, they exist all right."

Johnny stared in surprise. "'ow do yer know that? Wot makes yer so sure?"

"Never mind that for now. We must search the rest of the house because he could have put them anywhere, though I don't think he would have come in here."

"P'raps he hid them right at the top of the house." Johnny still hankered to get to the other side of that locked door.

"No, I shouldn't think so."

"What makes you so sure?" he asked again.

Hannah raised her hand at the sound of the parlour door opening and light footsteps. "Shh! Here comes Miss Caroline now."

The evening passed quietly; Caroline was preoccupied with her own thoughts and was not disposed to talk. Johnny read to himself and Hannah had some sewing.

It was not until the two women went upstairs to bed that Caroline divulged to Hannah the essential parts of her conversation with Lord Lonsdale, and begged her to recall even the smallest detail of all the time she had spent with her mother, right from the first day of her employment. "Anything and everything could be important, Hannah," said Caroline. "Try and remember, then I can tell Dashell when he comes on Wednesday. And I will do the same."

"I don't know if there is much more I can tell you, Miss Caroline, for I have told you everything already." And to think Lord Lonsdale had said he would search parish records in Sussex to find out the truth, if he had to. What a gentleman! And how he must love Miss Caroline. She could tell Johnny that and she could trust him to keep that sort of thing to himself.

Hannah had misgivings about Lord Lonsdale calling on Mr. Wardlock on Saturday. It would be just like that man to be cantankerous on purpose and refuse to divulge any information at all. And he had never given that stolen letter back to Miss Caroline.

Hannah had long noticed a difference in Mr. Wardlock. There was something so sinister about him, she dreaded having to attend to him, to speak to him. She had to be so careful for she could easily be dismissed for some slight fault. It was a little while before she fell asleep.

Caroline lay awake as well. She loved Dashell, had loved him all along, but never would she compromise him.

Chapter Twenty-Five
Dashell Returns To Windsor

Dashell left the house on Becket Lane with a heavy heart for he was hardly able to believe Caroline's revelations, but admired her for her courage and honesty. But how could Caroline's mother not have spoken to her own daughters? What dreadful secret had she kept all those years and that had even died with her? Perhaps their father had been a felon, a confidence trickster, some kind of criminal, or even worse—a murderer.

How was Dashell to tell his father he had to go to Sussex and would be absent for days, even weeks, and never mind the reason. He would do anything for Caroline, but would he defy his own father? It would cost him dearly to do so, yet it would cost him even more to lose the only woman he could ever love.

Dashell arrived back at Barrandale Park in time to refresh himself after his ride and went to join the others before they entered the dining room.

"I trust your business was conducted to your satisfaction?" enquired Barrandale politely after they sat down.

"No, not quite, sir," replied Dashell. "In fact, I am obliged to go to London again on Wednesday on the same subject."

"Indeed?" said Barrandale, surprised, wondering what was taking up so much of his son's time. No doubt Dashell would tell him in his own good time. Barrandale pursued another subject. "I went over the estate books with Mitchell today. He is a most able man and I will be sorry to see him go. You will meet with him tomorrow, as arranged?"

"Yes," replied Dashell, "we will spend the whole day together. Would you care to come with us? One of the grooms could drive you in the trap."

"Thank you, no. I will trust in your discretion."

Dashell sighed inwardly at that. This was placing another burden on his shoulders. "If you have no objection, sir, I would like to go through the books myself this evening."

"Of course. They are in my study."

Mitchell had kept very careful accounts but Dashell knew it was up to him to find ways for the estate to produce more. After an hour or so of careful reading he went to join the others.

"You plan to return to London on Wednesday, Dashell?" Lady Smythe enquired. "I thought to return then myself. You are so much stronger now, Randolph, and I have no fear in leaving you now. Perhaps I may have your escort, Dashell?"

"I would be honoured, Aunt Letty, but only so far as Hounslow as I am not going directly into the City."

Lady Smythe was surprised, but agreed, exchanging a puzzled look with her brother.

The next day Dashell and Mitchell went over the whole estate. Mitchell was very thorough and pointed out every aspect of the estate: grass and arable land; the home farms; labourers' cottages; fishing rights in the Thames; gardens and lawns; orchards and kitchen gardens; the rides, the avenues; timber trees; including the stables and all out buildings.

When Dashell and his brothers were still boys they had the run of the estate and knew every inch of it. Now after all those years it seemed so different. Hedges grown and thickened; coppices enlarged; ponds created or drained. Dashell was amazed how much trees had grown, even the one out of which he had fallen. How long had it been since he went over the estate? Too long, it seemed.

There was a stand of Scots pine trees which had been planted many years ago and were now at their prime just when they were so greatly needed. There were also other trees; oaks, beeches, elms, even birches. Some of them were selected for falling, and even an old walnut tree. There was always a demand for good wood, and while Dashell regretted having to give the order beggars could not be choosers.

It had been a long day, and Dashell learned everything he could and he had been very impressed with the way Mitchell had run the estate. He had not yet thought of any long-term means of working the estate except to increase flocks, herds and produce, and to plough under grassland, but he realized it required something more than that.

Dashell left the stables until last for this was the place he knew and loved the most, and he noticed one of the loose boxes was empty.

"Mr.Maxwell took Lively out a while ago, sir," explained Reuben. Dashell nodded. Trust Maxwell to be on a horse whenever possible.

They came to a beautiful grey filly born on the estate, named Daisy Chain because of an irregular oval of white spots on her near hind-quarter. "She has developed into a very fine animal," remarked Dashell, looking at the filly in admiration. He had a good eye for a horse.

"There's another thing too, sir," said Reuben. "When out in the paddock she runs for the sheer joy of it and she has a fair turn of speed."

"That's right, sir," added James, not to be outdone, "Raven, her sire, traces back to the Darley Arabian through Eclipse, and Eclipse was unbeaten in eighteen races. We reckon Daisy Chain has the makings of a flyer."

"So she should fetch a good price at that rate," said Dashell. Just then Maxwell came in on Lively. "Had a good ride?" Dashell asked.

"Yes, I did," enthused Maxwell. "Lively cleared a five-barred gate with ease. He's a natural. He can jump anything. He would make a first-class steeplechaser."

"I'm going back the long way round," said Dashell. "Care to join me?"

"Yes, all right. How did your day go?" asked Maxwell.

"Quite well, in a sad sort of way."

"You know," mused Maxwell slowly, "it's a pity we can't do something like breeding cattle or sheep because we have enough land."

Dashell came to a sudden stop. "Maxwell! You have given me an idea! Your remark about Lively being a natural, and the men saying Daisy Chain had the makings of a flyer. Instead of selling two damn good horses we will keep them and race them. Then with Raven's bloodline we can start breeding. I must go and discuss this with Father."

Out of sheer exuberance Dashell gave Maxwell a hearty slap on the back right between his shoulder blades, knocking the breath out of him. By the time Maxwell recovered and gathered enough breath to call out "You idiot!" Dashell was striding towards the house with a new spring in his step.

Dashell found his father in his study, who looked up as his son entered, laid down his pen and regarded him with interest. They talked together for some time about the estate and Dashell finished by speaking about the horses. "We can race Daisy Chain and Lively, and with Raven we can start breeding in earnest with the chestnut mares, the ones Mother had. You will still have your carriage horses, although they are getting on in years, but our horses have always had excellent care."

Barrandale smiled. "You are getting into your stride with the bit in your teeth."

"Father, I want that filly and I am willing to pay you one hundred guineas for her."

Barrandale stared at him. "The devil you are. You utterly amaze me. Do you think she is that good, untried as she is?"

"Yes, I do. And I also realise we will have to find a trainer somehow."

There appeared on his father's tired face the same look of dawning hope that Dashell seen on Caroline's face. "Perhaps you are right," said Barrandale. "I do agree that this is the way to go; as well as the other suggestions you have made for the estate."

Dashell was relieved. "Thank you, sir."

"Well, now," continued Barrandale, "Are you still planning to attend to your business tomorrow?"

"Yes, sir," replied Dashell. "I hope to have the rest of this matter cleared up soon. Incidentally, I shall be staying in Town, as there is nothing more I can do here and the men have their orders. That is, if you are agreeable."

Barrandale nodded. "Yes, I think everything has been covered. Then with your aunt also returning that means I shall be on my own, except for Maxwell."

"Has he said anything about his future, sir?" ventured Dashell.

"No, he has been quiet about it. But he is a sensible boy; and he has been helping me these last few days sorting out books in the library."

They joined the others and talked for a while until Simmonds came to ask if anything more was required.

Chapter Twenty-Six

Caroline Tells Her Story

The next morning Lady Smythe left in her carriage accompanied by Dashell on horseback. They made a brief stop at Hounslow, where Dashell bade her goodbye and set off for his real destination, trying not to show himself too eager as he knew his aunt had been wondering about him.

This time Dashell was more sure of his welcome. Hannah showed him into the parlour, where a luncheon table setting had already been set out.

Caroline extended her hand to greet Dashell and he resisted the temptation to kiss it. "If you please, Dashell, we will dine now. Or is it too soon for you?"

"No, not at all."

"It will give us more time to talk afterwards."

It was a pleasant meal with Dashell describing what he had been doing yesterday and their hopes for the future of the estate, and Caroline could not help wondering why he was telling her all this until she looked up and saw him smiling at her.

"We must have faith, Caroline."

For a fleeting moment she pictured herself as Lady Lonsdale and mistress of the estate, and then she chided herself because it was not likely to happen.

"When you left the other day, Dashell, you let me dare hope for the impossible. I will not think worse of you if you cannot make the attempt after all."

"How else are we to learn who you really are?" he asked. "Nothing you say will deter me."

"But—"

"If you mention this subject once more, my girl," said Dashell firmly, placing both his hands flat on the table, "I shall most definitely kiss you."

Completely taken aback, Caroline gave a frightened little gasp. "Oh! Then with that dire threat hanging over me I shall most certainly keep quiet."

Dashell grinned in delight. "Now I know why you love pink roses," he teased. "You match their colour so well."

"Dashell!" exclaimed Caroline, only too conscious of her flaming face. "You are impossible!"

"Mmm," was all he said.

"Some details you know already," Caroline began, after they finished their meal, and she had regained her composure. "Mother would never talk about our real father and we shall probably never know why she kept it a secret from us. Hannah and I have gone over everything we can think of, and she is quite certain that when she came into Mother's employment when she was fifteen, Mother had received a terrible shock and was fearful for Maude and myself. She would never leave us alone, almost as though she was terrified she might lose us.

"When Hannah came for an interview, Mother remarked she also came from Sussex and named some town or village. Hannah said she was so taken with the two infant children she was to care for that she did not hear clearly the name of the place Mother mentioned. She has tried and tried to remember, but can only recall an "ee" sound. Poor Hannah, she is quite distressed about it, especially knowing of your possible search."

"Well, she was not to know," said Dashell. "When did you and your sister suspect Wardlock was not your real father?"

"It was when we were about twelve and eleven years old. Maude and I had often heard remarks about children looking like their parents, but never heard it said about us, and we wondered why. We began to study Papa carefully on the few occasions we saw him and could see no likeness. In fact, Maude voiced the opinion she was glad we could not. The one time we did ask

Mother she became very upset and made us promise not to speak of it again, saying that she would tell us in her own time. Of course we did promise, although our silence was sorely tried. Neither Maude nor I slept much that night."

"What was your mother's attitude towards Wardlock?" asked Dashell, "if I may ask such a question."

"Much the same as ours," replied Caroline, "to be in his company as little as possible." She smiled at Dashell. "I do not mean to give the impression we had nothing in our lives. To the contrary we were very happy in our own way. When we moved to Fulham it turned out to be a blessing in disguise, although I'm certain Mother never said as much to Papa. By the way, I call Thomas Wardlock "Papa" for want of another name."

Dashell nodded briefly and waited for her to continue.

"Mother quickly made friends and was greatly liked as much as Papa seemed to be disliked, not that he ever made much attempt to be pleasant. Mother taught us our letters and numbers and how to read and write. She had a wonderful way about her and made everything so interesting. On our walks she would make us look at things. The light and shadow of clouds; flowers and leaves; how birds behaved; and everything about nature. She taught us to sing and play the piano. In fact she taught us everything she knew. We both adored Mother, although she could be very strict about our lessons. We were very happy amongst ourselves and our friends; yet Maude once described us as the kind of flowers that opened in the morning and closed at night, if you see what I mean. We read books to each other; all the usual fairy and history stories, and others like *Robinson Crusoe* and *Swiss Family Robinson*."

"*Swiss Family Robinson!*" exclaimed Dashell. "My brothers and I read that one summer during the holidays. That's how I got this scar on my cheek. We tried building a house in a tree and I fell onto a pile of wood below. We may even have read it at the same time."

"Perhaps we did." Caroline smiled again as she prepared to continue. "Johnny used to bring back discarded newspapers from the inn whenever he could, and we would read and study them and discuss world affairs as far as we were able to comprehend them. When Papa discovered that we were doing this he was most displeased. and said we were to stop because it was not ladylike. But he had not reckoned with Mother, and she could be very determined. Please tell me, Dashell, if I am boring you. I did not realize I had so much to tell you. And there is more."

"No, you are not boring me," Dashell told her. "I have listened to every word. In fact, I am convinced your mother came from a good background. She must have been taught all this herself for her to pass it on to her daughters."

"But what?" cried Caroline. "I have lain awake at night wondering what Mother knew but never dared to tell. But I will continue. When Johnny came to live with us, someone showed him how to catch rabbits and fish. It certainly helped with our house-keeping, as Papa was not exactly generous. Hannah told us that Mother once had quite a set-to with him and even showed him the bills and how much everything cost. We would go out into the fields and hedges and pick rose hips for syrup and blackberries for pies, and with our vegetable garden and old orchard we did quite well.

"Then one day Mother announced that she had entered our names at a School for Young Ladies in Kent, and that we had been accepted. We would go there in the autumn and be there for the whole year. Well, there was never a quiet day after that. The amount of material purchased and the cutting and sewing that went on was quite astonishing. Have you any sisters, Dashell?"

"No, only brothers," he replied. "But I do know all about this kind of thing."

"Oh? I suppose you mean lady-friends. It's my turn to tease you now."

"Oh, no. I was thinking of my mother and aunt."

"Touché!" she laughed. "Anyway, to continue. We asked Mother how she could possibly afford to send us, and we did wonder if Papa was helping, but somehow we could not see him doing that. She merely replied that she had saved all the money she was paid for giving singing and piano lessons. At the time we believed her."

"Did she not tell you the truth then?" asked Dashell incredulously.

"Oh yes, she did, but not all of it. But here am I forgetting to ring for tea. Do please excuse me. It must be all the talking I am doing. I don't usually talk this much."

"Really?" laughed Dashell. "You amaze me. You are a very unusual woman."

Before Caroline could think of a suitable reply Hannah came in with the tea tray, so she gave him a look instead. After pouring out two cups of tea and offering her guest a plate of little cakes, she sat down again. "As I have said, we were to be at the School for a whole year. We were very concerned for Mother, leaving her all that time and being so far away but Mother, being Mother, assured us she would be all right. When the day finally came for us to leave we hung out of the carriage window waving. We did not know it would be the last time we would see her alive.

"Maude and I loved every single minute at the School. We learned French and Italian and some German; we studied singing and piano playing more intensely, likewise painting and sketching, and the art of conversation, and we learned how to ride. In fact, we learned everything that young ladies of quality should know, although I say that myself.

"There is something which I shall be utterly grateful for until my dying day, and that is that Maude and I would take turns writing to Mother every Sunday, or sometimes we both did, telling her what we had done and learned that week, where we been, about the other girls, and the fun we had together. Hannah told us later that Mother lived from one week to the next waiting for our letters, and that she read and re-read them until she almost knew them by heart, then would take them out and read them all over again. We found our letters amongst her things after we returned, smudged from so much handling.

"About a month before our return we received a letter from Hannah. She was writing without our Mother's knowledge, and please not to be angry with her for doing so, but felt we should know our Mother was not as strong as she used to be. Mother's letters never gave any indication of this, although on studying them we saw that her writing was not as steady in her later letters as in her earlier ones.

"So we came home, delighted to be seeing Mother again for we had so much to tell her. Perhaps you can imagine our absolute devastation when we were greeted by a tearful Hannah who told us that our darling Mother had died the night before we arrived. We could hardly grasp or comprehend what she told us.

"It was a terrible shock. Nothing we learned at the School had prepared us for something like this. Never will I forget those days. Maude and I had to make all the arrangements for the funeral ourselves, although the vicar was very kind and helped us all he could, for Papa was surprisingly unable to do anything. We had no black mourning apparel so the vicar's wife kindly lent us some. My dress was a little too short and Maude's a little too tight and we had to leave the back undone, but she wore a shawl round her shoulders so nobody knew. It was humiliating that we could not do better for Mother, but we knew she would have understood."

"It all must have been very distressing for you both," said Dashell gently.

Caroline nodded, grateful for Dashell's understanding. "Yes, it was. The church was packed. Maude, who could sing like an angel, sang Schubert's *Ave Maria*. How she managed to do so without breaking down, I shall never know. She was very brave. Of course everyone was very kind, but to us it was just a black nightmare."

"What did Wardlock do while all this was happening?"

"Practically nothing, except to grumble at the cost of the funeral. Then he declared he had to go away for a time because the loss of his dear wife was too much for him. Actually, it was the best thing he could have done, and I feel no guilt in saying this." Caroline paused again, while Dashell shook his head once more in disbelief.

"When we went through Mother's things we discovered to our utter amazement a receipt for the sale of some jewelry we never knew she had possessed. We looked at the date on the receipt, and it was issued about twelve months before we entered the Academy. So that was how Mother must have paid our fees. The money she kept from teaching music was only part of it.

"We asked Hannah if she knew anything about the jewelry, for we remembered she had accompanied Mother into London at that time. She said they had gone to a jewelry shop on Oxford Street and she had waited outside. Mother took in a brooch because of a loose catch, or so she said, and came out looking very pleased about something, so Maude and I assumed she had received a very good price for whatever piece of jewelry she had sold. It amazed us that Mother had said nothing about the jewels she had kept hidden away all those years." Caroline looked at Dashell. "We found a whole lot more, you know."

Dashell stared at her. "Where did your mother get them from? Unless she had them with her all the time."

"We thought she must have. Anyway Maude and I agreed never to say anything to Papa about the jewelry, as Mother obviously had not."

"He might have wondered where the money came from."

"I don't think he cared," said Caroline. "He never asked us about it. Nor did we find legal papers of any kind. It was almost as though we did not exist." She was still unable to dispel the nagging fear that she and her sister could have been born out of wedlock. "If there are any legal papers, then Papa must have them. In fact, Maude and I began to wonder why we had attended the School. Possibly Mother wished us to meet young gentlemen of good family through the young ladies there. This may be what she had in mind when she said she would speak to us in her own good time.

"Then a friend from the School came with her brother to offer condolences, and then the brother called on his own. He was very taken with Maude and she was with him. Papa ordered him out of the house and forbad him from coming back. Poor Maude! She was devastated and Papa gave her no valid reason for what he had done. I know Maude tried to speak to him, but to no avail. I cannot tell you why. Then a day or so later Maude was found at the bottom of the stairs with a broken neck. I still cannot believe my darling sister did what she did; but it is said that one never really knows a person.

"Once more I had to borrow that black apparel, only this time we had a very quiet funeral. Mother and Maude were laid side by side in what appeared to me to be the darkest and dreariest corner of the churchyard, as Papa said he could not afford anything better. And if that was not enough, he also said he would reduce our house-keeping money now that there were two less people to feed. I do not know how we could have managed without Johnny catching rabbits and fish for us.

"Some of the young ladies who had been at the School with us came to pay their respects, and they could scarcely conceal their disgust and amazement when they saw how we really lived. It was utterly humiliating. I was so ashamed. I can hardly recall how I survived those days with my two dear ones taken from me. Hannah and Johnny were so kind and understanding, especially Johnny who did his best to cheer me up.

"I knew I had to get out of the house and earn my living somehow. With all I had learned I thought I could be a governess or teacher somewhere. Another alternative would be a lady's maid."

"I don't think becoming a governess or lady's maid would have been a wise choice," remarked Dashell casually.

"Why ever not?"

"Because, my sweet, you are far too beautiful. You would have devastated every male in the house, to say nothing of husbands running after you and jealous wives running after them."

"Oh, Dashell, don't be so foolish!" laughed Caroline. "Anyway, I should think being a governess requires brains, not beauty. Anyway, Hannah declared she would not be separated from me; and indeed, I did not like the thought of being without her. We had almost decided on becoming dressmakers or seamstresses when Johnny suggested we could open a tea shop, like the one round the corner here. It was like a revelation. It was the answer to everything, for we could now leave with a purpose.

"We began to make plans at once. Hannah still had relatives in Sussex, although elderly by now, so we decided to go there. Johnny said he would come with us and help all he could. We went through rooms and cupboards deciding what we would need and what we could sell or pawn. I have no hesitation in admitting this for we needed every penny we could find, such was our desire to escape from this terrible situation, for to stay was unthinkable. We had to be careful too, not to arouse any suspicion.

"Mother's clothing was too small for me so it was given to charity. I altered Maude's clothing to fit me for if I was to wait on tables I had to have a decent array of dresses. Johnny helped so much. He borrowed a pony and cart from a local farmer whom he had often worked for and took items to pawn, and he came back with a surprising amount of money. Even so there were many precious things I could not part with. There were some memories I would always cherish.

"Then one day I went up to London accompanied by Hannah, taking a piece of jewellery Mother had kept hidden, to the same shop she had gone to. We tried to hail a cab to return but none stopped, so we began to walk to the cab stand at the top of Oxford Street near Hyde Park. We had to cross the road and Oxford Street seemed to be unusually busy." Here Caroline stopped and looked at Dashell.

"I can tell you exactly what happened next," he said softly. "You came into my life and I have never been the same since."

"Dashell, please! Do not tease me! You know perfectly well what is at stake."

"I do not mean to tease you. I have never been more serious in my life."

Caroline gave her head a little shake. "I know my narrative has been a long one but I have tried to tell you everything, as you asked."

"Yes, it has been long but very informative," agreed Dashell, "and I admire you for it. Does Wardlock speak to you at all?"

"No. I see little of him because he takes meals on his own now. Anyway, Hannah and Johnny made me promise to use the back stairs whenever he was in the house to avoid meeting him."

"What!" cried Dashell, astounded at the novel situation of servants asking the mistress of the house to promise them something. "What else did they want you to do?" he asked, beginning to feel uneasy.

"Dashell, you are getting that 'look' again," said Caroline nervously.

"I must know," he insisted.

"Very well," she replied. "After that Monday afternoon, when we retired to bed, Hannah insisted that she would sleep in my room with me, which she has done ever since, and Johnny showed us how to wedge a chair under the door handle to prevent anyone opening the door from the other side." She stopped short at Dashell's gasp.

"Do you mean to say," he cried, "that they believe you to be in real physical danger?" He was beginning to think those two servants knew more than they were telling their mistress. "Caroline, I hardly know what to say. I am devastated. But I do agree that you must leave. I cannot think of you being here alone like you are."

"Yes, indeed I must leave for I have no alternative, particularly if Papa refuses to speak to you on Saturday." Caroline glanced at the clock on the mantelpiece, and silence fell between them.

"Caroline, my darling," began Dashell, "I am truly amazed at what you have related to me. No wonder you had that air of sadness when I first met you. Now I am even more determined to find out who you really are." He frowned slightly as though thinking of something, then his face cleared. "You could stay with my aunt who lives in Grosvenor Square."

"No, Dashell, but thank you. I will not compromise you or your family in any way."

"Very well," he sighed. He took hold of her hands which she did not withdraw this time. "I know you understand my search could take several weeks or even months," and paused as Caroline nodded, "so I want you to promise me something."

She looked up at him in surprise, "I will, if I can. What is it?"

"I want you to promise me, faithfully," said Dashell, giving her hands a gentle squeeze, "that you will not drift out of my life like a piece of thistledown and float away I know not where. It would break my heart to lose you. Promise me you will let me know where you go, where you are."

"I promise," replied Caroline solemnly. "But where should I write to?"

"Write to me at Barrandale Park, at Windsor. The London house is for sale and there must be no more missing letters. And now, dearest, I shall go. There is no need to get up, I will see myself out."

"Goodbye, Dashell, and thank you," said Caroline. "My darling," she whispered when she heard the front door close. She moved quickly to a window to watch him go. He looked up as he shut the gate, saw her, smiled and raised his hand. "May God go with you," she whispered.

Dashell walked briskly back to the inn and asked if Johnny was about.

"No, sir," replied Perkins, the head ostler, "he only works here part time and I do not know where else he could be," wondering why an obvious gentleman wanted to speak to a mere stable boy and a Cockney one at that.

Dashell rode back to Park Lane deep in thought. First and foremost was Caroline's safety and he could well see why she was anxious to leave. The time had come to speak to his father. It could not be put off any longer.

Chapter Twenty-Seven
Dashell Dines With His Aunt For The Third Time

"Welcome back, your lordship. I trust Lord Barrandale is in better health?" Matthew ventured to ask.

"Yes, he is very much better, I am pleased to say, Matthew," said Dashell. "He wishes me to inform you that he will be returning here tomorrow. Has anything happened during my absence?"

"Yes, indeed, sir," replied Matthew, and related that several parties had shown interest in the house. "There is one gentleman in particular and I believe an offer has been made, but of course the estate agent will be able to inform you about this."

"Any 'disinterested parties' at all?" asked Dashell, knowing Matthew would understand his meaning.

"Yes, quite a few, sir. Of course I refused them entry and insisted they approach the appropriate quarters. Not one of the parties returned, I regret to say." Matthew looked at his boots as though deploring the manners of people today.

Dashell knew why those people had come in the first place and was glad he had listened to Martin's advice. He looked through the inventories of all the rooms in the house. "You have done excellent work on these, Matthew. I will go through them in more detail when Lord Barrandale returns. Now will you give George this note to take to Lady Smythe? I will be dining with her tonight, but I do not expect to be back late."

Dashell could not help smiling to himself after George returned with his aunt's answer, as he wondered what his aunt would make of yet another request to dine with her.

Dashell duly called later that evening. "I will show myself up, Chadwick."

"Dashell," murmured Lady Smythe when he entered her salon, "this is the third time that you have asked to dine alone with me," albeit with tongue in cheek. "I am sure the servants will start talking."

Dashell grinned. "Let 'em," and then with perfect, utmost gallantry, he kissed first one hand and then the other.

His aunt was not fooled, however. "What's all this, Dashell?" she asked. "You either want something or you are up to something."

"Both, I fear, Aunt Letty. I need to talk to you. I very much need your help."

"You need my help? What do you mean?" Oh, no!" she cried, sitting bolt upright. "Surely Barrandale has not had a relapse. I could not bear it."

"He is well, and you know he plans to return tomorrow."

"Oh, yes, of course, how foolish of me."

The servants entered and began setting out the evening meal. Dashell deliberately turned the conversation to something else and his aunt astutely took the hint.

After they had finished their meal and the servants had gone, Lady Smythe re-opened the conversation. "Quite frankly, Dashell, we had plenty of time to talk at Windsor, yet you choose to come here again."

"I could not speak to you sooner, Aunt Letty, because I have only just this afternoon completed my unfinished business."

"Ah," said Lady Smythe wisely. "Both your father and I felt you had something on your mind over and above our family troubles."

Dashell was surprised. "You did? Was it that obvious? Did you discuss it at all?"

"No, only to remark about it to each other in passing one afternoon."

"Oh," said Dashell, relieved. "Yes, there is something I wish to discuss with you, and it is a long story."

"I might have known," sighed Lady Smythe. "If it is interesting I shall stay awake. If not, I shall fall asleep. Help me make myself more comfortable, if you please." Dashell obliged by plumping up her cushions, and she lay back and looked expectantly at him.

"It concerns a lady," began Dashell. "A very charming and beautiful lady." Those few opening words immediately caught Lady Smythe's attention. "You will remember when I visited you a while ago I was bemoaning the fact that I had not yet met anyone with whom I could form a lasting attachment."

"Oh, Dashell, so now you have! I am so pleased for you. Who is she, if I may ask?"

"It is not easy to answer that. I wish it was." He saw the look of surprise on his aunt's face, so he told her the whole story concerning Caroline.

Lady Smythe made no interruption save a brief question here and there. There was silence at first after Dashell finished his story, until he remarked with a lop-sided smile, "So you stayed awake after all. You must have found this interesting."

His aunt stared at him in horror. "May I say that I have never heard of such a story in my life. How can a mother not tell her own daughters the name of their father? Unless she was ashamed of him. What in the world had she to hide? Or was she ashamed of them? Could it be that they were born out of wedlock? Why else would she have kept so quiet all those years?"

"I must say I had thought of that," Dashell admitted ruefully, "but I don't think it likely. They were taught everything she knew and were sent to a reputable school. I think the mother knew exactly what she was doing. It was most unfortunate she died when she did."

"Amen," murmured Lady Smythe with a slight frown. "I have heard of that school and I believe it has a very good reputation."

"From what Caroline herself said, she and her sister loved every minute of it. That in itself says a lot."

"Ah, yes, that reminds me," said Lady Smythe. "What of the sister? You say she threw herself down the stairs because her gentleman caller was ordered away? It sounds as though she was a trifle unbalanced, and it could be family trait, if I may say so."

"Not having met the sister, I cannot answer that. But I can say that Caroline is the most balanced woman I have ever met. And the most courageous."

Lady Smythe could find nothing to say to that. But how romantic, the way they had met! Just a chance meeting, like the way she had said it could happen. And he so gallant. *But Dashell, why, oh why, could you not have met someone in the ordinary way, instead of that girl, which may only lead to heartache for both of you.* She roused herself. "Are you still determined to find out Caroline's real name? I must say I do not like the sound of the name Wardlock."

A muscle twitched in Dashell's jaw. "Yes."

"And how am I to help you? I must say I do feel sorry for the girl, especially with that man for a stepfather."

"I am wondering, Aunt Letty, if I could persuade you to let her come here until we find some quiet retreat where she can stay until I return. You know a lot of people and there must be some discreet person who lives in the country somewhere."

Lady Smythe frowned. "I thought you said she was leaving for Sussex. She may not wish to come here. Didn't you say she would not compromise you in any way?"

"I am not leaving her there if Wardlock refuses to co-operate. Goodness knows what that vindictive man may do."

"Dashell, do you fully realize what you are asking? This woman of yours coming here with one name and then leaving with another. How am I to explain that?"

"To begin with, she is not my 'woman'. She is very much a lady. And she will not be here long enough for you to have to explain anything."

Lady Smythe examined her fingernails for no apparent reason. "I hope you are not intending to make her your mistress, because if you are I will have nothing to do with this nonsense. And I can also tell you that a mistress can be very expensive."

Dashell swung round almost angrily, his face darkened. "I intend to make her my wife. She would never consider anything else, nor would I even suggest it."

"You know this could lead to second scandal if you are not careful, don't you?" persisted Lady Smythe. She pressed her hand to her forehead. "How Barrandale is going to take this I daren't even think." Dashell gave her a bleak look. "Have you said anything to him yet?"

"No," he replied. "I could not talk to him until I learned everything from Caroline, just as I could not speak to you until now. But I will tomorrow when he returns." Dashell was not looking forward to that conversation, but he would have to broach the subject somehow.

Lady Smythe groaned to herself. First Walden, now this, and Maxwell's future still to be resolved. What on earth was happing to their family? Everything was falling apart.

"If you do find out her real name her family might not consider you suitable. After all, you are not the wealthy eligible bachelor you once were." Lady Smythe felt she was clutching at straws.

"For which I should be thankful," retorted Dashell. "At least it weeds out the gold-diggers."

"Humph. I suppose so."

"And speaking of family, I have suspected for some time that the mother, Isobel, could have married against her family's wishes and they would have nothing more to do with her." Dashell turned to face his aunt. "It does happen, you know,"

"Oh, yes, indeed," she agreed. "I can think of instances myself." She looked at her nephew's determined face. "This search of yours, have you no friends who can help you? Maybe Maxwell could. Or what about the Ellersby brothers? Ellis I would certainly trust, and Martin too, for all that his brains rattle round like dried peas in a box."

Dashell gave a short bark of laughter. If only Aunt Letty knew of Martin's timely warning! "I think, Aunt Letty, it would not be wise to have too many people making enquiries. It would only attract attention. No, this is something only I can do, for her sake."

Neither of them seemed to have anything more to say, and Lady Smythe stifled a yawn. "I have kept you up late, Aunt Letty," remarked Dashell. I love Caroline dearly, and I had to speak to you."

"And does she love you?" she asked, hoping he was not going on this quest for nothing.

"Oh, yes," he replied, as he remembered that warm glow in his heart. He had not yet mentioned this to Caroline; time enough yet when he could add a few kisses while he did so. The mere thought made him smile while his aunt watched in wonder.

"So, my wise and understanding aunt, I shall leave you," he said, and kissed her goodnight. "Thank you so much."

"Yes, do please go, or I shall really fall asleep. And yes, I will do what I can to help, though I shudder to think what Barrandale will have to say."

Chapter Twenty-Eight
Lord Barrandale Returns To London

Lord Barrandale had asked Maxwell if he wished to come to London with him but Maxwell said he preferred to stay in Windsor to "think things over," so his father left without him. On arriving at Hounslow he stopped at one of the quieter inns. He was just about to leave when he heard someone hailing him. "Barrandale! Is that you, Barrandale?" He turned round to be greeted by an old friend. "Ah, it is indeed you." The gentleman's voice trailed off as he regarded Barrandale with some degree of horror. "Oh, my dear fellow. Have you been ill?"

"Allenby! How good to see you again. Yes, I have been somewhat indisposed lately," replied Barrandale, drawing himself up with dignity. He and Lord Allenby had known each other for years, and he wondered if their friendship would now endure.

Allenby drew Barrandale to one side. "I have been hearing some disturbing rumours, my dear fellow, and I must warn you that London is beginning to buzz."

Lord Barrandale's worst fears had come about, but he recognised Lord Allenby's offer of continued friendship and was moved by it. "You are very kind. I fear the rumours are indeed true and I must go and face them."

Allenby bowed in return. "I admire your fortitude. But come, will you continue your journey with me? We can talk together, and my coachman will see you to your door."

Barrandale was quite touched. He would have preferred to travel alone but did not wish to offend Allenby, who was very influential, and he would need all the friends he could keep. "You are very kind," he said again.

"Not at all, my dear fellow." So Barrandale stepped into Allenby's carriage while his own rolled away empty. Lord Allenby's conversation had been quite edifying, but he was still thankful to be set down outside his own door.

"It is good to see you here again, your lordship," said Matthew as he helped Barrandale out of his coat, and contrived not to show too much surprise at the change in his master.

"Thank you, Matthew. My son has told me of your concern; and that you have been keeping everything in order here,"

Barrandale was surprised to see Dashell come forward to greet him, who still had that preoccupied look about him. "I had not expected to see you so soon," he said, regarding Dashell somewhat curiously. They had by now gone into the sitting-room.

"I trust you had a pleasant journey, sir?" enquired Dashell.

"Yes, indeed," replied his father, and briefly described his meeting with Lord Allenby. "He had the goodness to invite me to dine with him tomorrow evening. I do not really wish to go, but feel I needs must as I comprehend this is his way of showing our friendship still stands. By the way, you are included, if you wish to come."

"That is most kind of him. Perhaps I will, if I have nothing else on hand." Again Barrandale regarded his son shrewdly with those all-seeing eyes of his. Dashell was well aware of this. Should he mention that matter so dear to his heart now? No, not yet. Mention other matters first. "Sir," he began, "I looked through the list of houses for sale before you arrived, and there is something that caught my interest. It seems a certain house was being built to some gentleman's specifications, and who died before it was finished. The builders are anxious to complete the house and are offering it at a very reasonable price. It is situated in South Kensington in the vicinity of Kew Gardens, and consists of the following rooms, and so on." Dashell looked up from the description of the house. "If I may say so, sir, I think we should ask the estate agent to follow this up for us. It sounds just like what we are looking for."

Barrandale demurred at first, stating that South Kensington was not too desirable a neighbourhood, but agreed that it was easily accessible to Windsor. "Very well, we will ask the agent to call here. I agree with you time is an important factor, and I trust we shall learn more of the offer made on this house. And I must call upon the bank tomorrow," he added as an afterthought. He fell silent for a few moments. "This house has been in our family for so many years, and so much has happened here. It . . . well, never mind, nothing can be done now." It was typical of him not to cast about laying blame but to take a philosophical attitude.

Dashell tried to think of something sympathetic to say without sounding trite, but his father asked him, "Are you dining out tonight?"

"No, sir. I was planning to stay in."

"So we will have each other's company then?"

Dashell seized his chance, for it was now or never. "There is a matter I wish to discuss with you, sir, perhaps after we have dined, if you would be so good." Now he had made a beginning, and there was no going back.

"Has this anything to do with your unfinished business?" enquired Barrandale mildly.

"Yes," Dashell replied, aware of that searching gaze. "It has now become a matter of some urgency."

"Indeed? Then I will be at your disposal."

That evening after they had dined and returned to the sitting—room, Dashell wondered how he could begin talking about his precious subject without stuttering and appearing foolish. The very fact his father expected people to be direct and come straight to the point just seemed to make matters worse, especially when he had so much to say.

"Before you begin Dashell," said his father, "please allow me to say this. It was something Allenby related to me while we were travelling together. It occurred one morning some days ago when he was near St.Paul's Cathedral. He told me a young man on horseback passed his carriage and stopped at some flower sellers on the cathedral steps, dismounted, and handed the reins to some child to hold.

"Allenby said there then ensued such a charming and heart-warming scene that he actually stopped his carriage to watch. Apparently this young man was very particular and searched until he found the kind of flowers he wanted. From across the road, Allenby thought they looked like forget-me-nots and pansies, both such delightful conveyers of certain messages. The young man then hailed a cab and laid the precious bouquets on the seat inside, handed a letter to the driver and proceeded to give directions. The young man paid the driver in advance and watched the cab until it was out of sight; and even from across the road Allenby could see the young man give a great sigh, who then remounted after giving the child a coin, and went on his way."

During this narration Barrandale looked everywhere except at his son, until at the end his gaze did finally come to rest on Dashell. "Is this the matter you wish to discuss with me?" he enquired with a gentle smile.

During this narration Dashell experienced a whole range of emotions until he jumped up, shaking his fists in the air. "Ye gods!" he almost shouted, striding up and down. "Is nothing private in this city?"

"Ah, so it was you," remarked his father, looking at him over his fingertips.

Dashell swore again. "Dammit! Why does everyone know everyone else's business? If you cough in the morning, everyone you meet in the evening has a remedy for it."

"A somewhat startling metaphor," remarked Barrandale "but I quite understand your meaning. I am intrigued," he continued, "as it is obvious there is the existence of a lady."

This revelation had shaken Dashell because he was so concerned for Caroline's protection. Would nothing ever go right for them! Not that he had any cause to doubt Lord Allenby, it was his son Lord Norris who troubled him, the same Norris who had led that laughing throng at the gymnasium. Allenby could casually say something to Norris, who would then take it up, repeat it, and fan the flame of gossip. And if that ghastly Hepplewhite woman got hold of the story! Dashell could be making too much out of it, but it hardened his resolve to go to Sussex, with or without his father's consent. He pulled himself together. "I am sorry for my outburst, sir. I do apologize, but I care very much for this lady and her need for protection, and this is why I must speak to you."

"May I ask if congratulations are in order?"

"No, not yet."

"Ah, the lady does not care for you. She does not return your affection."

"Oh, she does."

"Ah," said Barrandale again. "Then her parents object. Perhaps they do not now find you suitable and wish to terminate the alliance."

"The only parent is a very unpleasant stepfather," said Dashell, his mouth curling up.

"And he objects?"

"I am planning to speak with him on Saturday, although I know he will do so."

"I see," said Barrandale, who was not at all sure he did see. He recrossed his legs. "May I be permitted to know the lady's name?"

Now the truth must be told. It was the question Dashell has been dreading. He turned round to face his father and their eyes met. "The lady is known as Miss Caroline Wardlock, but that is not her real name. In fact, she does not know her real name."

Barrandale stiffened, with that steely look in his eyes. "Indeed?" he said coldly. What kind of woman was this, and how had his son become embroiled with her? And he wanted to marry her? "I think you owe me an explanation," he said icily. "Whatever else we may have lost, we have not lost our good name. You will tell me exactly what you mean by this. Pray proceed."

It sounded like an order. So once more Dashell told the story of how he had met Caroline.

"A few weeks ago I had tea with Aunt Letty," he began . . . and so on . . . finishing with being summoned home to Windsor and being compelled to leave Caroline. "I could only write and hope she would understand my absence."

"And did she understand?" enquired Barrandale gently.

"Caroline never got the letter," answered Dashell, and described how Wardlock had taken it and never gave it to her.

Barrandale had listened in silence, his initial anger dissipating into understanding and sympathy. "My dear boy, forgive me if you had to leave Miss Wardlock because I summoned you to Windsor. I had absolutely no idea, and you never said anything."

"What else could I do?" cried Dashell. "I had to put your concerns first because it affected the whole family. I was desperately anxious for Caroline alone in that house with that man, except for Hannah and Johnny. You have no idea how relieved I was about that, the two best and only possible persons who could really look after her." Dashell spun round on his heel at the sound of a faint chuckle. "Do my words amuse you, sir?" he demanded, his face flushed.

"I am sorry, Dashell, but in this one aspect they do. I have heard of servants being ordered to keep certain callers away or being used as messengers or go-betweens, but never have I known of servants encouraging or helping a romance."

Dashell laughed. "I had not thought of it like that," he admitted. "That Johnny is a Cockney boy with a heart of gold. He is quite trustworthy. In fact, I would trust him sooner than many others I know."

"Indeed?" said Barrandale, regarding him again with some surprise. Then he remarked about Caroline's mother struggling for the welfare of her two daughters.

"Yes," agreed Dashell, "I am fairly certain that Isobel married against her family's wishes, and who then would have nothing more to do with her. According to Hannah she appeared very fearful at first for her children and I believe she married Wardlock because she had no means of support, which raises the question, what about her first husband?"

"Over the years, according to Hannah, Wardlock gradually changed into a very unpleasant man, even almost sinister. Now after the deaths of her mother and sister, Caroline is most anxious to leave. Mindful of Johnny's warnings I waited until last Monday to see her. It was then she told me that she and her sister did not know the name of their real father. I was shocked, yet I admired her honesty and courage. I saw her again yesterday when she told me everything she could about herself. This is why I had to wait until now to speak with you."

"Surely there are documents, some certificates of birth?" asked Barrandale.

"It seems they are missing and I am sure that scoundrel Wardlock knows where they are."

"Have you considered the possibility," said Barrandale, trying to be delicate, "that the girls could be illegitimate, hence the mother's silence, and the fact that there are no documents?"

"Yes, I have," replied Dashell levelly. "One daughter perhaps, but not both."

Barrandale just shook his head in disbelief. "All that you have told me is astounding, beyond comprehension."

"I love her, Father, and I cannot bear the thought of losing her. Yet she will not consider marriage until she knows her real name. Don't forget, she is still under age."

"She sounds like a lady of great strength of character from your description. But have you considered that her family may not wish to be reminded of the existence of a daughter of the mother they abandoned? And what about the father's family?"

"Nothing is known about that, so all the more reason to bring her into this one," was Dashell's swift answer.

"Touché," murmured Barrandale, glancing at his son with approval. "So you are still determined to find out who Caroline really is?"

"Of course I am! Do you really think otherwise? I believe myself to be a man of honour, and I cannot desert her now when she has no one else to turn to, leaving her to wonder for the rest of her life."

"Does she mean so much to you then, this sweet paragon of yours?"

"Need you ask?" replied Dashell with a twisted smile. "If I would go to the ends of the earth for her, can Sussex be all that far?"

"Even if it takes you days or weeks or even months?"

"Even if it takes me days or weeks or even months. Do you remember the morning after you called me home when we were in the rose garden? You said you hoped that one day I would find such a love as you did. I could have told you then that I already had."

"And you still said nothing?"

"It was not the right time."

"That was noble of you, my son."

"Father, you are making it difficult for me to say what I want to say. I must ask for a lengthy leave of absence. Maxwell is home now so you will not be alone. I will go, sir, with or without your consent. You cannot prevent it."

Dashell went to lean with both hands on the mantelpiece, his head down, feeling mentally exhausted. He stayed in that position, during which time Barrandale studied this son who was so dear to him, as much a man of honour as another son was not. Dashell half-turned his head. "Father," he implored, "say something."

The leather chair creaked as Barrandale got up. He went over and laid a hand on Dashell's shoulder. "It is not my intention to prevent you. But before you go galloping across Sussex in all directions and utterly exhausting yourself, to say nothing of rousing the curiousity of the whole county, may I suggest that you obtain the very best map there is of Sussex, and go over it inch by inch. Draw lines if need be, and underline the name of every single city, town, village and hamlet containing that particular "ee" sound. Then write to the appropriate parish priests and ask them to look through their records. Surely one of them will have the answer you seek."

Dashell slowly raised his head at these words, then straightened up and turned to his father. "Why, this means I need not to go to

Sussex after all. This is wonderful! Why did I not think of this myself?"

"Because you are very much in love, so you tell me, and I believe that such a condition can—er—affect one's rational thinking."

Dashell laughed in sheer delight. "This is incredible! Just wait until I tell Caroline! Sir, I hardly know how to thank you."

"It is enough for me to still have you with me. And I must admit that your lady's story intrigues me, and I too am anxious to know how it will end."

Dashell came down to breakfast the next morning to find his father already seated. "I am still amazed at myself for not thinking of a map, sir," he said.

"You are too much a man of action, my son, you need to have something to do," replied Barrandale. "Are you not known in certain sporting circles, boxing I believe, as Dashing Dashell or Dashell the Dasher, or something like that?"

Dashell's jaw dropped open. "How on earth did you get to hear that?" Then on a sudden thought, he added, "If that was Norris, I'll have even more of a score to settle with him."

"Oh, I really forget now. It was quite some time ago. However, I am fairly certain it was not Norris, nor even Allenby." That was no comfort to Dashell. It left him wondering who it could have been and he was aware of his father smiling at him.

"Now to business," said Barrandale, laying down his napkin. "I have ordered my carriage for ten o'clock and I would like you to accompany me to the Bank. I have also asked the estate agent to call at his earliest convenience. Matthew can take the note by hand." He paused and looked at Dashell.

"And while Matthew is out he can purchase a map of Sussex," added Dashell eagerly. "I can hardly wait. I will spend the afternoon going over it as you suggest."

After luncheon Dashell settled immediately to his task. Drawing pencil lines one inch apart across and down, he pored over the map, carefully underlying all appropriate names of places and making out a list. At about quarter to three the estate agent called as requested, and father and son discussed property details with him.

"As you are still working on your map," said Barrandale afterwards, "I take it you will not be dining at Allenby's tonight?"

"Not I, sir," said Dashell glancing up. "I am not stopping until I finish this."

"Then I will say you have a prior engagement. That can cover many things." He then settled himself down to go through letters and papers that had come during his absence, looking up from time to time at Dashell.

Some time later Dashell finally laid down his pen and stretched his arms over his head. At last he had finished. He looked at his list and counted the names. All were within an area of approximately eighty miles by thirty. Two thousand and four hundred square miles! It would have been a daunting task indeed to have gone in person.

Chapter Twenty-Nine
More Happenings at the House on Becket Lane

Hannah had explained to Johnny that she had searched everywhere in the kitchen for those missing documents and was certain they were not was hidden there.

"So where do we look now?" asked Johnny. "What about upstairs?" he added, hopefully.

"Johnny, I have told you more than once the mistress had the attic place closed off," said Hannah, somewhat sharply. "Now, tomorrow morning" she continued briskly, "I will do both of Mr. Wardlock's rooms as usual as he will be here on Saturday, and we must not make him suspicious."

The next morning, Friday, Caroline dusted and tided upstairs while Hannah did Wardlock's downstairs room. Along either side of the room's fireplace was some wooden panelling with beautifully carved flowers and leaves. As Hannah passed her feather duster over the paneling she almost lost her grip on the handle as one of the feathers caught on a leaf. In trying to loosen the duster, Hannah caused the leaf to move.

In amazement she opened the tiny leaf on its equally tiny hinge to reveal a keyhole and stared with bated breath. Could this be the hiding place she and Johnny had been searching for? Considering the countless times Hannah had dusted that woodwork it was astounding she had never noticed this before. Perhaps it was pure chance the leaf "door" had not been properly closed, hence a feather catching in it, and how cunningly concealed it was in that beautiful carving! Hannah made a mental note of the position, for Johnny must be told as soon as possible.

Later Caroline and Hannah left for the usual Friday ladies' meeting. Hannah and Johnny had agreed between themselves not to say anything to Miss Caroline about their search, so somehow Hannah had to speak to Johnny when they passed the inn.

The two women had just turned the corner when they spied a certain Mrs.Grimshaw ahead. "Oh, no!" gasped Caroline, "Of all the people to meet. She talks so much and we'll never get away." Hannah, however, seized her chance. She said she must have dropped a glove and hurried back to the inn.

Luckily Johnny was around. He looked up at the sound of quick footsteps and was astonished to see Hannah. "Oh Johnny, you'll never guess! I think I have found that hiding place!" and hurriedly explained where while Johnny listened open-mouthed.

"'annah, me girl," he breathed, "Oo would've thought of looking there!"

"I must go, or Miss Caroline will be wondering where I am."

Caroline was still being gabbed at by Mrs.Grimshaw. "Oh, here is your maid back again," sniffed the latter, wondering at the liberty taken by such a person. Caroline turned round in surprise, not realizing Hannah had been absent.

"I dropped a glove, Miss Caroline," said Hannah, "and went back to look for it."

Mrs.Grimshaw could hardly conceal her impatience at having to wait for a mere serving-woman to finish some explanation. "As I have been telling you all along, Caroline," she said, wagging a finger in her face," it is high time you got married, a pretty girl like you. Why, I can think of any number of young men who would be only too willing to meet you."

Caroline, furious, had heard enough, and she hardly dared imagine the type of young men this woman might produce. "I would really prefer that you did not, Mrs.Grimshaw," she said more sharply than she meant to. "It is far too soon after the deaths of my dear mother and sister for me to entertain any such possibility. Good day to you, ma'am. Come along, Hannah."

She walked angrily away, feeling like a hypocrite, leaving Mrs.Grimshaw staring after her, her mouth open but silent for once. "That tiresome woman! What are you smiling at, Hannah?" she asked curiously.

"It was the look on Mrs.Grimshaw's face," Hannah chuckled, keeping the real reason to herself. A few minutes later they met up with a far more pleasant person and Hannah was quite content to walk behind while the other two chatted away.

At the end of the meeting the ladies began to leave and Caroline and Hannah walked back to the tea shop. "I'll never forget Lord Lonsdale coming in here looking for you, Miss Caroline," Hannah ventured in a whisper.

"Hush, now," Caroline whispered back, "or someone will hear you. But you are quite right, neither will I."

"Do you know what makes me sad," mused Caroline, as they slowly returned to the house. "It's leaving behind all the plants and flowers Mother loved so much."

"Like the pink roses," Hannah reminded her. When they had passed the inn Hannah had seen Johnny but he had not seen her. Back indoors she glanced at the kitchen clock and hoped Johnny would not be too much longer. One was never sure when that man would appear.

Johnny had been busy in a steady way during the afternoon, and all the time he kept looking at the stable clock and thought the hands would never move.

Samuel Cullen, the under-ostler, came over to Johnny as he swept the yard. "Hey, I'm sure I saw a cab pass just now."

"Wot cab?" asked Johnny, without stopping his sweeping.

"Your "horrible man's cab," said Samuel, who knew all about Johnny's dislike and distrust of Mr.Wardlock. "It has just turned round the corner."

"Wot!" Johnny almost screeched. He threw down his broom and dashed to the side of the lane just in time to see the cab disappear into the distance. Of all the times for him to turn up, just when Hannah had found that hiding place. "Damn and blarst 'im. He always means trouble when he comes early, an' Miss Caroline and 'annah are there by themselves. Oh, damn 'im." He turned to Samuel, who was listening with interest. "Samuel, I gotta go."

"What, now? You're stretching it a bit, Johnny, but I'll cover for you."

"Thanks. Yer're all 'eart."

Johnny raced along the lane to the house with his heart in his mouth, not knowing what to expect, except trouble.

Caroline had just gone to the linen cupboard for something and returned to her room, and she did not hear either the cab arrive or the front door opening. She left her room to go down the front stairs believing her stepfather to be out of the house. She descended a few steps and was shocked to see him in the hall looking up at her. Taken by surprise as his presence was so unexpected she clutched at the bannisters for support. Never had she seen such a malevolent expression on his face. Summoning her courage and with beating heart she drew herself up. "Good afternoon, Papa. You are early today."

He did not answer but began mounting the stairs slowly. His silence and manner alarmed Caroline and she stepped back until she was at the top of the stairs. Horrified, and wondering, she watched as he took a newspaper out of his coat pocket and started waving it at her.

"Has that man been here again?" demanded Wardlock. "And do not pretend you do not know who I mean. That fine gentleman of yours. Has he dared to come to my house again? Hah! I can see by your face that he has. And you were deceitful enough to encourage him behind my back. I will not have it! I forbid you to see him again, ever." He began hurling those same hateful words and insults he had used before; but Caroline had found a new strength, so he paused, angered that his words did not have the effect he expected.

He moved upstairs while he spoke, causing Caroline to back away from him, and again he shook the newspaper at her. "I read today in this very paper about his profligate brother, who has all but ruined his family."

"Do you think to insult Lord Lonsdale and myself?" asked Caroline with dignity.

"Pah!" he sneered. "Do not play the fine lady with me!" A cunning look came over his face. "Has he mentioned marriage to you?"

"Yes, as a matter of fact he has," answered Caroline coolly. She realized this was certainly not the time to mention Dashell's intended visit tomorrow, as it would only inflame him the more, and even make him refuse to see Dashell at all.

"You poor little fool," he sneered again. "Do you really think he means it? A fine son of a fine father to mix with the likes of you? Pah! A lonely church with hired actors to play their parts. It has been done before, you know." At once Caroline realized this must have been the way he had spoken to Maude. "I forbid you to see him again," he repeated. "Do you hear?"

"Yes, I do hear. And do not accuse me of deceit. Where is the letter Lord Lonsdale wrote to me which you took from the postman? You never gave it to me. Wardlock's eyes narrowed, and Caroline immediately saw her mistake in mentioning the postman, for it indicated enquiries had been made.

"Would you question me . . . your own father?" demanded Wardlock again.

"You are not my father!" Caroline now knew he would never reveal her true name out of sheer spite.

By now they both stood level on the landing; and as Caroline backed away from him and his menacing expression, she felt something brush past behind her and knew it must be Hannah.

Busy in the kitchen Hannah gradually became aware of voices and wondered who on earth Miss Caroline could be talking to. She carefully opened the door into the hallway and saw Mr. Wardlock halfway up the stairs. What in the world was he doing here? Why had he come home early? If he found out what they were planning to do it would spoil everything, and there was no knowing what he might do.

Hannah's one thought was to get to the bedroom and hide that linen bag containing the rest of those jewels. If he got his hands on them they would never see them again, besides being plied with a lot of questions. Likewise there was the linen purse containing their carefully saved money, and he would want to know how they had come by that as well. And if he stayed how on earth was Johnny to get into that downstairs room to find that hiding place? Oh, drat that man!

Hannah reached the top of the stairs muttering, "Good for you, Miss Caroline, you stand up to him and give him what for." She slipped behind her young mistress not caring if Mr. Wardlock saw her, entered the bedroom and thrust both linen bags into the deep pockets of her skirts.

Caroline and her stepfather now stood facing each other. She cool and proud, and he uncertain. "Do you think to treat me the same way you treated my sister?"

She now knew why her stepfather had come. Whatever he had read in the newspaper about Dashell's brother was his excuse to quarrel with her. She recalled all the pent-up grief and loneliness she had endured since the loss of her dear ones and began to feel loathing and disgust for this strange man who had never really wanted to be part of their lives.

"All she wanted was happiness and you cruelly denied it." Knowing that she would soon be leaving this house for good she no longer cared what she said. Anguished and tearful, she cried out, "You destroyed my sister. And your neglect and indifference sent our mother to an early grave."

Wardlock was enraged, "You dare to speak to me like that? To accuse me?" Lifting his cane, which he had carried with him, he struck out at Caroline. With a scream she saw the blow coming and raised her arms to shield herself, and the full force fell on her left forearm. Gasping in pain she attempted to defend herself from further blows but her left forearm was useless, and another blow caught her on the side of her head, stunning her. Seizing her right arm, Wardlock dragged her along to her bedroom, Caroline stumbling alongside, vaguely aware of hearing Hannah's voice. He flung her forward angrily and she struck the corner of one of the travelling boxes already packed, and was knocked senseless. Wardlock raised his cane to strike her again only to find his own arm seized by Hannah. "Leave her alone! Leave her alone! You have done enough!"

Wardlock only stopped because he felt strangely out of breath, and a puzzling little pain flickered along his left arm. Glaring at Hannah, who stood in front of Caroline, daring him to touch her, he slowly turned to go downstairs, followed by Hannah, who although she desperately wanted to tend to Miss Caroline's hurts, she was also going to make sure he left. She heard herself shouting at him but could hardly remember what she said afterwards.

When Johnny reached the house he noticed the front door had been left open. Ignoring the waiting cab he ran along the path, up the steps and into the hall. Hearing sounds and voices from upstairs Johnny prepared to race up but shrank back into the shadows when Wardlock turned the corner to come down. Trying to control his panting Johnny could only guess that something terrible had happened and that he was too late to prevent it.

A stone-faced Wardlock came down followed by a greatly agitated Hannah, who called out, "You wicked man!"

"Oh, Hannah, be careful," muttered Johnny. "You could get us dismissed on the spot, and then what?" He watched as Wardlock reached the bottom of the stairs and turned round.

"Woman," he called up to Hannah, "Lock her door and bring me the key!"

Trembling, Hannah obeyed, not wanting to rouse his anger again. She struggled upstairs and made her way to the bedroom. With a shaking hand she locked the door, and returned, feeling she could fall down if she was not careful.

Wardlock did not care about what he had done to his stepdaughter, but he did mind about the waiting cab costing him money. "Hurry, woman!" He snatched the key from Hannah's shaking hand, glanced at it, and thrust it into his pocket. "I shall be back later tonight," he snapped, and left the house. Hannah sank down onto the stairs, still shaking, and clutched the bannisters for support.

Johnny emerged from the shadows. "'annah," he began in dismay, "yer didn't go an' give 'im the key, did yer? 'ow are we to get in? There ain't annuver one."

Not knowing how Johnny had managed to come nor how long he had been there, she whispered through parched lips, "Bring me some water, please." He promptly disappeared into the kitchen and returned with a cupful. She gratefully drank some and felt better. "Take the cup back, Johnny. We must not leave anything lying about."

"The key," he persisted when he came back.

Hannah felt stronger. "Help me up, will you?"

"The key," he cried again, his voice anxiously rising.

"Don't worry," she said. "I turned the real key in the lock to make it click and then gave him the key to the linen cupboard instead. He won't know the difference and he won't find out for a while anyway."

Relief spread over Johnny's face. Oh, 'annah, you're a marvel! Good for you! That means we can still get into the room?"

"Of course! Come along, we must see to Miss Caroline. Oh, Johnny, it was awful the way that wicked man struck her with his cane."

"Wot? 'E did wot?" Johnny was aghast, and raced ahead of Hannah to unlock the door.

With anxious cries of dismay and concern they found their young mistress still unconscious on the floor. They lifted her tenderly and carefully onto the bed and examined her hurts: a large nasty bruise on her arm and cuts and bruises on her face.

"I can't believe it," gasped Johnny. "What the 'ell 'appened? Oh, lor', just wait until the Guv sees this."

Hannah quickly poured some water from the ewer on the washstand into a basin and began gently wiping the blood off Caroline's face with a soft cloth. "There isn't time to tell you now, Johnny, but it was terrible. It was a miracle you came. How did you know?"

"Samuel at the inn spotted a cab turn the corner an' told me an' I came as soon as I could."

"Thank goodness you did. Now listen, you must go and find Lord Lonsdale. You told me once you knew where he lived."

"Yes, I do. But suppose I can't find 'im. 'e could be out somewhere."

"If he's not there don't go looking for him. We don't know how much time we have before that man returns. Come back with a cab and we will take Miss Caroline to the Anglican Nunnery up the road."

"Why can't we take her there in the first place?" asked Johnny logically.

"I would rather have a city cab," answered Hannah. "A local man could start talking."

Johnny nodded. Then glanced at Caroline and asked anxiously, "Shouldn't she 'ave a doctor first?"

"No," said Hannah firmly. "I know I'm taking a risk, but Dr. Meldicott would want her to stay here, and she will not remain another night in this house if I can help it."

"You fink of everything." Then asked pointedly, "What about the other fing?"

"At the moment Miss Caroline is more important and Lord Lonsdale must be told. Nothing downstairs must be disturbed to make that man suspicious, so don't go looking now. Take all the house-keeping money from the jar. You know which one." By now she had gently dried Caroline's face. "Just look at all those bruises." She almost wept.

Many thoughts went through his mind as Johnny dashed downstairs. There would not be time to look for a cab, certainly not one with a local driver. Hannah was right. The only thing he could do was go himself. He quickly took off his work boots and put on his other lighter ones, which were much better for running. He scooped out all the money from the jar into his pocket without bothering to count it. Running through the hall he banged the front door behind him, to let Hannah know he was on his way.

Johnny had to pass the inn and hoped old Perkins would not see him. Once past he broke into a run. He had nearly four miles to go. He did not know what he would do if he saw that cab coming back, with Hannah there by herself with Miss Caroline lying so still and pale. Those blows on her head could be serious and what if she never came round? The Guv would never get over it. And he also had to get back into that house that night to find that secret place. And if he couldn't return in time then he would just have to creep in during the early hours of the morning.

He was about half-way now and kept at a steady jog. No use sprinting and getting winded.

The worst part was getting round Hyde Park Corner with all the wheeled traffic but he managed it.

Hannah had loosened Caroline's hair and dress to make lying more comfortable for her, and remained by the bed, loath to leave her. She reckoned that if Johnny found Lord Lonsdale and he came at once he should be here within an hour.

Thank goodness they had some boxes already packed. As Hannah moved about the two bags of jewels and money she had snatched up earlier knocked against her, but they could stay where they were for safe keeping. How thankful she was she had got to them in time! She turned her attention to the dresses still hanging in the wardrobe and these were carefully packed away into the second box and the lid put down. Smaller personal items for both of them were put into carpet bags.

Now Hannah could turn her attention back to the figure still lying silent on her bed. She felt Caroline's feet and they were cold, so she began chafing them hoping to induce some warmth into them, but to no avail. There were warm stockings packed away in the first box but Hannah did not dare spend time looking for them. Then she remembered the pairs of warm woollen socks each of the girls had knitted for Johnny some time ago. He must still have them and she knew he would not mind her taking a pair from his room.

Downstairs in the kitchen, everything she had been using were still as she left them and she hastily put everything away. The jar containing the housekeeping money was empty so Johnny must have taken it all. She went into his little room and rummaged through his small wooden chest, seized a pair of socks and hurried upstairs again, feeling as though the very silence in the house was menacing.

On returning to the room she found Caroline was moaning softly in pain, and had pushed the coverlet away. First slipping on the socks, Hannah rearranged the coverlet over her again and noticed how the bruise on her left arm and hand had grown more discoloured. In attempting to move the arm she realized it was broken and cried out in horror. And that fiend had wanted to leave her locked in her room! With tears welling up she began chafing Caroline's feet again and prayed that someone would come, leaving it to the Good Lord to know who she meant.

Chapter Thirty
Johnny Runs To Find Lord Lonsdale

Dashell turned round in his chair with his list of names in one hand. "Sir, do you know how many names have that particular "ee" sound?" he asked his father.

They exchanged startled glances at the sudden commotion at the front door. Thunderous knocking and violent pealing of the bell, and Matthew's footsteps passing along the hallway, and his outraged remonstrances. Matthew had opened the door to find a panting, disheveled boy who promptly put his foot forward to prevent the door being closed. Between gasps Johnny cried out, "Where is Lord Lonsdale? Where is he? I gotta find 'im!"

"Be off with you! How dare you come here!" retorted Matthew.

"I gotta find 'im! I must!" Johnny's voice rose in desperation, causing Matthew to blink in uncertainty.

"Hey, you, come back here!" cried Matthew, as Johnny forced his way in.

Dashell knew of only one person who would make such a commotion. He ran into the hall just as Johnny pushed his way past the outraged butler.

"I beg your pardon, sir, but the boy slipped past me. I will fetch George and have him thrown out," Matthew said, glaring at Johnny as he spoke.

"No, Matthew! It is quite all right. I know this boy." Dashell's remark caused even Matthew's well-trained jaw to drop open.

Still panting, Johnny stumbled forward, "Thank Gawd yer 'ere. I've run all the way from the 'ouse, 'e came back early an' you'v e gotta come, 'cos 'e damn well nearly killed 'er."

"What!" cried a stunned Dashell. He turned to Matthew who had remained on hand, still indignant, and astonished at a Cockney boy speaking so freely to Lord Lonsdale; and within the hearing of Lord Barrandale, too. "Matthew! My gig, immediately! And I want Stephen with me. And then come back with George."

"Yes, sir. At once, sir."

Dashell steered Johnny into the sitting-room and pushed him into a chair. Johnny could hardly speak at first, wiping his sleeves across his face, relieved the Guv was in after all. It was Lord Barrandale himself who poured a little brandy and water into a glass and handed it to Dashell, who took it with a quick look of thanks and then forced Johnny to swallow a mouthful. Johnny coughed and spluttered as the unfamiliar liquid went down his throat. "Blimey, Guv, what's that stuff?" he protested, but it helped to ease him.

"Johnny, what happened?" said Dashell. "Tell me quickly."

"Well, Guv. I don't really know it all. Samuel, that's the other ostler at the inn, saw a cab turn the corner and told me but I couldn't get away at first and then when I did I ran to the 'ouse and 'eard Miss Caroline scream when I got there and saw 'im coming downstairs and Hannah shouting at 'im and 'e told 'er to go back an' lock the bedroom door an' giv 'im the key but she gave 'im a different one and 'e sed 'e'd be back later an' then left. Hannah sed 'e hit 'er wiv 'is cane." Johnny's words came tumbling out almost without him pausing for breath.

"The blackguard," swore Dashell, clenching his fists. "But Caroline? Could you still get into her bedroom?"

"Yes, we found 'er on the floor an' put 'er on the bed an' 'annah sent me to find you." Johnny became agitated. "If only I could've got away sooner I could've stopped 'im an' she wouldn't be so 'urt," he cried. Again Johnny's words had come tumbling out, pressured by the anxiety of the whole situation. "Thank Gawd I found you," he repeated simply.

"I think you have been very brave, Johnny," Dashell said. "And running all the way here. Do you know how it all started?"

"No, Guv, only that when he comes 'ome early it usually means trouble. Hannah could tell yer more."

"One more thing, Johnny. Has a doctor been sent for?"

"No, 'cos 'e would make Miss Caroline stay in the 'ouse."

Matthew appeared in the doorway holding Dashell's hat and driving gloves. "The gig is at the front door, sir."

"Thank you, Matthew," he said briefly. "Now, one moment before I leave," and hastened into the writing room.

Johnny had not been fully aware of Lord Barrandale's presence until a slight sound made him look up. His eyes widened. *Blimey,* he thought, *he must be the Guv's farver.* He got to his feet awkwardly wondering what to say, if anything, which was unusual for him.

"So you are Johnny," said Lord Barrandale. "My son has told me all about you. You are a remarkable young man."

Johnny grinned cautiously in appreciation and, being careful not to say Guv this time, replied, "Lord Lonsdale is a real gent, yer lordship."

"Yes," said Barrandale with a smile, "I know."

They heard Dashell's voice in the hall. "George, take this note to Lady Smythe immediately. No reply is required."

He re-entered the room. "Johnny," continued Dashell. "Would you look for a four-wheeled cab, but not a barouche, and follow as soon as you can." Johnny sped away at once.

"You ordered your gig?" queried Barrandale. "Why? We have carriages here."

"Thank you, sir, but no," Dashell answered swiftly. "It would be impolite to turn down Allenby's invitation at such short notice. We cannot risk offending him."

"Quite right," said Barrandale. "So what shall I tell him about your absence?"

"Anything you like, except the truth, of course."

"Where will you take Caroline? You cannot bring her here."

"To Grosvenor Square. Where else?"

Dashell ran down the steps and into his gig, took the reins from Stephen and drove away.

Left alone in the sitting-room Barrandale went to look at the list of place-names Dashell had made. To his amazement there were over ninety containing that particular "ee" sound. Incredible! It would have been a tremendous task for Dashell to enquire about the knowledge he sought. What an undertaking it would have been. He marveled at his son's love for this girl; and at the devotion and help of two ordinary servants.

At Grosvenor Square Chadwick held out a silver salver to Lady Smythe with a letter on it, who froze when she recognized the familiar hand-writing. *If he wants to dine alone with me again I'll wring his neck*, she thought. Chadwick coughed slightly. "George informed me, milady, that no reply was required." *I really will wring his neck*, she promised herself.

Serenely, she opened the letter and read it through twice. "Chadwick, it seems we are having a guest arriving at very short notice, within an hour or two. Would you prepare the guest chamber with the adjoining room, for a young lady and her maid? It seems that the young lady could possibly be indisposed. That is all. Thank you, Chadwick."

Lady Smythe looked again at the note from Dashell.

My dearest, darling Aunt,

Caroline needs our help sooner than expected, as I have just received word she has been hurt by her stepfather. I am going to fetch her and her maid.
Father knows all.

Your adoring nephew,
Dashell

It was those last three words that really troubled Lady Smythe. Father may very well know all, but that gave no indication what Father thought or said. She read the note once more. *I'll give him 'dearest, darling Aunt'.* She settled down uneasily to await their arrival.

Johnny had trouble finding a four-wheeled cab for none would stop when hailed. Eventually he ran up to a cab stand and pulled one out of the ranks, thankful that the driver knew where to go. Once the cab was clear of the traffic round Hyde Park Corner, an impatient Johnny stuck his head out of the window. "Move it, will yer!"

Dashell, about fifteen minutes ahead, also had to use his skill to get round Hyde Park Corner and into Old Brompton Road. When the road was reasonably clear he urged Sparkle into a full gallop, his thoughts racing at the same speed. *Dear heavens, what has that fiend done to you? Why did I not persuade you to leave sooner? Caroline, my darling, I am coming.*

Chapter Thirty-One
At Becket Lane Again

In the upstairs room Hannah had lit some candles in the gathering dusk when she heard the approach of rapid hoofbeats. She cautiously opened a window and looked out and gave a cry of relief when a vehicle pulled up and an athletic figure leapt out.

Dashell looked up as Hannah called out, "The door is open, sir." Once in the hall he saw her with a light at the top of the stairs and ran up.

"What is this, Hannah?" Dashell hardly dared to ask. "Johnny said that Wardlock had hurt Caroline. He said he had run all the way to find me."

"Oh, sir, it was dreadful, dreadful. But come this way; the door on the right."

Dashell swiftly passed her and entered the room and saw Caroline's still figure on the bed. Bending over her while Hannah held a lamp he cried out in horror at the sight of the bruises on her face. "He did this to her?" he asked incredulously, his eyes blazing. "But why? What happened?"

"I do not know, sir. Only Miss Caroline herself can say. I heard raised voices and looked into the hall and he was on the stairs waving a newspaper, and saying something about a brother." Dashell swore inwardly that the family news had reached the papers. "Then I went upstairs the back way and heard Miss Caroline say something about her sister and mother. If I had not been there I don't know what he might have done." Hannah was quite overcome. "He could even have killed her."

"That's exactly what Johnny said." Dashell would have gathered Caroline in his arms but Hannah cried out, "Be careful, sir! Her left arm is broken."

Dashell slowly turned his head with such a bleak expression that Hannah took a step backwards. "Where is he? Where can I find him?" After daring Wardlock to hurt Caroline he had still done this!

"I do not know, sir. Even the mistress never knew where he went or what he did."

Dashell knew it would be useless to waste time pursuing the matter further because other things were much more urgent and important. "Johnny is following in a cab and should be here any minute. He told me a doctor has not yet been sent for."

"I had to send Johnny to find you first, sir. If that man came back and found Dr. Meldicott had been here when he thought this room was locked, I don't know what he would have done."

"Of course, Hannah, I understand what you are saying. As soon as Johnny comes he can go with Stephen to fetch this Dr. Meldicott. Caroline must be examined as soon as possible."

Hannah was much less anxious now that Lord Lonsdale was here. "God bless you for coming, sir," she said simply.

"Did you doubt my coming?" asked Dashell in surprise.

"Not for a moment, sir. I only feared lest Johnny could not find you. I don't know what I would have done on my own if he had come back without you. But what will become of us and all our plans to leave? Miss Caroline cannot possibly travel the way she is."

"There is no need to fear anything any more, Hannah. I have come to take Caroline away, and once she leaves this house she will never set foot in it again."

"But where will you take us, sir?" cried Hannah, looking at him in wonder.

"To my aunt's place at Grosvenor Square. I have told her the whole story; and when Caroline is well enough to travel she will stay in the countryside until she is quite rested. My aunt has some very discreet friends."

"God bless you again, sir, and this kind lady."

Dashell moved to the window and leaned out. "Here is a cab coming now," he said, and went downstairs and along the path to the gate to meet whoever it was arriving. Johnny jumped out of the cab. "We're 'ere," he said, rather unnecessarily.

"Thank goodness," said Dashell speaking urgently. "We must send for a doctor. Caroline has a broken arm and is still unconscious." Johnny's heart missed a beat at this further news. "Would you go with Stephen and fetch this Dr.Meldicott? You can show him the way." The gig moved away, while Dashell spoke to the cab driver before returning indoors.

"They have gone to fetch Dr.Meldicott," he told Hannah on re-entering the room. "Caroline will not have much longer to wait."

For want of something to do, Hannah moved quietly about, placing anything she could carry at the top of the stairs ready to be put into the cab. She had placed the two bags with the jewels and the money into a carpet bag which she was not letting out of her sight.

Dashell sat on the side of the bed to keep vigil. "This may not be the right time or place, Hannah, but I can never thank you or Johnny enough for what you both have done. I am still amazed how Johnny ran all the way to find me."

"What else could we have done, sir? Miss Caroline needed you."

Dashell smiled at that. "Do you think she loves me?"

"Indeed she does, sir. I know that for a fact."

But Dashell must hear that from Caroline herself. He held her good right hand against his cheek and felt an overwhelming love for her as she lay there looking so vulnerable. Those bruises on her dear face. Pray God she would be all right, that there would be no lasting damage.

Dr.Meldicott had just finished his evening meal when the gig pulled up outside his house and Johnny knocked on the door, which opened flush onto the road. The manservant answered and recognized Johnny at once. Dr.Meldicott heard the words, "Miss

Caroline Wardlock," and came out into the hall. "Johnny, did I hear you say Miss Wardlock has had an accident?"

"Please could yer come, Doctor. Miss Caroline 'as a broken arm an' some bruises, an' she's unconscious."

Dr.Meldicott did not like the sound of this, remembering her sister's accident. "Very well, I will come at once. I will order my man—"

Stephen, who had also come to the door, said, "It's all right, sir. I have orders to fetch you and bring you back."

Dr.Meldicott was even more surprised. However, it took him but a few moments to pick up his bag and other necessities before stepping into the gig. He wondered at the vehicle, not having seen it before, and at who could give orders and how the vehicle was at the Wardlock house in the first place. Johnny was left to find his own way back.

Dr.Meldicott turned to Stephen. "Who is your master?"

"Lord Lonsdale, sir."

That only induced more misgivings. Dr.Meldicott did not know Caroline even knew a Lord Lonsdale, an obvious aristocrat from the sound of it, and he frowned to himself. It was not unknown for a woman to be abused if she refused a man's advances, and then the man send for a doctor to appease his conscience, if he had one.

Arriving at the house there was a man waiting at the gate with a lantern. "I am so thankful you could come," he said. "I am Lord Lonsdale. Come with me, would you?" Dr.Meldicott knew the way well enough but silently followed Dashell into the house.

When they reached the bedroom Dashell handed the lantern to Hannah, and closed the door behind them, then went to lean on the bannisters on the landing.

"Oh, Dr.Meldicott," said Hannah. "Poor Miss Caroline. I was almost at my wits' end. It was dreadful, the way he struck her."

Dr.Meldicott thought he had assessed the situation at once. "One moment, Hannah, I must attend to my unfortunate patient first. Questions will come later."

Hannah held up the lantern and watched as the doctor examined Caroline's cuts and bruises, then turned his attention to the broken arm, which he deftly set and placed splints around it and bandaged it up.

Dr.Meldicott was puzzled when heard the sounds of footsteps on the stairs as though things were being carried, and recollected seeing bags and boxes on the landing. And there was also that cab waiting outside. He glanced quickly round the room and thought it seemed surprisingly bare. "It seems one blow glanced off her head and the other has caused some concussion," he remarked, "but I do not think there will be any lasting damage." While speaking he packed his bag and led the way to the door, beckoning Hannah to follow him. There were certain questions that needed answering.

Dashell, who had been waiting on the landing as patiently as he could, turned round as the door opened. "Tell me, doctor," he cried eagerly, "how is Caroline? Will she be all right?"

"She is comfortable enough, and yes, she will be all right."

"Thank you, I am more relieved than I can say. You have given me hope."

The good doctor was rather surprised. These did not seem to be the words of a guilty man. He looked sternly from Dashell to Hannah. "Did Caroline fall downstairs? No? Then how did she come by her injuries? Who is responsible?" He looked straight at Dashell, who met his gaze levelly, and then looked at Hannah.

Hannah smoothed down her apron. "It was Mr.Wardlock, her own stepfather."

Dr.Meldicott stared at Hannah in blank amazement. He had not expected this. "You mean Mr.Wardlock did this?" he queried. "I find that very strange indeed. But why?"

"I do not know, but both Johnny and I can bear witness to the fact, although neither of us saw everything."

Dr.Meldicott shook his head in disbelief, and wondered about the cab outside and the evidence of baggage, which suggested a pre-arranged flight. Had Wardlock tried to prevent an elopement? "And where is Wardlock now?"

"He left after leaving Caroline lying on the floor," Hannah told him stiffly, pressing her lips together. "He would have done more but I prevented him."

"I find this most disturbing, Hannah, astonishing, in fact. Why such vicious behaviour?" he asked again.

Hannah pressed her lips together again and cast her eyes down. "Only Miss Caroline herself can tell us."

Dr.Meldicott looked at Dashell. "And you, your lordship?"

Dashell had sensed the doctor was puzzled at his presence and explained, "Johnny came to find me. In fact, he ran all the way, and I left within twenty minutes and came straight here, while Johnny followed in a cab."

This was interesting news indeed. It suggested a strong attachment between this gentleman and Caroline, whom Dr.Meldicott had known since she was a little child. "So you were not even here at the time?"

"No. And I came here with the intention of taking this lady to a place of safety, for under no circumstances can she remain here."

"And where will that place of safety be? Because I want to see her again."

"With my aunt, Lady Smythe, who resides at Grosvenor Square," said Dashell. The two men had at last come to an understanding.

"I must point out that Caroline should not really be moved," Dr.Meldicott said, "and I will therefore not accept any responsibility."

"I understand what you are saying," said Dashell. "And now in my turn, may I trust in your discretion in all this? You may also apply to me for your fee at Barrandale House on Park Lane."

"You are most kind," the doctor murmured. Another surprise. Park Lane indeed! What was this attachment between this gentleman and Caroline? He glanced at Hannah and was somewhat reassured by her demeanour.

Johnny and Stephen had been taking boxes out to the cab. There was not enough room for the last one and it would have to be left behind, so it was hidden in the cupboard under the stairs to be fetched later at a safer time.

Dashell called out from the upstairs window, "Stephen! Come up here and bring a lamp from the gig with you."

Under the watchful eye of Dr.Meldicott, anxious for his patient, Dashell carefully lifted Caroline in his strong arms, murmuring, "Come, my darling, you are safe now." They left the room, Stephen lighting the way with the lamp, Dashell going downstairs one step at a time, not daring to risk a fall, followed by the doctor and Hannah, who carried the carpet-bag and the lantern.

Johnny, who had returned by now, opened the front door for them. He tugged at Hannah's sleeve and whispered to her about a box put in the cupboard under the stairs because it would not fit on the cab, and she whispered back to him that it couldn't be helped and there were other things to come back for anyway. He still whispered urgently that he would have to tell the livery stable they would not now be requiring that horse and cart ordered for Monday morning.

Still carrying his precious burden, Dashell stepped into the cab. Johnny took the lantern from Hannah as he helped her into the cab, leaving her to sit where best she could, while a very thoughtful Dr.Meldicott took his seat beside Stephen in the gig.

Johnny managed to wink at Hannah with a jerk of his head towards the house, and watched until both vehicles were out of sight before racing back indoors.

Chapter Thirty-Two

At Grosvenor Square

The wonderful elation Dashell had experienced knowing he need not now go to Sussex on that long search, had disappeared in the light of these recent events. He had eagerly looked forward to telling all this to Caroline—but now? There was no way of knowing what damage had been done; it was possible she could be unconscious for days. Such things did happen. Heartbroken, he held her as close to him as he dared. "Hannah, when I dreamed of holding Caroline in my arms I never meant it to be like this."

Hannah's answer was to shed some tears, which she mopped up with her handkerchief. "Please, sir, we must pray she will recover soon," she said, sniffing as quietly as she could.

"Hannah, there was obviously no time to speak to you earlier, but I must find out exactly what happened, and I must also speak to Johnny."

She swallowed hard. "Aye, sir, I can tell you more too, now that we are away from that man's clutches. Some things I never dared tell either of the two girls."

Dashell stared at Hannah in the darkness of the cab's interior, dimly lit by what little moonlight there was. "What do you mean?"

Before Hannah could say anything, a slight movement came from Caroline. "Oh-h-h, my head hurts. My arm hurts." Both Dashell and Hannah were overjoyed although the words were almost indistinct. There were some more indistinct murmurings then a little louder, as Caroline cried out, "Hannah! Hannah!" through her bruised mouth.

"I am here, dear." Hannah's touch seemed to soothe Caroline, who tried to murmur something before her voice trailed away.

"She almost regained consciousness," whispered Dashell ecstatically. "She will get better. But we must keep quiet in case our talking disturbs her." There was not much farther to go, and as Dashell pressed his lips gently on Caroline's forehead, it occurred to him that Johnny also knew more than he had previously said. Yes, Dashell would certainly speak to both of them.

The cab stopped outside Smythe House in Grosvenor Square. "Hannah," said Dashell "would you go and knock on the front door? I will wait until Chadwick answers." He knew people could be watching in curiosity from their windows at the sound of a vehicle stopping outside someone's door and he wanted to act quickly, for he knew from experience that curtains could twitch.

Chadwick must have been waiting, as the front door opened on Hannah's first knock and he came out with a lantern. Dashell carefully stepped out of the cab, and with a brief nod at the butler as he passed him, carried Caroline swiftly upstairs, leaving the unloading of the boxes from the cab to Chadwick's supervision.

Lady Smythe was waiting outside the guest room and stared over the bannisters as her nephew came up and swept past her. She gave a little shriek, "Is this your lady?" she gasped. For one fleeting moment she almost regretted allowing Dashell to bring Caroline here, particularly as she still had to face Barrandale.

She went into the guest room and whisked the bedclothes back as Dashell carefully laid Caroline down. She looked at Caroline's dishevelled hair, her crumpled dress, the bruises, and broken arm in a sling, and—oh, horrors!—those thick woollen socks. "In heaven's name what has happened? When you said she had been injured I did not imagine this." She saw the appealing look on Dashell's face.

"Aunt Letty, I beg you, please look after her," he implored.

"Of course I will. At least it appears she has been attended to by a doctor already."

"Yes," replied Dashell quickly, "His name is Dr. Meldicott, and he will be coming here in the morning to see her again."

"Where is the maid you said would be with her?"

As though in answer Chadwick ushered in Hannah, who was still clutching the carpet bag. Everything had been removed from the cab and the driver had gone away considering the money he had been paid was worth all the effort. Lady Smythe glanced at Hannah, taking in everything at once. Well, she certainly looked a decent kindly woman, as Hannah bobbed to her.

"We must see to this child before she gets cold," said Lady Smythe. She turned briskly to Chadwick, who had been waiting. "Hot bricks, Chadwick, and another blanket."

"I have already ordered hot bricks, milady."

"That was very thoughtful of you. Now, Dashell," she said, turning to him, "you must leave."

"I must speak to you, Aunt Letty."

"Not now," she frowned. "Wait for me in the salon if it is important." She closed the door on him and he walked away.

Important? Of course it was. In fact, it was wonderful. He could find out Caroline's real name much sooner than had been expected by simply writing to likely parish priests. No need now for his aunt to worry about anything.

Between the two of them Lady Smythe and Hannah removed Caroline's clothing and put on a warm flannel nightdress which had been in the carpet bag, then combed out her hair as far as they could without disturbing her head too much. The woollen socks were left on even after the extra blanket and hot bricks were brought up.

Hannah begged to offer her thanks to Lady Smythe. "So kind of you, Lady Smythe, as indeed is Lord Lonsdale," she said, and Lady Smythe graciously inclined her head.

There was nothing more to be done now that Caroline had been made as comfortable as possible, and Hannah had been sent down to the kitchen for something to eat, so Lady Smythe went along to the salon where a weary Dashell had seated himself in a chair with his legs outstretched. He had not even moved when Chadwick informed him that Stephen was at the door with the gig. "Did you wish him to wait, sir?"

"No thank you, Chadwick. Tell him to return." Stephen was a good fellow and had no doubt taken Johnny to the stableyard at Barrandale House before coming round to Grosvenor Square, and it really was no distance for Dashell to walk back.

He got to his feet when his aunt entered the room, who firmly closed the door behind her. Still horrified, and never one to mince words, she came straight to the point. "What in heaven's name happened to that girl? Hannah said her stepfather did this. But why was he so cruel? I am just appalled. Thank goodness she was attended to by a doctor before she came here, for goodness knows what explaining I would have had to make to my own doctor. It was a wonder her doctor allowed her to be moved."

"Caroline had to be moved," replied Dashell stiffly. "Under no circumstances was I allowing her to remain there. It was under Dr. Meldicott's supervision that I carried her into the cab. He did not think the head injuries were too serious; and Caroline showed signs of regaining consciousness while in the cab." He remembered his statement to Hannah that Caroline would never set foot in that Wardlock house again. He did not think his aunt would appreciate that remark right now and yet there was nowhere else he could have taken her.

Lady Smythe sat tapping her fingers on the armrest of her chair. "I hope you are right. And you said that this Dr. Meldicott would be calling here tomorrow to see her? I like the sound of him for that."

"Yes, he was genuinely concerned for her. But Aunt Letty, I have something to tell you."

"I hope it is not another long story, for I am too tired to listen. Yet I do feel quite sorry for the poor girl."

So Dashell explained what he had been doing earlier that day, upon his father's own suggestion, and he that could now write to likely parish priests.

His aunt's eyes, which had been closed, flew open as she sat up. "Do you mean there really is a possibility of learning Caroline's real name? That you could write, instead of going off on what might be a wild goose chase?" It made her mind a great deal easier that the suggestion had come from Barrandale himself, as it showed he had some empathy towards the situation.

"Now, Dashell, I really must go to bed," she said, yawning delicately. "And you must be tired too."

Dashell certainly was, from first feeling so elated, looking forward to telling Caroline about his new plans, then having to deal with all that followed. "I will just look in on Caroline before I go."

With a sigh his aunt watched him leave the room and then decided to follow him. He glanced round as she came to stand beside him. "Where is Hannah?" he asked. "Is she not here?"

"I sent her down to the kitchen for some refreshments." His aunt told him. "The poor woman looked so worn out. I will stay here for a while, as this girl should not be left alone."

"That reminds me," said Dashell, "Hannah intimated she had more things to tell me, and I am sure Johnny knows more too. And I would really like to know what happened this afternoon. Well, that will have to wait." Bending over he kissed Caroline on her forehead and unmarked cheek. "Look after my darling for me."

Lady Smythe just nodded and patted his arm, unable to speak.

Chapter Thirty-Three
More Happenings With Johnny

Johnny had raced back into the house which was now in complete darkness, and he had no idea how much time he had before Wardlock returned and he had much to do. The first thing was to fetch that lockpick he had kept hidden. Hannah would be appalled to know Johnny even had it, and never mind that he knew how to use it. Taking a linen bag from a kitchen drawer, he went into the downstairs room where Hannah had discovered Wardlock's hiding place.

The second panelling on the right side of the fireplace, Hannah had told him. Look for a leaf at eye level. Placing the lantern on the floor, Johnny ran both hands over the panelling carefully feeling until he found the leaf, and unlocked the tiny keyhole in a second.

He had not felt any hinges at all, just as Hannah had said she had not, so the whole panel must lift out. It would not budge. Then it must swivel somehow. Hardly daring to breathe he pressed first the left side, then the right side. It moved! He swiveled it wide open and the cavity behind it revealed a black metal box.

"Cor!" he exclaimed excitedly, almost forgetting to be quiet. "It's 'ere! We've found it! We've found it!" He was just about to seize the box with both hands when he remembered Finger's words of caution. "Yer gotta put it back exactly as it was or they'll know it's been moved."

Johnny lifted the box out, squatted on the floor and tried to open the lid, but it was locked. "Might 'ave known," he muttered. He paused a moment with the pick in his hand. After all his and

Hannah's searchings, this had to be the last hiding place. If not, where else? He turned the pick, closed his eyes, then raised the lid. He opened his eyes and caught his breath at the sight of a large amount of papers, consisting of newspaper cuttings and what looked like documents or legal papers of some kind. The very kind of things they had been searching for!

There was no time to look through them so Johnny put everything into the linen bag, re-locked the now empty metal box and placed it back exactly where it had been, swiveled the panel into place, re-locked it and closed the little leaf over the keyhole.

"That should fool the ol' buzzard," grinned Johnny to himself. "Serve 'im right for hiding somefink wot wasn't 'is in the first place." Holding the linen bag carefully with one hand, he picked up the lantern and hastily retreated to the kitchen.

Once there he glanced at the clock. Time was moving on and there was something else he absolutely had to do. He had to find out what was on the other side of that locked door at the top of the house. It was now or never. But first of all he had to hide that linen bag in his room, just in case. Then he ran outside to the garden shed for a spade.

Armed with this and the lantern he made his way upstairs to the landing and stood still for a moment, remembering what a terrible to-do it had been earlier. Well, Miss Caroline must be at that lady's house by now. And what a clever idea it had been of Hannah to switch the keys. Oh, no! The door to the linen cupboard was still open. He would have to wedge it shut somehow, otherwise 'is Nibs would see it was open and it would give the game away at once. He did not want to waste time going down to the kitchen for a piece of paper, so a folded table napkin tightly wedged underneath the door worked just as well.

The house was so still it was creepy. No wonder Hannah said she felt it was beginning to be haunted. Johnny shivered as though he was cold, and the flickering flame in the lantern made strange shapes on the walls. Bracing himself and casting away all fears, he quickly went to the door leading to the attic and pulled aside the curtain that kept out the draught.

He knew from previous examinations that the lock was too rusty for a key to turn, even if one was available. Placing the flat end of the spade between the door and the jamb he began to move it one way and then the other, trying to pry it open. It was a stout lock, but the wood began to splinter and finally gave way with a great deal of noise, as though in protest. With one hearty kick the door swung sharply open, hitting the wall hard behind, causing it to swing back again. Johnny pushed it open cautiously and held up the lantern.

There was a short length of floor, a narrow flight of stairs with a yawning expanse of darkness at the top, and a musty smell of years of un-aired rooms. Hannah had told him more than once that nothing was there, just empty unused servants' rooms, but he had to satisfy his own curiosity.

Bracing himself again Johnny made his way up to a small landing with three doors leading off it. The first two rooms were empty. Just falls of soot, a long-dead bird, and some old leaves, all of which must have swirled down the chimneys, and a broken window pane. Johnny felt let down, but perhaps it was just the existence of a locked door that had piqued his interest. Maybe Hannah was right after all.

Entering the third room he held up the lantern and looked about. Nothing. Empty. Just like the others. Disgusted and disappointed, all his hopes and convictions had come to nothing. What a waste of time. He turned to go and gave a hoarse shout of fear when he saw a face looking at him from behind the door.

His knees buckled under him and he almost dropped the lantern. Still shaking, he gaped at the face, which came from a portrait propped up on an easel, and stared back at him as though it had not seen anything for years. He took a closer look and felt the hairs at the back of his neck beginning to prickle. So that was why the door had been locked all those years! Probably to hide this from 'is Nibs. *Cor!* he thought. *Just wait till Miss Caroline sees this! And the Guv. And Hannah. What a surprise they would 'ave!*

The chimes of the clock in the hall echoing up to the attic brought Johnny back to reality. He must go. Still feeling shaky from shock he carried the portrait down the stairs, leaving the easel where it was. He pushed the splintered wood back with his feet before closing the door and pulling the curtain across again, hoping that in the darkness no evidence would be seen. His heart still thumping he gathered up spade, portrait and lantern and dashed away as though something ghostly might appear and escort him downstairs. It was with great relief that he kicked the kitchen door shut behind him. He returned the spade to the garden shed, picking up some dry sacking at the same time.

It had been a very exhausting time for Johnny. First there was his run from the inn to the house and encountering the situation there; then running to find the Guv and the journey back to Becket Lane in the cab. Helping Stephen to carry boxes out to the cab; then running back from the doctor's house. Ending with that final search for the missing documents; and then finding that long-hidden portrait, and—oh! What a start that had given him, and all this in a relatively short period of time.

Johnny was now feeling extremely hungry and somewhat light-headed, aided no doubt by the unaccustomed brandy he had earlier. There was only one place that held a remedy for these ailments: the pantry. Armed with a tray, a plate and a very sharp knife he made his way there. He returned with several slices of ham, buttered bread and some cheese and a jug of milk. After eating a few mouthfuls he jumped up and made a roll from the left over sacking, and pushed it against the door to the hall to prevent any flickering light from the lantern showing underneath.

When he finished his meal he put the tray on the draining board and took the linen bag from its hiding place. Sitting at the table again and pulling the lantern closer he looked though the contents of the linen bag and sure enough there were marriage and baptismal certificates.

Hannah, we did it! We did it! The Guv and Miss Caroline can get married now. Johnny was ecstatic. Pushing aside the newspaper cuttings, he pulled out another document. It was the last will and testament of Thomas Wardlock Physhe, dated only six months before. *What?* he thought. *That was just after Miss Maude's death. But that name Physhe. Sounds more like Fish to me. Huh, I always thought there was something fishy about 'im. I wonder what the old devil 'as written.* After Wardlock's behaviour he had no qualms in reading anything. The parchment was stiff and new and crackled when he opened it. The wording was short and to the point and written in flowery handwriting which was a little difficult to read.

> *I, Thomas Wardlock Physhe, being of sound mind,* (Hah! That's a laugh, snorted Johnny to himself), *do hereby leave the property known as Twenty-nine Becket Lane in the District of Fulham in London and all its possessions and attachments and contents, to Miss Davilla Spendham, of White Hart Lane, Camden Town.*

Then there were the signatures of Wardlock and the solicitor's two clerks, and the date. That was all.

Johnny's blood ran cold. There was no mention of Miss Caroline, Wardlock's surviving stepdaughter. Had he come back this afternoon just to quarrel with her? Had he come with the intention of killing her? Well, why not? He'd killed Miss Maude, 'adn't 'e? And did that mean Miss Caroline would have absolutely nothing? It must. And then that must go for Hannah and Johnny as well. All their clothing and every little item that belonged to them would no longer be theirs. Legally, the law would be quite adamant about that.

The very thought appalled him. And who was this Miss Davilla Spendham anyway? Some fancy piece of Wardlock's with that theatrical sounding name. *Huh, she must be ruddy hard* up to want the likes of 'im. Blimey, there was no accounting for tastes. They must be two of a kind, if you arsk me.

Once more the clock in the hall warned him time was passing. As he gathered up the papers something else caught his eye, another will dated many years earlier. He blatantly opened it.

> *I, Thomas Wardlock,* (there was no Physhe this time) *do hereby leave all my worldly possessions and the property known as Twenty-nine Becket Lane and all attachments thereto, to my wife and my two step-daughters during their lifetimes, to pass in due course to the last survivor.*

Now that was much better. Miss Caroline would now inherit the property, such as it was, and everything in it. Johnny hesitated a moment before making up his mind. He took the second will to the fire grate in the wall and set it alight, and watched as it crumpled into ashes, making sure every piece of paper burned. Now Johnny had got his revenge on old Wardlock as he had promised himself days ago he would. Should he tell the Guv about this? Or even Hannah? She at least would be horrified. But Uncle Joe's words came back to him.

Now he really had to go, but where was he going to sleep? It was too risky to stay in the house, which meant there was only one possible place left. Gathering up the bedding from his little room, Johnny took it out to the enormous hollow tree stump at the end of the old carriageway, returned for the portrait and the linen bag with all the documents, and his precious hoard of coins which he had been carefully saving for months.

It would be rather cramped in the stump, but he would be comfortable enough. Once settled, Johnny blew out the lantern. Exhausted, his head had hardly touched the pillow before he was asleep, and he never heard a cab pull up and then leave.

Chapter Thirty-Four
Thomas Wardlock

Thomas Wardlock's parents, Thomas and Millicent Physhe, were members of a travelling group of actors who went from place to place earning what they could, which was not always very much. His parents taught him to read and write, and other things they knew, such as card tricks, conjuring, sleight of hand, mimicry, make-up, and disguises.

So Thomas grew up in a world of make-believe and it completely intrigued him. It was fascinating how clothing, wigs, and different speech and accents could transform a person into someone else. He was not a particularly friendly person so he disliked playing jovial, happy characters, it was simply not in his nature to be so. He also discovered he had a talent for writing in a beautiful script.

The elder Thomas disliked his name "Fish" and tried to disguise it by spelling it "Physhe". The younger Thomas also detested that name and eventually adopted his mother's maiden name, calling himself Thomas Wardlock, although he never made it legal.

All this might have continued indefinitely had things not come to an abrupt end. After a very successful week some robbers set upon the actors and stole all their takings. Not only that, they smashed all their props and scenery and tore the clothing stored in their wardrobe. The actors suspected that a rival company had hired ruffians to do this, but nothing could be proved. Shaken and heart-broken, unable to continue, the little group disbanded and went their separate ways.

The elder Thomas never got over the shock and took to drink. The last the younger Thomas heard of his father was that he had fallen into a rain-filled ditch and drowned. He lost touch with his mother completely and never really knew what became of her. Acting was all knew and he soon joined another company.

Something else Thomas had grown up with was a constant, chronic shortage of money. The acquisition and the keeping of it began to create miserly traits in him, and he was loath to part with any money once he had it. Watching the aristocracy in all their finery and careless handling of too much wealth stirred greed in him, and he began to think of ways to relieve them of it by using his card tricks and sleight of hand. He drifted into gaming houses but soon learned to be careful. It became dangerous for him one night when he was forced to leave in a hurry. No matter. He merely changed his disguise and tried elsewhere.

Thomas discovered forgery was quite lucrative too, by writing false letters of credit or reference, by forged signatures on cheques, or forged certificates of learning. With his beautiful script Thomas began to write elaborate certificates of marriages, births, and even deaths if anyone wanted to "disappear". He found it easy to make a living this way. He would gain the confidence of some individual, put forward a scheme and eventually relieve the unfortunate victim of his money. But the perpetrator could not be found, of course, because his disguise had long been changed, or discarded altogether. Swindler or confidence-trickster would be good names for him.

Emboldened by his successes, Thomas felt it was time to join the gentry themselves and become one of them. To do this in a convincing manner he began to look around for a suitable wife. Not that he really wanted one, women did not particularly interest him, but he thought it would look better if he had one. He could hardly believe his luck when he heard of a young woman recently widowed with two infant daughters. Money was running short and she was at her wits' end to know what to do.

To this lady's utter astonishment she received a visit from a clergyman, who said he had been requested to call by a certain gentleman who was greatly distressed to learn of her predicament, and was willing to put forward an offer of a most delicate nature. This said gentleman was too embarrassed to come himself as the subject was so tender, so he, the clergyman, had offered to come and speak on the gentleman's behalf.

The lady listened in amazement and declared that such was her desperate situation that she hardly had any choice in the matter. Her remarks and grateful thanks were conveyed to the gentleman, and a meeting was arranged.

It was agreed that the marriage was only to be one of convenience for each party, although they would give the outward appearance of a married couple. They would live in the same house but nothing more was to be expected from either side. Unfortunately the gentleman did not like children, so he asked that the lady keep hers out of his way. With regard to servants, a cook-housekeeper had already been hired, as well as a coachman, but alas, the carriage would not be at the lady's disposal. There were plenty of cabs available if she wished to engage one, and she was free to come and go.

The gentleman would continue to conduct his business, which was of no concern of hers, and the lady replied that she would give music and singing lessons and any other tuition as required. Any remuneration earned would be hers. The gentleman agreed to this as long as he was not in the house when the lady taught her lessons, as he did not like noise. The contract was drawn up and signed by both parties. The marriage ceremony took place but was not conducted by the clergyman who had introduced them, nor was he to be seen anywhere. He had many commitments and had been called out of town, or so the gentleman understood. Clever as he was, Thomas could not be the officiating clergyman and the bridegroom at the same time.

So Thomas Wardlock conducted his business and the lady attended to the matters of the house and went out with him as required. The lady seemed as though she had been born to this, as indeed she had, but Thomas Wardlock was constantly learning his part. He was never fully accepted and it irritated him to see how well-liked his wife was.

In some ways the lady was amicably agreeable but in others she had a will of steel, especially in the matter of her nursemaid. The lady did not particularly like the woman and insisted on one of her own choosing. There was something else that had not occurred to Wardlock, and that was the price of food. The lady showed him the bills one day and he very grudgingly allowed more house-keeping money. He had grown up with the knowledge that money was tight and he hated having to part with it.

Wardlock had one close call with the authorities and the thought of prison filled him with dread, especially as his victim had thought he could detect a faint smell of greasepaint. Greasepaint! How were the authorities to know who they were looking for if disguises and aliases kept on changing? Badly shaken, Wardlock became terrified of recognition. He must be more careful to safeguard himself as his business was becoming too dangerous.

He bought a different house within the shadow of Fulham Palace. That was a clever move. Who would think of looking for him there? He had not liked the name of the house, and as he had purchased it on the 29th March, which happened to be his birthday, he perversely changed the name to just "Twenty-nine". His wife, of course, had to accompany him, and had Wardlock but known, this proved to be a blessing in disguise for the lady and her two daughters.

Ever thinking of ways to save money, or rather not to spend it in the first place, Wardlock dismissed the cook, and said the nursemaid, whom his wife had always paid, could take over, and the two girls were now old enough to help around the house. He sold the carriage and dismissed the coachman. He made arrangements for a cab driver to come and pick him up each morning through the week. The driver tried to protest but Wardlock threatened to expose the man's real name and shady past if he did not comply.

It was difficult to say when the bitterness and resentment really took hold. The very goodness of the lady and her daughters reflected his very humble beginnings, and Wardlock realized he could never achieve their level. Later his wife told him that she was going to hire a boy to live in and work around the house and garden. He grudgingly said the boy could come but he would have to earn his own keep, for not a penny would he give him.

Wardlock was also having serious concerns about his health. He had some slight dizziness and shortness of breath on occasions, and the thought of being unable to continue what he was doing horrified him. At one time his hands became a trifle unsteady and a forged signature on a bank draft was not as good as usual. It aroused the suspicions of the bank clerk and the presenter was detained and later arrested. Thomas Wardlock, of course, was implicated but could not be found. Once more he was badly shaken.

He had acted ever since he could remember, always adopting different characters at will. In time, had this caused his own personality to become overshadowed until he did not know his own true self? Or did he know his true self and acted to cover it up? Or was he unable to fathom out who he really was, and did he even care? Whatever it was, Wardlock was becoming confused and the acquisition of money was the only thing that mattered to him.

He had not paid much attention when he learned that his stepdaughters, Maude and Caroline, would be away for a whole year at a select school for young women. It was only after they left to go to the school that he wanted to know more about it. In the first place—why? What a terrible waste of money. And how could his wife possibly afford it? His wife merely replied that she saved the money she had obtained from teaching music and singing and needlework, as was agreed in their contract. Ha! So therefore it must have been quite a lot if she was able to continue paying her two servants as well. It was enough for the purpose, she said, and it was no concern of his how she wished to educate her daughters.

Wardlock was still not satisfied. So his wife had been quietly accumulating all this money and he had not known about it! And what was so special about these two girls that they required this grand education? All this preyed on his mind because he was so convinced there was more money—his wife must have more. He would wait for his chance and look in her bedroom.

One Sunday morning when his wife and her maidservant were at church Wardlock went into her room and began looking through her desk, and before long pulled out a leather case containing some documents. There was their own marriage contract, their certificate of marriage, his wife's certificate from her previous marriage, and the baptismal papers of the two girls. So his suspicions had been correct. There was more to this than met the eye. An avaricious look spread over his face. He would withhold these papers until he got some satisfactory answers.

His wife, however, refused to cooperate and asked, even begged her husband to return what did not belong to him. It was unfortunate that her deteriorating health prevented any further discussion, and then her death finally ended any chance of doing so. He showed, or even felt, very little emotion. In fact he felt cheated, this feeling of money being just beyond his reach. Nevertheless, he played the part of the bereaved husband very well.

Wardlock planned some kind of revenge on the hated gentry and an opportunity came sooner than expected when a young gentleman had called to see his elder step-daughter. How he had acted the part of the affronted father still mourning the loss of his dear wife. How he had enjoyed ordering the young man out of the house! Then his step-daughter had the audacity to question what he was doing, so he would teach her a lesson she would not forget, which succeeded far beyond what he had planned.

Surely the gods must have been with Wardlock, for another opportunity eventually came along for him to deal with the younger step-daughter. He had been to see his doctor once more demanding something be done about a recurring problem, only the fool could not pinpoint what was wrong. Wardlock had stormed out, declaring all doctors to be quacks, and this one in particular.

On returning home early he had encountered a carriage outside his house, which did nothing to improve his temper. However, the situation had been placed right into his hands. Ill or not, Wardlock had swiftly taken advantage, but everything went wrong. He had hurled insult after insult at his step-daughter, thinking the man would leave in disgust, but when that dark, angry face confronted his and their eyes met, he felt a cold shiver of fear and wondered if he had over-acted, for this young man had no intention of being ordered about.

Pah! What nonsense! He could act his way into or out of anything. By the next morning Wardlock had brushed the incident aside, except for that one little spot of fear or doubt that would not go away.

Again he thought the gods were with him when he took that letter from the postman a day or so later, a letter from this Lord Lonsdale to Caroline, which he had no hesitation in reading. How pathetic it sounded! Such feeble excuses! *Really, Lord Lonsdale, I would have thought better of you. So your words and threats to me meant nothing.* Wardlock discarded the letter by burning it in the brazier of a man roasting hot chestnuts, completely ignoring the man's indignant cries, as he watched the letter crumple to ashes.

Then a client of his of had left a newspaper behind and, not being one to waste anything, Wardlock read it through. He was reminded of the time he tried to forbid his wife and step-daughters from reading newspapers, only to have his wife confront him. Why, pray? She asked. And he vaguely replied it was unladylike. The real reason was the possibility they might see some article concerning a certain cunning trickster—himself—whom the police could never find, although they were diligently following every possible lead. Over the years Wardlock had carefully cut out and kept all these articles.

In that particular newspaper Wardlock had, there happened to be a paragraph or two about one of the sons of Lord Barrandale, a profligate and spendthrift from the sound of it. But was not this Lord Lonsdale another son of Lord Barrandale? The very man who had been at his house? Here was another opportunity that must not be missed. Now he could deal with the remaining girl and then be rid of all of them.

Returning to his house in haste Wardlock actually encountered the girl on the staircase, even more proof the gods were with him. But again something went wrong. He had not expected her to withstand him or speak to him the way she did. He was so incensed, that he could not recollect everything that occurred afterwards, but he did remember striking out with his cane and dragging the wretched girl to her room and throwing her to the floor, only to have the servant woman defy and thwart him. He also remembered demanding the key from the woman before leaving the house.

On his return later that evening Wardlock stepped slowly out of the cab and waited for it to leave, while he stared at the house. There was not a single light on, which did not surprise him, nor did he ever expect anyone to wait up for him. He opened the front door and felt for the candle and matches on the little table just inside. He had spent the evening, without a twinge of conscience, with female company and had perhaps imbibed a trifle too much. It required three matches, to his chagrin, before he managed to light the candle without burning his fingers, and the flame cast shaky shadows.

He stood at the bottom of the stairs and looked upwards. Insolent girl! How dare she accuse him so! And she had continued to see this so-called gentleman behind his back when he had expressly forbidden her to do so. He would turn her out onto the streets where she belonged, the common little piece, and he would dismiss that servant woman for her insolence, too.

He would also dismiss that wretched boy, whatever his name was. Came from the East End of London, did he? Well, that alone proved he would never be up to any good. He should never have allowed the boy to come in the first place. Well, it was late, so he would deal with everything in the morning.

He reached the top of the stairs somewhat out of breath. Confound that fool of a doctor, nothing the man gave him seemed to do any good. All was quiet as Wardlock looked towards Caroline's bedroom door. The fact he had left her lying on the floor troubled him not one whit. His lips curled in an unpleasant smile as he turned towards his own door.

Everything was as it always had been. He suspected nothing.

Chapter Thirty-Five

Father and Son

It was a bright, starry night which Dashell hardly noticed as he walked slowly and wearily back to Park Lane, still feeling Caroline's soft cheek against his own. He had done all he could and she was safe now, and the efforts of Hannah and Johnny were nothing short of amazing.

When Matthew opened the door to him and then enquired if he had yet dined, Dashell realized he had not eaten at all. "I believe Cook has kept something hot for you," said Matthew, glancing discreetly at his young master's tired, strained face. He had never known Lord Lonsdale so concerned over a woman before.

"Thank you, Matthew, I will have something. Has my father returned yet?"

"Yes, sir. Lord Barrandale is in the small salon. I believe he is waiting to see you."

Dashell smiled to himself. He knew exactly why his father was waiting to see him.

Matthew coughed slightly and said, "Stephen requested me to inform you, sir, that the young man who called here earlier today would not return with him tonight."

"Would not return?" repeated Dashell. Perhaps it was because he was tired after all the events of the last several hours that he felt a flash of annoyance, even anger. He was not used to being disobeyed. "Would you send Stephen to me." While he waited he went into the salon to see his father. "I trust you enjoyed your evening, sir?"

"Ah, yes, Dashell. I did, thank you," said Barrandale. "Allenby sends you his regards and hopes you might join him another time. I told him you had a prior engagement, and he has no idea what, of course. I was very discreet. How was your evening?" he enquired meaningfully, narrowing his eyes.

"Not at all good," Dashell admitted ruefully. Footsteps sounded in the hall. "If you would excuse me, sir, I wish to speak to Stephen. I will join you after I have had something to eat."

"Very well," said Barrandale. It must have been a trying time if his son had not yet dined.

Dashell went out into the hall. "Stephen, I understand Johnny did not come back with you tonight. Why was that? Do you know where he is?"

"He said he would not come back as he had things to do in the house, sir," replied Stephen. "He did not say what. I offered to wait for him, but he said no. That is all I know. I hope I did the right thing, sir" he added, seeing Lord Lonsdale's deep frown.

"Yes, of course, Stephen. I expect Johnny will be all right. Thank you, you may go."

Dashell's thoughts troubled him somewhat during his meal. He was uneasy about Johnny. Why had it been necessary for the boy to go back into the house at all? What else did he have to do? Surely he was not going to wait to challenge Wardlock. That would be quite foolish with a vicious man like that. Dashell did not wish to have to inform Caroline that Johnny had been injured too.

Dashell had to remind himself that Johnny was not his servant and therefore did not have to heed his orders. He had long ago recognised that Johnny was a law unto himself, and that he was a very resourceful young man, and he had to content himself with that. A few minutes later Dashell went to join his father.

"I need not inform you why I have been waiting," said Barrandale with a faint smile as Dashell sat down. "I am all agog to learn what has happened. I trust Caroline is all right?"

"She is as well as can be expected. And thank you for your concern."

Barrandale's eyes widened in surprise. "That does not sound like a good beginning."

So Dashell related all that had happened after he left the house in so great a haste: Hannah's fears at being left alone while Caroline lay unconscious; Dr.Meldicott being fetched and having to allay his fears, even suspicions; the journey in the cab to Grosvenor Square; and Aunt Letty's horror at the extent of Caroline's injuries. "I think Aunt Letty is somewhat apprehensive about explaining to you her involvement in the situation, but it was I who got her into it," concluded Dashell.

Barrandale had listened incredulously to everything. "Do you mean Wardlock just left that girl lying on the floor?" He shook his head in disbelief. "What a heartless scoundrel."

"As I was saying," continued Dashell, after a moment's pause, "when travelling back in the cab Hannah intimated to me that she had been keeping certain knowledge to herself, not daring to tell anyone. And I still want to know exactly what occurred between Caroline and Wardlock."

"What about this Johnny?" queried Barrandale. "I am still amazed he ran all the way from Fulham to find you. It must be what, three or four miles?" Again he shook his head in disbelief, then suddenly asked, "Where is Johnny?"

"I wish I knew," answered Dashell. "I told him earlier he could come here and sleep in the loft above the stables, as I did not want him to stay in that house overnight. However Stephen informed me just now that Johnny would not return with him. I have no idea what he could be doing."

After a few moments of silence, during which time Dashell had gone to stand by the mantelpiece with one elbow leaning on it, he slowly said, "Do you know, when I saw Caroline with her broken arm and those bruises on her lovely face, I felt that if Wardlock had still been there, that I could almost have killed him."

Barrandale looked up quickly at his son's darkened face and away again. "I trust you will reconsider that remark, Dashell," he said carefully, "for a scandal like that would kill me also."

Dashell was startled out of his reverie, appalled at what he had just said. "I do sincerely beg your pardon, sir. I did not really mean that, I—" he floundered to a stop. What a fool—how much he and his father would lose!

Barrandale yawned tactfully. "I think we had both better retire to bed. It has been a full day for both of us, and it is getting late."

Chapter Thirty-Six
Wardlock Calls at Barrandale House

Wardlock awoke in the morning later than his usual time and it took him a while to realise there were no sounds of movement in the house. Picking up his watch from his bedside table he gave an exclamation of surprise and got up to ring the bell. Where was that wretched woman with his hot water? She should have brought it long ago. After a few more minutes he rang the bell once more, but still there was no answer, which did nothing to improve his temper. He angrily flung on his dressing robe and shuffled into some slippers and went out onto the landing. It was quiet. Too quiet.

A suspicion began to creep into his mind. Going along to Caroline's bedroom he turned the handle of the door and pushed it open, at the same time remembering it was supposed to be locked and he had the key. He stepped inside and stared in amazement at the emptiness. Hurrying over to the dressing table he pulled out all the drawers, and did the same with the chest. All empty. And there was nothing hanging in the wardrobe, either. Except for the bed clothes, everything had gone as though spirited away. So that was why there had been no answer to the bell, that woman had gone too.

He turned to leave the room and stopped short at the sight of a key in the lock. Curiously he turned it several times and watched the bolt shoot out, back, out and back again. So what was the key he had been given? Shuffling to his room to fetch it he tried it in the lock. It did not turn. So which lock did it fit? The next nearest room was the one once occupied by Maude, who was obviously as bad as her sister. Hussies, both of them. Then he tried the lock in the door of the room previously used by his late wife. The key would not turn. He knew it did not fit his own lock, so that just left one other door, although he did not know what lay behind it. He tried the key and it turned with ease, revealing a linen cupboard. Again, he turned the key several times, locking and unlocking, opening and shutting the door, and in so doing dislodged the piece of cloth that had wedged the door shut. So he had been tricked! That woman had deliberately given him the wrong key so she could still get into Caroline's room. He would not forget that. Enraged, he gave vent to his feelings by kicking the door.

Where had they gone? How had they gone? There must have been a vehicle of some kind; and there was only one other person who would be involved. His lips curled back in a vicious snarl. He would pay a call on this fine gentleman friend of hers. To call upon the very people whose ranks he had once aspired to join but had never been accepted, because those same people sensed there was something about him that did not quite ring true. How right they were, and how he hated them for it.

He returned to his room and dressed hurriedly and left the house, slamming the front door hard behind him. He was half-way along the road before he realized that he had not shaved nor eaten breakfast, nor could he for there was no hot water, and arrived at the inn demanding some kind of conveyance. The inn-keeper, not liking the look of Wardlock, suggested he tried going down to the end of the road to get a cab there. Wardlock protested he could not walk that far, and indeed he did not look well, so the inn-keeper offered to send someone to fetch a cab for him, if the gentleman cared to wait.

Word was sent for Johnny to go. There was no sign of Johnny, Perkins grimly replied. He hadn't seen him since yesterday afternoon when he left early and without permission. Where was he, then? Perkins did not know, but when he did show up he knew of a well-known, well-heated place where all stableboys could go and that one in particular.

The situation was becoming critical when a cab came along from the direction of London. It was waved down but the cab driver shook his head to say the cab was engaged, and then half-turned round and raised his hand to indicate he would come back when he had dropped off his passenger. Thankfully, the inn-keeper went indoors and Wardlock was left to fume while he waited outside. The cab driver, pleased to have another fare so soon, returned quickly to pick up Wardlock.

Dashell had spent a restless night and by seven o'clock was out on Sparkle cantering round Hyde Park. He went round twice before he felt his head had cleared.

At the breakfast table Barrandale enquired what Dashell's plans were for the day, for he felt a certain person could possibly be calling and he would prefer Dashell to be present.

"I have already thought of that," said Dashell, "and yes, I will be here when he comes, after what he did to Caroline," he added savagely, only to look up and encounter a warning frown from his father.

Dashell was longing to see Caroline and to know how she was. However, decorum and set manners would not permit a call until much later in the morning. About an hour later, as though in answer to his thoughts, Lady Smythe's maid was sent round with a note to the effect that Caroline had spent a reasonably restful night, and that Dr.Meldicott was expected to call within an hour or so, as he had indicated to Hannah he would. Dashell knew his aunt well enough to know she was asking him not to call too soon, and that all was well.

Wardlock was still fuming when he arrived at Barrandale House. Curtly ordering the cab to wait, he rang the bell and knocked impatiently, then shrilled at Matthew when he opened the door, and demanded to see Lord Lonsdale.

Matthew was privately scandalized as yet another dishevelled person stood on the doorstep demanding to see Lord Lonsdale, but only worse this time. "If you care to wait here, sir," said Matthew impassively, "I will see if his lordship is in."

"Of course he is in. I know he is in. And I will not wait on the doorstep. I demand to come in." So saying, Wardlock pushed his way past the butler into the hall.

"What name shall I say, sir?" How did Lord Lonsdale come to know such dreadful people?

"Wardlock. Thomas Wardlock," he snapped.

Wardlock? wondered Matthew. That name sounded familiar. Where had he heard it before? Oh, good heavens, surely not that lady's parent. What in the world was happening? He really would consider handing in his notice if the daughter was anything like the father.

Impassively he opened the door to the library where both their lordships were writing. Barrandale had just finished one or two letters, and Dashell was still trying to draft one out to send to likely parish incumbents. Again they had both heard voices in the hall and had looked at each other significantly as Dashell laid down his pen. Before Matthew could make an announcement Wardlock had rudely pushed his way past him again, and with an apologetic look at Lord Barrandale, Matthew closed the door.

"You there!" cried Wardlock, addressing Dashell, and completely ignoring Lord Barrandale. "Where is my daughter? I demand to know where she is."

Barrandale thought he had never seen such a vile looking man before, and Dashell on his part was appalled at the change in the man. He had looked bad enough when he had first met him at Becket Lane, but now he looked ill and grey and shrunken somehow, and he must have left in a hurry for he needed a shave.

"Do you know where Caroline is?" Wardlock cried again, his voice rising. "And do not pretend you know nothing."

"Of course I know where she is, and I shall know where she is for the rest of my life."

"Hah! So she is here. So you did take her."

"Yes. I did take her, but she is not here. Caroline is in a place of safety."

"A place of safety indeed," sneered Wardlock. "Why does she need one? And how did she get there? Let me tell you, sir, you dared to enter my house and had the audacity to abduct my daughter."

"I entered your house and rescued your step-daughter, after you left her lying unconscious on the floor of a locked room with a broken arm," declared Dashell.

Wardlock blinked in surprise and gave a start at that piece of information. He had no idea he had broken Caroline's arm, although in the confusion he did remember raising his cane to her before that woman interfered. "How did you know she was injured anyway?" he asked. "Who told you?"

Dashell surveyed him with ever growing dislike. "Johnny ran all the way here to tell me." He said this to try and judge from the reply whether or not Wardlock had seen the boy, as he was still concerned about Johnny's non-appearance.

Unfortunately, Wardlock did not say anything. Instead he looked as though he did not believe Dashell, although his thoughts raged inwardly. That boy and that woman must be in league against him, considering the way they had both thwarted him. Another thought came to him and a crafty look spread over his face. "I understand you have mentioned marriage to her."

"Yes," replied Dashell. "It is my intention to marry Caroline."

Wardlock sneered again. "She is not of age and I will never give my consent."

Dashell realized in an instant his intended call to speak to Wardlock would have been absolutely useless. "Fortunately, we do not need your consent'" he said. "You are not Caroline's real father and we have our own ways and means of finding who was. When we have found her family we can then approach her nearest male relative."

That non-plussed Wardlock at first, until he slowly began to laugh, knowing he had all those documents and papers hidden away behind that secret panel. He must go back and burn them. "You will never, never find out. You cannot. It is impossible." His laughter became a high-pitched cackle causing him to catch his breath, which in turn reduced him to coughing. Father and son looked at each other in alarm. Barrandale for one did not want this man to become ill in his house and require assistance, but Dashell was too angry.

"You damnable scoundrel!" cried Dashell. "You absolute blackguard! By George, if you were a younger man I would give you such a thrashing—" He stopped short at the feel of a firm hand on his arm.

"Sir," said Barrandale in his cool, authoritative voice, "I find you quite disgusting and your presence here is extremely distasteful. You will leave, and you can find your own way out."

Once more Wardlock felt rebuffed. He had tried his worst with the gentry and had failed, and with Dashell pointedly holding the library door open, he was forced to go. A moment later the front door slammed shut. Dashell moved quickly to a window to make sure he really left, and watched as Wardlock swore at the cab driver and then lean out of the cab window, shaking his fist and mouthing obscenities.

Dashell turned round. "That man makes me feel positively ill. I do not know how those three women managed to live with him." Even as he said those words he recalled Caroline's remark that they saw very little of him. "Do you think he could cause trouble? He could deny he ever assaulted Caroline. He could say that she too fell down the stairs. They are rather steep, incidentally."

"I don't think so," replied Barrandale carefully. "There is the evidence of the two servants, and this Dr. Meldicott."

Dashell was not entirely satisfied. The evidence of mere servants was not always considered reliable or necessary. "I am sorry it had to come to this, sir, I must apologize for Wardlock's behaviour. I sincerely hope we have seen the last of him."

"Let me just say that, like you, I am thankful your lady is safe and out of that house, as you have so described it to me. Now, if you please, I shall return to what I was doing."

Dashell likewise turned back to his own writing, but found he could not concentrate. That tirade from Wardlock that he would never find out Caroline's true parentage had angered him, and made him all the more determined to search. But there was something else troubling him. After some minutes he put down his pen in exasperation. "I wish I knew where Johnny was. What can be keeping him? If he is not here in an hour or so I shall go to Fulham to see what I can find out. I can at least make enquiries at the inn."

Barrandale glanced up from his writing but made no comment. He was not going to point out the fact that it would also mean calling at Becket Lane and seeing Wardlock again. However, he did make one observation, "You seem remarkably concerned for that young man and his whereabouts."

"I owe him too much not to be," replied Dashell, thinking what a wonderful ally Johnny had proven to be ever since their first meeting in Becket Lane.

Chapter Thirty-Seven
Johnny Again

It was Wardlock slamming the front door that same morning that awakened Johnny, not fully at first. When he heard the sound of footsteps on the path and the creaking of the gate being swung open, he quickly struggled up to peer out of the tree stump, and grinned at the sight of Mr. Wardlock setting out along the road shaking his fist. Ha! He must have found that Miss Caroline and Hannah were no longer there.

Yawning, he stretched himself leisurely. He must have slept right through the dawn chorus for it was now bright daylight and he had no idea what time it was. He pulled on his boots, thinking he had to get to Park Lane as soon as he could with the things he had found, and wouldn't the Guv and Miss Caroline be pleased. But he had some things to do first, so he would have to leave them in the tree stump, although he hated having to do that. With a sigh he shook out his pillow and blankets and took them back to his room.

He was curious to know what it was like upstairs and went to investigate. The doors to the linen cupboard and Miss Caroline's room were open, as were the wardrobe and the drawers of the chest and dressing table. The old buzzard must have been hopping mad when he realized he had been tricked. Still chuckling to himself, Johnny went downstairs for a makeshift breakfast.

He would have to hurry. He would have to call on the postman and explain Miss Caroline had gone to stay with friends and Hannah was with her, and would he please keep any letters for Miss Caroline at the Post Office. He would also have to speak to the innkeeper and tell him he could not work at the inn any more. He was rather sorry about that since he liked being there. He put his breakfast dishes on the draining board alongside the ones he had used last night. 'Is Nibs would realize someone had been there and that would make him even more hopping mad.

Johnny set off at a run to the postman's house, thankful to find him in, and quickly explained the situation about the letters, and ran off again before he was asked too many questions. On his way back he stopped at the inn to speak to the innkeeper and pick up his pay for that week and to say he could not work there any more.

Again time was pressing. It would just be his luck to leave the house and meet 'Is Nibs coming back. Johnny was not afraid of Mr. Wardlock, he never had been, for he knew enough about street fighting to easily get the better of him.

He fetched the linen bag and the portrait from the tree stump and took them indoors. There were two other things he was going to take with him: the double portrait of Miss Maude and Miss Caroline and that nice picture with Windsor Castle in the distance the mistress had painted and which still hung in her bedroom. He knew both were very precious to Miss Caroline for he had heard her talking about them to Hannah.

Johnny went back to the linen cupboard for a pillowcase and put the three pictures into it and tied a stout cord round it with a makeshift handle. Then, with the linen bag tied round his waist under his coat, he left the house. The cheapest way to Park Lane would be to walk, but that package was too heavy and too precious. The other way would be to get a cab and arrive in style, which would mean parting with some coins but he would not mind doing that—not for the Guv and Miss Caroline. It would mean patiently waiting at the inn or going down to the stand at the end of the road.

Johnny chose to wait at the inn, and when a cab did come along he hailed it. It did not stop but he knew the driver had seen him. He stared at the cab as it passed, then quickly dashed to the corner to watch it go down the lane exactly as the other cab had done yesterday. It must be 'is Nibs coming back. They had just missed each other. What a laugh! Johnny waited for the cab to return and hailed it again.

"Where to?" enquired the driver as he pulled up.

"Barrandale House, Park Lane," replied Johnny.

"Gor blimey!" the driver cried, "I've just come from there!" glaring at Johnny suspiciously.

"Did you drop off just now a very bad tempered old man?"

"Did I ever," he exclaimed. "Picked him up right here a while ago, took him to that house and waited for him, and he came out cursing and swearing. Short-changed me, he did. I was damned glad to get rid of him." He eyed Johnny again. "Why do you want to know?"

"I used to work for him," Johnny said, with all innocence. "Well, can you take me then?"

"Show me your money first," the man growled. Satisfied at the sight of the coins in Johnny's hand, he jerked his head, and Johnny stepped into the cab, being very careful with the package, laughing to himself all the way to Park Lane. He paid the required fare plus a few extra pennies. He felt the man deserved them.

Johnny looked at the front door and the steps up which he had bounded only yesterday. It seemed much longer ago than that, as so much had happened. Making sure the linen bag was secure and hefting up the package again, he knocked on the door.

"Good afternoon," he said to Matthew, who came to answer the door, and remembering to be polite, "Is Lord Lonsdale in? I have some very important fings to show 'im."

Matthew, of course, recognized Johnny at once and glanced at the package. Any other time he would have told him to go round to the servants' entrance to deliver anything he was carrying, but he had learned enough from Stephen's guarded comments that something was "going on". "I shall enquire if his lordship is at home."

Matthew entered the room where both their lordships were sitting and with an apologetic cough to Lord Barrandale, announced, "Lord Lonsdale, the young man who came here yesterday wishes to see you. He says he has some very important things to show you. Shall I show him into a private room?"

Dashell gave a joyful exclamation and glanced at his father. "No, Matthew, show him in here. Where have you been, Johnny?" he cried, as the boy was ushered in. "What kept you? I was almost ready to go back to that house to look for you. Matthew told me you have something important to show me." Upon which words an astonished Matthew closed the door. Really, whatever next.

"Yes, Guv, I 'ave. Oh, good morning, your lordship," he said on catching sight of Lord Barrandale, "I'm sure."

"Good morning," replied Barrandale gravely, but with a hint of a smile.

Johnny handed the bulky linen bag to Dashell. "I went back to the 'ouse to finish looking for these," he stated simply. "'annah an' me 'ad been looking for them."

"What do you mean you had been looking for them?" queried Dashell.

"Well," gulped Johnny, "'annah was quite sure they existed, an' she told me yesterday morning where she thought they could be 'idden."

Dashell, still not fully comprehending, had emptied out the contents onto a table as his father came to join him, and both stared in amazement at the documents and the bundle of old newspaper cuttings that fell out.

Johnny could not help saying, "I 'ad a quick look at 'em to make sure they wuz wot we 'ad been looking for, beggin' yer pardon," his conscience pricking him for once.

By now Dashell had seized and opened a document and found it to be the birth certificate of Caroline's sister, and read: "Maude Eleanor, born to Isobel Louise, wife of Arthur Hemsley Waterton, gentleman, in the parish of Sutherfield, in Sussex County." One of the names on his list! He searched for the other one, "Where is it?" he cried. Barrandale had already found it and silently handed it to Dashell, who opened it with trembling hands. There it was, with the same wording. "Caroline Diana, born to Isobel Louise, wife of Arthur Hemsley Waterton, gentleman, in the parish of Sutherfield, in Sussex County." "Johnny, this is wonderful!" cried Dashell in amazement. "How and where in the world did you find them? Did Wardlock have them?"

"Yes, Guv, 'e did."

Dashell swore under his breath. "I knew it. And I would like to know how he got hold of them." He looked again at the document he was still holding. Caroline need not have any more doubts about herself. Her real name was Waterton, daughter of a landed gentleman, and she could now hold up her head in the eyes of the world. Dashell's own private fears the two sisters might have been illegitimate were now dispelled for ever. There was no need to pay any attention to Wardlock's threats to never reveal Caroline's true identity to block their marriage. Surely nothing now could stand in their way.

"Please, Guv." pleaded Johnny, "'ow is Miss Caroline? I 'ave to arsk."

"She is doing as well as can be expected," replied Dashell with an understanding smile. "Apparently Dr.Meldicott called at Grosvenor Square earlier this morning to see her, as he said he would, and is satisfied with her progress. He does not think there is any lasting damage. That reminds me. In the carriage yesterday Hannah told me she had some things she had been keeping to herself, not daring to tell anyone, but feels she can speak up now that Caroline is out of Wardlock's clutches. Do you know what this could be about?"

Johnny was quite non-plussed and could shed no light on the matter at all, except to say, "She was dreadfully upset when the Missus died, and cried a lot. She said she missed her very much. Well, we all did. It wuz terrible, just when Miss Maude and Miss Caroline came 'ome." He still felt Hannah had rather overdone the weeping; and was also puzzled and annoyed she had been keeping some things from him.

Looking at Johnny levelly Dashell asked, "And is there anything you have been keeping to yourself for the same reason, not daring to tell anyone?"

Returning that level look and suddenly appearing more like a young man than a boy, Johnny quietly said, "Yes, Guv, I 'ave."

"Ah, I guessed as much. And Wardlock again, I suppose," Dashell added as Johnny nodded. "I will get Hannah and you together later and we can talk about it. Maybe some more light can be shed on all this mystery." Dashell caught sight again of the package Johnny had so carefully set on the floor, which momentarily had been put to one side. "What have you got there, Johnny. Something else from that house?"

While Dashell and Johnny had been talking Barrandale had been looking through the newspaper cuttings, but put them aside at the mention of the intriguing package.

"Yes, Guv, an' just you wait and see." Johnny was so certain of the profound effect it would have. He had been longing to show what he had found and now he could hardly contain himself. He undid the cord, watched curiously by the two men, and with the widest smile he could muster, held up the portrait for them to see.

They both gasped out loud, and Dashell almost shouted, "That's Caroline father! It must be! Where did you find it?"

"It was 'idden in an empty room at the top of the 'ouse," explained Johnny gleefully.

"How did you know it was there?" queried Dashell. "Caroline never mentioned it to me."

"She did not know it was there. No one did, except the missus."

Dashell stared at Johnny, thinking there was a tremendous amount of explaining to be done. He took hold of the portrait and held it up for a closer look, then turned it round. There was writing on the back, somewhat faded, but still readable. "To my darling Arthur," he read out loud, "On the occasion of your twenty-fifth birthday". Twenty-fifth birthday," he repeated, "Why, that's just about my age." He turned the portrait round again and the eyes looked straight at him. Those eyes! Just like someone else's. There was no doubt in Dashell's mind that this was Caroline's father, and even though she greatly resembled her mother he could discern the likeness between her and this parent. Oh, just wait until she saw this painting for herself!

"Look at those initials in the bottom right hand corner," he said, pointing to them, "the same as the ones on that double portrait. ILW. Isobel Louise Waterton. Isobel Louise Wardlock." He watched as Johnny picked up that painting of the two sisters. "Oh, Johnny, don't tell me you even brought that one as well."

"Yes, I did. Guv. An 'ere's the one from the Missus's room. I 'eard Miss Caroline telling 'annah somefink about it once an'—well, I thought yer might like that one as well," he finished rather lamely.

Dashell could not help laughing. "Johnny, you just about think of everything." He held up both paintings. "Look at these, sir."

"I am looking," replied Barrandale. "I am amazed. Intrigued, in fact."

"Johnny," said Dashell, "I am truly grateful to you, more than I can say."

Johnny coloured up. "Thank you," he muttered, too embarrassed to say much else.

To break an awkward silence Barrandale called out to Dashell, "Come and finish looking at the rest of these documents I have been going through. Here is the marriage licence between Arthur Waterton and Isobel Frobisher and the one between Isobel and Thomas Wardlock; the birth certificates of the two girls; and the death certificates of Isobel and Maude. And here is the last will and testament of Wardlock. Rather old, it seems. Strange he did not make a more recent one." Neither of them noticed Johnny lift his gaze to the ceiling, looking as though butter would not melt in his mouth. It gave him quite a pious look. "We must, of course, give it back to him," remarked Barrandale.

"It will be the only thing we do give back to him, "said Dashell grimly.

That brought Johnny back to earth with a bump. Giving the old will back to Wardlock would prompt him to ask the whereabouts of the other one. *Oh, damn and blast,* he thought.

"But just look at this marriage contract between Wardlock and Isobel," continued Barrandale. "It seems absolutely strange, even cold." He waited patiently while his son read it through.

Dashell looked up in wonder. "Well, I'll be damned, begging your pardon, sir, but doesn't this explain so much that puzzled Caroline and her sister? Now I understand why they never saw much of him." Turning to Johnny again he said, "I am curious, Johnny. Where exactly did you sleep last night? Not in that house, I hope."

"Not on yer life, Guv, but near enough," Johnny replied as a wide grin spread over his face. "I slept in that 'uge 'ollow tree at the end of the driveway, by the road. Bit of a tight fit it was, an' all, as I 'ad everyfink wiv me. I knew 'e'd never fink of looking fer me there."

Both men laughed. "Quite ingenious," remarked Barrandale. "Now, Dashell," he continued, "I am sure you are most anxious to tell Caroline all this wonderful news, but before you go we must decide what to do with this brave young man, for on no account can he go back to that house."

Dashell agreed. "Perhaps Johnny could sleep in the stable loft? I am sure Reuben or Stephen could find a place for him."

Barrandale summoned Matthew and explained the situation, and Johnny was introduced to the other servants, who wondered at his being there.

Cook, however, was none too pleased at first at having a Cockney boy in her kitchen, thinking he would be more than cheeky and even scruffy—but orders were orders—and was agreeably surprised to find him pleasant and well-mannered. Needless to say, Matthew was greatly relieved to learn that Thomas Wardlock was only a step-father, no blood relation at all to Miss Wardlock.

Chapter Thirty-Eight
The Death of Thomas Wardlock

After the cab with its disgruntled passenger stopped outside the house on Becket Lane, Wardlock intended to waste no time in carrying out his plan of burning those revealing documents. There were two things, however, that had to be considered first. One was the fact that he got out of breath if he hurried too much, and the other was that he was getting very hungry.

He went up the steps to the front door carefully, grumbling to himself all the while, but still managed to slam the door angrily behind him. He would find something to eat first then take leisurely time to watch those papers burn. He cackled to himself at the mere thought of it. That fancy lord would never get the better of him, Wardlock would make sure of that. And that foolish girl would never be able to know her real name. How clever he had been at finding those documents, and when his wife refused to tell him where all her money was, dealing with her had been surprisingly easy. And the way the other girl had tripped and fallen down the stairs and broken her neck was too good to be true. Serve her right for daring to question his authority. However, it was a pity that the other girl had eluded him.

Wardlock went towards the door leading from the hall to the kitchen. The place reminded him again of his lowly beginnings, when at times the little group of actors he had been born into performed for the gentry and were sent to the kitchens afterwards for some refreshments. Pah! He was much better than they were. Had he not acted his way among them until he felt he was better than any one of them? Except for that faint feeling of rejection that never really went away.

He stopped short, taken by surprise at the sight of used dishes and cutlery on the draining board where Johnny had deliberately left them. Caroline and that other woman had gone, leaving only that wretched boy. It must have been him. And he had the sheer audacity to be in the house overnight. If only Wardlock had known!

Hunger prompted him again. He needed to find the pantry but did not know which door led to it. It so happened that the first door he tried opened into Johnny's little room, where he had dumped his pillow and blankets from his overnight stay in the tree stump straight onto his bed in an untidy heap. Wardlock recoiled in disgust, and turned sharply away. He realized at once that he should not have moved so quickly as the effort made him feel a little dizzy, and he leaned his hand against a wall and waited until his head cleared. Then he opened the next likely door which this time did lead to the pantry. Bread, some cheese and butter, some milk that was beginning to turn, and a leg of ham hanging from a hook in the ceiling. Only there was no knife to slice the ham.

Back he went to the kitchen to find clean utensils, for he was not going to use the ones left on the draining board. It infuriated him to think that boy had been in the house overnight, as he must have been, for where else would he have slept? After rummaging around he found what he wanted, returned to the pantry and began cramming food into his mouth. He ate quickly for it was too cold to stay there for long, and then returned to the kitchen where it was not much better. The fire grate in the wall was empty, except for a little pile of ashes which meant nothing to him.

He noticed the coil of sacking on the floor which had been pushed to one side when he opened the door to come in. It must have been put there to prevent any light from being seen under the door. That boy again! Why had he ever allowed him to come?

Enough time had gone by. Now Wardlock had to do what he really had in mind. It might be chilly here but there would be a fire set ready in his room as usual. He must go through those newspaper cuttings again and only keep the good ones, and burn everything else.

What incompetent fools the authorities were, and how brilliant he had been. He liked one particular article that said he should have made the stage his career. But not really, not to act given characters with words written for them in arranged settings. No, time and again he had created his own characters, words and situations. That, he felt, was the true indication of his greatness, and he had never been caught.

Wardlock crossed the hall to his own room, when something on the floor caught his eye and roused his curiosity. He stooped to look closer. Fresh gouge marks and scratches? Not all the way along, but as though some heavy object had been carried, put down because of weight, and then pushed, and the marks led towards the staircase. Curiosity now fully aroused he followed the marks and found a door under the stairs. He never even knew there was a door there. Oh! Perhaps this was where the money was hidden. He was still obsessed with the possibility of finding it. Eagerly he felt around and found the catch and opened the cupboard. Disappointed and disgusted he found there was only a very large wooden box.

He was about to turn away when he thought again that those marks on the floor looked fresh, and what was in the box anyway? He tried to tug it out but it was too heavy. Instead he tried lifting the lid.—Ah! it was not locked. Putting a hand inside, he felt fabric and pulled out a dress, and stared at it in amazement. He pulled out another, and then a third. Why would dresses, obviously female attire, be packed away like this? Whose were they?

His lips curled. Caroline! Who else's would they be? So that fancy man of hers must have bought them for her and she had accepted them. What a shameless little hussy! Had they been planning to elope? Then those words he had hurled at her days ago in the front room in the presence of Lord Lonsdale, had been correct. Wardlock had been right all along. What a pity that woman had interfered yesterday.

Wardlock fingered the dresses again. They were certainly not silk or satin, as might have been expected, but that was neither here nor there. He had no way of knowing his step-daughters had worn these dresses at that School, or that two of them had been Maude's and had been altered to fit Caroline. But he did know what he was going to do.

Carrying one dress with him Wardlock returned to the kitchen for that sharp carving knife still on the draining board and, holding the dress up, he sliced it from neckline to hemline, and let it fall to the floor. Still holding the knife he went back to the hall, sliced off the sleeves of the second dress and hacked at the hemline of the third dress. He felt inside the box again and found a fourth dress. He should have put Caroline out of the house long ago. Holding it up, he sliced it from top to bottom just like the first one.

By now the exertion was taking its toll. He had not expected to encounter the box under the stairs or its contents, and he was beginning to feel giddy again. He needed to go and sit down. Dropping the knife on the floor Wardlock made his way carefully to his room, sliding his hand along walls for support. He must keep his strength to do what he had to do, he kept telling himself. How fortunate it was he had taken those documents from his wife, and it was her misfortune she had been so tiresome about it.

Shivering slightly, for the room felt chilly, Wardlock went over to the fireplace to light the fire to get a good blaze going. A queer sound came from his mouth that was meant to be a laugh. Yes, he would get the last laugh on them all, the whole lot of them, including all those whom he had duped and cheated over the years. And in particular that Lord Lonsdale, who once had the audacity to threaten him in his own house, and that stupid girl who had dared to stand up to him. He would make sure they were never able to marry. Another odd sound came from him.

The fire was now strongly burning in the grate and he added some more wood. He pulled a little key from his pocket, unlocked the secret panel and swivelled it open, lifted the black metal box off the shelf and held it for a moment before placing it on his desk. He unlocked the lid and gave a shout of complete surprise and stared in open-mouthed amazement at the emptiness inside. How could it possibly be empty? His eyes must be playing tricks. Scooping his hands round inside produced nothing, nor did shaking the box upside down. Nobody else knew the box was there so how had everything disappeared?

Wardlock stumbled back to the shelf thinking he had misplaced the contents, but nothing was there. Had he taken them to his bedroom for some reason? He took a step or two towards the door but knew he would never be able to climb those stairs, for he was beginning to find it difficult to breathe. He returned to the box and stared into it, half expecting the contents to reappear. He brushed his hands across his eyes. Surely they must be playing tricks.

Only able to take shallow breaths he stood motionless, trying to think. That woman, that boy. Always that woman, that boy. Could they have found the box? How could they have found it? The fire crackled and shifted in the grate. They had won after all, and the newspaper cuttings would give Wardlock's game away. All his cunning and covering up of his tracks wasted. All his years of brilliant acting come to nothing. This was the final rejection. The final defeat.

Wardlock shook his fists furiously in the air and gave a long hoarse scream of rage. Then with a different cry, he clutched his chest as a violent pain seared through it and along his left arm, and he staggered about choking and gasping for air, then fell to the floor and lay still.

The fire in the grate burned itself out for want of attention.

Chapter Thirty-Nine

Dashell and Caroline

Dashell was eagerly on his way to his aunt's house, taking that precious document with him. How amazed and astonished Caroline would be!

Left on his own, Barrandale read the other documents again for interest's sake. *That's rather odd,* he thought to himself, *there does not appear to be a death certificate for Sir Arthur Waterton. I wonder if Dashell noticed.* He sighed and shook his head as he remembered Dashell's observation that as one mystery cleared up another one appeared. At least now there was proof that those girls were legitimate. He also knew his son would not rest until it was all cleared up, and prayed Dashell knew what he was doing.

With another sigh Barrandale turned his attention to the bundle of old newspaper cuttings, for there had to be some reason why Wardlock kept them all. Some of them were quite old, yellowing with age, and were in some kind of chronological order. As Barrandale read them he recollected seeing some of the articles himself in the newspapers, although he had not paid a great deal of attention to them at the time.

Dashell had not noticed anything missing among all the documents, as his mind was too full of the amazing fact that Caroline's real name was now known. Chadwick opened the door to him and Dashell promptly said he would announce himself before running upstairs.

He knocked briefly on the salon door completely startling his aunt. "Aunt Letty!" he cried, "you will never guess! Some wonderful news! It's about Caroline."

"I might have known!"

Dashell sat down beside his aunt and thrust the document into her hands. "Here, read it. We now know Caroline's real name."

She read the document in astonishment and glanced up quickly at Dashell. "This is incredible, amazing. How did you get this?" Wide-eyed, she listened as her nephew explained as best he could what Johnny had been doing yesterday and this morning, and then he described the contents of the linen bag. What was also exciting was that Johnny had even found a painting of Caroline's father done by her mother, who had hidden it for years in the upstairs attic. "But why all this secrecy?" Lady Smythe wondered. "Why did she not want her girls to know?"

"I would like to know that too," replied Dashell. "By the way, after Father and I have dined tonight Hannah and Johnny will be telling us all they know of the situation, for both of them have been keeping things back."

"One moment, Dashell, I am not missing out on any possible revelation of the truth. It's unthinkable. You and your father must dine here this evening, because neither I nor Hannah is going to leave Caroline."

"Very well," laughed Dashell, "and quite possibly more things may be revealed."

"Yes, that could be possible." Lady Smythe looked at the document again. "Waterton," she mused. "The younger daughter of some obscure country squire in some obscure village in Sussex. At least I am glad we can now put a name to that poor girl."

Dashell stood up. "I must see Caroline and try to get her to understand."

"Yes, and I must write a note to your father, and inform Chadwick there will be two more to dine here tonight."

Dashell entered Caroline's room quietly and saw Hannah sitting beside the bed. "Hannah," he said excitedly yet keeping his voice down, "you will never guess, although I am sure you will, but Johnny found those documents you had both been looking for."

Her eyes lit up in delight. "Oh, that's wonderful, sir! I knew he would."

"Look, here is Caroline's birth certificate. And we also have one for her sister Maude."

"So her name is Waterton. That means she need never use that other name ever again. That in itself is a miracle. And there is the name of the village the mistress mentioned, the one I could never remember. Oh, I can hardly believe it."

"And what's more," continued Dashell, "Johnny even found a painting of Sir Arthur Waterton hidden in one of the attic rooms."

"Well, I never," replied Hannah. "He was always asking me about that locked door leading to the attic. It would be just like him to go and find out. What a blessing he did."

A slight sound prompted Dashell to move to the bed and look again at Caroline's once lovely face, now discoloured with bruises. "How is she doing, Hannah?"

"Quite well, sir, considering the circumstances. Dr. Meldicott's sleeping potion has been keeping her rested."

Dashell nodded, feeling relieved. "I must tell her the wonderful news and hope she understands." He pulled over a low chair and sat down, while Hannah tactfully closed the door behind her. He clasped Caroline's right hand, "Dearest," he said softly, "can you hear me?" She moved her head slightly towards the sound of his voice and he thought he could feel a gentle quiver of her fingers. He was overjoyed. Surely this meant she would get better. "Caroline, your birth certificate has been found. We now know your real name. It is Waterton." Once more he thought he felt a slight quiver of her fingers. "Johnny also found a portrait of your father painted by your mother." The lid of her unharmed eye fluttered open for a moment and he fancied she recognised him.

In his eagerness Dashell went on speaking. "Dearest, there is nothing now that can prevent us from marrying. We will get legal consent somehow. You will make a beautiful Lady Lonsdale and you will be mistress of both our town and country houses, and all the gardens will be yours too."

Dashell went on to describe their estate and houses in some length and detail. He ended by saying, "Caroline, please say you will marry me, unless you would rather be the mistress of a teashop." He gave a chuckle at his own joke, half expecting a little smile from her in response. "Please say something to me, or does this mean you refuse me?" he wondered, stammering at the possibility. He took a close careful look at her, observing her regular breathing, and sat back. "Really, Caroline, I don't think you have heard a single word I said."

Indeed she had not, for the residue of the sleeping potion was still strong and she had drifted into sleep again. Dashell gave a little start when his aunt entered the room and he let go of Caroline's hand which he had been holding to his cheek.

"I hope you are not disturbing her, Dashell," Lady Smythe whispered. "You have been here quite a while you know."

"She is asleep. I was just about to leave anyway." Dashell bent down to kiss Caroline's forehead, cheek and hand again, watched by his aunt.

"The boy's besotted," she told her brother later. "I've never known the like."

Chapter Forty

Hannah and Johnny Tell All They Know

Some while later Chadwick announced Lord Barrandale. "Such was your summons and explanation, Letty, my dear," said Barrandale as he sat down, "I just had to come. By the way, Dashell, when young Faulkner comes he will be bringing that portrait with him. Everything else I have locked away in safe keeping. And how is the patient?" he enquired.

Dashell could have talked at length about that subject, but Lady Smythe wanted to hear more about the other things Johnny had found. Barrandale did not mention the apparently missing death certificate for Sir Arthur Waterton, deeming it wiser to wait until Hannah and Johnny had spoken. Nor did he say anything about his rising suspicions and misgivings after perusing Wardlock's old newspaper cuttings, for the same reason.

During their meal they talked of other things in front of the servants but when they returned to the salon they spoke of what was really uppermost in their minds. Lady Smythe's trusted maid sat with Caroline and had been told to inform her ladyship immediately if she felt any concern for her charge.

George had taken Johnny round to Grosvenor Square and while Johnny had only a few minutes to spend with Hannah, he had time to show her the portrait, who was still amazed at its discovery.

When Hannah and Johnny had been ushered into the salon and the portrait shown to Lady Smythe, she exclaimed at once, "Of course he is Caroline's father! How astonished she will be when she sees it." She turned to Johnny. "So you are the young man who found all these things?"

"Yes, yer ladyship," he replied, remembering Hannah's reminder about being polite.

"I am sure Johnny will tell us his story in good time, Aunt Letty," said Dashell, who was eager to hear it all himself, "but Hannah should begin first because we all want to hear everything."

"Before you do begin, Hannah," said Lord Barrandale, "and I know the others would agree with me, you are among friends, so do not be afraid to speak your mind."

"Thank you, your lordship," said Hannah, sounding relieved. So she began.

"I came into my mistress's employment when I was about fifteen. Even at that age I could see that she was very troubled and afraid of something and could hardly bear to let her children out of her sight, as though she was terrified for their safety. Naturally, I thought that Mr. Wardlock was her husband, the father of the two girls." Hannah spoke as though his name was distasteful to mention. "I was surprised at how cold and indifferent he was, but now I know it was no real marriage at all, just a convenience for both of them. Well, at least it provided a roof over my mistress's head, so I will say no more about that.

"For the first year or so my mistress was always very anxious to know if a particular letter had come for her. She must have written to someone expecting a reply, but which never came. I think it gave her a feeling of hopelessness until she made some supreme effort to be cheerful, as though she had made up her mind about something. She devoted herself to her two little girls and I believe it was the fact she had them that saved her.

"Then without warning or explanation, that man sold the house and bought the one on Becket Lane in Fulham. He dismissed the cook and said I could take over, knowing that the mistress had always paid me. He also said the girls were old enough to help around the house. He sold the carriage and dismissed the coachman. He also arranged for a cab to pick him up each morning to take him to the City. This unexpected move did prove to be a blessing in disguise for the mistress. She fitted into everything as usual, making friends wherever she went, but he did not, and he seemed to resent that fact. Not that he bothered that much to be friendly anyway."

As Hannah paused in her narrative, Lord Barrandale asked, "Did your mistress ever mention her first husband?"

"No, your lordship, I never knew there was a first husband. Then I overheard something when I fetched the two girls home from a birthday party which set me thinking, for I was beginning not to see any likeness between them and their supposed father. The mistress never mentioned anything to me, not that she would, and I resolved on my part to make no reference to the fact. If the mistress did not wish to take me into her confidence, then I would respect that too.

"After we moved to Becket Lane the mistress and I cleaned out the whole house, for it had been quite neglected, and the three rooms at the top of the house were shut off as they were not being used, and the door to them was locked. I never knew what happened to the key."

Johnny cried out, "That's why the door was locked! That was where the portrait was hidden. To fink it had bin there all these years and no one even knoo!" A look from Hannah silenced him.

"Perhaps I should mention here," continued Hannah, "that some people were amazed to learn the mistress was not a widow, that there was a husband somewhere in the background. But for all he did he might as well not have been there. He never said what he did or where he went, and I don't think the mistress ever asked him. I was hurt for her at the time although now I can see how it came about." Hannah paused a moment or two in her narrative.

"Please continue, Hannah," said Lady Smythe, "it has been quite edifying."

"Yes, milady," said Hannah. "My mistress was very accomplished. She loved singing and playing her piano, which she bought herself. She taught her own girls as well as taking in pupils. She also taught fine needlework and embroidery. She saved as much money as she could as though she had a set purpose in mind, which indeed I believe she had. Then she sold a piece of jewellery she had kept hidden to pay the fees for her girls to go to that Ladies' School.

"When the girls were accepted the mistress was sent a list of all the things they were expected to bring with them. Then it seemed the house was turned upside down, what with all the lengths of material bought and all the stitching that had to be done, for they would be away for a full year.

"It is surprising how tiring stitching all day can be, and the mistress would often insist we all went out for walks to get some fresh air. As well as being this busy she still taught her other pupils. It was then, I am sure, that my dear lady over-taxed herself, and whatever burden she had been carrying for so long likewise took her strength. In spite of her courageous gaiety and high spirits the years had taken their toll.

"Once the girls left, the house fell silent, and I know the mistress missed them dreadfully and I could see a year would be a long time for her to wait for their return. Then I became the one who insisted we went for walks to get some fresh air. I will always bless those girls for faithfully writing home each week. She would read their letters eagerly and sometimes she would read parts of them to me.

"Everything would have been all right if that man had not interfered, because he suddenly wanted to know more about it. Why had the girls gone away? What was so special about them? And how had my mistress managed to pay for it all? He demanded to know, but she just said that she had saved all the money she had earned from teaching, and reminded him she was under no obligation to tell him anything. She never mentioned any jewels.

"Then one Sunday morning when the mistress and I were at church Mr. Wardlock went into her bedroom to look for whatever he could find and discovered those documents, the ones he had hidden away and which Johnny and I searched the house for. That's why I knew he had them. He spoke to my lady later that evening and cruelly declared he would not give the documents back until she told him how much money she really had. She was greatly shocked by his going into her room and taking the documents and begged and pleaded for their return, but he still refused.

"Whatever my dear mistress had been striving and hoping for, and then having it so cruelly taken away, caused even her gallant strength and spirit to nearly break, and it was then that her health really began to fail. Oh, that hateful, horrible man! I beg your pardon, sirs and lady, but the memory still haunts me.

"Just before the girls were due to return I wrote to them, without my lady knowing, and told them that their mother's health was not what it had been. I tried not to alarm them and I was hesitant about writing in the first place, but was eventually glad I did so.

"Some time after I had written, my mistress and I were out walking and got caught in a heavy downpour of rain. We were quite drenched by the time we got back to the house. My lady must have caught a chill for by the next day she had developed a nasty sore throat and I put her to bed and made her stay there. The next day I sent Johnny for Dr.Meldicott and he came at once and left some medicine for me to give her. My lady beckoned me to her bedside and tried desperately to tell me something. I know now what she had tried to say, but at the time her throat was so sore she could barely speak and she was having difficulty breathing, and I simply could not understand her.

"When that man heard his wife was ill he seemed quite put out about it. Later in the day I heard his voice in her room again demanding that she tell him what he wanted to know. I was so angry at him that I went in, and he glared at me but left the room."

Hannah fell silent, restlessly moving her hands about on her lap.

"There is something troubling you, isn't there, Hannah?" asked Dashell. "What you referred to in the carriage yesterday."

She nodded. "Yes, sir, there is. The next morning when I went in to see to her I found my dear lady had died during the night. Oh, how I wish I had sat up with her! Please forgive me, I still think of it. I informed Mr. Wardlock at once and he came to see her and said something about his dear wife being at peace at last, and then he turned and left the room. That was all he said, not that I expected him to say much else.

"Once more I sent Johnny for Dr. Meldicott. The doctor did not seem too surprised for he knew how ill my lady was, and the bluish tone to her skin indicated she did have trouble breathing. But it is my belief my lady's death was not a natural one."

Her listeners cried out in horror. While Johnny burst out, "So that's why you cried all over the place. I always thought you overdid it. Now I know why."

"Johnny, please!" cried an embarrassed, exasperated Hannah, cutting him short.

"One moment, if you please." Barrandale's voice brought calm to the situation. "Now, that is a very grave statement you have just made, Hannah. Can you verify it?"

"Yes, Lord Barrandale, I believe I can," said Hannah regaining her composure. "Later in the day when tidying the room out of respect, I noticed something terribly wrong. On a chair by the window was a cushion cover with a cross stitch design of daffodils, which the mistress had stitched herself when she was a girl. It had been moved as though someone had picked it up for some reason and then thrown it back again, for it fell crookedly and the design was upside down."

There was a horrified silence as the underlying meaning of Hannah's words sank in.

Dashell was incredulous. "Do you mean to say," he said, "that Wardlock actually smothered your mistress?"

Hannah could only whisper, "Yes, sir, that is what I do believe. I have no proof, but glad I am at last to speak of it."

"And you said nothing of your suspicions to Dr. Meldicott?" continued Dashell.

"No, sir, I could not. I dared not. He would have questioned Mr. Wardlock, who might have dismissed me on the spot. I could not run that risk when the girls were coming home in a day or two."

Feeling a little more relaxed now that she had spoken of that terrible truth, Hannah continued her narrative. "I will always remember the girls' homecoming. They looked so joyous and happy, so ladylike and beautiful. Miss Maude called out "Where's Mother? Where is she?" and I had to tell them she had died while they were on their way home. Their happy looks changed to bewilderment and disbelief, just like a ship on a calm sea suddenly foundering on rocks. I never could bring myself to say exactly how she had died."

Johnny could contain himself no longer. "I know just 'ow yer felt about keeping quiet, Hannah, 'cos that's 'ow I felt about Miss Maude's death, cos that weren't real either." He came to a stop as four pairs of astonished eyes turned to him. "I mean, it weren't natural. She didn't throw herself down the stairs. She tripped over a thread he had stretched across the top steps, so that's why she fell."

Once more there were cries from the others. "How do you know there was a thread there in the first place?" asked Hannah. "You never told me."

"I had to keep me mouth shut. I couldn't tell you. He would have said I was lying and have me go to prison, and that would have meant me leaving you and Miss Caroline."

Dashell's turned pale and his blood ran cold. It could so easily have been Caroline who fell and not her sister.

Once more Barrandale spoke. "Johnny, you must give us an explanation."

So Johnny carefully described how he discovered the thread and what it suggested to him, and when he looked again it was no longer there. "It must have been him. Who else would have done it? And then to make sure he didn't do the same with Miss Caroline, early every morning I would creep up the back stairs to the top of the front stairs. There never was any thread, but there mighta bin. Then I would go back to bed."

Hannah stared at him. "I never knew you did that. Why didn't you tell me?"

"You were so upset about the missus' death," Johnny replied doggedly, "I couldn't tell you that as well."

"Does Caroline know about this?" asked Dashell.

Embarrassed, Johnny shook his head. "No."

"In the light of what we have heard," said Barrandale, "you all know what this means?"

"Yes," said Dashell bluntly. "That he is a murderer."

"That is what I do mean," continued Barrandale, "but there is no proof, at least nothing that would stand up in a court of law. Consequently, we must agree that nothing is to be said about all this. Let sleeping dogs lie."

"Hannah," said Dashell, "you told me a while ago that you slept in the same room as Caroline for her safety."

"Yes, sir, I did have that fear, and Johnny showed me how to wedge a chair under the door handle." She stopped short and stared at Johnny. "So that's why you wanted Miss Caroline to use the back stairs; in case there was another thread."

"Yes, but I couldn't tell you the real reason."

Hannah and Johnny then described their search for the missing documents, and Wardlock's quarrel with Caroline on the front stairs, and what more he might have done if not for Hannah's intervention.

"One more question, Hannah," said Dashell. "What can you tell us about the jewels Caroline's mother, Isobel, kept hidden all those years?"

"I cannot tell you anything more about them, sir. Even the girls never knew she had them. But thankful I am I hid them in time, for we would never have seen them again."

"Hannah," said Lady Smythe, "would you bring me the linen bag they are in. I may be able to recognize some. And now that you and Johnny have finished you may go downstairs for some refreshments. Tell Chadwick I sent you."

Chapter Forty-One
Dashell and the Others Continue To Talk

Lady Smythe emptied out the contents of the bag onto a low table Dashell pulled up for her. Necklaces, bracelets, finger rings, earrings, brooches. Gold and silver items. Emeralds, rubies, sapphires, diamonds, pearls and other precious stones. All worth a considerable fortune. She looked them over and then shook her head. "I do not recognize any of them. It was just a faint hope anyway. But I cannot help thinking that Isobel could have sold more and lived in relative comfort, instead of struggling in the way Hannah described to us."

"And how would the wife of an ordinary village squire be in possession of such wealth?" queried Barrandale. "They are not usually that rich, so perhaps she did marry beneath her, as one might describe it."

"So that supports my theory that Isobel married against her family's wishes," said Dashell, "and yet the jewels were hers in her own right."

"If she did marry without her family's consent they would certainly not have allowed her to take them," reasoned Barrandale. "And if she did they would have definitely wanted them back. That may explain why Isobel was so concerned about concealment, as Hannah observed when she first entered her employment."

"So what shall we do with them?" asked Lady Smythe.

"We must keep them in safety, of course," said Dashell. "As far as we know they belong to Caroline."

"That reminds me, Dashell," said Barrandale, "did you notice there was no death certificate for Arthur Waterton amongst all those papers Johnny found?"

Shocked and dismayed, Dashell stared at him. "No, sir, I did not. I was too taken up with Caroline's birth certificate. Surely the death certificate would have been kept by Isobel, unless she lost it. I wonder what became of it, unless he died after he abandoned her, if he did abandon her."

"Perhaps he did not die. Perhaps they divorced," said Barrandale.

"I hardly think so, sir. Isobel wrote on the back of the portrait, "To my darling Arthur," and that suggests great attachment."

"So therefore he must have died," replied Barrandale. "She would never have remarried if he had still been alive."

By now Lady Smythe had put all the jewels back into the linen bag. Watching her, there crept into Dashell's mind a small but real thought that since Caroline obviously came from a very wealthy family, they might not consider him, a penniless heir, as a suitable husband for their newfound relative. On the other hand, if they had such little regard for Isobel, they would not concern themselves about her daughter too much. Out loud, he said, "It is still strange that family from neither side came forward to help in any way. Isobel might have remarried just to change her name, as though seeking not only concealment, but obscurity also. It was most unfortunate it had to be with someone like Wardlock."

"I wonder," said Barrandale. "You could be right. She seems to have been an intelligent lady, as well as courageous, so she must have had her own good reasons."

"I suppose we should try and find her family, her next of kin," said Lady Smythe, "and what a storm that might bring about. They could be most annoyed at having some hitherto unknown, forgotten or unwanted female relative suddenly foisted upon them."

"Not when they learn about all those jewels," said Dashell sarcastically.

"It's all so very puzzling," she added stifling a yawn.

They continued talking until Barrandale observed his sister stifle another yawn, and indicated to Dashell it was time they left. "It is time for us to go, Letty," he said, standing up. "It has been a most illuminating evening. I am amazed at all the events that have taken place, and at the fortitude of those two servants. I feel sure that without them Caroline may not have survived."

Dashell thought so too, while Lady Smythe admitted, "I am becoming quite concerned for the girl after hearing more about her. What a dreadful man her stepfather sounds like. Am I forgiven, Barrandale, for taking her under my roof?" she asked, placing her hand on his arm, "for I do feel I have helped her."

He placed his hand on hers. "Of course, Letty, but what else could you and I have done when Dashell appealed to us for help?"

Dashell was deeply touched. "I thank both of you very much, and so will Caroline when she recovers." He kissed his aunt fondly on her cheeks and smiled at his father as they left to go downstairs.

Once they had gone Lady Smythe turned to go to the guest-room to look more kindly on the girl her nephew had found. Hannah was already in her night clothes and had been brushing out Caroline's hair as far as she was able. "How is she?" she asked, keeping her voice down.

"She is very quiet, milady. I am sure the sleeping potion is doing her good."

"The linen bag with the jewels and the painting are still in the salon. Would you bring them here for safekeeping. Good night, Hannah."

"Yes, milady. Good night, milady," replied Hannah with a bob.

The two men had walked slowly back to Barrandale House. "What an incredible story," said Barrandale. "So much has come to light and yet so much needs to be told. For instance, what became of Waterton's death certificate, and why did Isobel wish to remain in obscurity? Because it certainly seems like it. And that young Faulkner, what a remarkable boy he is."

"I know," agreed Dashell. "He seems to have the ability to be at the right place at the right time, and I feel honour-bound to reward him in some way. I will speak to Hannah about it and she may be able to suggest something. Also tomorrow," he continued, "I will write to the parish priest of the village of Sutherfield and ask him what he knows about the Watertons. It will be interesting to see what kind of answer he gives me."

"Ah, yes, you mean Caroline's next of kin."

Matthew opened the door so promptly to their knocking that he must have been in the hall awaiting their return.

"Has Johnny returned yet?" enquired Dashell.

"Yes, sir, some half an hour ago, replied Matthew, as he helped their lordships out of their coats. "Will you be requiring anything else tonight?"

"No thank you," said Barrandale. "I shall retire now." He turned to Dashell, "And you?"

"No, not yet. I want to sit and think awhile," and then decided he could do that just as well in his own room. "Oh, perhaps I will come up too."

It was not until he was actually in bed that Barrandale remembered he had not mentioned to Dashell his suspicions about Wardlock. It was too late now so it would have to wait until morning.

Chapter Forty-Two

Lord Barrandale's Suspicions

The next morning after breakfast Barrandale and Dashell were together in the library. Dashell was still feeling invigorated after his early morning ride around Hyde Park, and with the feeling that now at last Caroline's real name was known, he need not fear any discovery of her existence. The very fact she was in the care of Lady Smythe and with her own maid in attendance, would dispel any unkind rumours of her propriety. It had been his concern all along to protect her name.

Barrandale cleared his throat somewhat. "Dashell," he began, "I particularly wish to speak to you about something. I did not mention the subject last evening because what with everything else discussed I quite frankly forgot, and it was not an opportune moment in any case." Dashell watched curiously as his father produced the old newspaper cuttings. "I read through these when you left yesterday to go to Grosvenor Square and found them most revealing. I believe I know why Wardlock made a point of keeping them, and I would be obliged if you would go through them carefully. I would like to know if you come to the same conclusion as I have."

"Very well, sir." Dashell began with the earliest clippings while Barrandale sat and patiently waited. After several minutes Dashell shot a keen thoughtful look at his father.

"Remember what Hannah said, that even her mistress did not know where Wardlock went or what he did," Barrandale reminded him.

"Yes, and Caroline herself said as much to me," Dashell commented briefly. After several more minutes he concluded by saying, "I do remember seeing these articles from time to time in the newspapers but never paid a great deal of attention to them."

"That was exactly my response too."

"And your opinion is that because Wardlock kept all these cuttings, it suggests to you that he could be the person so long sought by the authorities?"

"Yes, it does," said Barrandale. "Except there is no proof, only supposition. I believe people keep cuttings about any given subject, and Wardlock might have kept these to pander to his own vanity. Our suspicions would never stand up in court, not that we would ever take it that far of course. That is not for us to do."

Dashell glanced back at the cuttings and began to shuffle through them. "There was a paragraph or two fairly recently—ah, here it is," he said, and read out loud:

> ". . . the perpetrator is very cunning and is obviously clever with disguises and has used one alias after another, which the Police have found most baffling and makes it almost impossible for the scoundrel to be caught. It almost goes without saying that there is no knowledge of his real name. He does not appear to have any conscience for he has ruined many people, and one wonders what he has done with all his ill-gotten gains. One also cannot help thinking that if the said person had taken to the stage for a living instead of a life of crime, he would have had a brilliant career."

Dashell put down the cuttings. "Does not appear to have any conscience," he repeated. "Well, he left Caroline on the floor of a locked room, didn't he? And that article said there was no knowledge of his real name. We know him as Thomas Wardlock, but according to that old will he called himself Thomas Physhe. I would think that is likely to be his real name, wouldn't you?"

"Yes, I agree that is a real possibility. And there is something else troubling me," said Barrandale gravely. "That man is ill and may not have much longer to live and we are in possession of his will, albeit an old one. If he is the person the authorities have long been looking for and that information comes to light, we could be accused of being accessories to the fact. We must therefore return that will as soon as possible. And I think these cuttings should be returned as well as they are of no use to us, and I would not wish them to be found in our possession either."

Dashell had listened to all this intently, and said, "There is that other matter too."

"Which is?"

"The fact that he killed Isobel and Maude. Why, we don't know, but I strongly believe he did. Hannah and Johnny are too honest and straightforward to make up such a thing. Besides, neither one knew the other's story, their reactions were too genuine."

"That is what you and I believe to be true, but again on no account can we say anything. It would cause a most unpleasant scandal if it was learned that we might be involved, and to have our names associated with the so-called "Phantom Deceiver," whom we know as a murderer."

"How do we explain to Wardlock how these items came into our possession?" asked Dashell. "He could well accuse us of stealing them." With a flash of grim humour Dashell reflected that Johnny himself could think of a plausible explanation.

"I'm afraid I cannot answer that," said Barrandale, wearily passing a hand over his brow. "I must leave that to you."

Dashell was immediately contrite. "I beg your pardon, sir, it seems my affairs are over-taxing you. When I first met Caroline I had no idea it would lead to all this. Of course I will go to Becket Lane. I will think of something to say."

"All I ask of you is that you be careful, discreet. Whatever that man has done in the past do not let your acute dislike of him over-ride you. Remember he answers to a Higher Authority than ours. Now," continued Barrandale, "here are the cuttings and the will, and here is Wardlock's copy of the marriage certificate and contract, which we don't need either."

As Dashell gathered up everything, a thought occurred to him. "That joint marriage certificate and contract, I wonder if it is genuine, knowing what a scoundrel Wardlock is." He spread it out on a table and they looked at it together.

"It seems genuine enough on the face of it," declared Barrandale. "The ceremony was held at a church in Camberwell, and the document signed by the officiating priest and two witnesses."

"That does not mean that they themselves were genuine," Dashell pointed out. "They could have been actors hired by Wardlock. It would mean looking through old records of eighteen years or so ago, but I am perfectly willing to do that. If everything is not valid, or if he gave a false name, then that would make the marriage null and void." Dashell began to fold up the document. "Wait a moment, there is something more. In the will he calls himself Thomas Physhe, but is known to us as Thomas Wardlock, and he wrote the will after he married Isobel. So again, which is his real name?"

"According to the newspapers he has had any number," Barrandale remarked.

"Well," said Dashell, bracing himself, "the sooner I go the better." He rang the bell for Matthew. "My gig, Matthew. I shall drive, and I want Johnny with me."

Chapter Forty-three

At Becket Lane Again - and Elsewhere

The gig was waiting at the front door with Stephen standing at Sparkle's head. Johnny was already in the gig, which had its hood raised as it was raining a little. "Thank the Lord for small mercies," Reuben muttered. "At least it will keep him out of sight," meaning Johnny. He was scandalized that Lord Lonsdale would even consider sitting next to a Cockney boy, and never mind what he had done, so Reuben had strictly instructed Johnny to keep any grin off his face.

Fortunately Johnny himself was feeling rather silent. The fact that the Guv wanted him to come with him could only mean they were going to Becket Lane, and that meant they would probably meet 'is Nibs again. He did not know the will and the newspaper cuttings were being returned, and if he had he might have had a few more qualms about that burned second will.

Dashell came out, stepped into the gig and drove away without saying anything. When they passed the Bishop's Head Inn, Johnny looked at it by turning his eyes. *Funny*, he thought, *only this time yesterday I was waiting for a cab and got the very same driver that had dropped off 'is Nibs.* He felt a grin coming which he quickly suppressed. He was not looking forward to seeing Mr. Nasty again.

Dashell felt he had really seen the last of Wardlock after that unpleasant call yesterday morning. But his father was correct, the documents had to be returned. When the gig stopped outside the house on Becket Lane, only then did Dashell tell Johnny what he was doing. "We are beholden to do this," he explained.

"Yes, Guv, I understand," replied Johnny gravely, feeling a sudden weight in the pit of his stomach. *Oh, 'ell*, he thought.

Dashell led the way up to the front door and knocked loudly. No answer. Again he knocked. Still no answer. He tried the handle. Locked.

"'E must be in," said Johnny doggedly. "Where else would 'e be? I can still get in through the side door, I know where the key is 'idden," and ran off to get it.

On entering the kitchen Johnny received the first of his shocks. He was halfway across the room when he realized there was something on the floor. At first he thought it was some sacking he had left behind. He picked it up and saw it was a woman's dress and it had been cut from top to bottom. It certainly had not been there when he left yesterday. Mr.Nasty! He heard further knocking and hastily ran into the hallway and opened the front door.

A rather annoyed Dashell took one look at Johnny and could see he was upset about something. "What's the matter?" he asked sharply.

For answer, Johnny showed him the dress he had found in the kitchen and then pointed at the others on the hallway floor. "They were the dresses they 'ad when they went to that school of theirs. I recognize the material." Four dresses, and all cut in some way. Was there no end to this man's spite? Then Dashell stepped on something hard. It was the handle of the knife, which Johnny hastily picked up. "'E musta used the knife I left on the draining board," he cried. "Ow did I know he would a fing like that. And 'ow am I to tell Miss Caroline and Hannah." He could not bring himself to confess he had left the knife out on purpose just to annoy Mr.Nasty.

"Where is Wardlock anyway?" wondered Dashell. "I am surprised he has not put in an appearance by now."

"He is usually there in his room," said Johnny, indicating which door.

Hardly bothering to knock Dashell entered the room and stopped short with a cry of surprise, and they both stared at a pair of boots sticking out from behind an armchair. They saw the open panel and the empty black box on the desk. So Wardlock had realized his hiding place had been discovered, which fact must have shocked and enraged him. So much so that he had some kind of fatal seizure. Dashell looked quickly round and saw the coat Wardlock had tossed aside, and laid it across his face. One had to be decent. Both Dashell and Johnny felt considerable relief at this turn of events, but for very different reasons.

Johnny would not now have to explain the absence of that second will. He also remembered the promise he had made to himself that he would get even with Mr.Nasty for what he did to Miss Caroline the afternoon of the carriage ride. And, wot's more, he had killed the Missus and Miss Maude. Johnny glanced again at the covered figure and felt no regret at all.

Neither did Dashell feel any regret. Wardlock had done his worst and failed. He had almost killed Caroline, and now she was free of him. Dashell's father had been right to insist the various items had to be returned. Dashell was more than thankful he had been too late to speak to Wardlock, but there was something else to think about. Wardlock's body could not just be left there, as a death had to be reported eventually.

"Johnny, is there a constable in this area?"

"No, Guv, I've never 'eard of one."

Well, it was a faint hope. "Show me where you found the black box."

Johnny was only too pleased to do so. He pointed out the little wooden leaf covering the keyhole which Hannah told him about, and how the panel swivelled about when he opened the hiding place.

Curious, Dashell peered inside the opening and said, "What's that? There seems to be something else. Did you look further inside?"

"No, I didn't, Guv," said Johnny in surprise. "I was in too much of a hurry." He reached his arm further in and touched something that felt like a package. "There is something else," he muttered. "I didn't have time to look further, I had to get away. Let's see if this other panel opens." Running his hands up and down the other panel he found a catch and opened it. Several more packages were revealed.

Dashell lifted one out and took it to the desk to look at it more carefully, and he wisely did not try to open it. He recalled that newspaper paragraph, *"One wonders what he did with all his ill-gotten gains."* Well, this must be some of them, he thought. He took out two more packages which had names, dates and amounts written on a label like the first one. "We must leave, Johnny, but before we do would you put those dresses and cut pieces back in the travelling box."

Johnny did so, thinking, *Trust that old buzzard to find em,* knowing full well not to speak ill of the dead. He closed the box and shut the cupboard door.

While Johnny was busy Dashell had been thinking. He returned the cuttings to the black box, but kept the will and the marriage contract in his coat pocket. He left the three packages on the desk with the black box. "Make sure both doors are locked Johnny, and give me the key to the front door and come to the gig."

Dashell fully intended to go to Scotland Yard, the headquarters of the newly formed Metropolitan Police. What with his father's suspicions and now his own, they had to be notified about Wardlock's body and the other things in that room. He made up his mind to be straightforward and lay his cards on the table.

The will stipulating that everything be passed from one female dependent to the other to the last survivor was all very well when it was written so many years ago, and Wardlock must have been a better man then, but that could not have included all those ill-gotten gains at the time of writing. However, a clever lawyer could argue that it did, and a legal battle could last for years and would probably use up all the money in fees anyway, besides infuriating many desperate people demanding the return of their money and valuables. The newspapers would keep things stirring and result in the very scandal he and his father were striving to avoid. Dashell also wondered, with all the different names Wardlock used, if that particular one used in the will was known to the authorities, meaning if Wardlock had used it elsewhere.

As he approached Scotland Yard Dashell wondered how well he would be received, as it was unheard of that someone from the aristocracy would actually go to the authorities. The will and the cuttings could hardly be considered decisive proof and he had already decided not to show them the marriage contract. It would not mean much to them anyway.

"You stay with the gig, Johnny." Dashell never liked leaving the gig unattended, even with a chain looped through the spokes of a wheel. He also did not really want Johnny with him.

If the constable on desk duty was surprised at the sight of an aristocratic gentleman, unattended by any servant, who asked to speak to someone in authority, and all this on a Sunday morning, he tried not to show it. He gravely asked the gentleman for his name and his eyebrows quivered slightly at the reply, and then requested the gentleman to wait a few minutes while he went to another room.

"Sir," he said to his superior, with a backward jerk of his head, "there's a gentleman asking to speak to someone in authority. Didn't say what about. Says he is Lord Lonsdale."

"What was that?" The inspector looked up sharply from the papers he was reading. The fact that such a gentleman had come to them voluntarily was indeed a surprise. Usually the Police could barely get through the doors of the aristocracy. He stared at his constable wondering if he had heard aright. "Did he give any indication what it was about?"

"No, sir. He just asked to speak to someone in authority," repeated the constable.

"Did he look drunk?" This was often the case when dealing with such gentlemen.

"No, sir, I wouldn't say so."

Inspector Cecil Cockburn had only been appointed as an inspector three months ago. He was very keen to get on but knew he needed more experience. "Ask Sergeant Springer to come, and then show the gentleman in." As the constable turned away he murmured to himself, "Lord Lonsdale? Son of Lord Barrandale? I wonder why he came here instead of asking us to go to him. I wonder what it's all about."

"Lord Lonsdale, sir," announced the constable, and shut the door behind Sergeant Springer.

Inspector Cockburn was even more surprised. He had not expected such a firm and resolute individual as this gentleman appeared to be. "At your service, Lord Lonsdale, I understand you wish to speak to someone in authority. I am Inspector Cockburn and this is my associate, Sergeant Springer." He indicated a chair to Dashell.

"Thank you, Inspector Cockburn. I will try to be concise although I have a difficult matter to approach." Dashell glanced at the sergeant and hesitated.

"Anything you say to me, Lord Lonsdale, you may say in front of my sergeant."

Dashell did not like that idea, but doubtless the sergeant would be informed by the Inspector in any case. And now that he was actually at Scotland Yard he hardly knew where to begin, and supposing he was wrong after all? "To begin with, Inspector, I wish to report the discovery of a body."

That caught the interest of the two men at once. "Do you indeed," drawled Cockburn.

"I went to call upon a man earlier this morning by the name of Thomas Wardlock but could get no answer to my knocking, but strangely the door was unlocked and I went in."

"Was there no servant?"

"The maidservant is with her mistress, who is staying with a friend. There is also a boy who works out of the house at times. Wardlock is—er, was—inclined to keep to himself."

"Oh, so you are well acquainted with the house, then."

"Yes, you could say so."

"So what did you do after you entered the house?"

"I knew in which room he was likely to be found, and there he was on the floor. I believe he must have had some kind of seizure."

"Did the other servant not find him sooner?"

"As I said just now," repeated Dashell patiently, "to the best of my knowledge Wardlock did not like to be disturbed. At times he preferred to attend to himself."

"Well, it all seems quite straightforward as far as I can see, Lord Lonsdale, but why did you come here if it appears to be a natural death?"

Dashell looked very steadily at Cockburn. "I may be quite wrong about what I am trying to tell you, Inspector, but I could not help noticing some packages on his desk with names, dates and amounts written on them, some which have been mentioned in the newspapers." Dashell paused as Cockburn's eyes never left his face. "In other words, could it be possible that the late Thomas Wardlock is the "Phantom Deceiver" the police have been looking for?"

If there had been a sudden violent thunderclap over their heads, or if the floor had opened up beneath them, the two men could not have been more dumbfounded. They stared aghast at Dashell, at each other, then back to Dashell. The inspector managed to find his voice and leaned forward, his arms on his desk with hands clasped. "If you are correct, Lord Lonsdale, how is it you are associated with such a person, may I ask?" he drawled, his eyes boring into him, "unless you are one of his victims?"

Dashell had been ready for a question like that. "No, I am not," he said. "I am betrothed to the younger of his two stepdaughters," he answered levelly, in spite of the fact Caroline had not actually said "yes" yet. "That is the only way in which I am acquainted with Wardlock. That was why I called upon him this morning to speak of the matter and to ask his consent. The lady is of gentle birth; and knowing the character of the late Thomas Wardlock I believe he presented himself to his late wife as something he was not, and deceived her, like all other people."

Dashell's next words stunned the two policemen even more. "There was a will on Wardlock's desk and I took the liberty of looking at it, for I knew the lady would be a beneficiary and she would not have objected." Really, the lies he was telling, it was almost bordering on perjury. "I noticed he used the name "Physhe". I wonder if that could be his real name." He got no further.

Cockburn, showing his worth now, snapped some orders to his sergeant who left the room immediately. "I can scarcely credit what you have been saying, Lord Lonsdale, but if those labelled packages are correct and match the names of some of those unfortunate people—" His voice trailed off. Then he realized he did not know where they were going. He had been so astonished at what he had heard he had forgotten to ask. A very bad mistake. "Where did you say we were going, Lord Lonsdale?" he drawled, as though he was just making sure. Another surprise at Dashell's reply. A quiet little place like that?

Johnny had stayed inside the gig because it was still raining, but at the sound of hooves and wheels he knew something was afoot. Dashell stepped into the gig and without a word he took the reins and drove off, followed by a police carriage containing Inspector Cockburn, Sergeant Springer and two constables, which in turn was followed by a hearse with a police doctor and two undertakers.

Dashell silently blessed the rain and overcast sky as the weather would keep most people indoors and churchgoers would be at home by now. He did not wish to be the subject of speculation and amazement as the three vehicles made their way to Becket Lane.

On arrival at the house Dashell would have led the way but the Inspector called him back. "One moment, if you please, we will go in first," he said, and took the front door key from Dashell.

Once inside the room Cockburn stood still, looking about and taking everything in. The packages on the desk just as Dashell had left them, the black box and the open panels, and then he turned his searching gaze to the figure on the floor. Going over, he whipped the coat off Wardlock's body. "Is this him?" he asked incredulously, staring at Dashell, who had now come into the room. Whoever Cockburn had expected it was certainly not someone as grey and thin and worn as this person was. In fact, Cockburn was not sure what he had expected. "Who put the coat over him? Did you, Lord Lonsdale?"

"Yes, I did," replied Dashell. "I thought it was the decent thing to do." Cockburn just grunted some reply.

The police doctor spoke up. "You say he must have had some kind of seizure, Lord Lonsdale. What makes you say that?"

"I understand he had not been well for some time."

"Oh. Well, I will make no comment until I have examined the body. When was the last time you saw him alive, by the way?"

"Yesterday morning. I had planned to call on him this morning on a personal matter, and on entering the room found him just as you see him now"

"Have I your permission to remove the body, Inspector?" the doctor asked as the undertakers were ready to leave, and Cockburn nodded. "I will make my report to you later, Inspector."

Cockburn had been quietly moving about the room while he listened at the same time, his sharp eyes missing nothing. He eventually went to the black box and took out all the cuttings. "These are very interesting," he remarked to his sergeant. "Looks like he kept them as references to himself. This could be further evidence he is our man, although I'm not sure a mere collection of newspaper cuttings will prove anything. I will take them and sort through them more carefully."

"Before you do anything further, Inspector Cockburn," said Dashell, "I would like to show you Wardlock's will and perhaps you might appreciate my concern."

Cockburn, annoyed at what he considered an intrusion, took the will from Dashell a little impatiently and quickly read through it. "So? It seems plain and straightforward to me apart from the fact it is dated some years ago, but that it not to say it is not legal.

And ah, yes, the name "Physhe", we will certainly investigate that. Is that all?"

Dashell was beginning to feel the Inspector was too sure of himself. "No, it is not. If you would allow me to explain. Wardlock's wife died some eighteen months ago from pneumonia, I believe, and the elder daughter a while later from an unfortunate accident. That leaves the younger daughter as the sole survivor. Therefore this property and everything in it or attached thereto, passes to her."

Cockburn and the sergeant looked at each other. What was Lord Lonsdale trying to say? That Wardlock's death was not a natural one? "I can see that, but go on," said Cockburn, watching Dashell carefully.

"Well, a clever lawyer could argue that the inheritance would also include everything Wardlock had kept hidden for years, all his stolen money, and such an argument could lead to a most difficult and awkward situation."

The Inspector relaxed when he caught the drift of what Dashell was saying and regarded him with new respect, especially as he himself had overlooked that point. Now somewhat mollified he said, "Thank you for bringing all that to my attention, Lord Lonsdale, but as these packages do contain stolen property we are quite within the law to remove them, so you need have no concern on that part."

Dashell in his turn felt relieved that the matter had been clarified, for Caroline's sake. "Thank you, you have put my mind at rest," he said, and put the will back in his pocket.

Meanwhile Sergeant Springer had turned his attention to more of the packages on the shelves and had brought a number of them out. "Sir," he cried, "would you come and look at these!"

Cockburn came at once to look and exclaimed in amazement, "The names! The dates! Just look at them. He even wrote down the amounts!"

"I recognize these cases from a while back," added the sergeant.

"I don't mind telling you, Lord Lonsdale," declared Cockburn, "that after years of searching for this man I could hardly believe what you told us earlier. We really owe you something for coming forward. With all his clever disguises we never knew who we were looking for. The descriptions given to us by those he had duped varied so much it was impossible to know. He certainly was a very clever and cunning man, I must admit. Incidentally, where did he keep all his disguises? They must be somewhere. We must look for them."

Johnny had been standing in the background so quietly all this time that he made everyone start when he spoke up. "Ekscooz me, Inspector, sir, but I fink I may be able to 'elp you."

Inspector Cockburn swung round. "And who are you?" he asked, glaring at Johnny.

"This is Johnny Faulkner," explained Dashell, "the young servant."

"Ah. Then what have you got to say? What do you know about it?"

"Well," explained Johnny, "at half-past nine every morning a cab would come and pick up Mr. Wardlock. He always looked his usual self when he left and he never carried anything with him. That's all I can tell you. I'm sure the cab driver could tell you somefink."

"Ah, so he had an accomplice. Was it always the same cab?"

"Yes, in the morning."

"And when did the cab return?"

"We never knoo when he'd come. Sometimes arternoons, sometime evenings. And it was different drivers then anyway."

"Sounds strange to me," reflected Cockburn. "Why live here? Why not just live in London proper and be done with it."

"I had wondered that myself," remarked Dashell. "Maybe he wanted to give the impression he was just an ordinary man attending to dealings in the City. I should think it is very quiet in Fulham. Nobody would think of looking for him here."

Cockburn fingered his chin thoughtfully. "You mean he could have been cunning enough to live in the shadow of the Bishop of London's Palace."

The two constables had been removing all the packages, supervised by the sergeant. "All the packages are now in the carriage, sir," he said, "and the hearse left some time ago."

"Very good, sergeant." Cockburn then turned his attention to Johnny. "Now, young man, we will be here tomorrow morning at half-past nine, or earlier, to position ourselves. We will require that neither of you be here. This is entirely a police matter."

"Before you go, Inspector Cockburn, there is still something else I would like to mention to you."

"Yes, Lord Lonsdale?" asked the Inspector, sounding more careful this time.

"The name Wardlock was how the mother and her two daughters were known in this area. I would ask you, for the sake of my betrothed, that this name not be used in connection with the man who was found in this room, as it is fairly certain it was not his real name. His death, of course, will have to be made known, but let it just be as a local person."

"Hmm, I see your point," replied Cockburn. "Actually, we have never come across the name Wardlock associated with any case involving, er, shall we say "Physhe". That is correct, isn't it, sergeant?"

"Yes, sir. As far as we know that name has never been used at all."

"And you ask this for the sake of the younger stepdaughter who is of gentle birth?"

"Yes, Inspector Cockburn, I do," said Dashell, and their eyes met in understanding.

"I think we can accommodate your request, Lord Lonsdale. We can be quite discreet at times, and you have been most helpful. Now, we will leave, and here is the key to the front door."

Dashell waited for the sound of the police carriage to die away before turning to Johnny. "That was good of you to speak up about that cab. I hope they find out more but I don't expect to hear anything more from them. Now before we leave would you show me the pin on the stairs you spoke about."

"All right, Guv," said Johnny, and led the way. Dashell felt for himself the pin in the wall still with a tiny piece of frayed thread attached to it, and then looked to where it had been attached to the other side of the stairway. Poor Maude must have been terrified at the sudden violent shock as she felt herself falling, being unable to help herself. He stared down the stairs, still thinking it could so easily have been Caroline instead.

"If yer like, Guv," said Johnny interrupting Dashell's thoughts, "I can show yer where I found that pickchur of Miss Caroline's farver."

Dashell bestirred himself. "Yes, do. I would like to see."

Johnny led the way and showed Dashell the splintered doorway, and how he had used the garden spade, and then they went up to the attic rooms. "I looked in these two rooms first and then tried this third one. The pickchur was propped up on this easel behind the door and looked over my shoulder as if it was a real person. Cor! It gave me such a fright I almost dropped me lantern." Dashell marvelled how the picture had been hidden up here for years, its whereabouts known only to one person. Then they returned to the landing.

"This was the missus' room," explained Johnny. It was barely furnished with just a coverlet over the bed. They saw the cushion with the embroidered daffodils, the very one that had been used to smother Isobel. Dashell could imagine the feeble struggles of the sick lady, and wondered what Inspector Cockburn would have said had he known of those two suspicious deaths.

On a sudden thought Dashell asked Johnny to show him around the rest of the house, just to see exactly what Caroline had inherited. He was rather aghast at its state of repair, or rather lack of it, and Johnny told him that Wardlock had hardly spent a penny on its upkeep. Dashell just shook his head. Why neglect your own property?

"Well, whatever the state of the house it all belongs to Caroline now," said Dashell. "What happens next can be discussed with her when she is better. You and Stephen can come in the carriage later to fetch that box under the stairs. Now I think it is time for us to leave and go to the inn for a meal."

That afternoon the carriage returned to the house for the box under the stairs, which was taken to Grosvenor Square, giving Johnny plenty of time to think about what he was going to say to Hannah about the cut dresses.

Also that afternoon Dashell informed his father that Wardlock had been found dead on the floor. "I admit I was quite relieved I was too late to speak to him." His father's eyes widened in surprise when Dashell said he had gone to Scotland Yard, but he explained at some length why he felt it was expedient to do so. "Inspector Cockburn and Sergeant Springer were greatly astonished, as you can imagine, but it shows your suspicions were correct, sir."

Dashell concluded by remarking that Caroline may well have inherited the house according to Wardlock's old will, but it was in such a poor state that it would be far too costly to repair and her inheritance could end up being quite worthless.

Chapter Forty-Four

The Cab Driver Tells All He Knows

Inspector Cockburn and Sergeant Springer came to Becket Lane well before half-past nine the next morning, and had the police carriage backed down the side lane out of sight.

The previous afternoon and evening they had read through old files and reports on known cases of victims of the "Phantom Deceiver," as the newspapers had called him, and matched them up with the names and dates on the packages. They also matched up the aliases he had used as reported by the said unfortunate people.

"Sir, it's a wonder he could remember all the different names he used," remarked the sergeant as they stood waiting. "He must have had an incredible memory."

"Just shows what a brilliant but misguided person he was," replied the inspector.

Before long they heard a cab approaching, and they looked at each other and nodded. So that boy had been right. They waited for the cab to turn round and come to a halt, noticing the driver looked at the house but made no attempt to climb down from his seat. The two policemen then appeared from their vantage point and the sergeant stood in front of the cab and held the horse's bridle.

"What the hell's going on?" cried the cab driver indignantly. "Leave my horse alone, will you? What do you think you are doing?" He glanced at the house as though expecting someone to come out.

"I am Inspector Cockburn and this is Sergeant Springer," said Cockburn. "Why are you here?"

"Whaddya mean?" the cab driver replied. "What does it look like? I'm here to pick up my fare, and he should be out any minute. If you have any questions, ask him." He scowled from one policeman to the other.

"Your fare will not be coming out," the Inspector told him. "He died on Saturday."

The man blinked in surprise. "He did?" he said, and then became cagey. "What do you want with me? I had nothing to do with it. "You can't pin his death on me."

"We believe he died from natural causes."

"Oh."

"Does the name Wardlock mean anything to you? Or the name Physhe?"

"I do not know anyone by the name of Wardlock or Fish," declared the man stoutly.

Cockburn became irritated. "Come, come, man, don't play games with me. You have been coming this time each morning to pick him up, haven't you?"

"Oh, you mean him," the man said, jerking his head at the house. "He told me his name was Solomon."

Taken aback, it was the turn of the two policemen to blink in surprise. How many more names had this man used?

"What do you know about him?" persisted Cockburn.

"Me? Not much. Why do you ask? Is he wanted? He must be or you wouldn't be asking."

"Yes, he is. Or was."

The man brightened as a realization fully came to him. "Hey, if this man Solomon is dead then I no longer have to come here to pick him up. I'm free. I'm free of him at last." He smiled as though a weight had been lifted off his shoulders.

"Ah," said Cockburn, "so perhaps you can tell us something. To begin with, what is your name?"

The man hesitated a moment too long before saying, "Seth Denby."

"I have a feeling that is not your real name."

The man shook his head wearily. "He said he would reveal my real name if I did not do what he wanted."

"Well, he's dead," Cockburn reminded him. "If you come clean with us it will go better for you. So, what is your real name?"

The man climbed down from his seat and the sergeant released his hold on the bridle. "My real name is Sidney Dobson."

"Sidney Dobson," mused the Inspector. "I recognize that name now. There was one particular case, you and two other men. They did the robbing while you waited with a cab. The man robbed sustained serious injuries, from which he died. Those two were caught but you got away."

Dobson nodded. "Yes. My wife was ill and I needed more money for her medicine. That's how I got involved, and I wish I hadn't. That's when Solomon made me change my name and get a different horse in case the other one was recognised. It made me wonder if somehow he was involved. Why else would he do that? When he moved here he made me come and pick him up, rain, hail or shine. I hated it in winter time, but what could I do? That devil had me where he wanted me, and when I tried to leave he just sneered and threatened to expose my real name. Then what would to my wife do if I was sent to prison? I think he just liked to be cruel."

"Well, a while later my wife died, although I never told him. Then my niece, a widow, and her two small boys came to live with me, and I kept quiet about that in case he wanted to hurt them instead."

As Dobson paused, Cockburn asked him, "Did you drive for him at any other time during the day?"

"No, which I thought rather odd, or maybe not. He probably didn't want me to know where he went. Anyway, there were plenty of other cabs he could hail. He didn't care what I did the rest of the day, and I never brought him back here."

"So where did he go? Do you know?"

"I would drop him off at the same place each time, and he would wait for me to go and turn the corner of the road. I know that because I could see his reflection in a shop window on the other side of the street."

Cockburn glanced significantly at his sergeant. Obviously this cab driver was intelligent, and both men had been listening carefully. "Go on," urged Cockburn.

"I decided one day to find out where he went."

"Oh, and how did you do that?" asked Cockburn.

"Well, usually I couldn't wait to get rid of him, but like I said, I decided to find out where he went. My niece's two boys were older now and growing up into real sharp 'uns, and I got them to understand what I wanted them to do. I told them where to be the first time and to be ahead of me. They had to be very careful not to make Solomon suspicious, and never mind if they lost sight of him in the crowd. They could start again the next morning where they left off. On no account were they to run after him. I told them to pretend they did not know me, just be like boys playing in the streets.

"I don't mind telling you, Inspector, those two entered into the spirit of things right away. They said Solomon moved surprisingly quickly and they did lose him a few times, so it took them several days to discover where he went, but they did find out."

"And where was that?" asked Cockburn, who was quite impressed.

"Quite close to Covent Garden, and you know how busy that area is. I actually drove past the place just to make sure and see for myself. I could hardly believe it, and the boys insisted they were right. It seems Solomon took a long way round through narrow lanes and would come out about a quarter of a mile or so from where I dropped him off. It didn't make sense. Why not go straight there in first place?"

However, it did make sense to both policemen. To arrive at one place as himself and then leave as someone else. This must be where he kept his disguises, and who would notice him in a crowded place anyway.

"How long ago was all this?" enquired Cockburn.

"About six months ago."

"Did you not think of going to the Police?"

"No, I didn't want to get involved, not with the likes of him. I wanted as little as possible to do with him. Look," said Dobson, getting somewhat anxious, "I came clean like you asked and I have told you everything I know. I have done bad things in the past and I will do time if I have to. I just want to make a clean start."

"Well," said Cockburn, "I must say you have been very helpful and co-operative and I will do all I can for you. Now you can take me and my sergeant to this place you discovered. Our carriage will follow you. One moment more, we will make a note of your address as we will probably have to contact you later." He waited while the sergeant made a note of Dobson's address, and also the cab's licence number. Then the two vehicles moved off.

The cab eventually pulled up outside some mean looking buildings with an alleyway running between them. "Is this the right place?" queried Cockburn.

"Yes," replied Dobson. The boys said there was a door at the back of one of the buildings."

With a grunt Cockburn ordered him to wait while he and Sergeant Springer marched to the back of the premises. They found the door, but of course it was locked, so they made their way to what looked like an office at the front of the buildings. Inside the dusty little room was a man sitting behind a desk. On the wall behind him was a board with the name "J. Turnbull" painted on it.

"Are you J.Turnbull, the owner of these buildings?" asked Cockburn

"Yes, I am," the man replied. "And who are you, may I ask?"

"I am Inspector Cockburn and this is Sergeant Springer."

"What do you want with me?" asked Turnbull, a little shifty-eyed.

"What do you know about the man who rented the room outside at the back?"

"Not much," scowled Turnbull. "I hardly ever saw him."

"What name did he give you?" Cockburn quite expected to hear another different name and he was not disappointed.

"He said his name was Gilpin," Turnbull replied, as Cockburn gave his sergeant a knowing sidelong glance, who gave his head a little shake in response.

"What else can you tell us?"

"Well," said Turnbull, scratching his head, "this Gilpin has been renting from me for quite a considerable time. He said he was looking after the overflow wardrobes of theatrical companies, who often borrowed from each other, and he was the custodian. I thought it sounded a bit rum but it was no business of mine, and the rent was always on time."

"Apart from that, did you see much of this man Gilpin at all?" asked Cockburn.

"No. I didn't want to either, he seemed an odd cove to me. He used to give me the shivers. I suppose he came and went when he wanted to. He didn't bother me and I didn't bother him. Come to think of it, the rent is due in a day or so, you can speak to him then if you want to."

"We can't speak to him. He died on Saturday," Cockburn informed him.

"Hey!" cried Turnbull. "What about my rent and all the stuff that must be there, whatever it is. What's to become of it? I don't even know what theatrical companies to contact. I'll probably have to sell everything."

"You leave all that to the Police," Cockburn warned him. "But now, have you a spare key for that door?"

Turnbull rummaged in a box and pulled out a key. "This is the one," he said, and marched off with it, closely followed by the other two. When they reached the door at the back he took one look and cried, "That is not my lock!" He tried his key in any case, but it did not fit at all. "Well, I'll be blowed. That wily old so-and-so must have changed the lock and never told me." Turnbull blinked in surprise at the other two, who showed no surprise at all. "The cunning old devil. The nerve of him. But where is the key for this one? What am I to do now?"

"You are not to do anything at all," warned Cockburn again. "You are not to touch that lock at all. Everything is now in the hands of the Police. But one more thing. Did anyone ever come to see this Gilpin?"

"Not to my knowledge. If anyone did I would not have known."

"So there is nothing more you can tell us?"

"No."

"Well, thank you for what you have told us. You have been very helpful. We will be back, and again do not touch anything." The two policemen turned to go leaving a baffled Turnbull scratching his head, looking from his key to the lock.

Dobson, still waiting with his cab, glanced anxiously at the two officers as they returned. "Am I under arrest?"

"No," said Cockburn. "You may go, but I suggest you begin your 'clean start'."

"Thank you, sir," he replied. "I certainly will," and drove off a happier man already.

At Scotland Yard Inspector Cockburn learned that the post mortem on the man now known as Thomas Physhe had been completed, and that he had indeed died from natural causes. A list had been made of the few items found on his person, among which was a ring with three keys attached.

Taking these keys and a search warrant they returned to the building, and Cockburn, with a significant look at his sergeant, fitted a likely key into the lock, turned it, and pushed the door open on well-oiled hinges. They stepped into a small, musty hallway, and then opened another door with the second key, which led into a room the contents of which fairly took their breath away. They beheld racks of clothing hanging up, shelves stocked with hats, wigs, false beards, boxes of greasepaint, and all kinds of other theatrical items. There were also mirrors on the walls to afford front, side and back views. When they examined some items they discovered that everything had been numbered.

"So this is where he kept everything," said Cockburn in wonder. "This proves he must have had some theatrical background. And we must follow up on that name Physhe." He looked at a rather bare desk, which had only a collection of pens and an inkwell on it.

He now turned his attention to a safe in one corner of the room. With another significant look at Sergeant Springer he produced the third key, which fitted the lock perfectly. He opened the safe, neither of them knowing what to expect, and removed a leather-bound book with lined pages, rather like a journal, and riffled through it. Astounded at what he saw he cried out, "Great heavens! Just look at this!" and handed it to Springer. Cockburn reached in and pulled out another book, which had older dates. "I can't believe it!"

"Looks like he kept a record of everything he did, sir," cried an equally amazed sergeant. "And I recognize several of the names of those he duped out of their money and valuables."

"Yes, so do I," said Cockburn, still going through some of the pages of the other book. "But there are some here I do not know."

"Perhaps some people never came forward," suggested the sergeant. "So that could mean there could be more cases than ever."

"Hmm, you could be right," agreed Cockburn. "But the sheer arrogance and conceit of the man, and actually all this will help us piece our cases together. Look how he noted his disguises by jotting down the number of each item he used. That's so he could keep a record of everything and not repeat a disguise unless he wanted to. Clever. Very, very clever." He snapped the journal shut. "Arrangement must be made to have all these things moved to Scotland Yard. It will take us days to go through them all. See to it, Springer, will you."

"Yes, sir. By the way, I wonder if there is anything else in the safe?" Springer bent down, reached right in and pulled out something. A wooden box containing engraving tools and some fine pens for writing script in a flamboyant hand. There were also sheets of parchment paper and some of fine vellum. Had this man been a forger as well? They both shook their hands in disbelief.

Sergeant Springer let his breath out slowly. "Inspector Cockburn, sir, if I may be so bold to remark, that if Lord Lonsdale had not come forward like he did, and if that young Faulkner lad had not spoken up about that cab, and if Dobson had not told us how he found out about this place, we might never have discovered all this."

"How right you are, except that would have left Turnbull wondering about his rent," said Cockburn with a slight laugh.

After a few days of painstaking enquiries, Sergeant Springer learned of an old disbanded group of actors originally founded by one Thomas Fish, who later spelled his name "Physhe", who had a son also named Thomas, who changed his name and then seemed to disappear, nobody knowing his whereabouts and what happened to him. *Ah*, thought the sergeant, *this must be our man*.

So it was that Thomas Wardlock died in the house on Becket Lane and Thomas Physhe was buried in some obscure police cemetery reserved for felons.

At the conclusion of all their work, Inspector Cockburn remarked to Sergeant Springer, "You know, this man certainly was brilliant. Brilliant. He could have had honour, fame and fortune, but he chose to go the wrong way. Strange."

END OF BOOK ONE

BOOK TWO—THE SEQUEL

DASHELL AND CAROLINE

The missing documents have been found and Caroline now knows her real name, yet mystery remains, with unanswered questions. Dashell, and his brother, Maxwell, travel to Yorkshire to find out what else they can. What they discover greatly saddens them.

On their return Dashell meets a previously unknown relative of Caroline, who thought he had no relatives. This person, in his turn, is astounded at what he is told, and helps to reveal more of the truth.

Amazingly, two other people come forward later to tell their part of the story. In the end everything is brought to light, including someone's cruel deception and spite towards Isobel, Caroline's mother.

Now that all the mystery has been cleared up, Dashell and Caroline can prepare for a joyful wedding.